nothing personal

nothing personal

the kincaids book two

ROSALIND JAMES

ISBN-10: 0988761963
ISBN-13: 9780988761964

author's note

table of contents

prologue

♡

Desiree was cold. She was so cold.

Her head hurt really bad, too, like something sharp was pounding into it. She tried to raise her hand to touch it, but the pain sliced through her chest, hot and hard, at the movement.

"Mommy," she whimpered. "Hurts. Mommy."

She could hear noises, long, low groans, but it was dark, and she couldn't see. Then she heard the voice, not mad anymore. Scared.

"Lacey? You OK? Lace?"

Desiree was scared too, so scared she couldn't have moved even if it hadn't hurt so bad. She was crying now, the tears trickling, warm and wet, down her icy cheeks. And she kept moaning. She couldn't help it. The same word, over and over.

"Mommy. Mommy."

♡

She woke up clammy with sweat, not sure if she'd said it aloud or not. The tears were there, hot, salty rivulets exactly like the ones in the dream, and the cold was the same too.

Because she'd kicked off her comforter, that was why, and the temperature had dropped, the previous day's sunshine merely the false promise of late October.

The sadness dragged at her, black and heavy, trying to take her down, under the waves. But she couldn't afford that, especially not right now.

She reached a hand out for the switch of the bedside lamp, sat up in the pool of light cast by the frosted art glass shade. Swung her feet to the soft surface of the area rug beside her bed and stood, shivering a little in the chilly bedroom. Pulled off her wet undershirt and dropped it into the wicker hamper, found another one in the top drawer of the mahogany bureau, settled it into place, and immediately felt better, less chilled. She sat down again and took a long drink of water from the glass on the bedside table, then switched the lamp off and scooted to the other side of the bed, the clean, never-used side. Pulled the sheet and down comforter up, making herself a cozy nest against the cold and dark.

The dream, sure sign of anxiety, still hovered around the edges of her mind, threatening the sleep she needed if she were going to be at her best the next day. And that wasn't going to work, so she set about replacing the dark images with a meticulous catalogue of every feature of her cottage. The chandelier in the living room, the rug with its floral pattern in shades of dusty rose and soft green, the small hand-painted wooden table that sat beside her couch.

By the time she got to the robin's-egg blue of her stove, she was fading. The last thing she saw before sleep took her was the antique glass doorknob of her bedroom, the rubbed, dark bronze fittings around it. Leading into this room, where she was warm. Where she was safe.

coffee break

♡

"Shoot."

Alec heard the soft exclamation, the clatter of multiple small objects hitting stone, and turned. Well, he turned the rest of the way, anyway. Because he'd already been half-watching her, had seen the moment when the important-man-in-a-hurry had bumped into her as she reached the doorway to the lobby, causing her to lose her hold on her purse in her haste to secure her coffee and laptop case.

Now, she crouched as best she could in the slim skirt and narrow heels, scrambling to retrieve the bag's contents, spilling out over the polished granite floor of the high-rise office building.

Alec stepped out of line and bent to grab a rolling lipstick, a tumbling apple. Handed them to her along with a little notebook, a couple of pens, the energy bar and the tiny container of Tic-Tacs. He let her pick up the travel toothbrush, the metal case with the pinup girl on it. He was pretty sure that was for tampons, because his sister had the same one, and that she'd rather get it herself.

"Thanks," she said, looking up with a smile that turned a little frozen when she met his eyes. That was puzzling. She looked down again, finished stuffing items back into her purse,

1

picked up her cup of coffee from the floor where she'd set it, and straightened.

He stood along with her. She was taller than he'd realized, her slimness causing him to misjudge her height from a distance. Only three or four inches shorter than his six-two in her heels, and they weren't that high. He'd already checked them out, along with the rest of her. Gorgeous honey-colored skin, great bone structure, clearly visible with her hair pulled back into a businesslike twist. Classy all the way around, in a deep brown suit with a pencil skirt and belted jacket that showed off her figure, and that he'd been appreciating. A deep yellow top underneath the jacket that contrasted with her auburn hair. And, he realized as he kept looking into them, a pair of truly spectacular eyes.

Tiger eyes. Brown flecked with gold, a deeper brown edging the rim. Tilting up at the outer corners, and he didn't think it was just the eyeliner. And he was staring.

"Thanks," she said again with a brief smile.

"Got your lunch, anyway," he offered. It was lame, he knew, but he had to say something, because he didn't want to let her get away.

"Yeah." She smiled a bit at that. "Didn't spill my coffee, that's the main thing."

Her voice was low, soft. Sweet. A little husky. Her voice said *sex.* Long slow kisses and cool white wine. And, much later, tangled sheets and breath returning to a heaving chest. That feeling you had when you were lying beside the woman who had just taken you all the way around the world.

Yeah, that's what her voice was saying. But those tiger eyes weren't saying anything of the kind. They were wary, watchful. The full, soft lips, painted a conservative rose, were curved in a cool smile.

Her voice said *touch me.* And her eyes said *don't you dare.* It was all very confusing. And the hair was standing up at the back of his neck. Something about her...Something...

"You've lost your place," she pointed out. "Go get your coffee. Thanks again." She turned and left the shop without looking back.

He considered following her, gave it up after a split second's hesitation, and went to get back in line. He had a meeting coming up, and the shot of caffeine would help, though he didn't really need it. He was fired up, and he was ready.

Because he wasn't some nerdy programmer, tongue-tied at the sight of a beautiful, confident woman. He was Alec Kincaid, poised at the start of yet another spectacularly successful venture, Master of the Universe.

And his touch was gold.

it's not personal, it's business

♡

"So there you have it," Alec said three hours later, sweeping the conference table with a glance that made brief contact with each of the venture capital firm's board members. He offered his best dazzling smile, proven one hundred percent effective to date in three out of three road shows exactly like this one. "That's Hal. The best virtual assistant software ever, the one that's going to reset the bar. Just a little something that'll change the world as we know it."

"You're asking for ten million." That was Ron Jacobs, EnVisitech Capital's managing partner. "That's over 120 percent more second-round funding than last time."

"Because it's 200 percent more project than the last one," Alec answered smoothly. Objection One, right off the bat, just as he'd anticipated. "And if you look back at Page 17, we're projecting a five-year ROI that's more than 250 percent higher than the projections I showed you three years ago. And that one paid off fairly well, as I recall."

"It did," Ron agreed, as the rest of the board looked back through their presentation packets, or gazed at Alec with unreadable expressions. "But there were some bumps in the road."

Alec made a dismissive gesture. "There are always bumps. Show me a startup without any bumps, and I'll show you...

Well," he laughed, "I can't even show you one, can I? Because they don't exist. But we'll sail right over those bumps. We've done it before, and we'll do it again."

Ron exchanged a glance with the man to his left, a finance wizard named Calvin Tang whom Alec had never cared for much. Buttoned up, like all finance guys. Focusing too much on the bottom line, and losing sight of the top line, of the limitless revenue potential that would pay the bills, and make all of them rich. Alec forced himself into patience, never his strong suit, and waited.

"We'd like a little more documentation. A little more... insurance. Regular assurance that AI Solutions is on track, and is going to stay that way," Ron said after a pause.

"Whatever you like," Alec promised easily. "We've got a new Ops guy just about to come on board who's got some pretty fantastic credentials, and we're ready to roll. You'll see all the reports you could wish for."

"We've got an alternative arrangement in mind," Ron said, and the look in his eye left Alec in no doubt, despite the mildness of his words, that he meant business. Ron wasn't a yeller, but he hadn't got where he was by being soft.

"Rae Harlin," he said now.

"Ray Harlin?" Alec said blankly. "Who's he?"

Ron smiled a little. "You've never heard of Rae Harlin? Not exactly keeping up with your industry journals, are you? Quite the up-and-comer, Rae, with all due respect to your candidate."

"On the technical side, I'd say I'm fairly current," Alec said, keeping his cool with some effort. "Operations, I'll grant you, I'm not up on all the latest." And he'd been out of the loop for a while, but that wasn't the kind of thing you reminded people about. Not when you were asking them for millions of dollars, you didn't.

"Exactly," Ron said. "Hence the insurance." He rose from his richly padded black leather chair with athletic ease, reminding

Alec that Ron, despite the gray hair, still played handball three times a week.

The older man stepped around the deeply polished mahogany table, walked across the large conference room with its panoramic view over the San Francisco skyline, and opened an interior door, leaning inside for a few words. Then stood back and held the door for a woman who walked past him and seated herself composedly, raising her gaze politely to Ron and waiting for him to continue.

Alec was never at a loss, but he was at a loss now. It was the woman from the coffee shop. What was she doing here?

"Meet the fourth member of your executive team," Ron said. "Rae Harlin, your new CFO."

"Oh, *hell* no." That was Joe, on Alec's left. The words were muttered, but Alec heard them. He'd been listening to Joe mutter since their freshman year of college. When he was writing code, Joe's patience was limitless. And when he wasn't, he could get a little…intense. He wasn't happy now, and neither was Alec.

"I have a candidate," Alec insisted. "A good one. You can see his resume on Page 34." He recited from memory, as always. "I prefer—*we* prefer to choose our own team." His glance to left and right took in not only Joe, but Brandon Matthews, in charge of sales and marketing for their fourth new venture. Fourth time lucky, Alec could feel it. Just like the third time, and the two before that.

"You can choose your own team, if you like," Ron agreed. His tone was affable, his eyes weren't. "And look for funding someplace else."

"We've done well with you, Alec," he went on when Alec would have retorted. "This isn't personal, it's business. At this level of risk, we want accountability. And we want adult supervision."

"Adult supervision," Alec repeated.

"That's right," Ron said. "We know you're good on the tech side, and so is your team. But it's not a frat house, and it's not somebody's garage. It's serious money, and serious business. We want to back your venture, but it's up to you. Accountability that satisfies us, or find yourself other funding."

"And, Alec," he said, pulling the younger man aside when, at last, the meeting was over. After Alec had pulled the mask back on, smiled and shaken hands across the table with Rae Harlin—who'd still barely spoken a word, just fixed those tiger eyes on him in a level, assessing gaze that he found oddly disconcerting—and promised her he'd call her later in the day to set up a time to meet. When she'd left the room with the rest of Ron's group and Alec's two partners, and Alec was preparing to do the same.

"I'm saying this to you alone," Ron said now. "But I'm saying it seriously. This part *is* personal. Keep it zipped. This industry's about to hit a wave of sexual harassment litigation that's going to make the last couple decades look like a company picnic. Companies have got to start toeing the line, or it's going to come back to bite them. That's one reason I insisted—and make no mistake, *I'm* the one who insisted—on Rae. You've always kept the work under wraps, though she'll be keeping a good eye on data security too. But privately, or not so privately, you—you personally—have earned yourself one hell of a reputation. Don't let it screw you up, or screw us up, or you'll regret it."

"I've never harassed a woman in my life." Alec forced the words out through lips that had stiffened. "What I do in my personal time is nobody's business but my own."

"Then," Ron said, "we have nothing to worry about, have we?"

paging chewbacca

♡

He hadn't even recognized her.

The ride down in the elevator had been a little awkward. Desiree had stepped inside first, and after a brief but obvious hesitation and a glance back at the open door of the boardroom, through which Alec still hadn't appeared, Brandon and Joe had followed her. The two men had kept their eyes on the floor indicator on the ride down, and so had she.

"Goodbye," she said with a quick nod as they left the car, receiving their unenthusiastic farewells in return. That was the way it was going to be, then. Well, nobody liked surprises. Anyway, Alec clearly called the shots, and she'd get her chance with him tomorrow. And she was more than prepared for that.

She left the two men behind, crossing the polished stone lobby with her usual assured stride, giving the bar across the glass doors a healthy shove and making sure her head was high, her body language confident.

Never look hurried, never look worried. Signs of weakness. And, girl, you never want to be showing weakness. Cassandra's words were as applicable today as when she'd first uttered them, the day Desiree had hustled up, breathless and apologetic, to meet Cassie in the library for a study date during their first year of business school.

Desiree turned the corner into the plaza and found an out-of-the-way wall to perch on. The square was nearly deserted in the late October afternoon, a breeze that carried the chill of autumn tumbling a few unswept leaves into a miniature whirlpool on the concrete, but the sun felt good. She reached into her purse for the energy bar she had somehow never got around to eating, unwrapped it, and took a bite. Only realized how hungry she'd been when she'd wolfed down the entire thing.

Once she had, she felt better. She fished her phone out, grateful that it had been in a zippered pocket when the contents of her purse had spilled. But she didn't dial the number right away.

Alec Kincaid. She'd thought she was prepared to see him again. Heaven knows she'd studied every single thing ever written about him, followed every iteration of his brilliant career in preparation for today. She just hadn't been expecting to meet him quite like that, or for how he'd looked. His dark suit perfectly tailored to his tall body, the silk tie, which some personal shopper had clearly matched to the exact hue of his eyes, shining deep blue against the white shirt. Photogenic as he was, the pictures she'd seen online and in magazines hadn't done justice to the man he was now. They could capture his features, the slightly tough look of nearly black hair against dark skin, the strongly delineated nose, the squareness of jaw that kept his regular features from being too handsome to be masculine. Ridiculously good-looking, yes. Boyish...no. Not even close.

He hadn't been quite that obviously muscular in those pictures, though, the close cut of the suit revealing rather than concealing his build, the breadth of shoulder and trimness of waist and hips. She'd heard rumors that he'd spent the last few months on some reality show. He must have got in some serious shape for it, or during it, or something.

But above all, no camera could have caught the essence of him, the way he dominated any space he was in, the way he drew every eye.

Charisma. From the Greek for "divine favor," the gift of the gods. To call it "charm," as some of the articles had, wasn't enough to express its effect in the confined space of a conference room. Alec was talented, no doubt about it. But it was the flash of his smile, the way he seemed to be looking just at you, the way you wanted him to keep looking, to hold his attention, the way *you* couldn't stop looking. That was what had rocketed him to stardom, or at least the tech world's version of it. In an industry dominated by former geeks, he stood out like a poppy in a field of dandelions.

No, she hadn't quite expected all of that. And scrambling over the floor of the coffee shop hadn't been her best moment, though she thought she'd come out of the encounter reasonably well. He'd seemed more flustered than she had, oddly enough. And he'd certainly been more flustered at the meeting, which was understandable. He'd had a shock.

And he hadn't recognized her. Their previous meetings had clearly had more effect on her than on him. And she'd changed more. That was putting it lightly.

♡

"Ewww. That is so sad."

Desiree heard the low-voiced exclamation, the giggles coming from the group of girls lounging on their towels on the grassy bank of the Bidwell Park swimming pool, just above where she had waded in, needing the shock of cold water after her sweaty bike ride. She didn't pay much attention. Not until she heard the boy's voice raised above the girls' laughter

"Paging Chewbacca. Come in, Chewie."

The giggles increased then, accompanied by a loud masculine laugh. Desiree glanced at the group clustered near the water's edge. Four or five girls, wearing the kind of cute bikinis she'd eyed wistfully in store windows, on equally cute figures. She'd bet they had called around, coordinated their outfits beforehand. Senior girls, probably. Clustered close to the knot of boys she saw here every time, as far out of her league as movie stars.

Although she'd never seen that one before. In the center of everything, shaggy dark hair hanging straight around features that were almost too pretty, but not quite. She could see that even without her glasses, not to mention the deeply tanned skin on a tall, slim physique that looked more Hollywood than high school, and had already had her sneaking glances in his direction.

They were the popular kids, the ones she'd seen before, hanging out at the pool as they did on just about every August day here in Chico, with the mercury beginning its steady climb toward the hundred-degree mark. Nothing new there, except that *he* was new. But not new like her. Not gangling and awkward and left out. They all knew him. And if they were the royal court, he was their king.

And every one of them was looking at her. The girls whispering and giggling again, most of the boys grinning. Desiree gave a quick glance down at the loud floral pattern of her one-piece, with its ruffle over the bodice that, her grandmother had assured her, made her lanky frame look curvier. She could tell her face was flaming, wanted nothing more than to be invisible, to sink into the ground and vanish without a trace. Because the prickling down her arms made it clear that something was very, very wrong. Please, God, let her not have started her period without realizing it.

She hadn't. But it was just about as bad. She realized to her horror that a couple stray—but very obvious—copper-colored curls were peeking around the bottom edge of the suit.

"We know she's a natural redhead, anyway. And, hey, gotta love a Nature Girl." That was the comedian of the group again, a beefy blond, the source of the loud laugh Desiree had heard earlier.

She didn't wait to hear more. She waded further into the river water, struck out with a breaststroke that carried her away from the group, and then concentrated on swimming back and forth across the extensive area, as wide as several pools. Letting the movement and the cool water carry away her humiliation, and the burning sting of her tears.

♡

And that had been a very long time ago. Time to let it go. Desiree lifted the phone, punched buttons.

"Hi, honey," she heard after the third ring. "How did it go?"

"It went fine," she said, her heart soothed as always at the enthusiasm in the voice at the other end. "All neat and tidy, contract signed on the bottom line. It'll be a good challenge for the next year or so, anyway, getting this thing up and running. And a pretty good signing bonus too. You sure you don't want to go to Hawaii this year? Lie by the pool in the sunshine and let some handsome young cabana boy bring you daiquiris?"

She heard the raspy laugh that always reminded her of the smoky taste of whisky, followed by the ever-present cough that came straight from the cigarette pack. "Oh, honey, what in the world would I do in Hawaii? I like Reno just fine. You keep sending me there, and I'm more than happy. Marti and I can't wait to get our hands on those poker machines next week. The Silver Legacy had better watch out, because I'm feeling lucky."

Desiree had to laugh herself. "They've probably got your picture up already in their security area. All primed to escort you out when you start winning big. All right, then. But if you ever decide you want to go someplace more exotic, you just tell me."

"If I get a hankering for the pool boy, I'll let you know," her grandmother assured her. "But what did Alec say when he found out? I didn't talk to Pastor Dave about it, because you said not to, but oh, Lord, it's been hard to keep that secret. I still think it's too bad Alec's not a doctor like his brother, but I know he's done real well. Was he excited to be working with you?"

"Let's say he was able to contain his enthusiasm. I was pretty much foisted on him, I told you that."

"But he has to know that you're the best," Dixie argued. "The way you've had all those articles written about you and everything."

"I don't think he's read those," Desiree tried to explain. "I'm not as much of a celebrity as you think, Grandma. The guys with the ideas, the entrepreneurs like Alec, they're the big stars." And some of them were meteors, streaking across the sky.

"Well, I'm proud of you," Dixie said firmly. "What's the name of the company again?"

"AI Solutions. It's kind of a little joke. AI stands for Assisted Integration, but everybody in the industry thinks of it as 'artificial intelligence.' The way computers think, like in the movies. And that's about all I can tell you right now, because it's all still a big secret."

"AI Solutions. I like it," her grandma decided. "It's got a classy sound to it, doesn't it? That's just great, honey. Go buy yourself something to celebrate. I meant to tell you, Target has some real good deals on sheet sets right now. But only till this weekend, then the sale's over."

Desiree smiled. Man, she loved her grandmother. "Thanks. Maybe I'll do that. What about you? Do you need anything?"

"Not a thing. I'm good."

"All right, then. Just let me know if that changes. Love you."

"Love you too, honey. Congratulations again. Oh, can I talk about it to Alec's folks on Sunday? And tell the girls, tomorrow night at pinochle? And say the name?"

"You can talk about it. The name's not a secret, and I'm officially on board, so you can talk about me too. I'll let you go. Lots to do. Talk soon."

She hung up, put the phone back in her purse, and headed north to catch the light across Market Street. She'd take a detour on the way home, she decided. Walk through Union Square, look in the Scheuer Linens windows, maybe even buy a sheet set after all. It wasn't quite Target, but it would do.

alec stays out of trouble

♡

" I'm not excited."

That was Joe. The words were flat, Joe's light blue eyes cold, his mouth unsmiling. The least animated person in the crowded, noisy wine bar. The place to be on Friday night, and the last place Alec felt like being right now.

"Want to go up to my place to talk about this?" Alec asked.

"What?" Brandon asked, his shorter frame perched one stool over, thighs splayed aggressively, eyes roving. "And miss out on the window displays? Dude, what happened to you up in Iowa?"

"Idaho," Alec corrected.

Brandon waved a dismissive hand, sent an appraising glance toward a young Asian woman standing with a couple friends next to a window, where they could be seen by the passing pedestrian traffic. Short skirt, long glossy hair, high heels. "Whatever."

He shoved a cuff up on the close-fitting dress shirt he wore over his perfectly distressed jeans and nudged the floor with an Italian-loafered toe, edged back on the stool and hit Alec with an elbow. "Nine o'clock," he muttered.

Alec glanced at the woman, smiled as she reached a hand up to touch her hair. *Bingo.*

He turned back to Joe. "I know you're not happy. Hell, I'm not happy either. But face it, we're stuck with her."

"You're telling me you couldn't work your mojo on the board," Joe challenged. "Did you even try, yesterday? Or today, for that matter?"

Alec shook his head. "Move on. It's a done deal. And she's good. I checked her out."

"I checked her out too," Brandon said. "Major ice queen. Give me a few weeks, though, bet I could melt that."

"On the team," Alec reminded both of them. "Get used to it. Get behind it. We have no choice."

"There's always a choice," Joe said. "She could quit."

"Don't even think about it," Alec ordered. "She's already looking for office space, lining up staff. It's been one day, and she's *on* it."

"She's not hiring programmers," Joe said with alarm. "You and I are doing that."

"Relax," Alec told him. "I worked out the reporting lines with her today. Look at it this way. She's going to take care of the scut work none of us wants to do, and she'll do it better than we would too. Win-win."

"Sounds to me like she'll be bird-dogging us," Joe growled. "Watching. Handing out employee manuals and making us sign sexual-harassment policies. All the crap we started working together to get away from."

"So you watch a video, sign a piece of paper," Alec said impatiently. He was more than done discussing this. "You don't have to worry your pretty head about the lease, that's the main point."

"My pretty head never did worry about that," Joe said, a reluctant grin finally breaking the frost in the craggy lines of his bearded face. He ran a hand over his smooth expanse of scalp. "That was your pretty head."

"Exactly," Alec pounced. "That's exactly it." Although he could already tell that she was going to frustrate the hell out of him, in more ways than one.

♡

He'd met her at a café that afternoon, as arranged. She'd already been there when he'd arrived, seated at a table with her coffee and laptop in front of her. Advantage to her, right there.

"First of all," he began when he'd got his own coffee and sat down with her, wanting to set the tone from the start. "I should make it clear that I accept that you've been…chosen for us. But it's up to you to fit in with us, not the other way around."

"Fit in with *you,* in other words. Got it."

"We're partners. We don't operate under that kind of hierarchy."

"Sure you do. It's just not explicit. And like I said, I've got it," she went on as he groped for an answer. "I have something I need to make clear too. It's my job to make your job easier, yours specifically. To free you up to do the things only you can do, and to make the operation run as smoothly and efficiently as possible. I'm not going to be trying to get in your way. Just the opposite. Does that make having me on the team a little more palatable?"

He looked into the remarkable eyes that met his own so squarely. Tried not to notice the fullness of her lower lip, or to let his gaze drift down to the V-necked blouse that skimmed over her pretty breasts, tucked into the impossibly slim waist of another pencil skirt. All of which he'd taken in at a glance when she'd stood to shake his hand, then tried not to look at again. And he definitely wasn't going to be noticing the smoki-ness in that low, soft voice. She was palatable, all right. But he still wasn't crazy about working with her.

He realized she was still waiting for an answer. "Hey." He summoned up his best charming smile. "I'm up for anything that makes my life easier."

"Good, because that's what I'll be trying to do. Although I should be clear about something else too. Doing what's best for the company isn't always going to mean telling you what you want to hear, or agreeing with everything you say. You're going to have to trust that I'm up on the legal side, that I know what kind of safety plan we're required to have, how we need to document the hiring process, how we ensure data security and legal compliance, and that I'm going to be implementing those best practices."

"My eyes are already glazing over," he complained. "As soon as you said 'legal compliance' and 'best practices,' you lost me."

She gave him her first real smile, and he noticed that she had a dimple, just to the left of her mouth. A little...hole, enticing him, begging for his tongue to investigate it. *Don't go there.*

"Let's not talk about it in the abstract, then," she urged. "Waste of time, don't you think? Let's get into it, and see how I can help."

"Sounds good to me." Get into that, and out of the danger zone.

"Two top priorities, the way I see it," she said, clicking the touchpad on her laptop. "Office space and personnel. Let's start with space. We're staying in the City? I read that you'd bought a place here, so I assume you're planning on locating the business here as well?"

"Yeah. We all wanted to move up here. Silicon Valley got boring. South of Market, if we can do it. If not, we can try farther west."

She nodded, made a quick note. "I think we can do it. I've been in touch with a commercial realtor I've used before, just to get a feeling for what's out there, and there are some options. I'll start looking at space over the weekend. How big are we talking? How many tech staff to start?"

"Fifteen or so, but we'll want room to grow."

"All right. Maybe 25 people altogether, with some extra space. One floor, or maybe half, depending on the size of the building. That's all I need to know for now. Let's talk staff."

And they had. By the time they'd finished, he'd been convinced that she *was* going to make his life easier. Although there'd been a couple of sticky moments.

"Computers," she said. "Mac or PC? Because I'll want to get the IT end rolling right away."

"Mac," he said. "Though the three of us have our own."

She shook her head. "Nope. No personal machines. Too much of a security risk. And I'm sure that's your major concern too, at this point. That's going to be up to you, how you keep your programmers from having access to all of the code. I can't do that part. But you've got compliance issues as well. We'll be getting site licenses for every single piece of software," she went on when she saw him opening his mouth to object. "And everything has to be clean and traceable."

"Brandon isn't going to be happy," he said. "He's a PC guy."

"Then maybe you want to go with PCs."

"No," he said immediately. "Macs." He saw her smile, and laughed himself. "All right. I'll admit it. I decide. But I still don't see why we can't make an exception."

"You can't have one rule for the guys at the top, and another one for the staff," she explained. "Everyone sees it, everyone knows it, and it's a morale killer. And like I said. Data security."

She'd been impossible to budge, and he'd given up, because he'd had to concede, annoyingly enough, that she was right. Though he wasn't about to tell her so, and she didn't rub it in, either, thank goodness.

And then there'd been the other moment. They were wrapping it up, and she was making a final note. He watched her slim fingers flying over the keys, said idly, "You must type a hundred words a minute. If people still measure those things."

"No idea," she said. "Pretty fast."

"Is there anything you don't do well?" he asked. "Because so far, I'm intimidated."

She laughed, low and soft, and there was that dimple again. "I don't cook."

"Me neither," he grinned back. "Guess we'd better not plan on moving in together, or we'll starve."

That sobered her up fast. "That's the kind of thing you can't say. The kind of thing Ron's concerned about. You're saying it to me, which is one thing, although still not OK, let me just make that clear. And with anybody else…no. That goes for all you guys. I'll be telling Brandon and Joe as well, because that example has to be set from the top too."

"I'll try. But it's hard."

"Because you flirt," she said, still matter-of-fact, to his annoyance. "But you need to stop. It's going to get you into trouble."

No way I can get you into trouble? It was on the tip of his tongue. But he didn't say it. He was learning.

She shoved her laptop into its case, zipped it briskly shut. "I'll let you know early next week what I come up with, space-wise," she said. "And meanwhile, I'll get working on the non-programming staff."

"Sounds good." He stood with her, left the little café. "You down here?" he asked when she turned right with him. "Parked close by? Taking BART? I'm not sure where you live."

"I'm headed this way," she said. Walked another couple blocks with him in silence, her thoughts clearly elsewhere.

"This is me," she said at the corner of Fremont and Mission, just a block short of his place. He considered inviting her to join him and the guys later, and immediately abandoned the notion. Really bad idea.

"I'll be in touch with you at the beginning of the week, just as soon as I've got some space for you to look at," she said. "And we can talk about next steps."

She gave him a wave, turned and stepped smartly into the Friday-afternoon pedestrian traffic crossing Mission. And, he realized, she'd never answered his question. He had no idea where she lived.

♡

"So, yeah," he told Joe now, taking another cautious sip of wine. He hadn't got back into the drinking habit, and his tolerance was way down. "We might as well look at the bright side. Now I have more time to spend programming with you. Speaking of which, want to do some paired stuff tomorrow? Here?"

"Here?" Joe looked around.

"Not *here* here. Upstairs. My place."

Brandon snorted. "Only you would call the Millennium Tower 'upstairs.' What'd this run you in the end, four million? Four-point-five?"

"Something like that," Alec said shortly. He hated talking about how much he'd spent on something. It always made him hear his dad's voice in his head—and not in a good way.

Brandon wasn't deterred. "Probably even more. These places are going for way more than the asking price. The celebrity factor, probably. You don't have some 49ers you need to hang out with tomorrow?"

"You've been reading too many press releases. I haven't even seen a celebrity yet. This is convenient, that's all. I had to live somewhere. Might as well be the best."

"Dude, if I had a place here, I'd be at the pool on Saturday, scoping out the talent, not programming in my apartment," Brandon said.

"Which would be why you're the sales guy, and I'm the idea guy."

"It's all wasted on you." Brandon sighed, his restless gaze sweeping the crowd again.

"Well, not all." The Asian girl was moving their way now, Alec saw, together with a couple of friends.

"We good tomorrow?" he asked Joe. "Uh…" He eyed the girl again, saw her look back at him, then away, flicking that shiny hair over one slim shoulder. "Eleven?"

"Sure," his partner said.

"The blonde's a babe," Brandon said. "Calling that, if you've got the Asian chick."

"You're a dog," Alec chided. He smiled at the women from his perch on the bar stool as the trio sauntered casually past. "Hey."

And that was the beginning of another beautiful, if brief, friendship.

absolutely habanero

♡

"OK, I'll bite." Desiree noticed with a bit of pride that she wasn't out of breath after the steep climb up the Filbert Steps. "What are they?"

Javier turned and saw her looking over the hedge. He set the zigzagging piece of white—plastic? onto the flagstones of his patio as Philip did the same. Whatever the things were, they matched.

"Our new dining chairs," he explained. "Aren't they fabulous?"

"Uh..." Now that he'd told her, she could see it. "Very... modern."

He laughed. "You have no appreciation, baby girl. Come sit in one. They're comfortable, I promise."

"One sec." She pulled her keys from her purse, opened her French doors and set her laptop bag and her purse on the kitchen floor together with the pink plastic bag containing her dinner, picked up on the way home from her favorite Chinatown hole in the wall. Locked the door again, then lifted the latch on the gate connecting her garden to the boys' and went on through.

She sat gingerly on the shiny white surface, bounced experimentally, felt the material give. No arms, of course. Arms must be out of style. "All right," she conceded. "They're surprisingly comfortable. But they're still…"

"Modern," Javier said. "Of this millennium. We have four more. Come see how fabulous they look with the table."

"Yup," she said when the guys had carried the chairs through the sliding glass doors, set them with the others around the ebony dining table with its metal edging. "Those are some chairs, all right."

"Hopeless," Javier sighed. "But I have to say—gorgeous new skirt." He waved her into one of the new…she guessed she really did have to call them chairs—as he and Philip took two others. "Donna Karan, am I right?"

"You know my weakness," she admitted, sticking her legs out in front of her and toeing off her shoes, wiggling her bare toes luxuriously. "Big meeting today. First time with Mr. Alec A. Kincaid."

"Excuse me. I'm just catching my breath," Javier said, pounding on his chest and then fanning himself extravagantly with one brown hand. "Is it hot in here, or is it just him?"

"What's the *A* for, anyway?" Philip asked with a good-natured grin across the table for his partner.

"Alpha," Javier said firmly.

"Alasdair," Desiree said through her laughter. "Alexander Alasdair Kincaid. Sounds like the laird, doesn't he?"

"Close enough for me," Javier agreed. "How hot in person? Are we talking jalapeño, or habanero?"

"Oh, habanero," she said. "Absolutely."

"But it's hands off, right?" Philip asked. "We being professional here?"

"Also absolutely. Anyway, I'm not much for standing in line. Or rolling down the assembly line, more like. Being processed and moving on."

"Ouch," Philip agreed. "So, not a prospect. Anybody else on the horizon? Hot date tonight?"

"Not hot, warm, or otherwise. Lots of work to do anyway. I'm going to be flat-out for a while here."

"How about breaking for Bette Davis in a couple hours?" Philip urged. "We're doing 'Now, Voyager' for our Friday night flick."

"With popcorn. And extra butter," Javier tempted. "Plus Pink Lady apples. Your favorites. Bought them just for you."

She smiled. "Wish I could. But no. I'm looking at office space this weekend, and...oh, gosh, so many other things too. I'd give you the list, but it's just way too boring."

"Not going to be too busy to take Anthony and Cleo next week, are you?" Philip asked as one of the Siamese who had been rubbing around the three pairs of ankles jumped into Desiree's lap, submitted regally to her stroking hand. "Because Cabo's calling our name."

"Are you kidding? Cat-sitting's the highlight of my upcoming social life."

Javier sighed. "You'd better get moving on that, because I tossed that bouquet to you on purpose, baby girl. You're obligated now."

"I am not. It wasn't even a real bouquet."

"It was a perfectly good centerpiece, and I used it on you. It's been six months. I'm counting on you to pull it out here, and so far, you're disappointing me sadly. How many times have we set you up in the past year?"

"Mmmm...four," she decided.

"And how many second dates have we had?"

"Hey. One of them I did," she argued. "But then I got busy. And I'm busy now." Besides, hanging out with a couple could make a person feel so...lonely, and she didn't need to feel any lonelier.

She got up, reluctantly dumping the cat off her lap in the process, bent down to collect her shoes from beneath the table. "Cool chairs, guys. And say hi to Bette for me."

♡

She used the gate again to pass through into her own little patch of paradise, the patio laid with sandstone flags, surrounded by greenery both planted and potted in terracotta containers, all of it shielding her from the sight of the locals and tourists who used the stairs outside her carved wooden gate as a shortcut, or a workout, or just a scenic walk. Gnarled wisteria vines as big around as her wrist climbed both sides of the arbor that would provide shade, along with the delicate scent of their drooping blue-purple flowers, to her small teak table and chairs when summer came again.

She unlocked her multi-paned French doors, turned one antiqued bronze handle and stepped into the kitchen, the blue hand-blown glass diamonds winking in the pale sunlight, faithfully providing their accents within the diamonds of copper-colored tiles that made up the backsplash of her small but functional kitchen.

No wiggly white chairs in her dining room, or anywhere else either, she thought as she passed through the compact dining area and on into the living room, with its single floral-patterned couch in faded shades of pink, green, and white, the non-matching pair of upholstered antique side chairs. Her bare feet sank into the comfy wool rug that extended nearly to the edges of the narrow-plank hardwood floor, almost to the point where it met the richly detailed molding that she'd repainted twice now to keep its white gloss pristine.

Her cottage, all nine hundred square feet of it, was where she indulged her traditional side, her feminine side. And her feminine side had better stay confined right to this spot, she reminded herself sternly, passing through into her bedroom, with its pale green walls and more white molding at floor and ceiling, unzipping her skirt and hanging it in her neatly organized closet, unbuttoning her blouse and putting it into the mesh bag hanging over the door for hand-washables.

She pulled on her favorite pink fleece sweatpants and a V-necked white T-shirt, went into the bathroom to get rid of her makeup and get comfortable in preparation for a solid evening's work before her meeting with the realtor tomorrow. Flipped the switch and experienced the delight she felt every single time the two small chandelier wall fixtures on either side of the ornate oval mirror blazed out in twinkling, shining crystal. Even after four years, she still got the same kick out of it all. It was girly, and it was over the top, and she loved it.

Her hair had remained completely under control, she saw with satisfaction as she pulled the pins out and allowed it to fall around her shoulders in glossy waves. And so had she. She'd come a long, long way from Chico, and from that blistering summer day when she'd first met Alec Kincaid.

Snap.

"Hey! Sno-Cone girl!"

Desiree looked up from the smudgy newsprint of the oversized test prep book, blinking behind her glasses, and turned quickly to the rectangular serving window of the Snack Shack. She'd been so engrossed, she hadn't heard the group approach.

It was the blond guy, she saw with a sinking heart. Sticking his head through the window, into her space, giving another snap to his fingers. With a bunch of the others behind him. The last people she'd have chosen to encounter again today. She could feel the color rising in unsightly blotches up her chest, into her cheeks as he recognized her and the smirk formed. She lifted her chin and looked him in the eye.

"What can I get you?" *To sustain you in your preparations for your promising career in urinal maintenance.*

"Hot dog," he said. "And a red Sno-Cone."

She nodded, picked up the tongs to put a bun into its paper boat, pulled the metal handle of the steamer door open and tried not to notice the hot, moist air that rushed out, doing its bit to contribute to the hot, sticky atmosphere that had her curls plastered to the back of her neck and patches of damp showing on the back and under the arms of her tank top. The little fan on the back counter blew the hot air around, but that wasn't helping much. She slipped the dog into its bun and closed the door.

"Everything on it?"

"Everything but onions. You never know who's going to want to kiss me." Another loud laugh, echoed by the girls along with a "you wish."

Desiree ignored it all, scooped relish, sauerkraut, and grated cheese, and handed the container across the counter. Packed crushed ice into the cone and pumped syrup with an efficiency born of two months of practice. Accepted his money and made change, still running the PSAT question through her head.

The math sections were easy, the reading comprehension not too bad. She even felt fairly confident about the writing. But the grammar stuff was still stumping her sometimes, and that had her worried. She only had a couple more weeks of summer vacation left, and her work schedule wasn't leaving her enough study time. A new school, three AP classes...She had to get through the whole book before school started. She *had* to. Because she needed a good score on that test.

The blond guy took his change, wiped his hand ostentatiously on his swim trunks, and murmured, not quite softly enough, as he moved to the ketchup and mustard dispensers and allowed one of the girls to take his place at the serving hatch, "Whoa there, Chewie." Which elicited a couple more stifled giggles from the girls.

In many respects Anna Karenina and Emma Bovary are very similar characters, but Bovary has the most spirit and determination. No error.

Desiree focused with all her own determination on the sentence. Was something wrong with it? Or was it a "no error"? It sounded OK. She got Sno-Cones for the two girls, trying and failing to suppress a flash of envy at the cute sarong skirts they'd coordinated to their bikinis, while she continued to ponder. She gave the open book, spread carefully over paper towels on the counter beside her, a furtive glance as the second girl turned away.

Then *he* was at the window. The hottie.

"Hi," he said. His chest looked even better up close, tanned and smooth. He brushed back a lock of straight dark hair that was falling over one bright blue eye, his white smile seeming to light up the cramped space. Desiree was uncomfortably aware of her own impossible hair, frizzing up now from her swim, the steam in here. Of the makeup she wasn't wearing, because it would have melted right off, and she wasn't that good at putting it on anyway. Of her sweaty forehead and upper lip, the green-striped ribbed tank and khaki shorts she'd bought from the end-of-summer clearance rack at Walmart. Both hanging on a figure that remained resolutely boyish, even though she'd turned sixteen in May.

"How're you doing?" he went on. "Don't pay any attention to Danny," he said in a lower voice. "He can be kind of a jerk at times."

She felt her color rise even higher. She'd been pretending he hadn't heard either time, since he hadn't laughed with the others. No chance of that now.

"What can I get you?" she asked. She couldn't do anything about her blush or the sweat, but she wasn't going to look beaten, not if she could help it.

"Hot dog, please. With everything."

He leaned nonchalantly against the edge of the window to watch as she prepared it for him, spotted the book on the counter. "Studying?"

"Yeah. The PSAT."

"You're going to be a junior, huh? You new? I haven't seen you around."

"New this year. How about you?" she asked boldly.

"Just graduated. I'm working this summer, just like you. Day off today, that's all."

She handed him the dog. "Two ninety-five."

He gave her a few bills, tossed the nickel and another dollar into the jar labeled "College Fund."

"Thanks," she said with surprise. High school kids rarely tipped.

"No problem. Working outside in summer is hard, I know. Not from personal experience," he grinned. "But my brother's doing yardwork. He keeps telling me how much harder it is than my cushy spot."

"Harder than this too," she agreed.

"Oh, I don't know," he said, the grin gone now. "I'd say this has its moments."

"Hey, Kincaid!" It was the blond guy, shouting from the shade of the nearby picnic table. "Quit flirting and get your ass over here. Because I know you can do better."

The last bit was uttered more softly, but it still came across to Desiree loud and clear. She felt herself go even redder, if that were possible. And did her best to pretend she hadn't heard. Again.

"I really need to quit hanging out with him," the dark guy— Kincaid—muttered. "Thanks for this." He lifted the hot dog in acknowledgment. "And good luck on the test."

it's lonely at the top

♡

Alec leaped to the curb the next morning just ahead of the slow-moving street-sweeping truck, its bristles whirling over the asphalt, and heard the roar recede behind him as he continued on. He'd intended to get a cab back from Debra's place, but had found himself walking instead. Maybe he'd hit the gym before Joe showed up. Because he was restless. The brisk walk— and the sex—had helped, but his mind kept drifting annoyingly off here and there, instead of focusing on the technical challenges that had had him fired up since the idea for the virtual assistant software had first exploded in his brain during a long afternoon of haying.

Here being the bombardment of noise, the roar of diesel engines and the ebbing and flowing *whoosh* of traffic, the battering *rat-a-tat-tat* of jackhammers, the blast of horns. And the constant visual stimulation, the rush of people on the sidewalks, the signs and posters and marketing slogans, all calling out to be noticed, clamoring that he pay attention. The voices, talking to him, talking at him, talking around him. And all the electronics. Texts and emails and phone calls and the ever-present Internet. The sheer level of stimulation that had been battering him ever since he'd come back from Idaho, back from the show.

Which was the *there*, the other place his mind kept returning. To the steady passage of long summer days filled with hard,
steady physical labor. The all-too-short nights, drifting into the
deep sleep of physical exhaustion with only the sound of the
wind, the snores of his loft-mates in his ears. The chance to think
his thoughts, even if those thoughts weren't always pleasant.

He reached the building, entered the cool quiet of the expan-
sive lobby, all soaring space and glossy hard surfaces.

"Hey, Julio." He nodded to the guy at the reception desk,
received a "Good Morning" in return, and swiped his keycard for
the elevator, stepping out a few swiftly-moving seconds later into
the hushed corridor of the 53rd floor, the six closed doors of six
luxury apartments staring blankly back at him. He'd met most of
his neighbors in the month he'd lived here, but nothing beyond
a "how are you?" in the elevator. Another single guy, a lawyer,
he thought, probably divorced, some retired couples. Nobody
around now, though.

Inside his own door, then, and into his apartment, dropping
his keys into the blown glass bowl on the hall table, his jacket
onto one of the starkly modern white leather couches. The high
gloss of the wide dark floorboards, the white walls, the richly
veined marble of the kitchen countertops at one end of the great
room, echoed in the darker marble of the dining table with its
stainless steel base. And, most of all, the floor-to-ceiling windows
lining the best part of two walls, more glass and white concrete
in the buildings opposite, all throwing glaring light back at him.

Maybe he should have paid more attention, thought it
through better when the decorator was asking him about his
preferences. At the time, he'd appreciated her businesslike questions, the ability to get everything set up fast, once he'd closed on
the apartment. Modern, clean lines, the best, but nothing fussy.
Check, check, check. But it was all kind of…bare. Sterile, even.

Sometimes he wasn't sure if he was in a home or an operating room. Or a morgue.

Because the quiet, he thought as he headed down the hall into the master bedroom, across the carpet—pale, of course—into the walk-in closet, stripped off his button-down shirt and slacks, dumped them into the pile on the floor and grabbed workout gear from a smoothly sliding lacquered birch drawer, was almost more oppressive than the noise of the street below. No birdsong, no rush of creek water or drip of rain from the eaves, no wind in the pines. Just...quiet, unless he was playing music to have something in the background. In the middle of the city, but separated from it by the best insulation in the world. Money.

What was he, a Boy Scout? He'd always been an urban animal, and he still was, he was sure. It was just the transition. He needed a workout, that was all.

a is for...apple pie

♡

"Six offices along these walls," Rae pointed out as they stepped inside the vacant space that took up half the twelfth floor of the office building on the narrow alleyway that was Stevenson Street.

"We've got this. Give us a few minutes," she told the realtor when the man would have accompanied them further, causing Alec to hide a smile. Her looks could very nearly be called fragile, but there was nothing the least bit fragile about her character, it was becoming clear. It was only Tuesday, and she'd already whipped her way through all the office space available south of Market. He had a feeling that he was going to find today's list pretty extensive, but that she'd be whipping through that too.

"I was going to show you my two or three best candidates," she told him as she led him across the cavernous open space, furnished only with industrial carpeting interrupted periodically by rectangular cutouts for electrical outlets, and dust motes that drifted in the occasional shaft of sunlight. "But this one is really head and shoulders above the rest. Best location, best space. And there's no point wasting your time."

He tried—and failed—to ignore the way her hips swayed in the black knit pants, or the way those pants had to stretch to fit over her small but deliciously...backside. How the plum-colored sweater hugged her willowy figure, which did have a few more curves to it in exactly the right places. Not to mention the neck that rose above the sweater's ribbed collar in a vulnerable, too-slender column, a few auburn tendrils escaping at her nape beneath the ruthlessly subdued twist. But he looked around him too, because this was important. When he was programming, he didn't care too much where he was, but it mattered to other people, he knew. And as much as he hated dealing with operational stuff, it was part of the job.

"Good light, but not much view," he pointed out, stepping through the doorway of one of the offices lining two sides of the floor. He went to one of the two large windows, looked across the narrow alley at the walls and windows of the building beyond. More hard surfaces. More glass.

"A little better from the corner offices," she said. "Come see."

"I thought, this one for you," she said when they were inside the larger office, which did indeed overlook the plaza across the way with its planter boxes and trees, although the leaves were turning color and falling now. And over there, between two buildings, a single patch of deep autumn blue that was the sky. "We could use the other corner office, which has only building and street views, as a conference room," she suggested. "Because I noticed you like to see green."

"You did?" he asked, startled. "When?"

"On Friday, when we were walking back from getting coffee, past that living wall with the water and all the plants," she explained. "You enjoyed looking at that."

"I can't believe you noticed."

She shrugged. "It's my job to help you be productive. Relaxed people are more productive, and if you enjoy looking at greenery, it'll relax you. Let me know which of the other offices should go to Brandon and Joe, if you agree on this space, and I'll walk them through here too, without you, and present it to them. A fait accompli is better, and that it comes from me and not you."

"So they can blame you?"

"Also my job," she pointed out. "To be the bad guy. So who's next to you? That one's a little more desirable than the others, has a little more view."

"Joe," he said at once. "If we don't write code, we don't have a product, that's the bottom line. We'll need to be close. In fact, he'll need to be in here with me, so we can do paired programming. L-shaped desk. A big one, because I need space. Dual 32-inch monitors, two keyboard trays, two good chairs. I don't want to have to use the conference room every time, and that should be available anyway, for when the programmers want to work together."

She made a note on her phone. "Got it. I'll be checking with the others about their requirements too, and I need to sit with you and go through yours in more detail. But before we get ahead of ourselves, let me show you the rest of the floor."

"Good for you?" she asked when they'd finished their tour and she'd called the realtor over at last to answer a few questions.

"Yeah," Alec said. "Soon as you can do it. And I have to say," he added, "if the rest of it doesn't require any more work from me than this, I'm going to think I've died and gone to heaven."

"You seem surprised. There's a reason Ron chose me, you know," she said calmly. "Give me a couple minutes to get the ball rolling on closing this deal, then maybe we can get coffee and go through my list. It's a long one," she warned, holding up her phone and surprising him not a bit, "but I'll keep it moving."

Alec glanced at his own phone. "Past eleven-thirty. How about an early lunch instead?"

"I've got a lot to do," she hesitated.

"So? You still need to eat, don't you? Eat and talk, and go through your list," he coaxed. "Simple. Efficient. We'll multitask."

She smiled reluctantly. "All right."

"There's a pretty good place right next door," he said. "La Rochelle."

"I thought, just grab a salad," she protested. "Not menus and waiters."

"I'm still catching up on my diet after my recent grueling experiences," he said firmly. "I'm not grabbing anything, and if I need to be relaxed to be productive, well, so do you. We're going to sit down, and somebody's going to serve us, and before you know it, you're actually going to be enjoying yourself."

"Wow." She opened her eyes wide. "This would be the Alpha Male CEO."

He laughed. "This would be it. How did I do?"

"Pretty good," she smiled. "I'll reserve judgment, though, until I see a little more."

And if that wasn't flirting, he'd never seen it. Which was interesting, wasn't it?

♡

"Would you like to see the dessert menu?" the waiter asked more than an hour later.

"No, thanks," Rae exhaled. "Not for me."

"I would," Alec said. "After all that work getting through your list, I'm feeling faint. I definitely need dessert. And you need a cup of coffee."

The waiter smiled, handed over the compact, elegantly bound menus. "Two coffees to start?"

"Sure," Rae capitulated, and the waiter nodded and turned away. "I can come up with a few more questions to use the time."

"Not the way it's going to be," Alec said after a quick glance down the menu. "My turn to ask the questions, Desiree."

She looked up at him sharply, and he saw the flash of awareness at the use of her full name, heard her quick intake of breath.

"Why didn't you tell me that your grandmother is one of my dad's parishioners?" he demanded. "I talked to my mom on Sunday," he explained, confused again by the expression on her face. Surprise? Relief? What? "And I remembered who your grandmother was. I see her occasionally at church when I'm home," he explained. "Mrs. Foster, right? Nice lady."

"Yes," she said. "She is. And she thinks the world of your dad too. Well, of both of them. But you go to church when you're home?"

He had to laugh. "You ask that like it's a choice." He looked up as the waiter approached again, bent to set down two porcelain cups of coffee. "Apple clafouti, please," he said. "Assuming that's pie."

"It's apple pie, more or less," Rae told him.

"I don't know why they can't just make pie," Alec complained as the waiter departed with their dessert menus. "Nothing wrong with pie."

And then he looked at her again, into the gold-flecked eyes that widened at the arrested expression in his own, and felt a nearly audible *click* as he made the connection.

"Sno-Cone Girl," he said. Then instantly regretted it when he saw the wince, followed almost immediately by the stiffening of her posture. Head high, shoulders squared, exactly the way she'd looked back then. And he was twenty years old again, sitting in the diner, watching her feelings being hurt yet another time, and hating it.

♡

"My parents have been bugging me to get a job all summer," Maryann had complained, sitting back in the red leatherette booth and winding a strand of shiny blonde hair around one manicured finger. Every bit of her still looking brand-new and polished despite a lazy Sunday afternoon of tubing down the

Sacramento River. Maybe that was the twenty minutes she'd spent in the restrooms afterwards, and the arsenal of makeup Alec knew she carried in her bag.

Ryan snorted from across the table. "Must've given up by now. It's August. Nobody's going to hire you at this point."

Maryann sighed. "My dad's been making me work in his office instead, and it's *soooo* boring."

Alec looked up at the waitress who'd come up beside the roomy booth in the Chico Diner, watched her pull an order pad out of the black apron she wore over her black slacks and flip it open with a practiced motion. The same girl who'd worked at the Snack Shack two years ago, the summer he'd graduated from high school, he realized. He'd seen her a few more times after that first day, clearly working all the hours she could get. Always with her test prep book on the counter, always sweating in the heat.

The red hair was pulled back tight into a ponytail now, and she was prettier, not quite so skinny anymore. Had grown into her features a little, though the glasses didn't do anything for her. She'd filled out some too, he couldn't help but notice. And she was still working, but at least she was doing it in the air-conditioning these days.

Maryann was continuing with her story as if she hadn't noticed the waitress's arrival. "I asked my parents when I was going to get a summer vacation, since I go back to school in three weeks. There's so much to do to get ready, you know? All that stuff to buy, now that I'm moving out of the dorms. Dishes, and furniture, and pots and pans. There's just so *much*, it's overwhelming. But they said since I'm only in the office a few days a week, this *is* my vacation. They just can't stand to see anyone else having fun, that's what it is."

Alec shifted a little with embarrassment, cleared his throat as the waitress jumped into the pause after Maryann finished speaking.

"What can I get you folks?"

"Chef's salad, please," Rhonda said. "And a Diet Coke."

Alec looked at Maryann. "I can't decide," she complained. "Do you have information on calorie counts?" She looked over the laminated card with a critical eye.

"Sorry," the waitress said gravely. Her face was composed, but Alec caught a twitch at the corner of her mouth. "I'm afraid I don't."

Maryann sighed. "Chicken salad, then, as long as the chicken's roasted. How do they prepare it?"

That twitch again. "I'm not sure, but it's not fried, if that's your concern."

"I'll have that, then. And the dressing on the side," Maryann instructed.

"And to drink?"

"Diet Coke."

The girl nodded, scribbled the order, looked at Alec.

"Meatloaf plate, please," he said. "And iced tea."

"Ugh," Maryann complained. "How can you even eat that, when it's so hot?"

"Easy. Besides, they make great meatloaf here. Don't they?" he asked the waitress with a grin.

"The best," she said, a little smile finally appearing. She took Ryan's order. "I'll be right back with your drinks," she told them, gathering the menus and turning toward the kitchen.

"At least I don't have to wear a uniform at work," Maryann told Rhonda, her eyes on the slim retreating back in its baggy yellow golf shirt, tucked into the black polyester slacks worn over sensible black shoes that wouldn't be winning any awards during Fashion Week.

"I've never had to wear one either," Rhonda agreed. "I'd hate it. How about you guys? Ever wear a paper hat, back in the dim dark days?"

"Not me," Ryan said. "Just the green apron, and you know how that turns you on. She sometimes makes me wear it when we go out," he told the others, "just to show me off. I hate when she objectifies me like that, but what are you gonna do. If you've got it," he sighed, shaking his mop of curly brown hair, "you've got it."

"Oh, yeah," Rhonda agreed. "You're a stud."

"You know it. I'm not saying working at Starbucks has exactly been glamorous," Ryan said as Alec continued to laugh, "but hey, I've learned how to make coffee drinks. And no paper hat, at least."

"Or a shirt with your name on it, embroidered above the pocket," Maryann said with a giggle. "That would be the worst."

"Nothing wrong with working for a living," Alec said. "I hear that some of the best people do it."

"How's that going, dude?" Ryan asked lazily, lifting the Coke that the waitress had just set down from her round plastic tray. He pulled off the top bit of wrapper and took a grateful sip. "Made your first million yet?"

"Not hardly," Alec said. "Thanks," he said to the girl as she delivered his own iced tea. "Just glad to have landed an internship, and one that actually pays, or it would've been the green apron for me too. Man cannot live on scholarship alone, not if man has to buy textbooks and the occasional pair of jeans, he can't. And at least I'm not digging ditches like Gabe."

"Really?" Rhonda looked interested. "Is that what he's doing?"

"No," Alec said. "But close. Landscaping." He shuddered theatrically. "Way too hard."

"I'll bet he's hotter than ever, though," Rhonda sighed.

"Hey." Ryan looked as affronted as an easygoing guy could.

"Yeah, hey," Alec said. "I'll point out here that *I'm* the cute twin."

"Hmm," Rhonda considered, her head on one side. "Yeah. You're cuter. But he has those big football muscles. Plus he's more smolder-y."

"I can smolder with the best of them," Alec protested. Then ruined it by smiling again.

"See?" Rhonda laughed. "You can't. You totally can't. You cannot smolder to save your life."

Alec laughed back. Damn, he liked her. Too bad she'd been dating Ryan since high school. Why couldn't he find a sassy girl like that? Because he kept going for the hot ones, that was why. And they were never sassy.

And Maryann was pouting now, because he was ignoring her. He sighed. This wasn't working out. But it was just a vacation thing, and she was *really* pretty. Too bad she had to talk.

♡

The redheaded waitress was at the table an hour later, loading used plates and cutlery onto her already-laden tray.

"How about dessert?" she asked. "Would you like to see the menu again?"

"Not for me," Maryann said. "That salad was *huge*. I couldn't even eat half of it." She patted her nonexistent stomach, and Alec caught a sardonic glance from Ryan.

"Me neither, thanks," Rhonda said. "I'm trying to diet." She sighed and didn't pat her stomach, which was indeed not quite as nonexistent as Maryann's.

"Not necessary," Ryan assured her. "More of you to love." He grinned down at her as she made a face back at him, his hoot of a laugh escaping when she elbowed him in the ribs. "I would, though," he told the waitress. "What do you have?"

"Chocolate cake, carrot cake, Boston cream pie, cheesecake," she recited. "And pie."

"Chocolate cake," Ryan decided. "Can't beat that."

"It's good," she agreed. She turned to Alec, still balancing her load of dirty dishes. "What can I get you?"

"Pie," he said. "My favorite. What kind do you have?"

She smiled. "Just about anything you could want. Apple, cherry, blackberry, pecan, strawberry-rhubarb, lemon meringue, chocolate cream, banana cream."

A tiny dynamo of a gray-haired waitress bustled up next to the girl. She had a coffee pot in her right hand, a pitcher of iced tea in her left.

"Alec." Her delighted smile creased the leathery brown skin of her face into a relief map. "Nice to see you. It's been a while. Is my girl here taking good care of you?"

Alec saw the dark color rise into the redhead's smooth, honey-colored cheeks. "I was just getting his dessert order," she said.

He knew he should stand up, but how could he, with the two of them standing next to the table, blocking his exit? He couldn't even shake hands, because the older woman's were full. He felt rude, and embarrassed, and uncharacteristically awkward.

"Hi, Mrs. Foster," he said, giving her a smile that he hoped would cover him. "I haven't been able to get home much this summer. How're you doing?"

"Oh, I'm just fine." She reached out and filled his iced tea glass from her pitcher. "How are things going at that fancy school of yours? Which one is it again?"

"Stanford," the young waitress muttered.

"That's right," the older woman said with pleasure. "We were all so proud of you, I can't tell you. My smart cookie here's got a real good scholarship too. Tell him, honey."

She shrugged, her embarrassment clearly matching Alec's now. "It's no big deal. It isn't anything like his. It's just here, Chico."

"Hey," Alec protested. "A good CSU scholarship *is* a big deal. Congratulations. That PSAT worked out for you, then."

"You remember that?" the girl asked.

"Dude remembers everything," Ryan put in. "He's got so much data stored in there, he's going to need to add an extra room pretty soon."

"You're a real smart boy, I know that," Mrs. Foster told him. "I'd better get to my tables, and let you get your dessert. You take good care of him, honey," she told the younger woman. "Nothing but the best for Pastor Dave's boy. Give my regards to your folks, Alec."

"I will. Nice to see you," Alec said, and she gave him one last smile and bustled off.

"So, pie?" the girl asked him. "Were you able to narrow it down, or would you like the list again?" Still embarrassed, he saw, but doing her job.

"Apple, please," he said. "A la mode."

"One apple pie a la mode, one chocolate cake, coming right up."

"I can't believe how high-calorie everything is here," Maryann said. "You'd think they'd have *one* healthy option."

"Hey," Alec objected. "Tasty food, big portions, cheap prices. Everything I look for in a restaurant. What's not to like?"

Maryann rolled her eyes. "No wonder poor people are fat."

She'd muttered it, her voice low. But Alec heard it, and so did the waitress, it was clear. Her posture stiffened, her shoulders went back, and the color flamed even higher in her face.

"Coming right up," she repeated, not looking at Maryann. Not meeting Alec's eyes. She turned and walked to the kitchen, still balancing the heavy load that must have had her too-slender arms aching by now.

And Alec, for the first time in his life, wanted to hit a girl.

♡

"I broke up with her that day. Just so you know," he said now.

"Who?" Rae reached for her coffee cup, took her time pouring cream and stirring, took a casual sip.

"Maryann. That girl I was with. What she said—it wasn't OK with me. But I know I didn't say anything at the time, and I should have, shouldn't have just sat through the rest of dinner like I did."

She shrugged. "None of us has much courage when we're young. You were with your friends, and your girlfriend. When you're a waitress, you get used to hearing things like that. She wasn't the rudest customer I ever had, believe me. You didn't owe me anything. And my grandmother...that was embarrassing for you, I know."

He reached out, wanting to touch her hand where it clutched the handle of her cup. The other, he suspected, was clenched in her lap. He pulled his hand back at the last moment, wished he knew what to say. "*You* had courage, and you were, what, that last time? Nineteen?"

"Eighteen," she said. At least she was looking at him again. "My first summer working in the diner, but not my last. I worked there all through college, with my grandma. And I'm not sorry. I'm glad." Her low voice had lost its usual softness, and her eyes were blazing. "Because you know what? I know things that lots of so-called successful people have never learned. I know how to work really hard. I know that low-paying jobs are usually tougher and more stressful and a whole lot less enjoyable than high-paying ones. And I know that if hard work was all it took to make it, this country would be run by people who take care of kids and clean houses and mow lawns. And so should you."

"I do know that, because I was raised right, just like you," he assured her. "Poor, but right. Don't worry. All appearances to the contrary, I know all that too."

life on the cube farm

♡

"Yeah, I did some good work with Ethan. Their code was spaghetti when I got there, but I sorted it out. Visicon was pretty chill, but the challenge is over now. Ready to move on."

The young man leaned back in the leather chair that had been delivered just yesterday, Rae having decided that furnishing the conference room was top priority for exactly this reason. The kid's jeans were appropriately skinny, the designer jacket over the black T-shirt clearly carefully chosen for its panache. Alec knew that none of these guys wore a tie anymore—hell, he never did either, not unless it was absolutely necessary—but he'd wondered, when he'd seen the retro black high-tops with their white rubber caps, if they hadn't gone a little far down the road. He was less than ten years older than—Simon, he thought with a glance down at the resume in front of him, but he wouldn't have worn jeans to an interview. Or tennis shoes.

Still, Ethan said the guy could write code, and Ethan was a friend of Joe's, so who cared if the kid was a little cocky? Alec had been accused of that often enough himself, and they weren't hiring Simon for his personality. But Joe could finish interviewing him. Because the whine of electric drills and the *thump* of partitions being wrestled into place that had provided an unmelodious

background to their afternoon had suddenly died down considerably, and he should probably check on that.

"Excuse me." He got up from the conference table, stepped
out into the hive of activity that was their formerly-open office
space, and pulled the door shut behind him. One team was
industriously setting up panels for what would become their
cube farm, but the other was standing idle. With Rae.

"This needs to be taken apart and redone," she was saying.
"I believe I mentioned that you should double-check with the
diagram as you go."

She was standing tall, her gaze steady and serious on the big
bearded guy in the orange T-shirt, dusty jeans, and work boots,
a kidney belt beneath his pot belly, who was hefting his drill,
clearly impatient to get on with it.

"I have an extra copy here, since you seem to have mislaid
yours." She held the sheet out to the guy, who made no move to
take it.

"Twenty units," he said. "Five blocks of four. I do this all the
time, lady. Go on back to your office and let us do the job. Piece
of cake."

"Not if the electrical fittings are in the wrong place." She
crouched under the unit he'd just finished installing with his
helper, who was standing by, a bemused expression on his face.
She got onto all fours, crawled under the desk space, and poked
at the fitting. "See that? Wrong orientation."

The guy was looking, Alec saw. He was looking at Rae's ass,
exchanging a grin with his helper, and Alec was at his side in a
few quick strides.

"Problem here?" he asked.

"I don't have a problem," Beard Boy said, glancing at him,
then back down at Rae's rear view. "I'm having a real good time."

"Well, unless you want this to be your last day on the job,"
Alec said as Rae climbed out again, dusting off the knees of

her pants, "you'll do the work to Ms. Harlin's specs, and to her satisfaction."

"And who would you be?" the guy drawled, his eyes sweeping Alec's white shirt and dark gray slacks, making it clear that he was less than impressed.

Alec folded his arms, paused a moment, and stared him down. "I would be the guy who signs the check." *And the guy who could kick your ass.*

Beard Boy grunted. Reached a hand out for the piece of paper that Desiree handed silently to him, looked at the spot where she was tapping one slim nail, its coating of clear polish gleaming in the reflected light of the overhead fixtures and still-uncovered windows.

"Switch these two panels around," she said. "And please double-check all the electrical fittings this time as I asked. I found a loose one under there, and I don't think your boss would be happy about a return service call."

"Talk to you a sec?" she asked Alec as Beard Boy snapped an order to his helper, began to loosen bolts.

Alec followed her perfectly straight back and set shoulders towards the break room. He could see her scanning right and left along the way, checking the placement of the other cubes being assembled by the second team against another copy of her diagram. Which she had on a clipboard. Of course she did.

She waited until they were inside the area to which, Alec realized, she'd had rubber matting, a water cooler, and a state-of-the-art single-cup coffee machine added since yesterday. With coffee. And tea, and hot chocolate, and who knows what else, all neatly slotted into their dispenser. And surely that was a new dishwasher and refrigerator. They hadn't been stainless steel before, had they? When had that happened? He'd bet the refrigerator had milk in it already. And everyone's favorite drink, too, which she'd somehow divined. He'd just bet.

Then she turned to him. "I appreciate the chivalry," she told him. "But I've got it."

"What?"

She sighed. "It doesn't exactly make me look stronger if you have to rescue me. I had it. Worst case, I'd have called his boss. I've done this before, you know."

Alec shifted from one foot to the other. "Sorry. But he was pretty...disrespectful."

"I work in the tech industry," she said. "Disrespectful I'm used to. He didn't actually grab my...he didn't actually grab me, which puts him ahead of a fair number of the guys at the last conference I went to."

"And that's OK with you?" Why wasn't she outraged? Because he was, just thinking about it.

"It's not the least bit OK with me. But I've got this," she repeated. "It's not that I don't appreciate your help, but I've got it. And you've got interviews, don't you?"

"Yeah." He pulled his phone out of his pocket and took a look. "Joe should be wrapping that one up, got another one coming in at two."

"Then go take care of that," she urged. "And let me do my job."

♡

He wasn't feeling quite so protective of her two days later. When he and Joe were in the conference room again, joined this time by Brandon and Rae herself.

"I appreciate how easy you've made all this for us," Alec said, trying to smooth the troubled waters and wondering for the thousandth time in his entrepreneurial career why he'd ever thought it would be easier to be the boss. "That setup software was a brilliant idea, and now I've magically got furniture in my magic new office, placed exactly where I wanted it. I even have blinds already. I can't tell you how long that took, last time. And that's great."

"But?" Rae's eyes were steady on him from her spot below Brandon at the table, Joe having chosen to sit across from her. Still hostile, Alec thought with an inward sigh.

"But…if we have to do budgets," he asked, "do we have to do them right now? When we've got so much else going on?"

"Why do we ever have to do them?" Joe muttered. "There are only three of us. Bunch of bureaucratic B.S."

"Four of us," Alec pointed out.

"Because you don't know whether you're overspending until you know what you've planned to spend," Rae said, looking at Joe. "I've made it as simple as possible. I've prefilled the spreadsheets with all the line items I normally see, and even included some ballpark figures for things like trade show expense and salaries. All I need to know is which trade shows you're thinking of going to, how many initial hires you've decided on, what software programs you want everyone to have. Which I need to know anyway," she pointed out, "so I can get them ordered and installed on all the machines just as soon as they arrive. Before your new staff starts showing up. But yes. I do need to get some figures in there." Her low, soft voice was still calm, the only indication of tension the barely audible click of her ballpoint under the table. "I'll need to show some preliminary financials to the board next week."

"You need to spend money to make money." That was Brandon.

"She doesn't get that. Going to be nickel and diming us. Like being nibbled to death by ducks." Joe again.

"I understand that you need to spend money, and so does the board," Desiree said. "But your last venture's financials were, frankly, a mess. The board never knew what was going on from one month to the next. They're pretty tolerant of change, but they absolutely hate surprises. And I suspect that dealing with me's going to be more pleasant than that scenario."

"Dealing with you definitely has its points," Brandon agreed, looking at her with a smile.

She gave him a cool look, and Alec heaved another inward sigh. Another gentle reminder was clearly called for. Because Joe hated her, and Brandon…didn't.

"Well." He set both palms on the shining surface of the table in a gesture of finality. "Sounds like we're doing budgets. I'll talk to you about it at ten, how about," he said to Joe, "before our next interview, and to Brandon, say, eleven-thirty. And we'll work it out."

"And any time you know there's going to be a variance," Rae said, "you just need to inform me."

"I knew it," Joe growled. "Staff meetings. The ultimate time-suck."

"I didn't say staff meetings." Rae looked at him levelly. "I said inform me. I'm two doors down from you. Stick your head in my door. Send me an email. Inform me."

"Man," Alec groaned when the other two men had left, and he'd put a hand out to stop Rae from leaving the room. He leaned back in his chair at the head of the table, rocked a little in the plush leather. "You really know how to clear a room."

"Hey," she said. "I never even mentioned the employee manuals."

♡

He was the one who stuck his head in her door a few days later. She was sitting with their new clerical person, who was industriously taking notes. Veronica, Alec remembered as the thin, somewhat mousy young woman looked up at his entrance and turned a predictable shade of pink. A lot of name for a fairly plain young woman. Rae liked her, anyway, and having a good-looking woman at the front desk would be asking for trouble with all those cocky young code warriors around, legends in their own minds.

"Can I interrupt for a few minutes?" he asked. "Get you to join us in the conference room, Rae?"

"Sure," she said. "Why don't you go on back to the desk, start familiarizing yourself with HR Hero's website," she told Veronica. "Look over the hiring forms, and the employee manual section too. We need to get that in place." She looked up at Alec with a gleam in her eye that had him laughing back at her. "Just as soon as possible, I'd say, wouldn't you, Alec?"

"Oh, absolutely," he agreed, stepping back to let Veronica scuttle past him, the color flaring even higher as she did, and waiting for Rae to join him.

"What's up?" she asked. "Decided on a staff meeting after all? Want to go over those budgets, maybe have me diagram your new hire decision matrix for you?"

"No, although I'm sure you could do it at the drop of a hat. I thought we'd get your input on our logo finalists."

"Oh, actual *fun* stuff. Sure."

"Hmm," she said when she was standing and looking down at the five designs, each printed on a separate piece of paper and laid out on the polished blonde surface of the conference table. "Do you have them smaller?"

Alec stood beside her, looked across the table at his partners, both leaning against the credenza that stood beneath the wall of windows, echoes of their recent heated discussion hanging in the room like a fog. Joe folded his arms and stared at Desiree, his posture clearly communicating that he, for one, wasn't interested in her input. After a few more uncomfortable seconds, Brandon shrugged and grabbed a single sheet of paper from the file folder behind him, leaned forward and slid it across the table to her.

She ignored them both, looked at each large image in turn, then studied it in its smaller size. Alec watched as she flipped first one image over onto its face, then, after another period of study, a second. The third followed, and then her gaze was moving back and forth, again and again, between the final two. Studying the small images again now, and back to the large ones.

Joe sighed, shifted his weight. If Rae noticed, she gave no sign. She rearranged the two images so they were side by side. Then moved them so that one was on the bottom, the other on the top. And then reversed the order.

"This one," she finally said, pointing to her choice.

"Too simple," Brandon began, but Alec put out a hand in a downward motion that silenced the other man.

"Interesting," Alec said. "Why?"

"Because it *is* simple," Rae explained. "Look, this one looks good, all big like this." She reached without hesitation for the blank page second from the left, flipping it over to reveal Brandon and Joe's top candidate. "But look at it small," she explained, tapping a nail on the piece of paper where the logos were reproduced in thumbnail size. "That's how it's going to be viewed, most of the time. You don't have a...a billboard with just your logo on it."

"You have a trade show booth with exactly that," Brandon argued.

"True," she agreed. "And what percentage of our eventual market is going to see our booth at a trade show?"

"She's right," Alec decided. *Our.* That was interesting. "And why this one instead of your other finalist?" Which had been his own favorite.

"That one's bold. But this one is more elegant," she said. "Especially larger, see?" She pointed to the full-size image again. "That other one, it...shouts at you, and isn't the whole point of this software that it's assisting you, sort of gently and unobtrusively? Running your life, but more in the background?"

"Like a really good secretary," Alec agreed. "Like they used to be, anyway."

"Everybody gets a wife," Brandon put in. "That's the idea."

"Hmm. I'd think hard about that image," Rae said, her tone dry as dust. "But anyway, this one caught my eye first, and I came back to it at the end, too. And when I see it alone..." She flipped her final also-ran over on its face, "I like it even more."

"I think we just got schooled, boys," Alec said with a grin.

"But don't go by me," Desiree said hastily, looking up to see Joe's frown, the spasm of annoyance that crossed Brandon's face. "I'm not a marketing expert. How about asking the others? We've got ten people out there already. Have them choose, and tell you why. That would be illuminating. They're all in your target demographic, surely. Or send your top three contenders out to a market research firm. Which you've already thought of, I'm sure." She looked at Brandon with an apologetic laugh.

"These just came *back* from the market research firm," Alec said. "With a strong consensus, which we weren't sure whether to accept."

"Because it was...?"

He smiled again. "Yours."

♡

He waited until she was well out of the room, then looked at Joe. "What?"

Joe shook his head, ran a hand that always looked like it belonged on a laborer, not the best programmer in the business, over his stubble of beard. Alec waited patiently. It could take Joe a while.

"Man," Joe finally said, "you've got to stop."

"Stop what?"

"Stop letting her do whatever she wants, just because you're hot for her."

Alec stared at him, speechless for once "What?" Joe said. "It's obvious. It's been the three of us for ten years, man. Ten *years*. And you and me for longer than that. And you're screwing it up. You're pissing it away."

"Do you feel that way too?" Alec looked at Brandon. "If you do, say it now."

Brandon spread his hands. "Hey, dude. What do you want from me? Do I think she's a tightass? Yeah, I do, but what CFO isn't? Do I think she's got a *cute* ass? Would I like to tap that? Hell, yeah. And I've never seen anybody as sharp on the ops side. Which is generous of me to admit, seeing as how she gave me the worst office. So, hey. Decorative, and doing the job. I'm good."

That was going to be Topic B. Meanwhile, Alec looked at Joe again. "Brandon's right," he told his best friend. "She's sharp on the ops side. And by the way," he added to Brandon, "I assigned the offices, just so you know. And you don't have the worst one, she does. Who's next to the break room? She is."

"But anyway." He dismissed that for the irrelevancy it was. "Yeah. She's sharp on the ops side. She's sharp on the financial side, too. Ron's been running companies longer than you and I have been alive, and she was his choice."

"And why was that?" Joe asked quietly.

"If you're suggesting that she's sleeping with him," Alec said, feeling the anger rise, hot, red, and unaccustomed, "you and I are going to discuss this offline."

He stopped, went to the door and shoved it closed. Nobody needed to hear this, and he needed the time to compose himself. He was always cool. But he wasn't cool now.

"Look, man," he said after a moment, looking Joe straight in the eye. "You're the best in the business. I wouldn't want to do this without you. I never have yet, and I don't want to start now. But you've got to trust me on the admin stuff."

Here it was, the elephant in the room, the issue Rae had put her pretty finger on right from the start. He was in charge. They danced around it, but it was the bald truth. He asked Joe's opinion, and he cared about it. But when it came down to the wire, he called the shots.

"So you're saying, get on board or go home," Joe said.

Alec winced inside, but kept his gaze steady on the other man. His partner and, besides his dad and his brother, the man he trusted most in the world. Could this really be it? One way to find out.

"Yeah," he said. "That's the bottom line."

Joe nodded slowly, gave his jaw one final scratch. "All right," he said. "I'm on board. I'm not happy, but hell, it's been too long, and I've trusted you to carry me this far."

Alec let out a breath he hadn't realized he was holding, tried his damnedest not to let his relief show. "All right," he said, and wished he could wipe his hands on his pants.

"One more thing," he told both of them. "That's it, on the mention of her ass. Or her looks. That's the last time. We clear?" He looked from one man to the other. "Because there's no place for that here, and that has to come from the top." Which Rae had said, he remembered. And once again, she'd been right.

the other woman

♡

"What's the deal with these boxes?" Desiree asked, touching one of the empty cardboard cartons with her toe. "They've been here since yesterday. Simon? Michael?"

The two young men turned reluctantly from Simon's cube, where they'd been consulting. Or maybe just chatting. "I brought some stuff in from home," Simon said.

She nodded. "Were you planning on taking the boxes home, then?"

"No. Just hadn't got around to getting rid of them."

"Well, get rid of them now, please. Flatten them and put them in the break room, and the cleaner will take them out."

She stood expectantly until he exchanged a speaking glance with his friend and got up, his reluctance obvious, and picked up the cartons. Once she was satisfied, she continued on her way back to her office, her mind returning to its ever-present checklist.

"Rae!" The call came from the reception desk, and she turned, already smiling.

"Hi, Claudine!" She retraced her steps as the blonde finished signing in, came over to her with the delight that made her so good at her job, and gave her a quick hug.

"We already bought it," Desiree teased. "Just to get that out of the way."

"Hey, I'm here on pleasure, not business," Claudine said. "But I noticed, and I was planning to call and say that if anybody needs any training, let me know and I'll get it set up ASAP. If I'd known it was you, I'd have called already. I didn't realize you were part of this outfit. My sources have let me down."

"It wasn't a done deal until the last minute," Rae explained. Although she *was* a bit surprised that it had been four whole weeks since she'd signed the contract, and Claudine hadn't found out. As regional sales manager for the most popular contact management software out there, Claudine knew everyone. And everything.

They'd first met when Claudine was working the booth at a conference, and Desiree had stopped by to ask some questions about the new version. She'd liked the other woman's no-non-sense competence from the start, but they'd really bonded when Claudine had seen Desiree sitting in a meeting room, waiting for a seminar to start, and had come over to join her. They'd started to chat, only to be increasingly distracted by the conversation of the two guys behind them. One dirty joke after another, each filthier than the last. Not Desiree's first such experience, and it wouldn't prove to be her last. Sharing it with Claudine had been an education, though.

"Hey, guys." Claudine had turned around with a toss of her blonde mane that channeled the cheerleader she most definitely hadn't been. "Winston, right?" she asked Guy #1. Claudine remembered every name.

"Uh…yeah," he said, crossing his arms, then uncrossing them again. "Oh. This is Noah."

"Noah," Claudine nodded while sticking a hand out for the other man to shake. "This is Rae. We're both pretty cute, huh?"

"Yeah," Winston said, looking more awkward than ever.

"Little tip for you," Claudine said, her bright smile never wavering. She inclined her head forward confidentially, causing both men to somehow sway towards her as well. "We're *really* impressed by the gentleman stuff. It's a woman thing. Keep it clean, win her…heart."

She'd winked, then, flashed an even brighter smile, and turned around again with Desiree. Winston and Noah had shut up. And Claudine and Desiree had formed a friendship that had lasted through that conference, and the years that had followed.

"I'm sorry I didn't know you were in town," Desiree said now. "I'd have got away for lunch. Well, coffee, anyway. Come on back and tell me what's new. I've got a couple minutes."

"Just a flying stop," Claudine followed Desiree toward her office, waving a hello where she recognized a face. "Portland tomorrow, then Seattle. But we have a few clients in the City I wanted to call on while I was here."

"Were we one of them?" Desiree was a little confused. She gestured Claudine into her office, noticed the missing shelf on her bookcase again. She needed to get the furniture guy back up here with that. Joe had one missing as well. Her thumbs typed "shelf" onto her phone, even as she took a seat behind her desk.

Claudine laughed and arranged her long limbs into one of the visitor's chairs. "Not exactly. A certain Mr. A. Kincaid I usually manage to pay a non-sales call on. Or maybe you could say that he pays one on me. Like I said, pleasure, not business. And honey, we're talking *pleasure*. That man can do things with his tongue that'll have you begging for mercy and shouting Hallelujah."

Desiree felt a jolt that had everything to do with…everything. Arousal, and jealousy, and confusion. None of which she wanted to examine right now.

"TMI," she said instead. "I'm working with the guy."

"And you don't think about doin' it with him? How can you help it?"

"I'm the straitlaced type. Hard-wired that way. So is it a serious thing? You and Alec?"

Another laugh. "Not exactly. Like I said. Non-sales call. Just a blonde having more fun. And yes, salon blonde counts."

And there was the man himself, one brown hand gripping the edge of the doorway as he swung his body around it, took a bouncing stride inside.

"Somebody told me there was a good-looking woman in the office," he said. "I thought I'd better come check it out."

"Hey, handsome," Claudine said, rising from her chair and bending to give Desiree a quick hug goodbye before turning to Alec. "You ready to get that drink?"

"Oh, you know it." Alec looked at Desiree. "Taking off," he told her unnecessarily. "Don't work too late."

"Have fun," she said, her smile feeling pasted on. Which was just stupid.

She was going over her numbers again, taking advantage of the quiet time. The outer office was dim and silent, even Joe having left a half-hour earlier.

She looked up at the sound of the office doors opening, then hissing shut again. Sat up a little straighter, her heart beating a little harder. The building had good security, she reminded herself, and you needed a keycard to get up here.

She could sense, rather than hear, someone moving around out there. If it had been Rosa, she'd have announced her presence with her usual cheerful call of "Cleaners!" That is, if her rolling cart hadn't done it for her. Desiree wished she'd left her office door open so she could see, then wished she'd locked it. She considered calling out herself, abandoned the idea fast. Sat still and hoped whoever it was would go away.

The suspense increased as the seconds ticked by, until she was literally holding her breath, staring at the door in frozen silence. And then there was a knock that made her leap in her chair, followed by the sight and sound of…just Alec, pushing the door open with a quiet "Rae?"

"Oh." She let her breath out with a *whoosh*, put both hands to her chest without even realizing it, felt the gallop of her heart. "You scared the hell out of me."

"Did I? Sorry. Didn't realize anyone was still here until I saw your light on." He looked at her more closely. "Hey. I really *did* scare you."

"That's OK." She reached for her water bottle, took a swig. "I just wasn't expecting you back."

Why *was* he back? It had sounded from Claudine's description like he took his time. Well, if they'd just had one drink, and then got into it…

Danger, Will Robinson. None of her business.

"Yeah." He perched on the edge of her desk, swinging a foot. "I stopped by to pick up some stuff. Why are you still here? It's after eight."

"First financials to the board tomorrow," she explained, trying not to look up into those eyes. Trying not to look at the strength of the thigh resting on her desk. Which didn't leave her a whole lot to look at. "Running through them again."

"Did you eat?"

"Uh…" She had to think about it. "No."

"Not dinner? Or not lunch *or* dinner?"

"Hey. I had lunch."

"Let me guess. An apple. *Maybe* an energy bar."

"You got the apple right," she said with a reluctant smile. She still felt jumpy, and a little shaky. She *had* forgotten the energy bar, she realized guiltily.

"All right." He got up, held out a hand. "Shut down and come on."

"What? I'm still working."

"Desiree." She jumped again at the use of her full name. She heard it so rarely these days. "You can take your laptop with you. And when you get home, you can sit up in bed, the way I'd be willing to bet you do anyway, and go through your numbers. But you're going to eat first. Come on, now. Shut down and let's go."

"You didn't eat anything yet?" She clicked her mouse to switch off, then realized the implications of that, what Claudine had said, and could feel herself starting to blush.

"Nope. Not a thing." If he'd noticed what she'd said, what she'd thought about what she'd said, he didn't give any sign of it. "And I'm starved. Take pity on me and keep me company. And then you can go home and look over your financials, although if you've made a single mistake, if you have to change a single thing before tomorrow…well, if you do, I'll owe you twenty bucks, how's that."

"Twenty bucks, huh?" She stuffed her laptop into its bag, opened the bottom drawer for her purse. "You have that much confidence in my accuracy?"

"Desiree," he said with a smile, walking through her door behind her and waiting while she turned the key, "I have complete faith in you."

♡

"The booth's going to look awesome," Brandon said, late the next morning. "And that setup should be a piece of cake." Well, it was nice to be appreciated.

"Maybe we could get into it in more…depth, over lunch," he suggested. "Could be a *long* lunch. I've got a brand-new Beemer just begging to be driven down the Great Highway. I'd love to have you try it out with me, see how fast we could go, how many laws we could break. I'll bet you're not nearly as buttoned-up as you like to pretend. Could be fun, don't you think?"

"Thanks," Desiree said, not looking up from her sketch. "But I'll be working through lunch."

"Sure? Might be nice to get away for a little while, get to know each other better. We're going to be working together really closely over the next few months. And I wouldn't mind getting even closer."

She looked across her desk at him at last, and the smile on his face left no doubt as to his meaning. Brandon had never heard of the soft sell. And he was attractive enough. Brown hair, stylishly cut. Round blue eyes, a bit of a snub nose, a boyish, open expression and cheerful grin that lots of women would find attractive, she was sure. And although he wasn't especially tall, topping her own five-nine by only an inch or two, he was in good shape, a shape that he displayed in European-cut slacks, dress shirts that hadn't come off the clearance rack, and the latest in Italian footwear, all a sharp contrast to Joe's jeans and running shoes.

Brandon dressed like Alec, she realized suddenly. Exactly like Alec.

She sighed, tapped the sheets of paper sharply together to align the edges, and set them aside. The layout for the booth that she'd better get ordered today, if it was going to be delivered in time. Because it was late November already, and with the holidays coming up…

She needed to deal with this first, though, so she turned her attention back to Brandon. "It's not a good idea. Not appropriate." Time to be direct, because the subtle approach wasn't working. "I appreciate your welcoming me, but I keep my professional relationships professional."

"You sure?" he pressed. "It's not inappropriate if there's no reporting relationship. If you're attracted, and I'm attracted, there's nothing to stop us. See, I read the policy, I didn't just sign it. Brownie points for me."

"Good for you. And I'm sure you read the next paragraph too, about unwelcome advances. You're allowed to ask once, and now you have, and I've answered." She kept her tone even. She didn't need to make another enemy here.

He put up both hands in a gesture of surrender. "All right. I get it. But for the record, any advances *you* want to make would be welcome. Just to put it out there."

"It's out there. Next item. Job description for your new marcom person. Let's work it up, I'll polish it and run it by you, and I'll post it this afternoon."

To her relief, he picked up the cue. Well, nobody could have called him stupid. A little persistent, maybe, but that was his job.

They were deep into it when she heard the single knock at the half-open door, and saw Alec stepping inside. He pulled his wallet from the back pocket of today's slacks—black, hugging his…physique very nicely indeed, and worn with a silvery-gray shirt that did wonders for his hair and skin.

Oh, yeah, he was doing something with his wallet too. He pulled out a twenty, waved it in the air. "Any changes?"

"Mmm…no," she admitted, his mock-concern teasing a smile from her.

He put the bill back into its slot within the slim strip of black leather and shoved the whole thing into his back pocket again. "Too bad I didn't set the terms better, but I'd say the next lunch is on you."

"It's on the company credit card either way," she pointed out. "All goes into the same category in the general ledger too. Which limits the scope of your victory considerably."

"But I have the satisfaction of winning. Which is never to be underestimated." He smiled down at her. "Got your energy bar today?"

She reached into her desk drawer, waved the pale blue-wrapped packet triumphantly.

"Not enough. Got to eat it too," he reminded her.

"Gotcha, boss." She sketched a salute.

He laughed again, then looked at Brandon. "Got a couple minutes later on? I had a flash on a visual in the shower this morning that I think is going to knock some socks off at the show next month."

Desiree had a flash on a visual of the shower that threatened to knock her socks off right now. She was suddenly very aware that she wasn't wearing any. Socks, that is. That only a pair of very tiny underwear lay between...her...and Alec's hand, should it choose to make its way under her skirt, up her thigh.

Which it wouldn't.

"Sure," Brandon said. "Soon as I'm done here."

Alec nodded again, rapped a farewell on the office door with a knuckle, and was gone.

"That was cozy," Brandon remarked.

"What?" Desiree wiped the foolish smile off her face. "Just a joke."

"Having lunch with me isn't appropriate, but having lunch with him is?"

"Because you *weren't* appropriate," she pointed out. "I told you."

"And he is."

"What did he say just now that was inappropriate? That he wouldn't have said to you?"

Brandon snorted. "That's his technique. Dude's had more tail than a peacock. And that's how he gets it. All casual and fun, just like that."

"Which is a *totally* inappropriate thing to say," she replied sharply. "Let's get back to this. Make sure you're all set up by the time of that show, so you *can* knock some socks off."

♡

But, she let herself remember once Brandon had left, dinner *had* been good. If it had been inappropriate, that had just been her traitorous imagination, getting away from her. Nothing Alec had done. Nothing at all.

He'd called a cab before he'd even ridden down the elevator with her, and it had been waiting by the time they'd left the lobby. Which had been awfully nice, and the place he'd taken her had been even nicer.

North Beach. More white tablecloths, more waiters. She'd have been impressed by how well the headwaiter had seemed to know Alec, how attentive he'd been, if she hadn't seen the bill slip from Alec's fingers into the other man's palm.

Well, maybe she'd still been impressed. Because it was just so...so *nice*. To lean against the worn brick wall in the soft light at the back of the little restaurant, to look into those eyes, so thickly fringed with black. To see the flash of teeth as he laughed, and to think about what Claudine had said. About his mouth, and about what he could do with it.

And she could have sworn that he was thinking about the same thing when those deep blue eyes had looked into her own. Even though he'd been nothing but a gentleman.

"You sure?" he asked when the white-mustachioed waiter made his second appearance. "Just soup? Not even a salad? Maybe chicken?"

"When I'm really tired," she found herself confessing, "knives and forks are too hard. Even salad's too hard. All that chewing."

"All right, then. Just Tuscan Beef Soup for the lady," he told the waiter. "But bring her some extra bread. And," she heard him say quietly to the elderly man, "if you could have them fill that soup bowl up a little higher, that'd be great. And bring it out right away?"

She'd spooned up every bit of the rich broth, the chunks of beef and vegetables, had dipped a second and then a third piece of bread in olive oil. Alec had watched it all without comment, while dispatching his own dinner with an alacrity that confirmed to Desiree that he really hadn't had dinner yet tonight.

And when they'd finished, he'd insisted, together with Giuseppe—of course the waiter's name was Giuseppe, because this wasn't romantic enough, the white tablecloth and the single red rose and the candle and the worn brick against her shoulder—he'd insisted that she order cannoli for dessert.

"Just one," he coaxed. "If you don't want it, you don't have to eat a single bite. But I think you need to taste whipped cream tonight."

"Don't you think she needs some whipped cream?" he demanded of the waiter, who smiled back at him, sensing, Desiree thought through a satisfied haze of red wine, succulent beef, and way too much potent testosterone, a truly magnificent tip.

"Definitely, the *signorina* needs whipped cream," Giuseppe agreed. "And we have the best."

She wasn't sure how you had better whipped cream than anyone else, but when the dessert arrived, she had to concede that this was the best.

Amaretto, one still-sane corner of her practical brain suggested, but that sensible voice was drowned out, oh so rapidly, by the sensation on her tongue, the silky smoothness of cream, the almond sweetness of the liqueur, the delicate drift of pastry and the deep dark pleasure of chocolate. And Alec, watching her as she allowed the rich concoction to drift between her lips, over her tongue, down her throat. Watching her, enjoying the sight of her enjoying herself, as if it were his tongue. His throat.

By the time he'd slapped a hand against the door of the cab that had again been waiting when they'd stepped out of the restaurant's front door, leaped back onto the sidewalk and raised that same hand in farewell, she'd been so lost in fatigue, wine, and lust that she could only sit back against the scarred leather and thank heaven that she hadn't actually kissed him. Or begged him.

♡

And thinking about it now wasn't doing her one single bit of good. She focused again on the job description she'd roughed out with Brandon for their new marketing communications person. She needed to get that posted, get the trade shows, anyway, off her plate and turned over to somebody else pronto. Once she got this done, she promised herself, she *would* eat that energy bar. Lunch break.

She felt a flash of irritation that Brandon hadn't been willing to take more of it on himself. She was going to have to be careful that he didn't take advantage of her. He had a good reputation—the trio's past three ventures had certainly succeeded spectacularly enough to send any sales and marketing professional's career sky-rocketing—but now she wondered how much of that had been due to his brilliance, and how much to the Alec Kincaid magic.

Her cell chirped, and she turned from the screen to which she'd added not a word, glanced at the display. Claudine.

"Hey, you." She leaned back in her chair to stretch a little. "You still around?"

"SFO. Waiting to board. Why didn't you tell me?"

"Tell you what?" She sat up straight again. Was Claudine upset that Desiree hadn't notified her of the job change? She hadn't seemed to mind yesterday.

"That you and Alec had a thing going on."

Desiree's mouth opened, stuttered over a protest as Claudine went on. "I'd have backed off if I'd known. I'm a little hurt, tell you the truth, that you don't trust me more than that. He's Prime cut, no doubt about it. But you're a friend."

"Wait. I mean, thanks." And there Desiree was, right back in the Confusion Zone. "But we don't. Have anything going on, I mean. Nothing personal. Just business."

"Uh-*huh*." The skepticism came right through the airwaves. "Which would certainly explain him turning me down."

"He did?" Desiree felt a surge of relief at getting the right answer to a question she hadn't dared ask, even of herself. "Well, I can imagine that doesn't happen to you very often," she hastened to add, "but it's nothing to do with me." She didn't say that she was sorry, because she wasn't.

"Only possible explanation," Claudine insisted. "Because I know it's not me. I've still got it. And he isn't exactly famous for turning women down. Turning them *over*, you bet. He knows it all, and he does it, too, six ways from Sunday. I could walk into any Women in Tech conference you'd care to name, ask who knows where his birthmark is, and count the show of hands. And then ask who'd like to see it again, and honey, that number would be exactly the same."

"All right, he's hot stuff," Desiree conceded. "And apparently more than a little slutty, I will just point out here. But everybody's entitled to an off night." Although he hadn't seemed like he'd been having an off night. Not while he'd been watching her eat whipped cream, he hadn't. A surge of pure lust at the memory had her doing some involuntary Kegels under her desk, and she actually shivered.

"And another thing." Claudine continued as if Desiree hadn't spoken. "Who did we talk about all evening? Not yours truly, beautiful and fascinating as I am."

"Me?" *That* was news. "He talked about me?"

"Where did I meet you?" The mimicry was clear. "How long have we known each other? And if you'd like to quiz me on my knowledge of how you've spent the past few weeks, your brilliant organizational skills, go right ahead, because I'm all clued in. Boring as hell, baby, and you know I love you."

"Oh." Desiree couldn't think of what else to say.

"But, Rae." Claudine's voice was serious now. "Here's a word of warning from a veteran of the trenches. He's a pro at this, and you're not. I'm not saying he's a bad guy. But I don't think the words 'I love you' have ever crossed those luscious lips, not unless he was talking to his mother. He's a good time, but he's not a good bet, not as a long-term prospect."

"He's not a prospect at all." Desiree was clear on that, whatever her body was telling her. "Even if I weren't working with him, he's not my type."

"Honey, that man is everybody's type."

"Not mine, he's not. I don't want a player. I sure as heck don't want to be played."

"You just hold that thought. Whoops. The Premium Star Alliance is boarding, and you know I'm premium."

"And a star." Desiree smiled, feeling extremely charitable and loving towards her friend. For some reason. At this particular moment. "Go. Talk soon."

She pressed the *End* button, looked across at the framed reproduction of Monet's *Water Lilies* that hung opposite her desk.

"Why," she asked the delicate purple flowers, "does everybody think I have a thing for Alec Kincaid? And why on *earth* would they imagine that he could have a thing for me?"

But the flowers just continued to float serenely on their placid pond, and said not a word.

And by the way. Exactly where *was* Alec's birthmark?

to grandmother's house we go

♡

"So that's next year's holidays decided on," Desiree said briskly. "Next item: closing the office over Christmas and New Year's."

They *were* having a staff meeting. Which Joe hadn't been one bit excited about, especially when he'd seen that horror of horrors, an agenda.

"What's this?" he'd demanded of Desiree, coming into Alec's office, where the two of them were working out software training plans, and waving the piece of paper. "I'll tell you what it is. Thin end of the wedge."

She looked at him, kept her voice level. "As I see it, you have three choices. One. I could send around an email asking all of you what you want to do about everything on that list. Everyone could "reply all," and we could go around and around and around about it for a day, until Alec made a decision. Two. Alec could make a decision all by himself. Or Three. We could all sit down together, spend fifteen minutes, you could voice your opinion, and Alec could make a decision *with* your input. Which would you prefer?"

He scowled at her a moment more, then smiled reluctantly, the stony expression softening. "All right. You got me there. Why do you have to be so damn reasonable?"

She laughed. This was *her* thin end of the wedge, and she was going to exploit it. "I don't know. Why do *you* have to be so damn stubborn?"

And that had made things a little easier, though he'd grumbled again when she'd stuck her head into his office to remind him of the meeting.

"One sec. I'm in the middle of something," he said.

She stood where she was for thirty seconds more, then stepped further into his office, the first time she'd entered his space since she'd had the furnishings set up. "Everyone else is ready," she told him. "Let's go, code boy."

"Witch," he muttered. But he smiled when he said it, logged off, and followed her.

"Thursday's Christmas Eve," she said now. "Two holidays, Thursday and Friday, same thing over New Year's. Do we close the office at five on Wednesday, the 23rd? Or a few hours early? Since we haven't had time to organize any kind of holiday party. And give people a chance to get wherever they're going, too."

"Good idea," Alec said. "What do you guys think? Two? Noon?"

"Yeah," Joe agreed. "Noon. Why not. Announce it now. Nice little present."

"All right. Let's do it at noon. You agree?" Alec belatedly asked Brandon.

"Sure," he shrugged. "Since I only have one person on my 'staff' so far, not that big a deal."

"All right." Alec looked at Desiree again. "Noon."

"OK," she said, making a note. "I'll send that around. Last thing. Reminder that anytime anyone steps away from their desk, they need to log off. I've noticed that hasn't always been happening, and that's a security breach, and a bad habit. I'll share with the two of you that we had multiple login attempts on Alec's account recently, and that's worrisome."

"Huh. Some cocky code warrior thinking it'd be funny to hack the boss, probably," Joe said. "Can't have thought they'd really get in."

"Oh, I don't know. Maybe they heard that he always uses some variant of his parents' address in there," Brandon said. "You still got that lazy habit?" he asked Alec.

"Not anymore," Alec said. "Rae already set me straight. Nobody's going to get in that way."

"Anyway," Desiree went on, "I'd appreciate if you'd remind your staff, and keep an eye out. I've been doing it, but it'll have more force if it comes from you too."

"It happens automatically after a few minutes," Brandon pointed out. "And it's a pain in the a—a pain in the neck to do it every single time you get up to talk to somebody."

"How long do you think it takes to slip a flash drive into a machine and press a couple keys?" she asked. "A few seconds to copy a file, or even more scarily, a few seconds to install a keylogger, and bingo, you've got code."

"We've got systems built in to check for that," Joe reminded her.

"And now we're going to have even more," she said. "As you know, we already allow no computers except the ones belonging to the four of us to leave the building. And starting today, there'll be a check at the security desk downstairs as well. Bags, backpacks, and turning out pockets, every time, to check for laptops, flash drives, any device that could store code. And that includes all of us. Nothing but a laptop for any of you, and you'll have to open up for inspection."

"What?" Joe stared at her. "Every time we leave the building?"

"Yes," she said. "Word's leaked out about what we're doing here, and there's a lot of buzz. Which is good, but you don't leave the Hope Diamond lying around. You install levels of security, and that's what we've done. Think of it as data hygiene. Good habits, like washing your hands after you use the men's room, which I also hope everyone's been doing, or I'd better start using a Kleenex every time I open a door."

Joe's bark of laughter broke the moment of startled silence. "I think you'd better use the Kleenex," he said. "Some of those guys are Neanderthals. But your point's taken."

"Good. Thanks. Because this is another one that has to come from the top, and requires your support. Alec, I'm calling you out right now on that first point, because you're the worst offender."

"Hmm?" He'd been looking at her intently enough. But not listening?

"Log off when you leave your computer. Please." She did her best to stay patient. After all, none of this was news to him, and he was probably thinking about code again. He'd been staying as late as she had, lately, though there hadn't been any repeats of their cozy dinner in the ten days since. But it sure was nice knowing that she wasn't on the floor alone. He sometimes came in to chat with her for a few minutes, too, when they were the only ones left. Perching that thigh on the desk, flashing that smile, the darkness outside her windows, the dimly lit office glimpsed through her half-open door all enhancing the feeling that they were the only two people in the world. And if that felt even nicer, well, that was her secret.

"Oh. OK," he said. And she had to be content with that.

♡

"So what are you doing over Christmas?" he asked that evening. When he was, yes, perched on the corner of her desk, swinging that leg, in gray slacks this time. And the usual dress shirt, white against the darkness beneath, open at the collar to show a brief triangle of skin.

She tried to sit back casually, to keep herself from leaning towards him. And was rewarded by a sudden vision of her

hands unfastening the next button on that white shirt, exposing another few inches of smooth brown, her fingertips lightly
brushing the chest she'd imagined touching so many times. Of
standing between those strong thighs while she did it. Of her
hands dropping to rest on them, how firm they would feel under
her palms. Because she would have to hold on, once he pulled her
in close to kiss her.

She shifted a little in the leather chair, saw him watch her
do it. And realized, in another flash of insight, that she hadn't
worn pants to work since they'd finished moving in. Because she
longed with every traitorous cell of her being to stand between
those thighs while he slipped his hands under the fine wool of her
skirt, stroked slowly up the backs of her bare legs until she was
pressed against him, until he held a cheek in each big palm, until
he was pulling her tight against his body, rubbing her against
him in exactly the place, in exactly the way she needed him to.

"What?" she asked. What had they been talking about? She
realized that his eyes had dropped to her breasts, and was suddenly aware, to her horror, that not only had she worn her sheer-
est, laciest underwear today, but she'd worn the matching bra as
well, the one in the nude color that made her look...well, nude.
And that she'd watched herself in the cheval mirror that stood in
one corner of her bedroom as she'd put them on, as she'd lingered
over every languorous movement, just so she could imagine him
watching too. Just like he was watching her now.

Watching her nipples harden, that was what he was doing.
And the yellow silk blouse wouldn't be concealing that one bit.
More like showing it off. Exposing her. Her insistent body, and
her wayward thoughts.

Why hadn't she *thought* about that when she'd slipped the
thing on? Or at least when she'd buttoned it up, her fingers
sliding over the fine texture that only silk could provide, and
watched herself doing it? Or more correctly, why hadn't she *not*

thought about it? What was she *doing?* Her fantasy life was way out of control, and right now, it was about to go straight over the edge.

"Huh?" he asked, not seeming any clearer on the topic than she was herself.

"What did you just ask me?" This was getting ridiculous. What were they, Abbott and Costello? Who was on first?

♡

Alec tried with a herculean effort of will to drag his mind back from the danger zone. From the place he'd gone as soon as he'd seen her pupils enlarging, that sweet, generous mouth softening and parting, her full lower lip dropping a little, revealing just a flash of pink tongue and small white teeth.

And then his gaze had traveled, out of his control now, tracing an irresistible path down the honey-colored skin of her throat, along the draped vee of neckline on that silky yellow blouse he'd been looking at all day. To the outline of the perfectly rounded, perfectly pretty breasts beneath. And the telltale points that formed as he watched, just asking for his palm to settle over one of them. Asking for his thumb to flick over it, again and again, while her mouth opened wider, her head went back. While he held her, his other hand tight around the curve of her beautiful ass. While he kissed the vulnerable, slim column of her throat, closed his teeth gently over the place where her neck met her shoulder.

He could almost feel the shudder that would run through her while he did it. Because he was watching it right now, the shiver she couldn't suppress. And imagining how it would feel to reach under that slim knit skirt, to touch her through the flimsy silken barrier that was no barrier at all. Until he slipped his hand inside to explore the soft, secret places underneath, to feel the way she would open to him. Open for him.

"What did you just ask me?" That was her. This was what was actually happening. She wasn't begging him. She wasn't asking him for it at all. She was trying to get him back on track.

"Oh." He struggled for composure, dropped a forearm, as casually as he could manage it, over his thigh, shifted position a little. Cleared his throat. "I said, what are you doing for Christmas?"

"Oh." She got busy straightening some papers on the desk that, as far as he could tell, didn't need straightening. "Going to my grandma's."

"This would be the grandmother in Chico? Mrs. Foster?"

"Yes. How about you?"

"Same. Not going to your grandmother's, that is, but spending the holiday with my family. I'm driving up there Wednesday afternoon with Joe. He doesn't have family close, so he usually comes home with me for the holidays. You want a ride?" he found himself offering. "Save you the drive? We'll be coming back Sunday."

"Oh. No." She was back with the papers again. "No, thanks, I'd better drive myself. Besides..." and this time a smile curved that luscious mouth, and her dimple peeked out again beside it. She'd eaten all her lipstick off, this late in the day, leaving her full lips exposed, soft and pink and vulnerable and...Damn. *Stop thinking about her lips.*

"I don't think Joe would be too excited," she was saying, and he dragged his mind back once again. "It might not be too comfortable, four hours with him hating on me from the back seat."

He laughed. "Hey. It might not be that way."

"Oh, I think so. Coming between the two of you again, getting in the middle of your beautiful bromance?"

"You never know. He might make *you* sit in the back seat."

The smile was gone, her posture stiffening a bit. "Could be. So I'll drive myself. But thanks."

"Wait," he said in alarm. "It was a joke. Of course you'd sit in the front. Joe's really a good guy, you know. And anyway, that'd be up to me. You'd sit in the front."

"I know it would. I mean, I know I would. Never mind. It's just that…" She stopped, shrugged. "I don't like to ride in the back. A thing I have."

"Oh. OK." He was still confused. But whatever was wrong, maybe he could tease her out of it. "So you're driving yourself. In, let me guess. Your silver Corolla."

"Nope." But she was laughing a little, and her shoulders had lost their rigid set.

"You're right. Way too flashy. Your *white* Corolla."

"Hmm." Still smiling. "Maybe you don't know me quite as well as you think you do."

"Could be," he said with a grin of his own. He loved watching her let go of that caution, that ever-present focus. Letting herself have fun. "Maybe I'll find out. Catch you riding your Harley down Third Street in your leathers. Though I still think it'd make sense to go together. And, just to get all wild and crazy here, maybe we could even get together for coffee, since we'll both be there."

She sighed. "It's called a personal life, Alec. We both have them, and it'd probably be better if we kept that separate from the work, don't you think?"

No. "Yes. Sure. OK." He eased himself off her desk, grateful that he could safely stand up again. "Speaking of which, I'd better get back to work, let you finish up too." Because although the arousal still lingered, what he was mostly feeling now was rattled. Off-balance. And, for the first time in a long, long time, completely unsure of where he stood with a woman.

spirit of the season

♡

The arm came around from the front. She watched the hand beneath the buttoned shirt cuff groping towards her, shrank against the seat again, pulled her legs as far to the side as they could go.

The questing fingers finally touched a piece of white paper that was lying on the floor, and the hand closed around it and scrunched it, the paper wrinkling up.

There was a jerk that flung her away from the window, and then they were going sideways, spinning around, and there was a screeching sound that went on and on, and somebody screaming. And then the *boom,* the crunch that cut the screaming off, even as she felt the wrench of something grabbing her hard around the middle, the crack as her head hit the window, the sharp pain blossoming, hot and red and spiky, until it filled every bit of her.

And it hurt really bad, and she wanted her mom. But her mom didn't come.

♡

Her sobs woke her. She was lying in bed, the tears wet on her cheeks, her head aching as if she had hit it just that moment and not twenty-five years earlier.

She rolled towards her bedside table and reached for her water glass, grabbed a corner of the sheet and wiped it across her eyes, over her cheeks. The dream was still there, vivid in her head along with the pain, and she switched on the lamp to chase it away, sat up and reached for her phone to check the time.

Four o'clock. The witching hour, when the bad things came back to haunt you.

♡

"Tell my girlfriend that I missed her. Give her a big smooch for me."

"I will." She smiled at Philip as she slammed the trunk of the car on her suitcase, then reached out for him, felt his arms wrapping around her, squeezing her tight, and had to blink back a couple tears at the comfort of it.

And then Javier, giving her a hug of his own. "Merry Christmas. Drive safe. And oh." He reached for the red bag he'd set on the sidewalk beside the car, handed it to her with a flourish. "Something to make Christmas Day a little more festive."

"Ooh, champagne," she said with a quick peek. "Cool. Thanks, guys. We're going to be two loopy ladies after we toast with this."

"Hmm." Javier tapped a finger against his chin. "You *could* use it for that, or you could invite Mr. Alexander Alpha Kincaid over and get toasted with *him.*"

"Which would be...hmm. Yeah. A *very* bad idea."

"Really? Because, baby girl, excuse me for saying it, but you need to get laid. You're getting dark circles under your eyes."

She had to laugh. "And sex helps with that? Really? I never heard that one."

"Gets the blood flowing," Javier assured her. "Sends oxygen to all those important places. Like your...brain."

"Oh, yeah. My brain. I'll remember that. Gotta go. Merry Christmas, guys. Have a great one."

"Bye." Javier gave her one last kiss on the cheek. "But if you get that man under the mistletoe, take that chance. Oxygen. Blood flow. I'm just sayin'."

♡

Philip and Javier were almost the only people who had touched her at all during the past two months, bar the occasional hand-shake, she realized as she drove off with one last wave out the car window. She hadn't been able to get back to Chico since she'd started the job, even for Thanksgiving. Which would have been all right, because her grandmother always came to visit her for a few days in December. Ostensibly to walk around Union Square, look at the decorations in the store windows and the big tree, exclaim over the huge, decorated marble lobbies of the grand office buildings, and go for a ladies' lunch on the top floor of Macy's, have tea with little sandwiches and cakes. But actually because it was a time when it was better to be together.

But this year, her grandmother hadn't come.

"The drive's getting a little long for me," Dixie had told her. "So you'll have to go see all the lights for me, and tell me all about it."

"Are you not feeling well? What does your doctor say?"

"Oh, I'm fine," Dixie insisted. "Nothing to bother a doctor about. I'm not sick, just a little tired. Just getting old."

"You aren't old, Grandma. You're not even seventy-five yet."

Her grandmother laughed, the familiar smoky whisky sound. "Well, then, just say I'm old enough to deserve a rest, how's that? I get to lie around on the couch all day and eat bonbons if I want, I'm such a lady of leisure. I'll miss our treat, but that'll make it even nicer to see you, and hear about all that important stuff you've been doing."

Desiree laughed herself at that. "If you want to hear about me yelling at the phone guys to check the lines, I guess I could tell you about that. I don't do the exciting parts, all the big meetings and the important people. That's Alec's job."

♡

But she wasn't thinking about Alec when she'd left the congestion that was I-5 on the day before Christmas Eve and was riding the back roads, quiet and empty, lonely or peaceful depending on your point of view, a series of right angles and straight lines arrowing across broad stretches of pancake-flat farmland, bringing her ever closer to Chico. The branches of the trees in the fruit and nut orchards were bare now, the sky a wintry pale, the heater on against the chill that even the Central Valley couldn't escape in late December.

It was the dream that had brought it back. The dream. The back seat. And Christmas approaching.

♡

She'd struggled and struggled on that long-ago December morning, her face getting hotter despite the chill in the apartment, her hands getting clumsier, her hair falling in her face because she didn't know how to get the barrettes to shut. She got the tights on at last, but they felt funny, and they pulled at her legs, and she didn't know how to fix them.

She went to the door of her room, peered out. He was there, sitting at the kitchen table, looking down, with a glass of something brown next to his hand. Maybe it was apple juice. She'd got herself a bowl of cereal when she'd got up, but she hadn't been able to find juice, and her dad had been asleep, she'd seen when she'd tiptoed down the hall and peeked into the bedroom. Maybe he'd made some juice, though. Maybe she could have some, because she was thirsty, and her legs were scratchy.

"Dad?"

He raised his head and stared at her, but his eyes were funny. She moved tentatively into the little kitchen, shifted from foot to foot.

"What?" he finally asked.

"I can't do my tights right." He'd told her to put on a good dress. After that, she'd thought, maybe he'd take her to see her mom. So she'd put on her Christmas dress, the one she and Mommy had found in the thrift store. It was green, and soft, and you could pet it like a cat.

"You can wear it for Special Occasions," Mommy had said, "when you want to be extra-pretty. When you go to birthday parties."

Desiree had known that she wouldn't be going to birthday parties, but she hadn't told her mom that, because it would make her mom sad. The pretty girls, the ones whose headbands always stayed on over their shiny hair, the ones with cute shirts that said *Princess* in sparkly letters, they were the ones who opened up the white envelopes in class, and giggled and talked about going to get manicures. Desiree wasn't sure what manicures were, but she knew that skinny girls who were too tall and had red hair and glasses and raised their hand every time didn't get them.

But her friend Olivia would invite her to her birthday, she thought hopefully. She probably would. And maybe she could wear her dress then. And at Christmas. And now.

So she got the dress off the hanger and unzipped it and pulled it on, and reached behind her and found the little end of the zipper at last and pulled it up from the bottom, and then scrunched her arm down and pulled it up from the top. So that was good. But then she tried to put on the tights, and she kept getting the foot all twisty, and she felt like she was going to cry. But she didn't want to cry, not if she was going to see her mom.

So she went in the kitchen and asked her dad, but her dad just looked at her.

"They look fine to me," he said. "Go put your shoes on."

"Then do we get to go see Mommy?" she asked.

His face twisted up, and her stomach felt funny again, like she was going to throw up.

"No," he said. "She's gone."

"But when can I see her?" she asked again. Maybe it was because they couldn't go in the car, because the car was gone too.

"Maybe we could go on the bus," she said. She and Mommy took the bus sometimes. The bus went lots of places, she knew that.

He shoved his chair back with a sudden movement and a screeching sound that made her jump and tremble, and she wrapped her hands together and twisted them in front of her.

"We're not going to see her," he said. He stood and picked up his glass of juice and took a big drink. And she wanted to ask him for some, but she didn't, because she wanted to know about her mom.

"But *why?*" she asked, trying not to cry. "Where did she go? When is she coming home?"

"She's dead!" he shouted, and he banged the glass down on the table, and Desiree shrank back against the wall of the kitchen as he continued to shout. She pulled her arms together in front of her and put her elbows in front of her face and her hands over her ears, and now she couldn't help it. She started to cry.

"She's not coming back!" He was still shouting. "She's dead, and she'll always be dead!"

And Desiree pressed and pressed and pressed herself into the wall, and tried to disappear.

♡

That had been the worst thing. But then her dad had gone away, back to his room, and she had gone back to her room. And later on, she had heard the sound of the doorbell, heard her dad opening it, and then she heard her grandma's voice, and her grandpa. She wanted to go out and see them, but she didn't, because everything was wrong, and she didn't know what she was supposed to do.

So she sat on her bed. She put her feet together so they lined up exactly, and held onto the edge of the bed, and looked down at her shoes. At the cutouts in the toes that had the red around them, that her mom had bought for her with her new dress. Her party shoes. She pressed them together, stared down at her red cutouts, and listened.

"Where's Desiree?" That was Grandma Dixie, and her voice wasn't right either. It wasn't all laughing and bubbling like usual, it was sharp, like the pain in Desiree's head, that still pounded in there like somebody was hitting her.

Tap. Tap. Tap, went the spikiness in her head.

"I don't know. In her room." That was her dad.

"In her *room?*" Her grandma again, and her voice was even spikier now. And then the rumble of her Grandpa Henry's voice, deep and slow. His voice still sounded the same, just slower.

And then her grandma was there, in her doorway. Coming over to her, and her face was still her grandma's face. It was still right.

"Oh, honey." Grandma Dixie was crying too, but her tears were warm, and they fell on Desiree's red hair that was still not in barrettes, because she didn't know how. Her grandma sat down on the bed with her, and Desiree was gathered in her skinny arms, pressed into her warm chest.

And she cried and cried and cried, and her grandma cried some more too.

And then her grandma fixed her tights.

♥

Now, she passed the Mexican restaurant, and the tire shop, and the last few orchards that remained this close to town, and turned in at the sign for Country Club Estates. Slowed to ten miles an hour, inched around the kids on their way to the playground. Waved a hello to Mrs. Chang and Mrs. Sanderson, out for their evening stroll, and received waves and smiles in return.

She went around the final curve, pulled to the curb. Saw her grandma's car parked beneath the neat carport, and smiled a little at the sight of it. Alec had got the white Corolla right, he'd just got the generation wrong.

Her grandma had a new lawn ornament, she saw. A donkey, a basket on its back planted with pink petunias, standing amongst the neatly trimmed bushes that filled the tiny area at the front edge of the mobile home. Well, he could keep the windmill and the gnomes company.

By the time she'd emerged from the car and gone around to the back to pull out her suitcase and the gifts she'd brought, her grandmother was coming down the wooden steps of the deck that Grandpa Henry had built for her when Desiree was a little girl. Dixie wasn't hustling, like she usually did, and she rested a hand on the wooden banister as she descended. But her smile creased her thin face, caused her rosy cheeks to round into apples.

And then her grandmother was reaching for her, her bright brown eyes sparkling with joy, and Desiree felt the lump rising in her throat again as her grandmother's arms enfolded her. She was home for Christmas.

the first noel

♡

She was surprised the next day, and a little alarmed, too, when her grandmother suggested that they skip their usual midnight service and go to church on Christmas morning instead.

"It's getting a little hard to stay up that late," Dixie admitted. "Besides, it's good to shake things up now and then. Keep me from turning into a boring old lady."

Since Dixie was wearing her silver sneakers at the time, smoking one of her endless Virginia Slims, her bright red lipstick drifting into the creases around her lips, and caroling merrily along, out of tune and not caring a bit, with "Grandma Got Run Over by a Reindeer," Desiree didn't think there was any danger of that.

"How's your dad?" Dixie asked when the song ended, peering through her reading glasses and poking the needle through another bright red cranberry, pulling it along the long thread to join the others.

"Fine, I guess." Desiree put her own needle through a kernel of popcorn, but it disintegrated in her fingers.

"You talk to him for Christmas?"

"Yeah, he called me."

"Is he still working at the Ford dealership?"

"I think so. We didn't really talk that long."

Her grandmother put the needle down, looked at her over her glasses. "Did he ask for money?"

"When does he ever not ask for money?" Desiree destroyed another kernel and gave up on the popcorn for the moment. "Well," she amended, "he hinted. You know, that it was too bad he couldn't come visit, him and Marybeth, because plane tickets are so expensive these days. Because he's missed me so much." She stabbed at another kernel, felt the satisfaction when her needle sank through the plump crispness, and pulled it down the thread.

"Did you give it to him?" her grandmother asked quietly.

"No." She stabbed another kernel. And she got this one too.

♡

So there had been no late-night carol singing, no warm light shining from midnight church windows. Instead, Desiree was making her annual church visit, singing "The First Noel" together with the rest of a packed house on Christmas morning. Which was fine. Although it had been a little disconcerting to see Alec in the first pew, together with what must have been his entire family. He hadn't noticed her, but she hadn't needed to wait for him to turn around to recognize that dark head.

Of course he was here. His father was the minister. She was sure that this was a command performance, just like it was for her. She'd say hello afterwards. How hard could that be? And then goodbye. And then she'd go home with her grandmother to start their Christmas. To open the presents in front of the little artificial tree, looking fairly bedraggled by now, but not replaceable.

"It's got plenty of life left in it," Dixie had protested when Desiree had suggested buying a new one, maybe some new ornaments too. "And what would I put on it that I'd like better than these things? Christmas is about memories, and my memories are right here."

So it was the shabby little tree again after all. With the pop-sicle stick snowflake, painted white and covered with silver glit-ter that had mostly fallen off by now, that had been her gift to her grandparents in first grade. And the canning ring, her seven-year-old gap-toothed picture filling the middle of it, hanging from its limp red ribbon. And all the rest of them, each one lov-ingly unpacked, reminisced over, and hung with ceremony last night. Plus, of course, the long strings of popcorn and cranberries they'd created with an extra bowl of buttery popcorn nearby "to keep us going," as they'd done every year since Desiree could remember.

They'd play cards later to the accompaniment of Dixie's col-lection of country Christmas CDs, and, eventually, she'd help her grandmother cook dinner. Not turkey, of course. Just chicken. She couldn't remember the last time she'd had turkey. Not since they'd become a family of two.

And she would know that somebody loved her. That some-body thought she was perfect the way she was. That she was spe-cial. That she was irreplaceable. And she'd know she had some-body to feel that way about too.

She felt her eyes misting over as the last sweet notes of the carol faded away. It was the music, and the smell of the evergreens that decorated the ends of the pews, and the time of year. It always got to her, lowered her defenses, left her open and exposed.

And after the service, it wasn't hello and goodbye after all.

Alec had been standing with the rest of his family at the edge of the heating system's reach, just inside the church door, while his father stood on the porch and shook hands, offering a word to every member of the congregation on their way out.

"Desiree." Alec's smile looked genuine. "See, I knew we were destined to meet when we were up here. And Mrs. Foster." He shook hands gently with her grandmother. "Nice to see you again, ma'am. Merry Christmas."

She beamed back at him. "Merry Christmas to you too. I hope you're taking a real vacation while you're here with your folks. Seems like every time I talk to Desiree, she's working, no matter how late it is. Maybe you can persuade her to that it's OK to have some fun, and she doesn't have to work quite so hard. But then," she added with a chuckle, "you probably do it too. It's really too bad. You should both be out enjoying life. You're only young once."

Desiree saw the smile that Alec's brother wasn't quite quick enough to hide. Because that had to be Gabe, standing beside a pretty brunette. He was a little shorter than his twin, but still plenty tall, six foot or so. Quite a bit broader, too. Those were some *shoulders*. Not as handsome as Alec, but, wow. Just as hot.

"I keep telling Alec that myself," he said gravely, the humor still lurking in the dark blue eyes that were a perfect match for his brother's. "Introduce us, bro."

"And you and Alec work together, Desiree?" the brunette, who turned out to be Gabe's fiancée Mira, asked once Alec had complied.

"Our CFO," Alec confirmed. "Runs our operations, too. Desiree's the real boss. Pushes us all around." He shot a sly glance at Joe, who smiled a little at that, nodded a hello to Desiree and came over to meet her grandmother, all politely enough. He'd come to church too, then. Quite the member of the family.

Alec's sister, too. Alyssa, that was her name. She'd been a year behind Desiree in school, which would make her three years younger than her brothers. Just as good-looking, the same blue eyes and dark hair, and, luckily for her, Alec's slim build instead of the bulk of her father and Gabe. She'd played a lot of sports in high school, and she'd been surprisingly friendly for one of the cool kids. That was about the sum of Desiree's recollection.

A few more minutes of chat, then Alec's mother, bidding farewell to a young couple with a baby and coming over for her own introduction. Still a remarkably handsome woman, her hair a light brown to her husband's black, medium height and slim where he was towering and burly, and the source of her children's blue eyes.

It was all a little overwhelming, this parade of Kincaids. And then the last parishioner had left, Alec's father had stepped inside, duty done, to join the group, and Desiree and Dixie were still there.

"We should go," Desiree said. "Let you start your Christmas."

Dave Kincaid laughed, a booming sound that resonated all the way to the arches of the high ceiling, to the tall stained-glass windows and traditional wooden pews. "This is actually a fairly big part of our Christmas," he pointed out, eyes teasing. "Still got a good dinner to eat, though. That's another big part. But how are you, Desiree? I don't think I've seen you since last Christmas. I've stayed caught up through your grandmother, of course. And I hear you're doing some good work, keeping our bad boy on track."

"Trying to," she said, unable to resist smiling back. "He's pretty much a law unto himself, though. But I do try."

"Hey," Alec protested. "I'm all buttoned down these days. Nose to the grindstone. It's all about the job."

"Hmm." Desiree had to tease a little herself. *"All?"*

"Most." He grinned down at her, and she had another of those flashes of heat, right there in church, with his parents watching. And Susie Kincaid's sharp blue eyes didn't miss a thing. Desiree caught the way Susie's gaze met her husband's, and she cringed a little inside.

"We should get going, Grandma," she said again.

"Before you go," Susie put in. "We'll be doing a big lunch tomorrow, one last day with all the kids around. Would you two like to come over and join us?"

"Oh," Desiree instantly demurred. "I'm not sure..."

"Oh, please do," Susie insisted. "It's quite the coincidence that you and Alec have ended up working so closely together, isn't it? I'd love to hear more about how it's all going down there. You know we can't get that much out of Joe," she said with a laughing glance across at him that elicited a grin in return. "And Alec never tells me anything, of course. So do come. Noon?"

Desiree glanced down at her grandmother, saw her smile of pleasure, and succumbed. "Yes. Thank you. That'd be fun."

"I'll bring my Pistachio Jell-O Salad," Dixie decided. "That way you won't have to worry about dessert."

"Oh, don't bother," Susie urged. "It'll mostly be leftovers anyway, and I have Gabe to help me, and Mira now too. Which is lucky, since I've never been able to get Alyssa to care a thing about cooking. And I've got Dave, of course, to do the really dirty work, get the meat off the turkey carcass for me. We're all set."

"So what's your job?" Desiree asked Alec. "Where are you in this picture?"

He heaved a sigh. "They let me take out the garbage and set the table, that's about it. I'm a total menace in the kitchen. Sometimes I'm allowed to wash dishes, but only if we're not using the best glasses."

"Well, we'll look forward to seeing your table-setting job, then," Dixie told him with a twinkle. "That'll be a treat. And I *will* bring my Jell-O salad. My mama always told me, never show up empty-handed."

♡

"I'm going to need a couple things for my salad," Dixie said the next morning.

Desiree took another sip of coffee, thought longingly about a latte. She was too relaxed to go hunt one down, though. Her third day off in a row, and she felt like she could lounge around in her bathrobe all morning long. She sure got lazy fast when she gave herself the chance. Good thing she almost never *did* have the chance. She'd never get anywhere.

"What?" she asked belatedly.

Her grandmother had been bending to look through the cans in a kitchen cupboard. She stood up, gave her chest a little pat, and sank into a chair next to her granddaughter. "I'm out of pistachio pudding mix. And Cool-Whip and crushed pineapple, too. I used the last of it when I made my salad for Pinochle Night last week. I'm going to have to go to the store."

"I'll go," Desiree said. "But maybe..." She hesitated. She remembered that lunch with Alec, the dinner too. She had a feeling that Pistachio Jell-O Salad wasn't going to be his favorite. It sure wasn't hers.

"Maybe I could buy a cake, or some brownies, or something," she suggested. "So you wouldn't have to cook again. That way you could take it easy today."

Her grandmother flapped a hand at her. "Oh, pssh. I could make my Jell-O salad in my sleep. And the best part is, making a double recipe's just as easy as making a single one. It'll be real Christmasy, once I put the maraschino cherries on top. I'll put it in the red Tupperware, and it'll be, whatchamacallit. Festive."

"All right." She might as well succumb to the inevitable. And Alec's parents, veterans of hundreds of church suppers, had probably eaten Dixie's Jell-O salad before. In fact, based on his mother's alacrity in declining the offer, Desiree was sure they had. "Need me to go right now?"

"If you don't mind. WinCo's got pretty good prices these days. Walmart's cheaper, but WinCo isn't bad."

"I'll go to WinCo, then." Because the Chico Walmart on the morning after Christmas—not exactly a prime vacation destination. "But you know," she added, giving it her usual valiant effort, "you don't have to shop at the very cheapest place anymore,

Grandma. You can even live it up, go to the deli. Whatever you want. If you need more money to do that, you just tell me."

"Go buy fancy things I don't need? Why would I do that? Besides, you should be putting that money away for a rainy day."

"But I *have* it," Desiree pleaded. "Really, Grandma. It would be OK."

"It's never OK to waste money," her grandmother said firmly. "It's enough to know that I'm not going to get it all rung up, and then have to ask the girl to put something back. That's good enough for me."

And that had been the end of that discussion.

"Do you need anything else?" Desiree asked when she'd pulled on a pair of jeans and grabbed her jacket.

"No, we should be fine. Plenty of leftovers from Christmas dinner."

Yes, there was some dry chicken left. And gravy that had come out of a packet, and cranberry sauce wiggling in the bowl, its cylindrical shape imprinted with the indentations left by its can, and frozen green beans mixed with undiluted cream of mushroom soup, with weird fried onions sprinkled on top. All of Grandma Dixie's traditional Christmas favorites.

She'd buy a bag of lettuce at the store, Desiree decided, some fresh vegetables, and make a salad to go with the chicken tonight. She loved her grandmother more than anyone else in the world. But no question, Dixie Lee Foster was nobody's idea of a gourmet cook.

eating the jell-o

♡

Desiree brought the car to a stop, set the brake and reached behind her for the big red plastic bowl, its lid carefully sealed to protect her grandmother's decorative touches. She stepped out onto the tree-lined street as her grandmother did the same, a bit more slowly, beside her.

No sidewalks here. Smaller, older houses on big lots, and none of the yards would be appearing in any ads for professional landscaping services. It was all a little shabby, a little sleepy. But there was nothing the least bit sleepy about the scene in front of her.

It was all motion and noise, the *thwack* of the basketball on the asphalt, grunts and exclamations and pounding feet. Alec's brother and sister darting to left and right, juking and feinting, dribbling and passing a basketball to each other with obvious skill, guarded by Alec and Joe. Alec in Gabe's face, aggressive, bumping his twin, his hands reaching out to grab a ball that Gabe, clearly not a bit intimidated, continued to deny him.

"Come on, Dog Head," Alec taunted as Gabe pivoted, dribbled around him in a quick series of moves. "Shoot."

But Gabe didn't. Instead, he fired the ball to Alyssa. No match for Joe in size or strength, but with some skills of her own. She whirled, and the ball left her hands, sailed between

Joe's outstretched arms, arced up and fell through the basket with a *swoosh.*

Alyssa whooped, did a little booty-shakin' dance across to Gabe, and bumped hips with her brother. "Nothin' but net, baby. Nothin' but net."

The backboard looked like it had seen some years of hard use. Covered with flaking white paint, it was fastened onto what must once have been a telephone pole that had been sunk into one corner of the big driveway, facing out onto the street. Desiree could easily imagine six or seven teenage boys out here, their size and their energy and their noise spilling out into the neighborhood. The silence must have echoed when Gabe and Alec had left home.

There wouldn't have been room to play in the driveway anyway, not today. Not with four cars in it. An older sedan that must have belonged to the siblings' parents, an SUV with some splatters of mud, a little yellow subcompact. And the gleaming black Mercedes that could only have been Alec's.

The man in question grabbed for the ball, turned to throw it in to Joe, and saw Desiree and her grandmother for the first time. Sent the pass to his brother instead, who grabbed it with quick, sure hands, and jogged over to greet the women.

"Hi," he said with a grin as he approached. He lifted the neckline of his faded gray T-shirt to wipe the sweat from his face, exposing a few inches of flat abdomen that had Desiree staring despite herself. His dark hair was mussed from the game, and he hadn't shaved yet today, the shadow of beard showing black against the tanned skin of his jaw. And yes, those dress shirts had been hiding some serious muscles. The bulge of biceps and triceps was barely visible under the edges of his sleeves, but the thin cotton fabric couldn't conceal the shape of his shoulders, and there was nothing at all covering up the heft of his forearms. He wasn't as bulky as Gabe, but those arms were *fine.*

And the rest of him wasn't bad either. He and his brother clearly had more than those blue eyes in common, because they could both sure fill out a pair of tight button-fly Levi's.

"Good thing you showed up," he told Desiree, interrupting her inventory of his...charms. "Excuse to retire with honor. Joe and I were getting our butts kicked."

"Only because Joe won't guard me, because he's afraid he's going to hurt a girl. Or maybe just touch her," Alyssa said, coming up with a laugh of her own. "Hi, Mrs. Foster. I'm glad you could make it. And hey, Desiree."

Joe looked down at Alyssa with his usual unreadable expression, his shaved head shiny with sweat. "Or maybe because I know that's the only way you could beat me, and I know you want to win."

"Oh, you were *letting* me win out of the goodness of your heart, because I'm such a delicate flower? I think not. You just got challenged to a game of H-O-R-S-E, tough guy. We'll see who can shoot."

"I didn't say you couldn't shoot," he said calmly. "I said you couldn't beat me."

"You're on. Soon as lunch is over, I'll be beating you with a stick. Prepare to whimper."

He smiled a little at that, but didn't bother to answer.

Alec looked past Desiree and Dixie, then back at Desiree again. "Not a white Corolla."

"Nope."

He laughed. "Not a Harley either. But you're right. A red Mini...not what I'd have expected. Maybe I *don't* know you as well as I think. Because I'd say you've got an unexpected frivolous side. And a feminine side too."

"Gee, thanks," she said wryly. "Glad you noticed."

"Oh, I noticed." He reached out for the bowl in her arms, and she surrendered it to him. "This must be the famous salad," he said. "Come on inside. Cold out here."

"You have a good Christmas, the two of you?" he asked as they walked behind the others up the long driveway to the house. Her grandmother really had lost a step, Desiree had already noticed, was a bright, bustling little sparrow no longer.

Still as cheerful as ever, though. "Oh, we had a wonderful day," she assured Alec. "Christmas dinner with my special girl, what could be better than that? How about you?"

"Good too. Family time. And a chance to catch up with Mira, because as you've heard, our family's getting a little bigger."

"She not a basketball player?" Desiree asked.

Alyssa heard that and laughed. "Not nearly tough enough."

"Hey." That was Gabe. "She's plenty tough. Just not aggressive. Two different things, tomboy. Plus, she and Mom are in there cooking and making wedding plans, and that's serious business on both counts."

He mounted the steps to the back porch, checked out the tread of his running shoes. "Better take off our shoes, or we'll get it from Mom."

"Oh." Dixie looked around. "I'll just find someplace to sit."

"Not you, Mrs. Foster," Alec said with a smile. "Just us disreputable types." He pulled off his battered sneakers, tossed them into the pile next to the door. "In fact, I'm feeling a little embarrassed, being all grubby like this when you and Desiree came over looking so pretty. Going to have to go clean up before lunch."

Desiree looked at him sharply. Was he making fun of her grandmother? All right, the red acrylic sweater with its Christmas-tree applique might not be the most elegant fashion statement, but she knew with what care her grandmother had dressed for this lunch, how pleased she'd been at the invitation. Her best white blouse, her neatest pair of black polyester slacks, the brooch pinned onto the sweater that she pulled out of the closet with delight and ceremony every year, just before she got up on the stepladder to hang the lights. Her grandmother had always made it Christmas, no matter how little had been under the tree, and if Alec was laughing at her…she couldn't *stand* it.

"I like your pin," Alec said now, holding the door for the two of them. "It looks like an antique. Is it special?"

"It is," Dixie beamed, stepping onto the shining yellow linoleum of the laundry room. "Special, I mean, but not an antique. Just old, like me. It was my mother's. I think the best things are the ones that remind you of someone you love, don't you?"

"Yes. I do." He smiled down at her, and Desiree breathed a sigh of relief. It was OK. It was going to be all right.

"This is really good," she said when they were sitting around the dining room table, both its leaves, Susie Kincaid had told her, in place now to accommodate "my favorite time of year. When my kids come home." The leaves were certainly needed today, with nine of them crowded around the tablecloth cheerfully printed with green holly sprigs.

"Just Turkey Tetrazzini," Susie said. "A pretty fancy name for turkey noodle casserole. And leftover everything else, too."

"Hey. You dissing my favorite meal?" Alec demanded. "I always asked for this when it was my turn to choose our birthday dinner," he explained. "I never understood why my mom thought it was funny."

"Just that it's what you do with leftovers," Susie said with a laugh. "And we had plenty of those today, even with all these hungry men in the house. Plus Alyssa, who does her share too. But even so, Dave got a little enthusiastic on the size of the turkey this year."

"It's good," Desiree said again. "It tastes a little smoky?"

"That would be the smoker," Dave told her. "I do the turkey, and I like to try something different every time. And this year that was smoking, thanks to the new barbecue Alec gave me for Father's Day. And even though I said I didn't need the big one with all those bells and whistles," he told his elder son, "I'll admit that I've enjoyed it."

Alec grinned. "I had to contribute an equal amount to the Relief Fund before he'd even take it. Turned out to be the most expensive Father's Day present I ever bought. Remind me never to give you and Mom a cruise, Dad, because it just might break me."

"Speaking of the Relief Fund," Dave said, "I wanted to tell you, Desiree, congratulations on that scholarship fund of yours. You've made quite a difference to at least two girls that I know of."

"Really. That's terrific." That was Mira, Gabe's fiancée, a quiet woman with a warm smile. "How does it work?"

Desiree shrugged with embarrassment. "It's still small. It's just something I set up with our old high school a few years ago, for a girl who's planning to major in business."

"The Henry and Dixie Lee Foster Scholarship Fund," Dixie pronounced proudly. "Although why on earth she'd name it after two people who were lucky even to graduate from high school, I can't imagine. I wanted her to give it her name. She's come so far, I thought that'd be an inspiration to those girls."

"I named it exactly right," Desiree said. "And I'm pretty clear that I was able to go to college because I had a place to live so I didn't have to pay for a room, and a scholarship to pay for some of the rest. I just want to give some other girl that same chance. It doesn't take that much to make the difference between going and not going."

"Between believing," Mira said, "and not."

"That's it," Desiree said. "That's it exactly. When I opened the envelope, when I saw that somebody was willing to give me all that money. *Me.* That they believed in me. I'll never forget how I felt when I first read that letter. That's when I knew it was all going to happen."

She stopped, embarrassed at the passion that had risen in her voice. "But it's still small," she repeated lamely. "Just a start."

"Can you tell me how to contribute?" Mira asked. "I'd like to help."

"Sure," Desiree said with surprise. "It's always just been me, but that'd be great."

"I'll contribute too," Alyssa said. "Not that I've got much, but I'll give what I can. Better than nothing, right?"

"You don't have to," Desiree said. "Not if it's a hardship."

"No," Alyssa said. "I want to. Because, yeah, the true riches are in the wealth of the spirit," she said with a laughing glance at her parents, "but try telling yourself that when you're sixteen, and you've got the wrong clothes anyway, and then you get changed for P.E. and you've got the *completely* wrong underwear. 'Hello, Fruit of the Loom,'" she mimicked. "'Three for five dollars! Special on Aisle Five!' Man, I wanted some of those lacy matching bra and underwear sets, didn't you, Desiree? I *coveted* them. Don't you buy them these days and wish you had a couple of those cheerleaders in the dressing room with you, so you could show them how much better your body looks than theirs now? Don't you think they should have that event at high school reunions? We should suggest it, because we'd both totally win. Booyah." She pumped a slim fist.

"Thanks." Desiree was laughing now, and so was Mira. "The Lacy Underwear Revenge Derby. That would be an *awesome* event." And that made the other women laugh harder, and Susie and Dixie were chuckling too, and Alec and Gabe were grinning, and even Dave was smiling a little. And Joe was frowning across the table at Alyssa again. Oh, well. Joe was always frowning.

"Here's what I want to know," Desiree asked. She was probably getting way too relaxed here, and she'd probably be sorry on Monday, but too bad. "Why doesn't it matter to guys, the clothes, I mean? Why didn't it matter for you, Alec? Because you were obviously cool, and hot, and all that good stuff back then. That was fairly clear. I'm sure you were too," she told Gabe. "Sorry. I never saw you, so I don't know."

"Nope. Never in a league with the pretty boy," Gabe said. Which brought an immediate, inarticulate protest from Mira that had him laughing and giving her a quick kiss. "I know you like me better," he told her. "And I'm counting on being able to keep you fooled a little while longer, until I get that ring on your finger and it's too late to change your mind."

"I tried," Alec pointed out. "She didn't want me. I can't help it if the woman has no taste. And to answer your question," he told Desiree, "It's because a guy can wear a T-shirt and jeans, and he's good. What we're wearing today, Gabe, aren't they about what we wore in high school?"

"In fact," Gabe answered, "I think these are *exactly* what we wore in high school. As in, I think I wore this same pair of pants. Opened the drawer today, and there they were. The shirt goes back that far too, for all I know. A little tight, come to think of it." He plucked at the thin, faded fabric stretching over his broad chest.

"I thought that same thing," Alec agreed. "Thought, did this shirt shrink? Guess we've both got a little bigger since then. We should probably toss some of that stuff."

"Yes," Desiree heard herself saying, "that'd probably be a good idea. You guys should definitely stop wearing your shirts so tight." And was rewarded by a quick, startled look from Alec, followed by a smile that started slow, then grew as he met her eyes.

"I really need to get you all to clean your rooms out," Susie said with a shake of her head. "That's pathetic. What do you think this is, a hotel?"

"I think having the wrong hair might have been the worst, though," Desiree said. *Let's get off the topic of tight T-shirts.* What had she been *thinking,* saying that in front of Alec's parents? Not to mention Joe. Not to mention *him.* "Even worse than the underwear." And now she was talking about underwear again.

"Yeah, the hair was the worst," she went on in desperation, trying to keep herself on safe ground, "because everybody sees your hair all the time. At least you didn't have that problem, Alyssa. I always admired your hair."

"Thanks," Alyssa said, pushing a glossy dark lock behind her shoulder. "But I admired *you.* The way you seemed…above it all. Like none of it ever got to you, not even the Mean Girls. And I'd like to help with your fund. Call my part the Clothing Stipend. They can buy some new underwear, anyway. And yes," she said with a glance across the table at Joe. "I said 'underwear.' Twice. Maybe even three times. Get over it."

"Stop baiting him, Alyssa," Susie said calmly. "You're terrible."

"How are your own philanthropy plans coming, Alec?" Dave asked his son, changing the subject. "Get that going yet?"

"Haven't had a chance to decide exactly how to set it up, or even what I want to do," Alec said. "Got the money earmarked, just busy, you know, with the new company and all."

"Earmarked isn't going to feed any hungry kids," his father told him bluntly. "Earmarked isn't going to send anyone to college, or get a family off the streets, or stamp out malaria, or whatever it is you decide to do. And I notice you had time to shop for that fancy new car last spring."

"Well, actually, I didn't," Alec said. "I rode with somebody who had one, he let me drive it, I liked it, so I called a guy and bought it. I have a feeling this wouldn't be quite that easy."

"Maybe you should get Desiree to help you set it up," Gabe suggested, humor lurking at the corners of his mouth. "She seems to have it down."

"I can't ask her to do that. She doesn't work for me, she works *with* me. There's a difference." Alec sounded a little defensive, Desiree thought. A little beleaguered.

"I'd be happy to help, if I can," she jumped in to assure him. "When you're ready. I did a lot of research before I set up my little thing. But what, you have a foundation planned?"

"I can hardly avoid it, can I?" he asked ruefully. "Not with my conscience sitting around the table with me."

"Perils of the PK," Alyssa said. "You can run, but you can't hide."

"Preacher's Kid." Alec, explaining again. "And," he sighed, "I think I've just figured out where my first contribution is going, because I'm not going to get out of this house without pledging it somewhere. You'd better tell those girls at Chico High to keep their GPAs up, because that scholarship fund is about to get a whole lot bigger."

♡

"Thanks for coming over," Alec told Rae an hour later, leaning down so she could see him and putting a hand on the window ledge. Damn, this was a tiny car. He hated to think what would happen if she got into an accident with anything bigger. Which would be just about anything at all. "You too, Mrs. Foster. Nice to catch up with you. And be careful on the drive back to the City tomorrow, Rae. Going to be a zoo out there."

"You too," she said. "See you Monday."

"Yeah. See you then."

He stood back and held up a hand in farewell as the two of them drove off, walked back toward the house. To the sight of his brother, leaning against the wall, bouncing the basketball on the driveway. Joe and Alyssa were still on dish duty, then.

"You are so screwed," Gabe said with satisfaction as Alec approached.

"What?"

"You can hardly see straight, you've got it so bad. Told you it would happen, and bro, it's happened. Cover your ears if you don't want to hear this, because I'm going to say the word. You're in love."

"I am not in love." Alec felt the punch of it straight to his gut. "I'm just...attracted."

Gabe snorted at that with the contempt it deserved. "Tell that to somebody who didn't just watch you eat the Jell-O salad."

"What are you talking about?" It was a losing battle, he could feel it, but Alec did his best.

"The squishy green stuff? The mini marshmallows? The maraschino cherries on top? There was Cool-Whip in that, I'll swear it."

"So? Maybe I got less finicky while we were out in the backwoods."

"Nope. That was true love. Because you asked for seconds."

"Hey." Alec gave it one last try. "You ate it too."

"Yup. Twin bond, right there. If you're going to be suffering, I'm going to be there with you."

"It doesn't matter, though." Alec leaned back against the wall himself with a sigh, and gave it up. "Because it can't happen. We're working together."

"Never stopped you before."

Alec shrugged irritably. "This is different. It wouldn't look good for me, not to the board, not to the industry, if we did it and everyone found out, but I'd survive it. Hell, I have before. But for her...she wouldn't. She's supposed to be the adult supervision. She's got this reputation built up, all based on keeping everybody focused, keeping it all about the business. She gets involved with me while she's working with me, her credibility's shot, because of *my* reputation. It would push her career right off the tracks."

"And you don't want to do that to her."

"Of course I don't. And it's worse than that, because I don't even know if she's interested. Well," Alec corrected himself, "I know she isn't, not interested in pursuing it, I mean."

"Has she said so?"

"Does she have to say it? She's made it clear, trust me."

"So what are you going to do?"

"What *can* I do? I can't exactly quit. And I can't push her into something that's going to hurt her. I guess I just go on like this. But is that even possible?"

"Is it possible to restrain yourself? I don't know. Is it? Who else are you sleeping with?"

Alec glared at his brother. "Nobody."

"Nobody at all? How long are we talking here?"

"More than two months. Not since the day we had our first meeting. Well," Alec amended, "that day, maybe, there was somebody. That night, I mean. But not since then. I've said no. I mean, flat-out no. Which makes no sense, if I'm never going to sleep with Desiree anyway. If I'm never even going to get to *touch* her. But I couldn't help it. I got to the point, and I just…I said no."

"You've never even touched her?" Gabe zeroed right in on the main point. "Not once? Never kissed her?"

"No. Didn't I just say? No. We can't."

"Never touched the stove," Gabe mused. "And yet you're pretty sure it's hot. Imagine that."

"You're supposed to be helping," Alec charged him. "Why else am I telling you all this? Where's your Hippocratic oath?"

Gabe looked at him, his expression serious now. "OK, then. Here you go. Here's my best shot. I'm not sure what the answer is going to be for you guys. I don't want to sound like a Hallmark card, but if it's meant to be, if it matters enough, you'll work it out. And nobody ever actually died of sexual frustration, you know. It just feels like it. Oh, and another thing?" he added as

Alyssa burst out the back door, grabbed the basketball from him, and began dribbling around the parked cars, Joe following behind her at a more leisurely pace, nodding to the brothers on his way out to the makeshift court.

Gabe waited until Joe was out of earshot, then continued. "If you ever do have this conversation with her, here's a tip. The part about not sleeping with anybody else sounds good. But don't tell her about what you did on the day of your first meeting. Just say, 'since the day of that first meeting with you.' Going to go over a *lot* better."

"Do you think I'm stupid?" Alec glowered at his brother. "I have a little experience here, you know."

"Yes, you do," Gabe replied cheerfully. "At casual sex, you've definitely got me beat. At being in love? Not so much."

casual sex

♡

"So how was the drive back? I kept an eye out for ridiculously tiny red clown cars, but I didn't see you."

He was grinning at her again. And sitting on the edge of her desk again. And looking good again. She needed to tell him to go away. Yeah. She needed to tell him that.

"Hey." She leaned back in her reclining desk chair, stretched out her legs in the skirt she'd worn on purpose this morning, just because it stopped an inch above the knee. And watched his gaze drop to her bare legs, right on cue.

She swiveled a little, felt the skirt inch up just a little bit more. "Thirty-five miles to the gallon on the freeway. How much does your car get?"

"Less." Still smiling, but his eyes had kindled, and he'd shifted position a bit. And she felt powerful, and feminine, and pretty damn sexy. She swiveled again.

"It was nice of your mom to invite my grandma and me to lunch," she said. "I enjoyed that."

"Yeah. I enjoyed seeing you too."

"You're different, with your family," she said.

"Am I?" He was still smiling, but it was the kind of smile she could imagine a jungle cat might have on its face just before it pounced. Because he looked just that intent, and that dangerous. "How?"

She shrugged, leaned back a little more, pushed off with a toe. "More relaxed. More...normal."

He laughed at that. "More normal? What does that mean? That I'm abnormal, normally?"

"No." She forgot to be sexy, sat up again. "Just...successful. In charge. Rich. None of which is exactly normal."

"You aren't doing too badly yourself," he said, "and you're pretty normal. Well, except for the efficiency thing."

She shrugged. "Not in your league, not that I'm not thrilled at getting this far. But not in your league, and you know it."

"Well, now you know that we come from just about the same place," he offered. "Which should help. Now that we've sat with our families and eaten lunch together."

"Including a delicious Jell-O salad," she pointed out.

He made a little face, rubbed his ear. "Uh...yeah. Thanks for bringing that up. Because what the hell am I supposed to say?"

"I don't know." She had to laugh at his expression. "I can't wait."

"If I say that I liked it," he complained, "she'll make it for me again next time. And if I say that I didn't, I'll have insulted your grandmother. And I may be slow, but I'm not stupid. I already figured out that that'd be a deal-breaker."

"Yes. That would be."

He paused a moment. "So, can I ask? What's the story with that? With you being with your grandmother, I mean."

"You don't want my sad life story, Alec."

"Yes, I do. I really do."

All the heat was gone, and she felt the familiar walls closing in, the door slamming shut. She glanced at her computer. "It's after eight. I need to go home, and so do you. And this is..." She hesitated. "This is dangerous, and stupid."

"Huh? What?"

She looked up at him sitting there, looking so good. Like every fantasy she'd ever had, of a strong, handsome, good man who would whisk her away from all the struggles and all the worries and all the heartaches in her life. Like every dangerously enticing escape she'd ever yearned for, when life was so scary, and so lonely, and so damn *hard* that it seemed like she'd never make it.

And she knew it was time to draw the line. No matter how much fun this was, how much she'd thought about him, and dreamed about him, and wanted to do more. No matter how much she wanted him to show her what it would be like to do everything. Six ways from Sunday.

"Alec." Time to say it. "You need to stop sitting on my desk. We need to stop this, this flirting. I know you do it all the time, but it's not appropriate, and I'm not..." She stopped, went on again. "I'm not in your league in this either. I can't flirt, not the way you do. Not for...for nothing."

"You think that's what I'm doing?" He actually looked shocked. Hadn't anybody ever called him on this stuff?

She sighed. "Of course that's what you're doing. I'm not saying you're a bad person. I like you a lot. But I don't have time or space in my life for casual relationships. And this *matters* to me, this job. You can just move on to the next project, the next big deal. But everything I do, every single job, it has to *work.* This is my *life.* Because we don't come from the same place, not really. You've got a net, don't you see? I don't have a net. I don't even have a rope. I've just got me here to keep me from falling. And not just me, my grandma too. For you, this is fun. And for me, it's life and death. It matters."

"I know it matters." He looked more upset than ever now, actually distressed. "And I know it isn't casual. None of it. Not the job, and not me. I'm not just flirting."

"So, what?" She could feel the tension gripping her shoulders, her thighs, tightening her throat so her voice came out pinched, instead of her usual calm, measured tones, but she couldn't help it. "You want to have sex with me? Is that what you're saying?"

"You must know I do." He stood up, shoved his hands into his pockets. "I guess I haven't been as cool as I thought. But, yes. Since we're putting it on the line, I want to have sex with you."

"Well, that's not going to happen." She clicked on her computer to shut it down, pulled out her purse, her laptop case. "I need to go home. It's late."

"And that's it?" he demanded. "That's all the talking we're going to do about this?"

"What else is there to say?" She stopped fiddling with her things and looked at him squarely. "It's all a sort of game for you, I get that. And lots of women are fine with that. They know the rules, and they know how to play. But I don't. I'm just not that kind of person. I'd get hurt. So, since I know it's really all the same to you," she said, the pain in her chest telling her that she was right, that she had to end this now, "go choose somebody else to play the game with, OK? Because I'm an amateur, and I'll lose."

"Desiree—"

"No." She stuffed her laptop into her case and pulled the zipper closed, shoved the strap over her shoulder and stood up. "I mean it, Alec. This has to end. This is done. And my name," she said fiercely, pushing past him, feeling the tears threatening, knowing she had to get out of there right that minute, "is Rae."

♡

Alec walked out of her office behind her, feeling like he'd been hit in the head with a brick. Watched her pull her keys out of her purse with fingers that trembled, lock her door, and walk across to the exit without looking back at him. Back straight, as always. Head high. And hurting. He could see it, and it was killing him.

He walked back into his own office, dropped into his chair. Swiveled to look out of his window at the plaza below, empty and forlorn in the occasional lights set into the pavement, casting half-circles onto the concrete and brick. The wind blowing through the bare branches of the newly-planted trees. And Desiree, her foreshortened figure appearing amidst them, on her way home, alone in the cold December dark. To wherever she lived, which she'd never trusted him to know. Just like she didn't trust him to know her, or to care about her either.

He'd always thought he was so smart, only involving himself with women who were willing to play by his rules, to keep it casual, to keep it fun. And now, when he wanted more, when he wanted it all, he couldn't have it. Because of everything he'd done before, because she thought this was the same old thing. Another flirtation. Another fling. Another fun time for Alec Kincaid, Master of the Universe.

It was so ironic, he could have laughed, except that it felt too bad. And he couldn't see how to change it, or how to fix it. How to show her that she mattered, that she didn't have to worry about falling. How to be her net.

a hostile work environment

♡

Desiree walked through the office, the fluorescent lights working overtime to combat the dark gray skies and steady rain that were turning a late January morning into something that looked more like night. Her automatic sweep for trouble spots found empty fast-food wrappers and Dr. Pepper cans littering Simon's cube. Again. And he was lounging against the reception desk, talking to Veronica. Also again.

"Excuse me," she said when she reached the two of them.

"Back to the salt mines," Simon told Veronica. "But remember what I said."

"One moment." Desiree put a hand out to stop him, stepped away from the desk a pace or two, kept her voice low. "When you get back to your desk, please dispose of your trash. We don't want ants in here."

She saw the sullen expression, but didn't let it deter her. Waited for his answer, which was nothing but a nod, but at least it was there.

"Don't let him waste your time," she warned Veronica once Simon had headed back to his desk.

"Oh, no," the young woman said hastily, and Desiree could see the flush growing. It was heady stuff, she knew, working in an office full of young single men. Veronica seemed to have got over her crush on Alec, his clear lack of encouragement having had its effect, but Desiree had seen her eyes following Brandon more than once in recent weeks, and that was an even worse idea. And Simon…She sighed.

"I know it can be tough to know how to say it," she coached the younger woman now, "but you can always go with, 'Well, I'd better get back to work.' And then you look at your computer and click your mouse."

Veronica flushed a little more, hearing the reprimand under the advice as Desiree had meant her to, and uttered something inarticulate and apologetic.

And that was enough, Desiree judged. Time to move on. "How's it going working with Thomas?" she asked next, and all right, maybe that *was* a bit of a nudge. Thomas Hsieh, the quiet young IT whiz she'd hired to provide the in-house tech support Alec had insisted on, had been working out well, and she'd decided on Veronica as his backup. A good opportunity for the young woman, who, despite her romantic tendencies, was bright, a good, hard worker, and eager to get ahead, the reasons Desiree had hired her in the first place. And if Desiree thought the two of them would make a nice couple, that was merely a bonus.

"It's fine. I'm learning a lot," Veronica assured her, and that didn't sound like romance was blooming. It was really a shame that women were so often attracted to bad boys, and that bad boys were so often, well, bad. But she wasn't a dating service, and Veronica's foolish heart wasn't actually her responsibility, so she left it there.

♡

Alec rapped once on Rae's door, stuck his head inside. Not out for lunch, of course. He'd figured as much. Intent on her computer, as always, but she looked up at the sound and gave him a smile. A cautious one, the kind she'd been offering him for a month now, ever since she'd drawn the line.

"Got a sec?" he asked.

"Sure." She pushed back a bit. She was wearing a long brown sweater today, falling open in gentle folds over a matching brown top, stretchy cream-colored pants, and boots. All very covered-up, very winter-weather-appropriate, very professional. Man, he missed her skirts. The top and pants were fairly tight, but still.

He took a seat opposite her. "We need to add some programmers," he began.

She nodded, clicked her mouse a couple times, started typing. "How many?"

"Eight."

"Same ad? Same basic requirements?"

"Yeah."

More typing. "I'll be recruiting on some Women in Tech sites. We need to make a genuine effort. You've got fifteen guys out there now, which doesn't look great. I need to know you'll be giving female candidates equal consideration."

"Of course. Not our fault, though, that startups are full of young guys. Not too many grandmas doing cutting-edge programming."

"I know the statistics. Equal consideration. That's all I'm saying."

"And I'm answering. Yes. Of course. Moving on, can we fit that many more without going to another floor?"

"Up to seventeen more," she assured him. "Lots of room."

"You sure? It doesn't look that way to me."

She swiveled and pulled out the big horizontal file drawer in her credenza. Reached an unerring hand out for the file she wanted, shoved the drawer shut, and swiveled back to Alec again.

She laid the file on the desk, opened it and pulled out a large sheet of paper, folded neatly down the middle. Spread it out on her desk facing him.

"Here and here," she pointed. "That's where your two new four-person cube setups go."

"Oh. OK." Of course she'd already figured this out.

"We'll have to take out that communal work space to do it," she went on. "Move them into the conference room for group work. Probably just as well to keep things a little more contained. A little more professional."

He nodded agreement. "And on that note, you'll probably want to get somebody different to do the installation."

She gave him her first real smile of the day, and there was that dimple again, winking at him from the corner of her pretty mouth. "Well, I could just sic you on my pal with the power tools. You could take him outside and beat him down for me."

"I could." He smiled back, saw her own smile grow. "And I would, if it would make you happy."

She looked down again, made a business of folding up her drawing and putting it back in the folder. "Actually," she said, "I'll get them to do the work on a Saturday, keep the disruption to a minimum."

"Probably pay double," he pointed out.

"Hey. You poaching on my territory? I'm the one doing the cost-benefit analysis. You're the big idea man. You just go back there and have ideas, write some brilliant code." She flapped a hand at the door. "I'll handle this."

"Yes, ma'am." He ducked a chastened head, grinned at her, saw the answering smile escaping her stern expression, and laughed.

"One more thing," he said. "The Super Bowl is on Sunday."

"Yes," she said gravely. "I'd heard that. But thanks for the reminder."

He laughed again. "You never make it easy, do you? But, yeah. The Super Bowl, and then, you know, that other thing. The premiere of my show. *America Alive: 1885.*"

"I'd heard that too. I've seen the promos. I've even taken a look at the website. No escape, because my neighbor thinks you look good on TV. He has that picture of you and your brother as his screen saver, and he tells me he's not the only one. Imagine that, you've got fans already, and the show hasn't even started yet. You could have a whole new career."

She seemed to catch herself, went on after a moment. "Besides, I've okayed all the bills for the PR blitz, remember? Good work getting on a reality TV show right before you launched a new venture. That's some good marketing right there."

"Well, even if you weren't planning to watch," he said, "at least I know your neighbor is, that there'll be an audience besides my mom and dad. What a relief. I poll pretty well in the gay demographic, that what you're telling me?"

"That's the word I'm getting," she said, the smile peeking out again.

He grinned. He loved it when he could get her to relax like this. It had been way too long. "Good to know. But anyway. Brandon and Joe are coming over to my place for the game, and then the show, and we thought you might like to join us."

In fact, neither of his partners had been thrilled at the idea.

"What?" Joe had objected when he'd brought it up the previous Friday night at Ziggurat, where they'd repaired as usual at the end of the workweek. "It's always been the three of us. Why?"

"Because she's on the team," Alec said. "Because look at us. Doing this again." He gestured around him. "This is exactly what women complain about. That they're shut out of the informal stuff where a lot of the discussion happens, where the decisions get made. Besides, she's got a lot to offer, and we should be taking advantage of that."

"She's operations," Joe argued. "We tell her what we need in support, she makes it happen. She doesn't need to be in on the decisions before that."

"Oh, I think it's a little more than that," Alec said. "Look at the logo. Look at the trade show stuff. She's got one hell of a marketing brain, and let's remember that we're marketing a consumer product. Women are going to make up half our market. That's a change for us. We've got a resource, and I want to use it."

"I know you want to use it," Joe growled, but he subsided at Alec's warning glare.

"Thanks, man." That was Brandon. "You saying I can't market to women? Just because I don't have …ovaries?" he amended at the last moment, after another glare. "That's some vote of confidence."

"I'm not saying there's anything wrong with what you're doing," Alec said as patiently as he could. Even though, yeah, maybe so. Rae's contributions had been tactful, matter-of-fact, but they'd been on-target, and she was doing as much to move their marketing efforts forward as Brandon was, which was telling Alec something right there, something he wasn't going to be able to ignore much longer. Which was going to be pretty damn tricky, because Brandon was a partner.

But now wasn't the time. "I'm saying, she's on the team," he said again. "And that I'm inviting her."

"And that we have to watch our language, and not offend her delicate sensibilities," Brandon muttered. "This should be a real fun time."

"You can't make dick jokes, if that's what you mean," Alec agreed. "Which aren't that funny anyway. You might think about moving past that."

He shoved himself back from the little table, wanting to be out of here, out of the crowd, the warmth, the noise of a hundred chattering voices, about eighty of them looking to get lucky, and most of the other twenty wishing they were free to try. "I'm going home. Who's in the office tomorrow?"

"Me," Joe said. "Got a couple things to run by you, too."

Alec nodded, looked at Brandon.

"I'll be working from home," the other man said. "Got a hot date later on tonight. I'm not planning on being too available in the morning, because she can't get enough."

"Yeah, I needed that information," Alec decided. "Thanks for that. See you tomorrow, then," he told Joe. "I'm out of here."

♡

"Anyway," he said to Rae now. "Would you like to join us?"

"Well..." she began, but stopped as he held up a hand.

"One sec." The voices had been there, on the edge of his consciousness. Two of them, coming from the break room next door. They'd been getting louder. And now they'd intruded fully.

"Talk about somebody who needs to get laid. Maybe if she got worked over hard enough, it'd loosen her up."

A laugh at that. "Yeah, but who'd volunteer? When I first started, I thought she was hot, but, damn. I mean, a woman in authority, sure. You know, thinking about getting the upper hand. But you'd have to have balls of steel to take that on."

"Stick it in her mouth, she'd probably bite it off."

"Avoid the teeth, yeah." They were both laughing hard now. "That'd be Helpful Hint Number One for the poor bastard."

"Pretty fun to think about how you'd do it, though," the first voice said, and Alec had recognized Simon. Of course. "A couple nights to wear her down, I'd be doing her any way I wanted."

Alec was at the door now, and Rae had risen to join him. He glanced down at her, saw her face draining of color as the conversation went on.

"Oh, yeah," the other man scoffed, and that was Simon's pal Michael. Following along, as usual. "You'd be so screwed."

"Naw, man, she would be. There's only one way guaranteed to loosen up a tightass like that. The hard way. That'd be sweet."

"Dude, you're sick." Michael, laughing. "Braver than me, that's for damn sure. I get a chill just thinking about it."

"The tougher they are, the harder they fall," Simon assured him.

And then Alec was around the corner and inside the break room. Michael was facing the door and saw him first, began making frantic gestures to his friend that Simon was apparently laughing too hard to notice.

"Or should I say," Simon went on over another gurgle of laughter, "the sweeter it is when you get them bent over the back of the couch, begging you to do it harder."

Michael finally got Simon's attention. The young man turned in his chair, black eyes widening with shock behind the stylish glasses.

"Oh, hey, Alec," he said, tried a casual smile that came out on the sickly side.

Alec sensed Rae entering the room behind him, saw Simon turn an even nastier shade, reach a hand up to comb through the black hair flopping over his forehead.

"Well, back to work," he said to Michael. Got up and dumped the plastic container that had held his lunch into the trash container under the sink.

"No." The anger turned Alec's voice to ice. "Clean out your desk. You're fired." He looked at Rae. "Get building security up here right now."

She looked back at him for a moment, then nodded and obeyed, turned away to speak rapidly into her phone.

"What?" Simon asked, actually rocking a little. "What for?"

"You know what for. Creating a hostile work environment."

"What the fu—? Because I joked around a little on my lunch break? You telling me you can't even tell a joke anymore? Hostile for who?"

"For me." The rage was, if anything, getting worse, and Alec wasn't sure how much longer he could keep his hands off the son of a bitch. "Because I find any environment with you in it hostile as hell. You make me sick, and you're out of here."

"You can't do this," Michael argued.

"The hell I can't. You're all employed at will, and I just exercised my will. You want to make it two for two?" That shut Michael up fast, just as Alec had known it would. Punk.

"I'll fight this. This isn't the end," Simon warned.

"Oh, yeah. It is. Unless I meet you in an alley somewhere." Alec never lost his temper, but he was losing it now, and badly.

"Yeah, right." Simon was still trying to bluster. "You and what army?"

Alec could barely get the words out. "No army. Just me."

♡

"Are you sure?" Rae asked when they were back in her office again. One of the security guys had made it up there fast, had stood over Simon as he emptied his desk into a carton Rae had supplied, had walked him out the door. "Simon's got great credentials, and I thought he was doing well. You could get him back, give him a warning. Kind of hard to have this happen right now when you're trying to get more staff, not lose any."

"I'm sure." She'd have the guy back after that?

"Well, you'll need to write it up," she said. "I only heard part of it, but I'll put down what I got too. Although we should do it as a layoff, not termination for cause. Still good to have the backup anyway, just in case."

"You mean I don't even get the satisfaction of firing his ass?" Alec was still stirred up, even if she wasn't. He took a few paces around the office, stood over her desk.

"Not unless you want to spend your time in a phone interview with the Department of Employment," she said. "Or, worse, in a hearing. Not worth it. He's gone, and you've sent your message. And you've defended my honor again, thank you very much. It's all done. Let it go. And quit looming over me, because I hate it, and it's not helping. Sit down."

"And that's it? That's as upset as you're going to get?" he demanded. But he sat.

She looked at him levelly, but he could see the color that hadn't yet subsided from her cheeks, hear that pen clicking under the desk. Over and over, the faint sound like the beat of the pulse he somehow knew was hammering as hard as his own.

"I can't afford to get upset," she said. "I work in tech. That's the way it is. When things come up, I handle them. If I'm going to run to the ladies' room and cry every time, I'm not going to be very effective."

"Did you ever do that?"

"Many times, in the early years. But I've had to grow a much thicker skin. No choice."

"Why do you do it, then?" he pressed. "Why not move to some other industry that's more female-friendly? Why put yourself through it?"

"You trying to fire me now too?" She was smiling a bit, her posture not quite so rigid.

He laughed in surprise, felt a little better himself. "No. Please don't quit on me. Just wondering."

"This is where the money is." She was serious now. "This is where the opportunities are. I can't afford not to take my opportunities. If they come at a price, well, doesn't everything?"

"All right." He looked at his watch. "After one. Have you eaten?"

"What? No. Not yet." She looked confused at the change of subject.

"Then let's go out," he urged. "Grab some lunch. That was nasty, and we both deserve a break."

"Alec…"

He held up a hand. "Nothing personal, just business. I'm exercising my authority again, since I'm on a roll here, and saying that I require an offsite meeting. And if we happen to be eating while we have it, well, I'll never tell."

She smiled a little at that. "An offsite meeting. OK. Give me five minutes."

He nodded with satisfaction. "Come get me when you're ready."

♡

"I guess you've had to get used to guys hitting on you at work," he speculated.

"If you could even dignify it by calling it that." They were in the little Mexican restaurant tucked into the alley, and Alec had been right, this *had* been a good idea. Vibrant framed fabric art hanging against yellow plastered walls, red chairs, tables inlaid with bright, colorful tile, it was all cheering her up. And the food was just as rich and colorful, satisfaction to body and soul. She spooned up another chunky bite of the soup he'd suggested. Cubes of avocado, generous clumps of shredded chicken, and strips of fried tortillas in a deep red, spicy broth, a wedge of lime squeezed into the bowl at the last minute. Lots of calories, but then, she didn't usually have to worry about that. One advantage of forgetting to eat so often.

"And having them say things like that about you because you're so obviously unavailable, too," he said. "Kind of damned if you do, damned if you don't."

"That would be it. You can either be a slut or a bitch." She saw him wince at the words, but went on. He'd asked, and she'd tell him. "That's the way it is. That's the choice. I prefer to be a bitch."

She thought about it a moment longer, took another spoonful of soup, savored it. "And I want to make it clear that I do appreciate the way you've stood up for me. But I have to be able to handle it. I can't wring my hands and wait to be rescued, and I'm not willing to let it drive me out of the industry. So I handle it."

"You do. But you shouldn't have to."

She shrugged. "That's the way it is," she repeated. "Have you ever asked yourself why I go by 'Rae' these days?"

"Because Desiree sounds too sexy? Sorry." He held up a hasty hand. "I know, I said the word. But you asked, and that would be my guess."

"That, or...not. 'Undesirable Desiree' ring any bells?"

He made a little business of taking a spoonful of soup himself, lifted his napkin to his lips. "I'd forgotten that."

"No, you hadn't. You never forget anything."

"All right," he admitted, "I hadn't. But you're not undesirable now. So that can't still hurt."

"You think? But you're right, I changed some. And no, you can't be too sexy, but you want to be attractive. Who you're really trying to be is that cheerleader who'd never go out with those guys in high school. Well, they went out with you, obviously," she amended. "But all the rest of those guys, no."

"I've dated a few cheerleaders in my time," he admitted. "But I don't really get it."

"Desirable, but unattainable," she explained. "Totally confident, and too good for them. It intimidates them."

"Intimidates the hell out of me, I'll tell you that," he agreed with a smile. "When did you figure that out? When did you...change?"

"Business school." She smiled a little herself, remembering. "I got there that first day, and I was kind of a mess. They assigned me an apartment with someone I didn't know, because I didn't know anybody. She took one look at me, and...Makeover City."

♡

The temperature had been hovering close to a hundred, she remembered, when she'd got off the train that late August day.

She'd dragged the two big old hard-sided suitcases off the platform and through the station, getting more and more flustered as they fell over again and again, their tiny wheels causing them to overbalance on the uneven surfaces and forcing her to shove them upright every time. They weren't exactly the latest thing, another Salvation Army purchase. But that didn't matter, because she was here.

"Help you, miss?" a porter had asked, but she'd declined. She didn't know how much you were supposed to tip, and just the thought made her nervous.

She reached the curb at last. She was sweating, her hair coming loose from her ponytail, tendrils flying around her face, sticking to her cheeks. She saw the cabs lined up and left her suitcases on the sidewalk, walked around the back to reach the driver's window of the closest one.

"Excuse me," she asked, leaning down to speak to him. "Can you take me to UC Davis?"

He stared at her. "Front of the line."

"Oh. Sorry." So she'd dragged her burdens to the front with her glasses sliding down her slippery nose in the heat, convinced by now that everyone was staring at the girl with the suitcases who didn't even know the rules for taxis.

This driver, to her relief, nodded at her request. He opened the trunk and heaved her bags inside without too much of a grimace, and she sank into the sticky plastic of the back seat with relief.

She pulled out her map, directed the driver to the front entrance of the block of furnished apartments. He heaved her bags out again, and they fell over again, and she wrestled them upright again. Paid the driver the amount she had anxiously watched mounting on the meter, and remembered to add the tip. And that had been her first taxi ride.

By the time she'd made it over the sidewalk, up the elevator, down the bumpy concrete walkway with her bags to the red door of Apartment 3C, she was even more nervous. And even sweatier. She knocked on the door. She'd never met her roommate, but she knew that she'd arrived already.

The door swung open to reveal a gazelle-slim young woman even taller than herself, her skin the color of cinnamon, her hair pulled back from her face with a band and springing around her head in perfectly organized chaos.

"Cassandra?" Desiree wiped a sweaty hand on her tan shorts, then stuck it out. "Hi. I'm Desiree."

Cassandra stared at her in disbelief. "Oh, *hell* no."

♡

Which had not been a great start. But it had been followed by Cassie's help dragging in Desiree's suitcases. And her refusal to let Desiree unpack them.

"You are not wearing any of these ugly-ass clothes," Cassie declared when Desiree had heaved the first green plastic case onto the bed and opened it. "Because I'd have to look at them."

"That's what I have, though," Desiree said, shoving her glasses up her nose yet again.

"You ever hear of contacts?" Cassie demanded. "Hair products? A damn *salon?*"

"I can't afford all that."

"You can't afford not to do it. Why are you doing this, business school I mean?"

"What? Uh…to get someplace."

"Uh-huh. An investment in your future."

"Exactly."

"Well, this is the exact same thing. An investment that's going to pay off. Nobody's going to take you seriously like that. They're going to take one look, and then they're going to look away, look at somebody else. And there's no reason for it to be that way. You've got good skin. Good hair, if you'd do something with it. And a good figure, just like me, tall and slim, good for clothes. You carry yourself well too. Again, just like me. We get you fixed up, you're going to go a lot further. In school, internships, jobs. It's an investment. You got some money saved?"

"Yes," Desiree faltered. "For living expenses. And I'll be getting a job. Which I'll *need.*"

"Uh-huh. What kind of job?"

"Waitress. That's what I know how to do."

"We get you fixed, your tips are going to double," Cassie said. "This is where it starts, your new life. Right here and now."

"By the time I started class three days later," Desiree told Alec now, "I had a new wardrobe—well, a few new outfits, anyway—that didn't cost nearly as much as I'd thought, because Cassie taught me about the beauty of the consignment store. I had new hair, and contacts, and makeup. And everything she didn't teach me in those three days, I learned from her over the next two years. She was right about everything. She was my guru."

"Well, she did a great job. She still helping you pick out your wardrobe?"

"No, unfortunately. She's working in the U.K. now, brand manager for one of the big packaged goods companies. She's a star. But my neighbor shops with me sometimes, when I need an opinion. The one who thinks you're hot."

"My fan club," Alec agreed. "And she wasn't the only future star in that apartment. Where did the two of you graduate?"

"Davis," she said in confusion. "Like I said."

"No. In your class. Let's have it. The dirty number."

"She was number three."

"And?" He made a beckoning motion. "Come on, Desiree. Give it to me."

She laughed and surrendered. "Number one."

football, beer, and reality tv

♡

"Gee, Dad, I've hardly been able to sleep all week, I've been so excited for today," Brandon needled, walking into the foyer on Sunday afternoon and handing Alec a six-pack. "My very favorite thing, watching football with women. Hope you bought some chick snacks."

"And what would those be?" Alec asked calmly, leading the way into the kitchen and shoving the beer into the huge stainless steel Sub-Zero fridge that didn't have all that much in it besides, well, beer. He handed Brandon one of the bottles he'd already chilled, pulled out another for himself.

Brandon went over to sprawl beside Joe on one of the over-sized white leather couches. Joe nodded at him without speaking, finished putting away his laptop. He and Alec had taken a couple hours to go through a few things together, multitasking as usual.

Brandon grabbed a taquito from a plate set on the stone surface of the massive coffee table and took a crunchy bite. "You know." He waved the crispy roll through the air like a cigar. "Teeny-tiny vegetables on a special hand-painted plat-ter. Little round tomatoes and baby carrots. Hummus dip, weird nasty whole-grain chips. Light beer. All that low-cal-orie shit."

"Does Rae look like somebody who has to count her calories?" Alec popped the top on a beer for himself and carried it back out, glanced at the 80-inch screen hung against the white wall opposite. Still just talking heads yapping about strategies and tactics, filling time. "And what do you care anyway? You put the "miss" in "misogynistic," you know that?"

"Oh, that's good," Brandon said. "That's very good. Did you think that up in the weight room today, or is that one right off the top of your head?"

"Damn, you're cranky. Still upset that I did the presentation at the conference? I thought we were good with that. Or are you just not gettin' any?"

Brandon laughed, took a long swallow of beer. "Nah, just messing with you. And I'm getting plenty. No problems there. Haven't seen you down in Ziggurat lately though, any day but Friday, or anyplace else either. You got somebody stashed away someplace? Getting serious on us?"

"Not hardly. Busy working, that's all."

"Never stopped you before."

"Yeah, well, maybe I'm getting old. Matching digits now, thirty-three. Maybe I'm starting to feel like one of those old guys driving around in his 911 convertible in one of those stupid English tweed caps that are supposed to make him look like some kind of suave international playboy, when everybody knows it's covering his bald spot."

"Hey," Joe objected.

"When your bald spot's your whole friggin' head, you aren't allowed to take offense," Alec told him.

He was interrupted by the buzz of his phone, picked up. "Yeah, thanks, Anthony. Send her on up."

"She's here," he told the others unnecessarily, feeling a little flutter of nerves that had him pretty damn astonished at himself. "So not so much of the 'chick snacks' jokes."

Brandon lifted his beer and the other palm, ducked his head in subservience. "I live to obey you, O Powerful One."

Alec went to the door, opened it and waited a minute or so. Heard the *ding* of the elevator, saw her step out, look around. Cream-colored leggings under a long, soft, clingy sweater, a cautious fraction more casual than her workday attire. Her hair was still up, though. He was beginning to be obsessed with the idea of seeing it down. He wanted a look at those curls. Well, to be honest, he wanted to wrap his fingers around those curls.

"Hi." He stepped into the hallway to meet her, took the paper bag she offered, looked inside to see a bottle of chilled white wine. "Thanks for coming. You didn't have to bring anything."

"If I didn't want to drink beer," she said, "I figured I might."

He laughed. "Wine, I've got. Snacks, even." *Including* cut-up vegetables, which he pulled out of the fridge once he'd ushered her inside. He'd been fairly specific with the catering company about providing "some stuff a woman would like."

"Just don't ask me to make a three-course dinner," he said, setting the platter on the marble-topped breakfast bar together with the—well, the bowl of hummus, "and I'm good." He got out a stack of plates, too. Women liked plates.

"Yeah, me too," she said. "But *I'm* good as long as you have popcorn. That's my favorite."

"Got that. Buttered, though."

"Buttered's how I like it. The more the better."

"A woman after my own heart." He smiled down at her. Thought about watching her lick the butter off her fingers. Or he could do it. Yeah, that'd be good.

"Hey, Rae," Brandon said, not bothering to get up. Joe stood, though, courtesy of Alec's parents, who'd drilled the same manners into Joe over the years that they'd instilled in Gabe and himself. They were good at that.

He could see Desiree's shoulders tensing a little as she greeted the others, though as usual, her face and voice betrayed nothing. She set her bag down on a stool, leaned against the breakfast bar while Alec opened the chilled white wine she'd brought and poured her a glass. She took it from him and wandered over to the floor-to-ceiling windows that covered half of two walls of the living room, coming to a dramatic point. He watched her stop and stand at the apex as everyone did, look out at the piers, the towers and suspension cables of the Bay Bridge, the water beyond, gray against the gray sky on this drab February day.

"Here we go," Brandon said, picking up the remote and turning up the volume on the speakers discreetly placed in the walls. "National anthem."

Alec indicated the matching easy chair sitting at right angles to the two couches, seated himself next to Rae, across from Joe and Brandon. They watched the overly dramatic musical interlude in silence, followed by the flyover, the segue to the inevitable overpriced commercial.

"Sometimes I wonder why I still watch this thing," Alec commented as lemurs scampered across the big screen, for some bizarre reason. "Another of those things you do because everybody else does."

"Excuse to eat popcorn," Rae said, taking a handful from the big bowl on the coffee table. She did manage to get through a fair amount of it during the first half, Alec noticed with surprise. And she didn't ask any stupid questions, either.

"Holding," he heard her say quietly once, just as the official blew his whistle, tossed the yellow flag.

"You know football," he said. "Dixie a fan?"

She smiled. "Forty-Niners all the way, win or lose. My grandpa was too. She wears her hat while she watches the games."

"Of course she does," he teased. "Got a big red-and-gold foam finger too, I bet, that she waves every time they get a touchdown."

That made her laugh. "Close."

♡

"So what do you think of Alec's place?" Brandon asked her when the game was over and they were waiting for the premiere of the show to begin. "Pretty sweet, huh?"

She looked around, and Alec could see the hesitation. "Great view," she said at last.

"Great *view?*" Brandon challenged. "That's it? Know how much it costs to get into this place, or how much a couch like this runs you?"

"Man, that's real classy," Joe said. "Maybe Alec should've left the price tags on. Rae could've been adding it all up in her head, so she could figure out exactly how impressed to be."

She ignored all that, to Alec's relief. "I'm more of a traditional furnishings kind of girl," she explained. "My neighbors give me grief about it all the time. They say I have grandma taste."

"Well, I can see why," Alec said. "You've got a grandma, after all. And that's OK. This didn't really turn out the way I wanted. I mean, it's what I thought I wanted, but I'm not so sure now. A little hard-edged, I guess." He laughed. "When you see the show, you'll get an idea why, at least I'm guessing you will, because I imagine that's how they'll spin it. Talk about your cognitive dissonance, coming home from that."

"Really," she said. "What was hard to adjust to, besides the modern furnishings?"

He shrugged. "Like, I drove back by myself, because Gabe was with Mira."

"Spoiler alert," Joe pointed out. "You just clued Brandon in."

"Kind of hard to hide that you're engaged to your co-star," Alec said. "At least from your family and friends. You and Rae already knew, because you've both met Mira, so what the hell, now Brandon knows too. I'm sure it's a major plot point, and that they'll make sure everyone starts getting the idea right from Episode One."

"But you drove yourself back," Rae prompted.

"Yeah. Decided to go down through Idaho, see more of it, because it's actually a really beautiful place. Which was fine, except that I kept getting honked at, and then realizing it was because I was going 50. I even got pulled over once by a cop for a sobriety test, I was driving so slowly. That was all fairly new. I usually have the opposite problem."

"Yeah, you've had a speeding ticket or two," Joe agreed, reaching for another potato chip.

"My insurance agent would tell you so. And I kept stopping to eat at places with neon beer signs and antlers on the wall, guys in John Deere caps, and being just fine with that."

"Still not going to tell us whether you won?" Brandon asked. "Not that half a million would have mattered much to you. But you know, a few hundred thousand here, a few there, and before you know it, you're talking about real money."

"Winning mattered, though," Alec assured him. "It mattered a lot. Wait and see. Because I'm *sure* that'll be part of the storyline."

♡

"Wow," Rae said as the credits rolled over the *America Alive* logo. "That looked like some hard work, unless it was in the editing."

"Not in the editing," Alec said. "There's no way to show how hard it really is, physically, not to mention every other way. The hardest thing I've ever done, bar none."

"Harder than DataQuest?" Joe asked, referring to his and Alec's first venture, begun when they were still at Stanford. When they'd subsisted on Red Bull and tortilla chips for what had felt like weeks at a time, and sleep had been a precious luxury.

"No contest," Alec assured him. "You want to know how easy our lives are now? Go back to 1885 for a few days, never mind a couple months. That whole training period, I'd wake up and my entire body would be one giant ache."

"The blonde chicks were hot, though," Brandon put in. One too many beers, Alec judged, because that wasn't his first comment on the subject, and Brandon usually had a little more class than that in mixed company. A *very* little. "That must've been some consolation. You put some moves on there? Sure looks like they were up for it."

Alec frowned at him, gave him a quick, sharp shake of the head. He hoped they weren't going to include that in the storyline, but he had a bad feeling that they would. At least they hadn't shown it today. But when they did…Why hadn't he thought more at the time about what he'd be showing the world, six months down the road? What he'd be showing his parents? What he'd be showing somebody like Rae?

"Time for me to go," she said, getting up from her chair. "But thanks. That was some entertaining viewing. The show, I mean, not so much the Super Bowl. I prefer a little closer game, but maybe that's what we'll get with the show, Alec. Some real competition?"

"Yes," he said, standing up himself. "I'm allowed to say that, at least. And that I think you'll be surprised."

"I'll look forward to it. Thanks for having me over."

"I'll walk you to your car."

She laughed. "That'd take a while. I didn't bring it."

"I'd be glad to give you a ride home," Joe put in, surprising Alec. "Or to BART, or whatever."

"No, I'm good." She waved a hand in the guys' direction, and Alec walked her to the door.

"Sure you're OK?" he asked when he'd opened it for her. "Because it's dark, and it'd be no trouble to drive you." Not that he knew where she lived. He could have accessed her employment file, of course, but he hadn't. Because he'd wanted to know badly enough that it had felt too much like stalking to check it out.

"I'm fine on my own," she insisted. "I'm used to it."

The elevator doors opened, and she stepped inside. He raised a hand in farewell and watched the doors close, then headed back into the apartment.

"You sticking around?" he asked Joe. "I'd like to run through a few things with you. Rae was right, I guess, about the game being boring, because I got an idea in there about how we can punch through that roadblock with the error-handling subroutine."

"Sure," Joe said.

"And that's my cue," Brandon said, getting up himself. "I think I hear my mother calling. Anyway, you wouldn't want me to watch you guys logging in. That'd probably violate three or four of Rae's rules right there, and she'd have to give me a spanking." He laughed, bent over, and gave himself a slap. "Owww, baby. Maybe that's enough reason to do it, what do you think?"

"I think," Joe said without looking up from where he was bent over, pulling his laptop case from behind the couch, "that you should shut up."

"Or I might guess your super-duper special passwords," Brandon went on, ignoring him, "even without my Secret Decoder Ring. Come to think of it, Rae should probably crack down on the two of you, do a brain wipe after you work together. I thought nobody was supposed to have all the pieces, and yet what do you know, somebody has to. Wonder if she's thought of that, that there you both are, all clued-in and cozy? I'd call that a serious security breach."

"Got to trust somebody," Alec said. "For my part, I'll stick with Joe. Take some snacks if you want, before you go." He was grateful that Brandon lived close, in another of the towering condo complexes that had sprung up south of Market, and had walked over, because he wasn't in any shape to drive home. "There are some sandwiches left. And, you know, your favorites. Baby vegetables and hummus."

"Taquitos," Brandon decided, heading into the kitchen and opening drawers. "Where are your ziplock bags?"

"Uh...not sure," Alec said, willing himself to relax. Just Brandon and his mouth, giving it a little extra today because he was a little drunk. "Imee rearranged things, I think."

"Never mind. I found them." Brandon dumped a few of the little rolls into a bag. "I guess it'd be way too much to expect you to have any little plastic containers for guacamole and bean dip."

"Just take them. I won't be eating them."

Brandon did, added a couple rolled sandwiches to his bag. "Bachelor dinner. I need to find a woman who can cook."

"They have to stick around to cook for you," Alec pointed out. "You get that when you actually, you know, *date* them, and they invite you over for dinner. You never get that far."

"Because he's too busy running away in the morning," Joe said. "Afraid he'll have accidentally married somebody, or promised her a second date."

"*Me?*" Brandon protested. "I'm not the only one here who specializes in casual. Can't help it if I'm better at it than Alec."

"Yeah, right," Joe snorted. "He might be casual, but they cook for him. He gets a little tickle in his throat, some girl's over here with her homemade chicken soup. You've got a ways to go, grasshopper."

"Well, if we don't get started," Alec told Joe, "we're going to be here till morning. Stick what you don't take back in the fridge, Brandon, so Joe and I don't die of food poisoning. 'Mysterious loss of startup brain trust: foul play suspected.' Little would they know it was because Brandon left the potato salad out."

"More likely to think we killed ourselves in despair over being beat to market because we're too damn *slow*," Joe growled.

"OK, I'm going." Brandon shoved the fridge door shut. "Don't have to tell me more than seven or eight times. See you guys tomorrow."

♡

And then Alec and Joe were alone, opening their laptops together, as they'd done so many thousands of times, over so many years. Alec logged into the cloud-based server, then hesitated.

"Does Brandon seem like kind of an…" he began.

"Asshole?" Joe asked, not looking up. "Yeah."

The startled a laugh out of Alec. "But is he worse?"

"Not sure," Joe said, and this time he did look up. "Maybe it's just that you've changed, so he looks worse."

"Ouch. I was that bad?"

"No. But close, sometimes. Let's go." Joe opened the file, and they lost themselves in solving the mysteries of code. Again, as always.

♡

"All right," Alec said, sitting back and stretching a couple hours later. "That's a fairly good start. I'll be able to give it some more time tomorrow."

"Hope so," Joe said, going to the fridge to refill his water glass. "Seeing as how you canned my best programmer."

"Hey, I told you. No choice."

"He was that far over the line?"

"Yes. He was. If you'd been there to hear it, you'd have done the same thing. How's Michael been since then? I almost fired him too, in the heat of the moment. We going to need to?"

"No. Not that bad," Joe said. "At least, yeah, he was pissed. You know how tight he and Simon were. But he wants the job, and let's face it, with Simon gone, he's in the Number One spot, got access to the best stuff, building that resume. He's not going to walk away from that, or to risk it."

He took a seat again, started packing up, and spoke without looking at Alec. "But you and Rae are getting pretty...corporate, aren't you?"

That one took Alec by surprise. "Corporate? Not the word I was expecting."

"That too. But doesn't it all feel a little stifling, all these rules, doing it by the book, having it get so big? Don't you miss the gunslinger days?"

Alec got up himself, took a restless turn around the room. He'd been sitting too long, needed another workout before bed. This was the downside of always meeting at his place.

"No," he said, grateful for the opportunity to put words to the feelings he'd been having for a while now. "I want to do bigger things. And bigger things mean bigger companies. Not even sure I want to keep starting up and selling out, tell you the truth. Maybe I'd like to actually run something, you know, grow it, expand the product line. As long as I had somebody to do the boring parts, of course," he added with a grin for his partner.

"Like Rae, you mean." Joe's eyes were watchful, and he wasn't smiling back.

"But I'm not planning on leaving you out," Alec said, realizing where this was going. "Hell, the more I get wrapped up in running the show, doing the whole visionary-founder deal, the more I need you on the tech side."

"Yeah, well," Joe said, finishing off his water. "As long as I'm happy just being your tech side. Maybe I do still want the startup rush. Who knows, maybe I'll decide I want to do it on my own, be the big boss, end up with a fleet of classic cars, one of those stacked garages for them underneath my mansion, not just one lousy Audi."

"I'd hate to lose you, man," Alec said, completely sobered now.

"Looks to me like you'd have compensations."

"Is it that obvious?"

Joe considered, taking his time as always. "Obvious to me, anyway. And I'm not exactly Mr. Sensitivity, so if I'm seeing it…"

"Well, I'm not the first guy in history to have a thing for a woman he works with," Alec said. "And sure as hell not the first to get flat nowhere with it. So just quit shooting off that big mouth of yours about it around the office, and we'll be good."

He got a smile out of Joe at that, because Joe could give clams lessons. But Alec reminded himself that he'd better figure out how to keep his partner challenged and on board, because he needed him. And Joe might be quiet, but he was anything but passive.

Joe slung his laptop case over a broad shoulder and got up to leave. "Yeah. Quit gossiping. I'll keep that in mind."

affairs of the heart

♡

"I thought I'd better check in before things got all wild and crazy," Desiree said nearly three weeks later, leaning back a little in her desk chair and smiling into the phone as if her grandmother could see her. "Because Pinochle Night's at your house tonight, isn't it? How are the preparations going?"

"Oh, pretty good."

That didn't sound like Dixie's usual enthusiasm. "Everything OK?" Desiree asked. "Is Mrs. Sanderson counting cards or something? You have to watch that woman like a hawk, I know."

And there was the wheezy, whisky laugh, to her relief. "Oh, no, nothing like that. Just been a little tired this week, got a little indigestion."

"Did you check with Dr. Alberts?"

"For what? My stomach's bothering me, that's all. And I wore myself out some, I guess, doing the gardening the other day. But I got all that nasty oxalis up. That spring rain brings those weeds right out."

"Maybe you should call him," Desiree persisted. "The doctor."

"If I'm not better by Monday, I'll think about it," Dixie conceded, and that was as much as Desiree could get from her. "But right now, I'm going to lie down on the couch and have a nice rest before the girls come over. I'll be fine."

♡

Desiree was putting the finishing touches on the report that would accompany the latest financials when her phone rang again. She reached for it with an exasperated sigh, looked at the screen. Dixie again.

"What?" she asked teasingly when she'd picked up. "I *told* you she was counting cards."

But it wasn't her grandmother who answered her.

"Desiree? Honey, it's Marti Sanderson. Your grandma's just gone to the hospital in the ambulance."

"*What?*" Desiree was already grabbing for the drawer pull, reaching for her purse. "What happened?"

"Her heart, I think," Mrs. Sanderson said, and Desiree heard the worry in the quavering voice. "We'd just got there. She got up to get the drinks, and she collapsed. Fell right on down."

"Is she..." Desiree couldn't say it. "All right?" Knowing that she wasn't, and praying all the same.

"Oh, honey, I don't know. But you'd better come."

She left her laptop open, her notes scattered. "I'm coming," she said. "I'll be there as fast as I can."

She hurried around the corner of the desk, caught her hip on the edge, and stumbled. Her purse flew from her hand, her phone dropping to the floor, and she was there, scrabbling for it. "Mrs. Sanderson? Are you still there?"

"I'm here, honey."

"I'm coming. Fast as I can. Call me if you hear anything, will you?"

She hung up, picked up her purse, grabbed for the rest of her things and stuffed them back into it. Where were her keys? She found them, finally, under the desk. Got to the door, shut it, and fumbled with the key, but her hand was shaking, and she couldn't fit it into the lock.

"Going so soon?"

It was Alec, coming out of the break room with a Red Bull in his hand. The only one still here other than Michael and Joe, after six on Friday night.

"I…" She was still trying to fit the key. "I have to go. To Chico. My grandma…"

"Whoa." Alec's hand was on her shoulder. "Rae. What's wrong? What happened?"

She gave up on her keys, turned to him, saw the concern in his eyes, and almost lost it. "She's been taken to the hospital. They think…her heart. But I don't know. I have to go."

He took the keys from her hand, locked the door, handed them back to her. "I'll drive you. Let me grab my stuff. We'll be out of here in two minutes."

"No. I have to go. I can't…"

"Desiree. Sit down." He guided her to an empty cube, sat her in its chair. "You can't drive yourself. Two minutes. Wait."

She waited, because she didn't know what else to do. Her car was at home, and home was too far away, even if she got a cab. So instead, she watched him walk briskly to his office, then watched the door until he emerged again, jacket on, laptop case slung over his shoulder, and came back to her.

"Let's go," he said. Within fifteen minutes, he'd walked her to his car and was pulling out of the Millennium Tower's underground garage. And that was where the progress stopped, because they were immediately caught in the rush hour traffic heading for the Bay Bridge.

She pulled her phone from her purse again with clumsy fingers, tried to punch 'Chico Hospital' into the navigation bar, but couldn't do it.

"*Damn* it," she breathed, feeling the agitation rise. "Come *on.*" The tears were close now, hot and sharp beneath her lids, and Alec glanced across at her.

"I need to call," she said helplessly. "I need to find out what's happening. And I can't make it work."

He nodded. "Hang on." Pushed a button on the leather-wrapped steering wheel with his thumb and said, "Call Dad."

Another few seconds, then Dave Kincaid's deep, rich voice filled the car, and Alec was explaining the situation in a few quick sentences.

"I'll call right now," Dave said. "Back to you in a few minutes."

Alec hung up, glanced over at Desiree again. "Dad knows everybody," he promised. "If there's anything to find out, he'll find it out."

The minutes ticked by, neither of them saying anything, because there was nothing to say. Just the litany running through Desiree's mind, *Please let her be all right,* over and over again, as the traffic inched across the bridge approach, not even on the span yet, and she watched the red brake lights winking on and off ahead of her, and wanted desperately to hurry, and couldn't, because they were stuck.

The chime of the phone through the big car's speakers made her jump.

Alec punched the button again. "Dad? Got you on speaker."

"She made it to the hospital OK," Dave said. "That's all I know. Probably all there is to know. I'll head on over there now, and keep you posted. How far out are you?"

"A good four hours," Alec guessed.

"I'll keep you posted," Dave said again. "And Desiree?"

"Yes, sir?" She heard her voice trembling with relief and the tears she couldn't completely hold back anymore, because her grandmother was alive.

"You hold that good thought," Dave said. "Your grandma's a strong lady, and so are you. You say a prayer and let Alec take care of you, and don't despair. I'll be right back to you just as soon as I get the word."

♡

The drive was endless, and at the end of it, her grandmother was still alive.

She and Alec sat for another hour in the surgical waiting room, and Dave Kincaid sat there too, and they waited, and Desiree felt as if she were going to wait forever, cycling between dull numbness and restless anxiety. But when the middle-aged woman in the green scrubs came into the room and called her name, there was no question which emotion was uppermost.

Alec was up with her, she barely registered as she approached the doctor. She was searching the woman's face for the expression that would give her the news, not seeing it, and knowing that it couldn't be. It couldn't, because she couldn't stand it.

Please, she prayed as she took what felt like the longest walk of her life. *Please.*

"Your grandmother's in Recovery," was the first thing she heard, and she sagged, and knew she would have fallen if Alec hadn't put an arm around her to hold her up.

"She's a lucky woman," the doctor went on. "That this happened when she had someone with her, and they called the ambulance as fast as they did, which meant that we were able to begin thrombolytic therapy right away too. Clot-busting drugs," she explained.

Desiree nodded. She'd heard all this. And she knew what the doctor hadn't said, too. That if it hadn't been Pinochle Night, her grandmother would have collapsed alone. And that she would have died.

"We did go ahead and do the angioplasty, and we put in a stent to relieve the blockage," the doctor went on. "She came through it well, and the damage wasn't severe, so all in all, you've got about as good an outcome as you could hope for." She smiled a little, the fatigue evident now, well after midnight. "Like I said, she's in Recovery, and best case, we'll keep her for another couple days, but we'll need to see."

"Can I see her?" Desiree asked.

"She'll be taken to Intensive Care," the doctor said. "On the fourth floor. But you won't be allowed to visit until morning. You should think about going home and getting some rest. You can come back as early as six."

Desiree shook her head. "No. Can I sit in their waiting room?"

"Of course." The woman put a hand out and touched Desiree's arm. "Your grandmother's a sick lady, but she's a tough one too," she said, and the sympathy made Desiree's tears well. "I'll come check on her again tomorrow, and then we'll see."

♡

Alec could feel the trembling in Rae's body as he led her back across the room and lowered her into her chair. She immediately leaned forward, circled her arms over her knees, and held on.

"Desiree," he said. His arm was still around her, his hand rubbing over her shoulder, and he'd never felt so helpless. "Oh, baby."

She shook her head violently, and he could feel her shaking under his hand, and still she was bent double, hanging on so tight. He looked helplessly at his father.

"Just hold her," Dave said quietly. "Wait."

So he held her and waited until the shaking had lessened, until she finally sat up again and he could pull her into him, because he couldn't help it, and hear the shudders of the sobs she was still trying to suppress.

"Thanks. I'm OK," she said at last, sounding anything but, and pushing herself upright, away from him. "It was just...hearing she was all right."

"Of course it was." He let her go, but he kept his arm around her shoulders, because he had to. "And now we should take you home, to my parents'." He looked at his dad, got the nod of approval. "For a few hours, at least. You need some rest."

"No." She stood, and he stood helplessly with her. "I'm waiting wherever they let me. Close to her."

So he stayed with her, all that night. Dozed in the uncomfortable chairs, checked on her every time he woke, and saw her sleeping and waking too. And in the morning, she was able to see her grandmother, and that was better. Alec got her to go to breakfast, and coaxed her to eat twice more during that long day, during which her grandmother was transferred to a regular room on the cardiac care floor, so Rae could sit at her bedside and hold her hand.

Alec watched some of the terrible tension leave her over that long day. And still she didn't cry.

guy number one

♡

"This is it. Turn left up ahead. The Country Club sign."

He'd wondered if she'd fallen asleep, she'd been so quiet. He'd been about to say something, to wake her up to ask the way before he drove right on out of town.

She continued to direct him, though, a right turn, then a left. He pulled to the curb at the spot she indicated, clicked the button to release his seatbelt. But she didn't follow suit. Instead, she turned towards him in the dark, seemed to be hesitating. So he waited.

"Do you think you could come in for a while?" she asked at last.

"Sure. Or I could take you to my parents'," he suggested again, "if you don't want to be alone. You know they'd be happy. It'd be better, Desiree. Really."

She shook her head. "No, I want to be here. But...could you come in? Just for a few minutes?"

"Sure." Although this wasn't exactly the way he'd pictured her inviting him back to her place.

He followed her up the sidewalk, climbed four wooden steps onto a neat little deck, and waited while she fished in her purse for the key, opened the door and flipped the switch. The light cast by a standing lamp revealed her exhaustion, the shadows under her eyes, the pallor of her skin. And he knew that, what-ever help he could be to her, that was what he was going to do.

She stood, looking irresolute again, in the middle of the shabby little living room, furnished with a single faux-leather recliner, a yellow couch with a red and black afghan folded over the end, a wooden coffee table with curved legs. The dinette set standing a few feet away, the compact kitchen beyond it, to the right of the front door. The layout completely familiar to Alec, and the whole place not that different from the mobile home where his own family had lived when he'd been in middle school. Right down to the framed piece of needlepoint hanging against the veneer paneling. *God Bless Our Home.*

"I need to take a shower," she said vaguely, clearly dead on her feet. "If you want…" She gestured towards the kitchen, let her arm fall again. "A beer or something. It's Miller Lite, though."

"I'm fine," he assured her. "You go take your shower." He'd gone by his parents' earlier in the day and showered, pulled clean clothes from the dresser that his mother, luckily, still hadn't cleaned out. But Desiree hadn't had a break at all.

He was sitting on the couch, leafing through a copy of *Good Housekeeping,* when the sound of running water stopped. The magazine selection here was pretty similar to the one in the hospital's waiting room. In fact, he'd read this same issue there, had already checked out the article on "Seven Ways to Make a Statement—Without Spending a Bundle." If he ever needed to stencil anything, he was all set.

He heard the bathroom door opening. And then a dull thud, a gasp. And was up and into the hallway leading out of the living room before he'd finished registering the sound.

She was leaning face-first into the space between the bath-room door and what was obviously her bedroom, her arms hug-ging herself in desperation, her head wedged into the corner. Wrapped in a pink terrycloth bathrobe, her feet bare. And crying.

"Desiree." He pulled her away from the wall, turned her gently around. "Oh, baby. Shhh. Come on, now. It's OK."

She shook her head blindly, wrapped her arms around herself even more tightly, literally trying to hold herself together. He didn't know what else to do, so he walked her back to the living room, pulled her down onto the couch with him. And then he held her while she cried.

She tried to talk a few times, but never got beyond, "It just… I'm just…" before the sobs took her again.

"I know," he said, his hand smoothing again and again over her wet hair. "I know, baby. But it's going to be all right."

At last she sat back, her eyes and nose streaming. Sniffed hard, wiped her hands over her wet cheeks.

"Here." He looked for tissues, couldn't see any. Got up and went into the kitchen and found the roll of paper towels, ripped a few off and carried them back to her.

She took them from him, set about the business of mopping up. She was breathing through her mouth, her cheeks and nose were mottled with red, and her eyes were puffy. And he could feel her pain all the way inside his chest. All the way to his heart.

"I was in the shower," she finally said, her voice even huskier than usual from her tears. "And I thought, my grandma's going to *die*. She's going to be gone, and I'm going to be…" She swallowed, and he could see the moisture leaking again from her swollen eyes. "I'm going to be alone. And I can't…I don't think I can stand it. She's all I have." The tears were back in force now. "She's the only thing."

"She's going to be all right, though," Alec said, wishing his dad were here. Or Gabe. Somebody who knew how to say the right things.

"But sometime," she said again. "She's going to die." She gave a watery little laugh that turned to a hiccup, blew her nose again. "Well, that's stupid. I mean, I know that. But I didn't...I didn't really *know* that, before."

He wasn't his dad, and he wasn't Gabe, so he went with what he had. "She's going to be mad at you, you know," he said conversationally.

"What?" She stared at him, horrified.

"That you've already got her dead and buried," he explained. "I'll bet she tells you that you'd better not be thinking you're getting your hands on her good stuff, because she's planning to be around for a long time yet."

That shocked another laugh out of her, and this one sounded more genuine. "I bet you're right." Her smile was wobbly, but it was a smile. "She's probably thinking right now that she'd better get out of the hospital fast, before I make off with her special sombrero-shaped chip-n-dip server."

"Or her red Tupperware Jell-O salad bowl," he agreed with a grin. "Because I *know* you've been coveting that."

She smiled again, and he put his arm around her, pulled her close, and kissed the top of her head. "I'm not trying to make light of how you feel," he tried to explain. "But you're so tired, and that makes everything look so much worse. Get some sleep, and I'll come back and take you to the hospital again in the morning. I'll bet she'll be feeling a whole lot perkier by then, and you will too."

"OK," she sighed. She straightened, and he let his arm fall. "But..." She looked at him again. "Would you mind staying with me? I can sleep in my grandma's room," she hurried to explain. "And you could sleep in mine. The sheets are clean, and there are a couple new toothbrushes in the bottom drawer in the bathroom, even. I mean, if you can. If you wouldn't mind."

"I wouldn't mind. Of course I wouldn't mind." Sleeping in her bed? Again, not the way he'd imagined it, and this clearly wasn't the time, but still. "And you have extra toothbrushes up here?" A little more teasing might be just what the doctor ordered. "Let me guess. There's an extra razor too, and not because of all the guys you've brought back here. Are your grandmother's spices in alphabetical order now, because you got bored over Christmas?"

"No." She was smiling back at him, because he'd got it right, had known what she needed. "They already were. And you're right. You're Guy Number One."

♡

"Alec."

He struggled out of the depths of sleep, wondered for a moment where he was. And then he saw the shape of her, pale against the darkness, standing beside the bed, and remembered. Desiree.

"What?" He pushed himself up on an elbow, blinked a couple times. "Can't sleep? Bad dream?"

"Can I…" Her voice was hesitant again, husky and low. "Can I get in bed with you? Would you…could you just hold me?"

Was this some kind of horrible nightmare? One of those ones where you were trying and trying to get to the airport, but you could never quite make it?

"Uh…" He cast his mind around wildly, but couldn't find any answers. "Sure." He scooted over, flipped the covers back. And saw her, felt her sliding in beside him. Coming closer, and he felt the touch of her feet on his calves, and flinched.

"Sorry," she said, pulling back. "Cold feet." Which was nothing to how he was feeling right now.

You can do this, he told himself desperately. *Man up.* She needed him to hold her, and that was all, and that was exactly what he was going to do. Right the hell now.

"It's OK." He rolled onto his back, pulled her close. "Come here."

She nestled into him. Her feet were still cold, and the long, slim arms and legs felt cool against his skin too. He shifted to his side, ran his hand down the narrow surface of her back, felt the rib of the skinny undershirt under his fingers, and was reminded of that first day he'd seen her, in the Snack Shack. And felt a rush of tenderness that almost overrode the heat that was consuming him now. A heat that she had to be aware of, because she was pressed close, and she was killing him.

"Could you..." Her breath was soft on his cheek. "Could you kiss me?"

He could, and he did. Pressed his lips gently to hers in the dark, to that full, soft, sweet mouth. Felt the shock of it, like the touch of a live wire, all the way through his body.

She sighed, and her mouth opened a little, and the kiss was heating, his tongue touching her upper lip, tracing the fullness of her lower one, and he could sense her tightening against him, her body as sensitized as his own. He could swear that he could feel what she was feeling, his tongue slipping into her mouth, tasting her, his mouth moving over her own. His hand drifting down her back, coming to rest on one firm, round cheek, sliding over the cotton underwear. His fingers touching the soft skin of the crease at the back of her thigh, rubbing over the edge of the fabric, tracing its contours. All the way down to the silk of her inner thigh, then back up, again and again.

He had her leg pulled over his hip now, and she was pressed tight against him, and he was still kissing her, more and more deeply, wanting every bit of her. Wanting to be inside her with a desperation he'd hadn't felt since he was sixteen.

And then it hit him, like a bucket of cold water right to the chest. His hand froze, his mouth lifted from her own.

"Shit."

She didn't respond for a moment, frozen too. Then scooted back from him in a hurried motion. "What?"

"I don't have a condom."

"Oh." She sat up. "Oh," she said again, and she sounded so lost. "Anyway, we shouldn't...This is such a bad idea. What am I *doing?*" She was working herself up again, he could tell.

He reached for her. "Desiree. Wait." Pulled her down next to him, leaned over to kiss her, gently this time. Soft on her mouth, then her cheek. He brushed her hair back, kissed her temple. "Baby, no. It isn't. It isn't a bad idea. Not if you want to do it, it isn't. It's a good idea, you and me. I promise."

"Oh." She sighed. "I do. I do want to do it." She had her arm around him, her hand stroking his upper back as if she couldn't resist, any more than he could resist touching her. He'd been sleeping in nothing but a pair of briefs, and he could almost picture the trail of sparks she left behind as her hand moved over his shoulder blade, down the length of his spine, back up again to trace the curve of muscle at his shoulder. "Could we...anyway?"

"No." He wished the answer could have been anything else. "Even though it's been months for me, and I've been tested. And I'll bet it's been a while for you too, hasn't it?"

He heard the little hitch of her laughter. "Months would be a safe bet." And he was *glad.*

Why the hell *didn't* he have a condom? He was always prepared. But he hadn't been, not since...when? Not since well before Christmas, anyway. Since he'd finally realized, on some level, that he wasn't going to be taking advantage of anything that came his way, so there was no point.

"But I'll bet you're not on birth control, are you?" This was the un-sexiest conversation he'd had in bed in years, but it mattered.

"No," she said softly, and he could hear the regret, and what sounded like...shame?

"Baby. It's all right." He kissed her again, took her lower lip between both of his own, pulled it into his mouth, and felt what it did to her.

"It's all right," he told her again between kisses, his hand moving over her back again, reaching to pull up the undershirt, tracing the top edge of her underwear now, low on her hips, around to the front, stroking over velvet skin, feeling her tremble at his touch. "I can still make you feel good. Lie back, now, and let me do it."

She didn't answer, but she had shifted onto her back, and he could sense that her thighs had parted, that she had abandoned her qualms, surrendered to this. Had surrendered to him, and he felt another surge of excitement, hot and dark, somehow existing right alongside his concern for her.

If she wanted it, he vowed, he was going to make it good for her. He moved onto one elbow, kept his fingers tracing over her abdomen. Leaned over to kiss her again, and he could finally do it exactly the way he needed to. With her underneath him. On and on, taking her little noises of surprise and pleasure into himself, feeling the faint shudders running through her, the urgency in the mouth that opened under his own.

He went slowly, and he was gentle for just as long as he could be. And he was as thorough as he knew how to be, because he wanted to touch every inch of her, and he wanted to kiss her everywhere, and he wanted to make it the best she'd ever had.

He lingered at her neck, just as he'd thought about doing so many times. And he'd been right, the spot above her collarbone, that hollow where her neck met her shoulder was her favorite. Just kissing her there, using his tongue and his teeth on her, had her shifting beneath him. Especially when he reached under the undershirt, sent his hand slowly up, stroking closer and closer, felt her moving harder, squirming now, until he was at her breast.

When he finally had his hand there, his thumb stroking over the nipple that pebbled under his touch, combined it with the stronger pressure of his teeth closing on her throat, she arched her back and cried out. And by the time he'd pushed the fabric up under her arms and had his mouth on her, his tongue busy, his teeth grazing her tender flesh, he found that her sensitive neck had only given him an inkling. Because with every place he touched her, every inch his mouth covered, he pushed her higher.

Finally, he got both hands under the undershirt, pulled it over her head.

"I'm going to take off your underwear now," he told her, reaching for that final strip of cotton. "Because I need you to be naked. And I need to touch you. I need every part of you to be mine."

Her only answer was to lift her hips, to help him. He moved down the bed as he pulled the things down her long, slim legs, dropped them on the floor. He started at the bottom, ran his hands up her calves, then up higher, his thumbs on the soft, delicate, secret skin of her inner thighs, the place he'd always wanted to touch. And he'd been right to want it. In fact, it felt so good, he did it again. Down, and then back up. Going more slowly with every inch he covered.

And then he touched her. So warm. So wet. So open, wanting it so much. So he gave it to her, and she writhed and cried out and lifted into his hand.

And after a while, that wasn't enough either, and he had to put his mouth on her.

He pushed her legs further apart with a hand on each thigh, held them there as he began. Carefully. Slowly, because he wanted this to last. Wanted every moment of it to feel even better than the moment before, until the fire took her, and consumed her. Until she burned.

And if she'd been responsive before, she was wild now. He was holding her down, spreading her wide, moving faster, harder, past the time for gentleness, and her hands were stroking frantically over his shoulders, in his hair, and she was calling out.

And then, all too soon, long before he was ready for it to be over, her cries reached a crescendo, and the spasms had begun, so strong that he could barely hold her.

He kept his mouth hard on her, increased the stimulation, and he thought she was going to levitate right off the bed, her back arching, her shoulders rising until she was nearly sitting up, her thighs straining against the firm restraint of his hands. On and on for what felt like minutes, until she subsided with a few final shudders, her cries turning to moans, then sobbing little breaths.

He moved up her body, took her mouth again, thrust his tongue deep, and kissed her the way he wanted to be inside her, invading every silken space. He knew that she could taste herself on him, and he wanted her to. To know where he'd been, and what he'd done.

He lifted a hand to her face, stroked a thumb over her cheek, felt the wetness there, and came back to himself fast. Rolled off her, onto his side.

"Desiree." His voice sounded strained, and no wonder. "Are you all right?"

"Yes." It was a sigh. Her hand came up to touch his chest lightly, and he could feel the languor of it, the fatigue. She stroked him once more, then her hand fell away. He heard her breath deepening, and knew that she was asleep.

the morning after

♡

Desiree came out of the bathroom, not sure what she'd find. She'd woken to the soft sound of rain on the roof, a gentle drumming that had almost lulled her back into sleep, until she'd remembered. Her grandmother, the hospital. And Alec.

He was sitting at the kitchen table, his laptop open in front of him. He looked at her as she hesitated in the entrance to the living room, and smiled. Not a grin, just the very sweetest smile.

"Hi," he said.

She pulled the sash of her robe tight with both hands. "Umm...hi." Well, this was awkward.

"Want some coffee? I hope you don't mind, I went ahead and poked around until I found it."

"Sure." But she wasn't really paying attention. Her purse wasn't on the end table next to the door where she always put it. Had she left it at the hospital somehow? When had she last had it? She couldn't remember, and felt a hot flash of panic.

"What's wrong?" he asked with his hand on the refrigerator door, watching her wandering around the living room.

"Did you see my purse? I need my phone. Did I leave it? Do you remember if I had it?" The panic was taking full hold now.

"It's right by your bed."

"Oh." She realized why he knew. That he'd have seen it, because he'd slept there. But that didn't matter right now. She needed to call.

"But your grandma's doing fine," he said before she'd even made it to the hallway again.

She stopped, turned. "She is? How do you know?"

"Called to check, soon as I got up. She had a good night, and everything's looking good. Still asleep, though."

She sagged with relief. Meanwhile, he pulled the mug from the microwave, filled it from the coffeemaker, waved it enticingly in her direction. "Coffee right here," he coaxed. "You have to come sit with me to get it, though."

She had to smile. She couldn't help it. She sat down opposite him at the dinette, picked up the cup he set before her. "You heated my milk first," she realized.

He looked confused. "Wasn't that right?"

"How did you know I like it that way?"

That sweet smile again. "I've been watching you heat up your milk for months now, remember? I know what you like."

She took a sip of the pale brown stuff. No sugar, and nearly as much milk as coffee, exactly right. He really *did* know what she liked, in more ways than one. But then, she'd liked everything.

She sneaked another peek over the rim of her cup. Same soft flannel shirt in a deep blue plaid he'd been wearing the day before, the neck of the white T-shirt showing underneath, but the shadow of dark beard above was gone. He'd found the pack of disposable razors too, then. She remembered the scrape of whiskers against tender skin in the dark, and shivered a little.

Another determined sip of coffee. No choice. They had to talk about this.

"About last night," she said as briskly as she could. "I put you on the spot, I realize that. I know you wanted to comfort me, and I appreciate it."

He wasn't smiling now. "You didn't put me on the spot. You gave me the chance I've been wanting for months."

"You didn't even get anything out of it, though." Direct was always the best way. "I fell asleep. So if you want me to… reciprocate."

He stared at her with what looked like anger. "What are you saying? That I did you a favor, and you're willing to pay me back? Is that it?"

She could feel the color rising in her cheeks. "I didn't mean that. I just meant…" She reached for her coffee cup again to give herself time to think, but something went wrong, and it tipped. She grabbed for it, but not before some of the hot liquid had spilled.

"Shit." He jumped up, came back with the sponge and mopped up, then tossed the pink rectangle back into the sink. And then sat down across from her again and faced her squarely.

"Desiree." His eyes forced her to hold his gaze. "I wanted to make love to you. And for the record, yes, I got something out of it. I enjoyed the hell out of it. And if you want to do it all again, and add a little bit more in there too, I'm more than up for that. In fact, you can bet that the first store we pass on our way to the hospital, I'm going to be pulling into that parking lot and visiting the Family Planning aisle so I'm ready if you do. And if you don't…" He stopped and took a breath. "I'm going to be pretty damn disappointed."

"I need to… *We* need to think about that, and talk about it." His words had filled her with a rush of heat, but she set them aside for later, because something else was nagging at her. "But I don't understand how I could have done that when my grandmother was in the hospital. How could I have even wanted to?"

"Because you needed somebody to hold you." He reached for her hand, his thumb rubbing over her knuckles, and she felt the pleasure of even that simple touch. "Seems fairly natural to me."

"That's what I told myself." She couldn't meet his gaze anymore, looked down at the wet spot that remained on the table, rubbed at it with the side of her fist. "When I asked you. But when you did, I wanted more. I wanted to have sex with you."

He laughed. "Well, I wanted to have sex with you too, so that makes us even, I guess."

"But when I'd been so upset," she insisted. "So sad. It seems wrong."

He paused a moment at that. "This is when I wish my dad were here," he muttered. Then hurried on at her obvious shock, "Not to discuss this exact topic, just to know the answers. I'm not sure, but it still seems normal to me. Maybe you wanted to feel connected. Maybe you wanted to feel alive. Any of that sounding good?"

"Yeah," she said with a sigh.

"Or maybe," he said, still holding her hand, a coaxing smile starting to grow, "maybe you're as hot for me as I am for you. No, on second thought, not possible."

"That one. That could be it." She could feel her own foolish smile beginning. "Or all of the above."

"Then," he said with a little upward tug on her hand, "come on over here and kiss me good morning."

♡

Sitting in a man's lap, she discovered, felt even better than she'd imagined it could. His thighs made a warm, deliciously firm seat, and it was a satisfyingly long way around those shoulders. The nape of his neck felt pretty good under her fingertips, although it had to compete with his back, and his arms too, because she wanted to touch him everywhere. And holy habanero, but the man could *kiss*. Long, slow, and everlastingly patient, no rush to move on to anything else. Like he could sit here and do it all day.

"What time is it?" she sighed against him at last.

"Mmm," he said, his mouth at the corner of hers, licking into her dimple, which felt just absolutely delicious, and her mind drifted again. "Eight, maybe. Around there."

She pulled away fast. "*Eight?* How did I sleep that late?"

"What? It's not exactly two in the afternoon. Are you telling me you never sleep in?"

"Yes. Till seven." She stood up, ran her hands through her hair, which was falling around her face in a wild profusion of curls, because she hadn't blow-dried it last night. "I need to get dressed so we can go to the hospital."

"Your grandma isn't even going to get her breakfast till nine," he said, shifting gears with an obvious effort. "I checked. And you need to give her a chance to make friends with all the nurses. So yeah, go ahead and get dressed so I can take you out to breakfast, because I'm not about to eat in that cafeteria again. I have some things to talk to you about anyway. Some plans I have."

♡

Forty-five minutes later, they were sitting in a café—but not the Chico Diner. She hadn't felt up to seeing everyone who knew her, knew her grandmother. Let alone explaining the hospital, or explaining Alec.

"And besides," she'd told him, "their coffee isn't that good. True confessions." Which had made him laugh.

He'd brought her here for breakfast instead, and she was feeling a lot more like herself now that she had a little makeup on, had her rowdy hair subdued again. Even though she was wearing snug, faded jeans and a close-fitting long-sleeved shirt with a scooped neckline, all soft oranges and browns, the kind of casual, slightly sexy clothes she'd never imagined Alec seeing her in. But there'd been no help for it, because she didn't keep that much up here. And after all, he'd seen her in her bathrobe, and a lot less now too. Well, he'd *felt* her, anyway. In the dark. He'd sure done that.

He hadn't seemed to mind her fashion choices, had looked her up and down and given her a slow, satisfied smile. Although he *had* expressed a little disappointment about her hair.

"Sorry I don't get to see this anymore," he'd said when she'd joined him in the kitchen again. He'd touched a hand to the nape of her neck, twisted a curl around his finger. "I liked it."

"All wild like that?" she'd asked in surprise.

"I like you wild."

Which had made her go liquid inside again. And that was why they were going to get this straight, right here in this coffee shop, because she needed to keep her expectations from getting away from her, and she couldn't stand the thought of him explaining to her, a day, or three, or seven from now, that it was over. Kindly, because he was always kind. Letting her down easy.

"Right," she said. They'd placed their orders, and had cups of coffee in front of them once again. "I'm going to try to say this better. There's no undoing what we did. Anyway, I liked it. I want to do it again, the…whole thing this time, and then that'll be it. Back to normal, which is for the best. And anyway," she hurried on at the look on his face as he sat staring at her, his cup halfway to his lips, "that's how you do things, and that's fine. Better for me too."

He set his cup down without taking a sip. "How do I do things, exactly? Enlighten me."

"You're casual." She looked right back at him. "It's just for fun, and it's short. Which suits me fine, because we can't have an office affair."

"You're right," he said. "We're not having an affair. That's not what I want."

"What?" She was completely confused now. "I thought you said…You seemed like you wanted…"

And that was when the waitress bustled up with their food. Eggs and toast for her, potatoes and bacon added for him. Alec thanked her abstractedly, but didn't start eating. Instead, he waited until she'd turned away, then looked at Desiree again, dark brows drawn down in a straight line over those blue eyes.

"When did I say I wanted an affair?" he challenged. "Let alone a...what? A fling? A hookup?"

"What, you're telling me you want a relationship?" She sighed. "Come on. I know you don't. And it'd be risky on so many levels anyway. If people found out, if it ended badly and we were still working together...it's such a bad idea."

"It's not a bad idea. You said that last night, remember? And remember what I told you? It's a good idea. It's a *great* idea. But I don't want a 'relationship.' I hate that word. I want a..." He seemed to be searching for the word. "A romance. That's what I want. A romance. I want to hold your hand, and bring you flowers, and walk barefoot on the beach with you, and take you away for the weekend. I want to thrill you. I want to sweep you off your feet."

You just did. She had to remind herself to breathe. And that he was a master at this. He did it all the time, and boy, did practice make perfect.

But it was all right, because she wasn't naïve, or a fool either. She was a rational, logical, disciplined woman who never let her dreams get away from her. He wanted to make it last a while? Well, she could figure out how to handle that, how to make it work out. And she deserved it. Surely she'd earned a little indulgence for once.

She felt like a dieter who'd spent years trying not to look at the tempting treats in the bakery window, turning away from the box of donuts on the break room table. And now, here was Alec. Not just a tasty snack, the entire buffet table. The richest, darkest, most decadent chocolate cake, slathered in a thick layer of chocolate buttercream, a little rosette of frosting piped on top, begging you to lick it off your fork.

For once, she was going to go ahead and have dessert, and she was going to savor every bite of it. But she wasn't going to mistake it for dinner.

But she didn't say any of that, because she wasn't a fool.

"All right," she told him, and if her smile was a little foolish all the same, well, she couldn't help that. "Yes, please."

His own smile grew as he looked back at her. "All right," he repeated. "Good."

"But we have to be careful," she warned. "Not to show anything at the office. Not to cause any talk. Any speculation at all."

"Well, no more than there already is, anyway," he said. "I should tell you that Brandon and Joe already have a fair idea of how I feel about you."

That made her sit up straighter. "That's not good. You know how iffy things are still with Joe. And Brandon...what? You guys talk about me?"

"No of course not, not the way you mean. I don't do that, and I don't allow it either, remember?"

"That's right," she said, relaxing a little. "Sorry, got carried away for a moment there."

"I know it's tricky," he reassured her. "But they know I haven't got anywhere, and I won't be enlightening them. As long as you can contain your desire for my body, restrain yourself from actually ripping my clothes off during those budget meetings, we're good."

"Well," she said, and her breath was coming a little faster now, "it could be hard, but I'll try."

"Maybe we'd better get it out of your system, then." He'd stopped smiling. "Work it out of you before we go back in there, so you can control yourself."

"Maybe we should." She could almost taste that buttercream, and oh, did she want it.

He cleared his throat, shifted a little on his side of the table. "But right now, we need to eat, so we can go see your grandmother. And think about what the doctor said, about getting someone to stay with her once she comes home."

"Oh." The 180-degree turn had her head spinning. How had she forgotten, even for a few minutes? All the heat and humor were gone, and the worry was back. "Do you think your dad might know of somebody, or how I could find somebody? Somebody who can cook, and who can help her with her rehab, and who isn't going to drive her crazy either." She pressed a hand to her temple, felt the throb of the pulse that had started hammering away there, right on cue. "I can start calling agencies tomorrow, I guess. Nothing's going to be open today."

"Desiree. Wait." He was holding up a hand, smiling at her. "Hang on. And *eat,* would you? I already had a thought, and did some checking. I think I've got the answer."

"You?" She couldn't have been more surprised. But she did take a bite of toast.

"Me. Don't look so shocked. It pains me. I *am* a CEO, you know, much as you enjoy bossing me around and pretending you're in charge. I do have some ideas once in a while. I haven't got here just by being good-looking and charming."

"All right." He'd teased the worry away, and she was smiling at him again, and eating too. "Let's hear your answer."

"You remember Lupe, from the show? The older lady on my homestead?"

"Sure. Of course." She was confused. "She knows somebody?"

"She *is* somebody. A home health worker," he explained. "And one hell of a fine cook. She didn't have too much to work with out there, but she made beans and cornbread taste about as good as they could. And I had a chance to taste some of her Mexican cooking too, afterwards, and let me tell you…" He sighed and took another bite of scrambled egg. "I'd be pretty happy to be eating her *huevos rancheros* right now. She'll get your grandma on her new diet, and happy to be there. Jolly her into going for her walks. Everything she needs."

"But she's…where?" Desiree was only slightly less confused. "And how do you know that she'd be available, or that it would work out?"

"Well, on the first one, because I already called her and asked," he replied promptly. "She's at a bit of a loose end right now, between jobs, and her daughter Maria-Elena off to college. Lupe 'lives in' sometimes, so that's not new either. I told her all about it, and she's up for it. I'll bring her out from Minneapolis, if you want her, that is, and you'll be all set."

"Oh no, you won't," Desiree said immediately. "If that's the answer, I'll fly her out. Why on earth would that be your responsibility? But you think she'd be better than someone I'd find here?"

He'd frowned at her insistence, but he didn't pursue it, just went on. "I already checked with my dad too, and he didn't know of anybody good who's available right now, short notice like this. And I *know* Lupe. You have to understand, it's different out there. She was sharing a 250-square-foot log cabin with three other women, and two of them were no joy, I'll tell you that. And even the other one was a whole lot more hard-headed than your grandmother could ever hope to be. If she could get along with the personalities out there…well, your sweet grandma's going to be a piece of cake."

"That Scott, you mean. He seemed like kind of a jerk."

"Yeah. You could say that. Being out there pushes you right to the limit. The physical part, and being away from everybody and everything you know, and the game. You see what people are all about. And what *she's* all about—it's all good."

"You're sure?"

"Do a phone interview, anyway," he urged.

"My grandma doesn't like spicy food." Could it be this easy?

"So you tell Lupe so, on the phone. See if you like her answer," he coaxed. "Give it a try."

♡

She'd agreed, in the end, and he'd felt a surge of relief that was way out of proportion to the event. That he'd been able to take some of the weight off her shoulders, chase that worried frown away. Although he'd still rather bring Lupe out himself. Especially since it was going to be expensive if they did it today, and he had a feeling it was going to be today, tomorrow at the latest.

But for now, they were on their way to the hospital, with two out of two issues working out exactly the way he'd hoped. After a quick stop at a convenience store on the way, that is. Because restraint was one thing, but he was only human, and if he were touching Desiree again tonight without being able to be inside her…he didn't think he could stand it.

"By the way," he said, swinging into the hospital lot. "I may have given the nurse the impression that we were engaged this morning."

"*What?*"

"Information to family members only. So I'm afraid you're my fiancée for the moment." Which, to his surprise, hadn't bothered him one little bit to say, to the nurse or right this minute. "I might even have to hold your hand in there. For verisimilitude."

"Verisimilitude."

"It means 'credibility.' Wasn't that in the PSAT study guide?"

"I know what it means." She still sounded upset. "I thought the whole point was that we were being discreet."

"In the office. Not a whole lot of overlap between here and there, though, is there? I'd say we're safe, pretending. Or telling the truth. Whichever."

He pulled into a space, and, of course, by the time he made it around the car, she'd already hopped out, pulled the hood of her jacket up to shelter from the persistent rain. He opened the umbrella he'd taken from beside the front door of the mobile home this morning, held it over her head as they made their way towards the entrance, avoiding the puddles as best they could. And she still hadn't said anything.

"You saying you don't want your grandma, or my family, or anybody at all to know we're dating?" he pressed at last.

"We're not dating. We haven't been on a single date."

"Hey," he said firmly. "Last night was a definite date. A pretty good one, too. And I have a feeling that our next date is going to be even better."

♡

"Whoops," he leaned down to whisper in her ear when they stepped off the elevator into the polished hallway of the Cardiac Care unit. "Our cover's blown already."

Because there was his dad, who wouldn't have had to be a rocket scientist to figure out where Alec had spent the night.

"Desiree." Dave took her hand in his own huge paw, gave it a squeeze. "I've just left your grandma, and she's feeling much better. Just had her breakfast."

"Thanks," she said, and Alec could see her relief at the news.

"How are you doing?" his dad asked her. "Did you get some sleep?"

And now Alec could see the red creeping up. "Yes," she said, keeping her composure as always. "Thank you for all your help, and for coming over this morning again. I know you're busy."

"That's my job. And in this case, my pleasure," he assured her. "But I do have a meeting over at the church, so I'll say good-bye and let you get in there to say good morning."

He let her go with a last squeeze of her hand, and she took off down the hall. And Alec watched her go, those soft, worn jeans all but painted onto the long legs.

"Good idea of yours, getting that help set up," Dave told his son.

"Yeah, thanks," Alec said with the pleasure it always gave him to know he'd made his dad proud. "Hope it works out."

"Bring Desiree over for lunch, dinner, whatever, when you all get a break here," Dave instructed. "But get in there now and look after her."

"Which one?" Alec wondered when his dad had walked past him, on his way out.

Dave heard him, though, turned back. "Oh, I'd say both of them now, wouldn't you?"

And then he offered his oldest child a smile, stepped into the waiting elevator and punched the button, and Alec was watching the doors slide shut.

One thing you could say about the Reverend David Kincaid, he knew how to leave his audience with something to think about.

♡

Dixie *was* feeling better this morning, Desiree found. Well enough to argue.

"I'll quit smoking," she agreed with the doctor who had come by on her morning rounds. That was one down, anyway. "If it's a choice between watching my granddaughter walk down the aisle someday and cigarettes now, I guess I've made my choice."

Desiree focused on her grandmother, tried to ignore Alec sitting beside her, the word "fiancée" still echoing in her head.

"That's good, Grandma. Good choice. What else?" she asked the doctor.

"Giving up the cigarettes is a start," the woman said. "But you're going to have to make some additional lifestyle changes, Mrs. Foster. Medications are one thing, and don't get me wrong, they're miracle drugs. But you have to do your part too. A new diet plan, an exercise schedule. I'm not telling you to run a marathon," she said, raising a hand at Dixie's look of surprise. "Easy walks, short at first, building up. You'll need someone with you for that, and all the rest of the time too at first, like I told your granddaughter yesterday. We want you moving, but not overdoing. And not driving either, not for a while."

"I've always taken care of myself," Dixie objected. "I'm feeling fine, or I will be soon enough. I wouldn't know what to do with somebody waiting on me."

"Not negotiable," the doctor said. "You don't have somebody there, it's a nursing home. You choose."

Dixie sighed. "Desiree's been hammering away at me already. And Pastor Dave said the same thing, and I guess he knows. I guess I'm beat."

Desiree had to smile. Dixie could argue with her doctor, but if Pastor Dave said it, that was different.

"We've got it set up," Desiree told the doctor. "No nursing home needed." She'd called Lupe Garcia from Alec's car after breakfast, anxious to get something set up right away, but determined not to make the wrong choice merely out of convenience. The other woman's warm manner, though, combined with Alec's assurance, had carried the day.

"Lupe's coming out this afternoon," she told Dixie once the doctor had left the room again. "I'll take you home in the morning, stay with you for another day or two until you're comfortable with her, and then she can take over."

"Oh no, you won't. If she's coming today," Dixie went on over Desiree's objection, "and I'm stuck here till tomorrow, why in heaven's name would you have to be here too? You'd think the nurses would have something better to do, the way they're in here all the time checking this and that, asking me my birthday like they're scared I'll have gone senile in the last hour. And what about Alec? He needs to get back to work. I'm not *his* grandma, just some tiresome old lady with a contrary heart. He's spent enough of his time on me."

"Hey," Alec objected. "Maybe I'm enjoying myself. Nothing I like better than hanging around with beautiful women."

Dixie snorted and flapped a hand at him. "Go on. You're too charming for your own good."

"He *is* going back," Desiree persisted. "Later tonight, that's the plan. And I'll take the train home in a day or two. It's all set."

"No, it's not, and no, you won't." Dixie was firm. "Both of you are going home today. I've got Marti and Iris coming by later to visit, and Pastor Dave stopping by again, and heaven knows who all else. I'm going to have to start charging admission. You've got me all set up, and you need to get back to those important jobs of yours. Bring this Lupe to meet me when she comes, and then scat."

"Grandma..." Desiree said helplessly. Looked at Alec, who raised his eyebrows at her.

"Stubborn independence seems to run in the family," he remarked.

"That's right," Dixie said. "I may have a weak heart, but the rest of me's still independent as the dickens. I mean it. Scat."

detour to truckee

♡

" Whew."

Alec could hear the weariness in the sigh as Rae leaned back in the passenger seat that evening. It had been a long day. Her grandmother had shooed them out of the hospital room eventually, telling them that "an old lady needs her privacy," which had made him laugh.

Rae had wanted to clean the house, go grocery shopping, but he'd put his foot down. "That's what Lupe's going to be here for," he'd reminded her. So she'd settled for clearing space out of her drawers and closet, washing the sheets on her bed for the other woman, which he'd had to concede was probably a good idea. They'd personalized those sheets fairly well the night before.

And Lupe herself had come in that evening full of calm competence, reassuring him that his memory hadn't been faulty. She'd given him a warm hug, a kiss on the cheek.

"Just as handsome as ever," she'd teased. She and Desiree had taken to each other right from the start, and if Alec had caught a speculative look on Lupe's face from time to time, at least she hadn't said anything. Hadn't warned Rae off him, as far as he could tell, which he had to confess he'd been a little worried about. The meeting with her grandmother had gone well too. Anyway, what he'd told Rae was no more than the truth. If

Lupe had been able to handle the personalities and the tensions of *America Alive,* dealing with one old lady, no matter how stubbornly independent, would be a piece of cake.

They'd seen Lupe settled in, said goodbye to Dixie, stopped by his parents' for dinner. All good, but it had taken time and energy, it was already eight and long since dark, and Rae was drooping.

"You OK?" he asked her now. "Go ahead and lean that seat back if you want, go to sleep."

"Maybe *I* need a nursing home," she tried to joke. "Or maybe you want to keep going, drive me all the way to Mexico."

He glanced across at her again. Made his decision, took the exit. "Well, Mexico might be out, but no reason you can't take a day off."

"What? Alec, no. I wasn't serious." She struggled upright. "Where are you going?"

"America's vacation wonderland. Truckee."

"Truckee? What? Why in the world?"

"Gabe. My brother," he explained. "And Mira. Nobody to bring you cocktails in the pool, but people to take care of you, and you can sleep in—past seven, even."

"I cannot take time off. Get right back on that freeway, Alec. I mean it."

"Nope. Another executive decision. I'm kidnapping you."

"You are not kidnapping me. That's ridiculous."

"Yup. I am. Bet you've worked every single day since you've started, haven't you? Every Saturday? Every Sunday?"

"That's what it takes. You know that, because I'll bet you've done the same. And if I need to get back, you *really* do."

"Hey, I got some work done. Wrote some pretty brilliant code, if I do say so myself, right in that waiting room. We'll leave before noon if you want, and you can put in a couple hours tomorrow afternoon if you absolutely have to. But we're going to Truckee first."

"We can't just barge in on them." She was weakening, he could tell.

"Another good try, but you still lose. Gabe's my twin. I'm allowed to barge. I'll call first, how's that."

"And that's going to be all right with Mira too?"

"Yup. It is."

♡

He'd worn her down, in the end. Had called, at her insistence, received the welcome he'd known would be there. And she'd finally relaxed. He'd put some music on, had been able to feel her calming as if he were touching her, had sensed the moment when she'd fallen asleep.

He'd driven the back roads, then the freeway again with her there beside him, the big car eating up the dark, cold miles of flat orchard land, and foothills, and, finally, mountains, and tried to imagine what it would feel like, almost losing somebody who mattered that much to him. His mom, his dad. His sister, his twin. And found that his mind wouldn't even go there, shied away every time it got close.

And he had four people. She had *one.*

"I've led a charmed life," he'd said to more than one interviewer, leaning back and flashing a smile that usually worked fairly well on both men and women. "I'm a lucky dog, and I know it."

He'd said it, secure in the knowledge that it wasn't true. That even though he might have had more than his fair share of brains, and, all right, looks too, he'd worked hard for everything he'd earned. That nobody had ever handed him anything.

But in fact, he'd been given so much. Because he'd gone to bed every single night, in whatever cheap place, whatever modest neighborhood his family was living that year, secure in the knowledge that his parents were handling things, that they were holding him safe. And Desiree, he was beginning to suspect, hadn't.

♡

It was after eleven by the time he nosed the big car into the driveway behind the red SUV. Rae pulled herself upright as he shut off the engine. "Where are we?"

"Here. Truckee. You slept the whole way." Nearly three hours. That should help.

She climbed out of the car while he pulled the bags from the trunk. Wrapped her arms around herself and shivered. "Brr."

"Shock to the system," he agreed. "Actual winter. Careful, it's a little slippery." He moved both bags to his left hand, grabbed her hand with his right, and negotiated the driveway, the snow banked to its side sensed but not seen in the cloudy dark. The windows ahead shone warm and welcoming, though, and a light by the front door cast a glow onto the wide wooden porch.

He used the doorbell, because it wasn't just Gabe anymore. Only a few seconds, and the door opened, spilling another pool of warm light into the cold and dark, and there was his brother.

Alec stepped inside behind Rae, shoved the door shut against the cold, and set the bags down. Put a hand out to the one already extending to him, performed their special handshake, and knew that he hadn't come here just for Rae.

He gave Mira her own hug and kiss next. "Hi, pretty girl." He stood back with both her hands in his. "Looking good. This boy still treating you right?"

"Mine," Gabe said as always, making Alec and Mira laugh, as always. "Get your own. Oh, wait. You finally did."

"Working on it," Alec corrected him, interpreting the lift of his brother's brows without too much difficulty. "You remember Desiree, Mira."

"Of course. I'm so glad Alec brought you to us," Mira told her. "It sounds like you've had such a rough time. I talked to Susie yesterday, and she told me what happened. How's your grandma doing?"

"Much better," Rae said. "She's going home from the hospital tomorrow."

"Pretty mild, then, as MIs go," Gabe guessed.

"Heart attacks, he means," Mira explained. "Speak English, not doctor, Gabe. But why are we standing around here? It's late, and Alec and Desiree must be exhausted. We don't have the guest bedroom and bath done yet, I'm afraid, but the trailer's still hooked up. And I'll just pull out a sleeping bag and extra pillow in case you need the couch, Alec. Come on, Desiree. Let's get you settled."

"That was tactful of her," Alec remarked after Mira had picked up Desiree's bag again, ushered her through the house and out the side door to the little travel trailer that sat in the yard, relic of Gabe and Mira's early days of home renovation. Alec had used it himself, the last few times he'd been here. It actually made a fairly good guest suite, complete with bathroom and kitchenette.

"Yeah," Gabe grinned, leading the way to the kitchen. "I would just have asked, 'One bed or two?'"

"Not sure myself," Alec admitted. "Been a hell of a weekend."

"Not quite your usual style," Gabe suggested.

"Nope. And I need to give her a little space right now. Use your bathroom a sec?"

"Sure."

When he came back, Gabe was sitting at the heavy pine table in the kitchen.

"Remodel looking good," Alec commented, running an exploratory hand over the brick wall behind the stove. "This turned out great."

"Yeah, Mira was right to want to keep it. Got a cabin feeling to it still, the whole thing, doesn't it?"

"And I know how you two like that." No stainless steel here. White appliances, cabinets made of light wood with porcelain pulls, a polished but scarred wide-plank wooden floor covered by rag rugs. It looked—and felt—intensely homey, the kind of place you could imagine your grandparents having lived for the past forty years. He could easily see Mira and Gabe here just that long.

He sat down across from his brother, felt the relief of it.

Gabe looked at him a moment, then shoved himself back from the table. "I'd say it's time for the good stuff," he decided. He pulled a tall bottle out of the cabinet above the stove, grabbed a couple of thick-bottomed glasses from another, poured a generous amount of amber liquid into each. He added a bit of water, sat down across from his twin and handed one across. "Medicinal. Cheers."

Alec took a sip from the heavy tumbler. "Single malt. Nice. Splashing out, bro."

"Christmas present from a grateful patient, appreciating that he gets to ski this year," Gabe explained. "Or maybe a down payment on the next time. He's pretty clumsy."

Alec laughed a little at that. "Job insurance."

"You know it." Gabe took his own sip, rolled it over his tongue appreciatively. "So. Desiree."

"Yeah." It was a sigh. "She just takes my heart and..." Alec set his glass down, put his fists together, and made the motion. "Twists it, just like that. Over and over. And I'd rather it was me. That I could take it for her, you know?"

"Uh-huh. I do. That's why they call it love."

"I didn't know it would feel like that, though. I thought it was supposed to feel *good*. But this weekend..." Now Alec's hand was on his chest. "It actually hurt me, here. Physically, I mean. Nobody said your heart would literally *hurt*."

Gabe stared at him in astonishment. "Uh…have you ever listened to a single song on the radio?"

Alec waved that away. "I just figured that was, you know, romantic stuff."

"For women, you mean." Gabe guessed correctly. "Well, I guess you found out."

"So is that how you feel?" Alec asked.

"Oh, yeah." Gabe looked up, alerted by something Alec hadn't noticed.

Sure enough, Mira appeared in the arched doorway a few seconds later, paused at the sight of the two of them. Alec saw the softening on his twin's face, the answering glow on Mira's.

"I've got Desiree settled out there," she told Alec. "She called the hospital, too, checked on her grandmother, so all's well, and I'll say good night. Don't rush, though, Gabe. Stay and talk to your brother." She gave them both her sweet smile, turned and left them alone.

"When she looks at me like that," Gabe said after a few silent moments spent contemplating the amber liquid in his glass. His eyes met Alec's. "When I know she feels that way about me, I think, how did I get that lucky? How do I keep on deserving her? That's what it's all about, bro. That's it."

He got up, tossed off the last of his drink. "So my advice? Go let Desiree know how you feel. And do whatever it takes to be the man she needs, because if you love her, it's worth it."

Alec rose too, set his glass in the dishwasher next to his brother's. "I'll do that. See you in the morning."

He'd always been the older brother, even though it was only by twenty minutes. Always. Alec watched his twin heading out of the kitchen as if he were following a beacon, and wondered. When had Gabe got so far out ahead of him?

the planner makes his move

♡

His fingers hovered for a moment above the keypad, his eyes shifting to the torn-off piece of notepad, its creases smoothed out carefully, lying on his kitchen table. He hadn't wanted to risk putting the number into his phone, much less a computer, even a personal one. Data could be traced.

This phone call could be traced, for that matter, even if he deleted it from his call history. If somebody checked, that is, and why should they? Anyway, the number he was calling, he'd been assured, was secure.

He'd been through all this already, the planner reminded himself. His tracks would be covered. More than covered.

No risk, no reward. He made his decision, punched in the number.

"Middle of the night," the voice on the other end said. "This had better be good news."

"It's good news." The planner kept his voice low, even though he was alone in the apartment. "I've got thirty-five percent of the alpha version ready to send you. You can have it tomorrow if you play this right. And you want to. The stuff I saw today… this is dynamite. Kincaid was out all weekend, and he'll be gone tomorrow too. That's my chance, and I'm taking it. Piece of cake, and getting the beta's going to be just that easy, because he isn't nearly as smart as he thinks he is, and I've got somebody set up on the inside to provide camouflage."

"A third of the alpha isn't going to pay the bills," the voice said. "Including yours. What good is that to me?"

"Down payment," the planner insisted. "I'm sticking my neck way out here. I need some incentive, or should I say a million incentives, or it's not going to happen. And don't you want to see what you'll be paying for?"

"I thought you had a way to cover your tracks." The voice was sharper now. "This can't lead back to us. And that inside help had better not know what's going on either. I told you, you share this with anybody, you've just cut your chances of getting away with it by a factor of ten."

"I've got it. Nobody else knows, and they won't, because that payoff's all mine." He'd lost control here somehow, was out of the driver's seat. *You have what he wants,* the planner reminded himself. *You're selling, not buying.* "Down payment. A million, or I hang up and you can do your R&D the hard way."

"Two hundred fifty K," the voice said. "After we see the alpha."

"A million," the planner insisted. "First. Once I get the wire confirmation, you'll get the code. Not before."

"Five hundred. And that's generous. We *can* do our own R&D, you know."

"Not like this, you can't." If he backed down now, he'd just slashed his final payment, the one that was going to set him up on an island someplace where the sun always shone and the girls had sweet smiles and long dark hair. The one that was finally going to get him what he deserved, what he'd been denied. What Alec had.

"This is big," he promised now. "This is going to change everything, you'll see. A million, or I hang up."

"Seven-fifty, and that's as high as I go," the voice said, and the planner felt the sag of relief.

"Seven-fifty," he agreed. "I've got the wire instructions right here."

"Offshore, I hope. No trail."

"You think I'm stupid?" The familiar rage flared hot.

"No, I think you've never done this before."

"And you have?"

The low chuckle came over the line. "Of course we have. You think you're the first? You think you're that special? You ever read the news?"

That was an unpleasant shock. "What are you doing?" the planner asked in alarm. "Sniffing around everyone with access to anything big? That's going to get you caught. And once they've got you...I could be twisting in the wind."

"Relax. Of course we aren't going to everyone. Only the ones with something we want to buy. And the ones we think will sell it."

He heard the contempt, and his anger rose again. "I told you why I'm selling it. It's not about the money."

"Right." The voice was dry. "Revenge."

"That's right. And living well is the best revenge." The fear and anger subsided, overridden by buoyant satisfaction at the prospect. It was going to be so sweet to watch it all go down. "Seven-fifty. I see the money, I send you the code. And when I deliver the beta, it's ten million, like we agreed." He was sorry, now, that he hadn't asked more.

"We'll talk about that when we get there." The voice was firm, and that was another shock. He wondered if he should press it now.

Wait until he sees the alpha, he reminded himself. *Then I can ask whatever I want. Raise it to twenty.*

"Give me the email address," he said now. "Once you check this out, you'll see what it's worth."

182

The chuckle at the other end had him bristling. "You really are an amateur. Thumb drive, bubble wrap, box. You ready for the address? And don't put it on your computer."

"I'm not an idiot," the planner retorted. "Go." He wrote, then recited the address back. A suite number. In reality, probably a mailbox in some anonymous storefront.

"Good," the voice said. "Send the box, shred the address. Good for one time only anyway. Don't input it *anywhere,* do you understand me?"

"Sure you don't want me to eat it?" The insult rankled.

"No. I want you to shred it, and this phone number too."

"How will I contact you, then? When I've got the beta?"

"Don't worry," the voice said. "We'll be in touch. We know where you live."

travel trailer

♡

Alec climbed the metal steps to the trailer's narrow door, pushed it open. He heard the sound of water running, saw her suitcase set on the bench that ran along one wall, and put his own bag down next to it. He considered turning on another light, dismissed the idea. The dim illumination provided by the single bedside lamp would do just fine, however this worked out.

He looked at the double bed that took up half the space in here, the flannel sheets folded back neatly over the top of the puffy down comforter encased in a cover woven to look like a Navajo blanket. Not too cold right now with a space heater chugging out the BTUs, but they'd be glad enough of the cozy bed later that night.

If he were sleeping in here, of course. He eyed the folded sleeping bag and pillow lying ready by the door, thought about sitting on the bed, and took a seat instead on the bench next to the little dining table. Leaned back, let all the remaining tension flow from his mind and body, and waited for Desiree to get out of the shower.

♡

Desiree turned the water off, shoved the curtain covering the tiny metal stall to one side, and reached for a fluffy white towel. It wasn't a long reach. Mira had told her that she and Gabe had lived here all autumn. That must have been cozy.

She toweled herself dry, used the lotion Mira had left on the triangular shower shelf along with shampoo and conditioner. Pretty good service at this hotel, considering that they'd been last-minute guests.

She took her time combing out her hair, wrapped the towel around her as best she could, wishing she hadn't left her old robe at her grandmother's. She twisted another towel around her head, opened the door of the cramped bathroom, saw Alec sitting in the shadows beyond the bed, and just about closed the door again. Paused for a long moment, then came out, hitching her towel around herself.

"Guess that answers that one," he said resignedly. "Looks like it's the sleeping bag, because we obviously need to work up to this again. Dinner, wine, candles, all that, see where we get. Where you want to go."

She stood at the foot of the bed and looked at him. Leaning against the wall, long legs stretched in front of him, arms crossed. All that power on a leash, held back tight because he thought she wasn't ready for it.

Well, he was wrong. She knew exactly where she wanted to go. And she knew that she wanted him to take her there.

She came the rest of the way around the bed, sat down on its edge, facing him. Took the turban off her head and threw the towel over by her suitcase. It didn't quite make it, fell to the floor, but she barely noticed. She reached both hands to her hair, ran her fingers up through it, lifted it behind her, and let it fall. Drew her arms down slowly, and saw him sit up straighter, pull his feet in, and push off his bench without even seeming to realize it.

"What kind of a kidnapping do you call this, then," she asked him, "if you're not even going to ravish me?"

♡

So he ravished her. Still slowly, still carefully, but oh, so thoroughly. He started by pulling her up to stand, taking her towel off and tossing it. She had no idea where it landed, because she wasn't looking.

"This is my favorite kind of ravishment," he murmured, pulling her head gently back with a fistful of hair, closing his mouth over the side of her neck and biting. "The kind where you start out naked."

He took his sweet time with her, kissing, touching, stroking, until her legs were trembling underneath her. Every time she thought about stepping back so she could unbutton his shirt, he kissed her again, moved his hand to someplace even better, and she got distracted.

At last, though, she had one hand running through the short hair at the back of his head, thick, dark, and soft as the pelt of an animal, feeling so good under her fingers, and had managed to get the other hand under his T-shirt, trailing over the smooth skin of his back.

"Alec," she sighed, lifting her mouth from his with difficulty, shivering at the feeling of his hand cupping her bottom while the other one took its leisurely time at her breast. His thumb was moving, he had her on her tiptoes, and she was melting inside. "I need to…take your clothes off. I need you naked too. Please. I don't need you to be so careful, or so gentle either, not tonight. I need you to hurry."

He kissed her one last time, then stepped back from her, leaving her rocking down off her toes. He stood back and looked at her, a slow smile growing. "Mmm. I don't think we're going to hurry. Because how much fun would that be?"

"Alec…"

"No," he said. "No hurrying. I think you're still kidnapped, and that I've got some more ravishing to do. I think you'd better pull the covers back and lie down on that bed, don't you? Right in the middle, because I'm going to need room if I'm going to ravish you the way you deserve."

She opened her mouth to say something, then closed it again. Who was she kidding? She needed more, and if this would get him naked faster, it was exactly what she was going to do. So she turned around and did it. Lay down in the middle of the bed, started to pull the sheet back over her.

"Oh, no," he said. "No covers. I want to look at you."

So she lay there, naked, a shiver of anticipation running through her, and waited for him.

He sat down on his bench again, pulled off his shoes and socks, then stood.

"I've got all this work to do still, though," he said, his hand on the top button of his shirt. "I'm going to need some inspiration."

"What?" she asked, her anticipation replaced by confusion.

"Why don't you put your hand on your breast," he suggested. "Show me what you do when you're alone. When you're thinking about me, the same way I think about you." He was undoing buttons now. "Because you do think about me when you're lying in bed, don't you?"

"Yes." She could feel the heat rising from her chest, up her throat, into her cheeks. "I think about you."

"Then show me." He finished unbuttoning. "Put your hand on your breast, Desiree. Please. Show me what you do."

She couldn't believe she was doing it, but she did it anyway. She started with her fingertips on her stomach, traced them up her rib cage, then, slowly, over the curve of her breast. Circling. Teasing.

She'd never been voluptuous, never the kind of woman men stared at on the street, but seeing the hunger in his eyes as he watched her hand move closer made her feel like that. Made her feel powerful, and so sexy. And watching him pull off the flannel shirt, revealing the arms she hadn't seen since that basketball game, was a pretty good incentive too.

He stared as her hand closed in. As it circled, then came back, drifted teasingly over the erect nipple. The sensation of it, the way it set up answering echoes straight to her center, the look in his eyes, they were all pushing her higher, and she shifted on the bed, felt her thighs parting as she kept on.

"Other hand, now," he said, standing in his white T-shirt and jeans, his feet bare, watching. "Put both of them up there and show me how you do it. Because you're so beautiful, and that looks so good, and I want to watch you."

"I need some inspiration too," she managed to say. "Take off the T-shirt first, then maybe I'll do it."

He smiled. Got both hands under the hem of the white tee, and pulled it up and over his head. Not making any kind of performance of it, but what a show it was anyway. The narrow waist, the flat brown belly she'd seen in a brief flash, now fully revealed to her with its hard horizontal ridges, the extra, delicious diagonal slash of muscle on either side, dropping into the waistband of his jeans, asking for her fingertips, her mouth to trace it the whole sweet way down.

Her gaze would have stayed there, but it had to move to his chest along with the shirt. There was no choice, really, because the slabs of pectorals, the bulge of shoulders needed to be looked at. And his arms. The sculpted shapes of biceps and triceps, the dark, silky hair revealed as he lifted his arms over his head. All of it. She wanted to touch it all, move her mouth over every bit of him.

"Both hands," he reminded her, and she did it for him, because he wanted it, and she did too. Her hands stroking, circling, the liquid fire pooling inside as she saw his gaze hot on her, the breath rising and falling in that broad chest.

"Tell me," he said as his hands went to the top button of his jeans. "Tell me what you think about when you're doing that at night, at home in bed."

"I think about you," she whispered. "About you."

"About me what?" He was unbuttoning, but he'd slowed down, somehow. "Come on, Desiree. Help me out here. Inspire me."

"About you...touching me. At work." She wouldn't have thought she could blush more, but she could tell that she was, and it didn't seem to matter, because saying the words was making it even better. "When I come into your office, I imagine... that you put me on the desk. When I wear a skirt..."

He'd finished his unbuttoning at last, was shoving the worn jeans over his hips. They were falling to the floor, and she was seeing the thighs she'd imagined so often. Just as strong and hard as she'd pictured them, dusted with black hair. And he was in his briefs, and they were...really something.

"Move that hand down now," he said, looking down at her with so much heat in his eyes, making her feel like the most desirable woman in the world. "Touch yourself. Show me how you come. Show me now, Desiree. And tell me the rest."

Her hand moved, barely aware that he'd told her to do it, just knowing that she had to. Because he was pulling off the briefs now, and that was better than she'd imagined too.

"I think about you," she said again, her voice soft and husky as she watched him watching her. "I think about you putting me on your desk. Unbuttoning my blouse, and... touching me."

"Mmm. That's what I do. Yeah, I can imagine that. That's good." He was reaching into his overnight bag for the paper bag with the box in it, ripping the end off, and pulling out a packet. "Keep going. What am I doing now?"

"You're…unfastening my bra, and holding me. Kissing me there." Her own hands were doing pretty well themselves, but it was watching him that was doing it.

"I'll do that," he promised, rolling the condom on, and she couldn't look away. "We'll lock the door, and I'll do it all to you. Tell me what happens next."

"You…" She was having trouble talking now. "You push me back on the desk. So I'm on my back. And you shove my skirt up. And you…"

"Tell me. Tell me right now, and I'll come over there and do it to you."

"You…stand between my thighs. And you…" She was climbing now, her entire body straining with effort, and she was gasping. "Alec. Please. Come do it."

"Not until you tell me. Not until I watch you come. Come on, Desiree. Come on, baby. Say the word. Tell me what I do to you."

"You…" she got out. "Oh, Alec. You…fuck me. Please."

And then she was there, and her hand was still moving, and he was moving towards her too. Coming over her, sliding inside, hot and hard and so deliciously much of him, while the contractions were still gripping her, and gripping him. And it was as if he started it all over again. She held onto him, felt him filling her, so much better than she'd ever imagined.

He pulled one of her legs around his waist, was reaching around to touch her, and it got even better. Still moving slowly, his other hand twisted through her hair, his face urgent and beautiful above her, a dark archangel, falling fast.

"Do you want to know what I think about?" he murmured in her ear.

"Oh," she moaned. "Yes."

"When you come into my office," he said, still moving, his hand still on her, his fingers going unerringly to the perfect spot,

"I make you lock the door. I have you come over to my desk, tell you to get on your knees. I'm hearing the guys out there, all talking and working, not knowing what's going on. That in my office, you're on your knees, unzipping me. You're taking me in your mouth, and I'm holding your head, and you're taking me so deep. All the way inside. I'm looking down at you, watching you do it. And it feels so good."

"You need to teach me," she got out through her rising excitement. "How to do it the way you want it."

"So much I want to do," he said. "I want to love you every way there is. Desiree. I want you so much."

And then he wasn't talking anymore, because they were both past that now. She had both hands around his back, stroking over all that muscle, that smooth dark skin. Down his sides, his arms. Holding him, and loving him. Feeling him move in her, the heat and the fullness of it. He was saying her name again, and she couldn't say his, because she couldn't talk anymore, because it was all too much. Until she was calling out, broken and urgent, and hearing his answering groan as he emptied into her.

♡

"Damn." He was lying on his back beside her, breathing hard. Had pulled the covers over them, finally, because their bodies were cooling down now, the heat dissipating. "I always knew that would feel good. But it felt..." He laughed a little. *"Really* good."

She was laughing a bit herself. "Mmm. What would you call that, though? Self-service ravishment?"

"Hey." He felt the slow grin growing. "I serviced you pretty good."

"Eventually." She leaned over him, kissed his chest, ran her hand over it, and that felt good too. "I've never been kidnapped before, though, so I'll admit that I don't know the rules."

"That's right." He smoothed a hand over her damp curls, twined one around his finger, exactly as he'd always imagined doing it. "Luckily, I'm an experienced kidnapper."

He considered staying where he was, changed his mind with reluctance, flipped the comforter back and swung his legs around.

She reached for him. "Don't go," she protested. "Stay with me."

He leaned over and kissed her, slow and soft. "Just going to take a shower," he promised. "Then I'll come back and sleep with you, so we can keep the monsters away."

"No monsters tonight," she said. "I'm good."

"I wasn't talking about *your* monsters." Which made her laugh, exactly as he'd hoped.

Then he stood up, but she had a hand around his thigh, was pulling him back to sit again. "Alec. Wait."

He began to turn, stopped at the touch of her mouth at the very base of his spine. Then her tongue, licking over the sensitive skin there, making him shiver.

She ran a slow hand down his back, stopped at the bottom, her fingertips delicate against his skin, and touched her lips to him again.

"Now you can go take your shower," she told him. "Now that I've kissed your birthmark."

you only need one

♡

"Morning."

It looked like Gabe and Mira were finishing up breakfast. Alec sighed a little as he shut the side door behind him. One of these days, he was going to have to learn how to cook. Oh, well. That's what restaurants were for.

"Mind if I borrow a couple things? T-shirt, underwear, socks?" he asked his brother. "And a laundry bag?"

"Sure." Gabe pushed back from the table, handed his brother a plastic bag taken from a wire basket nailed to the cabinet door under the sink, and led the way into his bedroom. He opened a few drawers and pulled out neatly folded items, handed them to Alec in a stack.

"It just gets worse and worse," Alec complained. "Not only do you have a special holder for your grocery bags, you fold your underwear."

"I do." Gabe clearly wasn't the least bit disconcerted. "Prepare to be shocked, because I fold Mira's too. I match up her socks and fold the tops over. I am Laundry Man, and I am proud."

Alec snorted. "Good thing you found each other."

"So." Gabe sat on the bed and watched his brother strip down. "No sleeping bag."

"What was that thing you said to me once?" Alec wondered, buttoning the fly of his jeans again, pulling the clean T-shirt over his head and yanking it down. "Oh, yeah. None of your business, and you know it."

Gabe laughed. "So you got that figured out? The working-together thing?"

"It'll work out." Alec sat beside him and pulled on the clean socks. "I'll make it happen."

"You always do," Gabe agreed. "The Midas touch. Not always as easy with those tricky human emotions, though."

"No worries." He was on top of the world this morning. It would work, because he would make it work. "I'm good."

♡

When they got back to the kitchen, there was a cup of coffee waiting for him in a white stoneware mug.

"Thanks," he told Mira, taking a grateful sip. Strong, black, and scalding, exactly the way he liked it. "I was telling Gabe last night, the remodel turned out great. Very homey."

"It's nice, isn't it?" she said, looking around with satisfaction.

"It looks like there should be, I don't know, things hanging from the beams in the ceiling," he said. "Like in the cabin. A side of bacon, maybe some of those plants." He gestured. "You know, bunches of them, hanging upside down."

"Herbs," she said with a smile. "I think we'll pass on the bacon, but Gabe's going to make me raised beds in the spring so we can do some gardening, so who knows? You might see your herbs drying in here someday. He says he'll build me a fence, too. I thought, sunflowers, sweet peas up against it. Won't that be pretty?"

"Let me guess," Alec said. "A white picket fence."

"That's what I want," she said happily. "And then a dog."

He had to roll his eyes at that, he couldn't help it. All they needed was the two-point-five kids, and they'd be all set.

"Want to come up for the weekend, late April maybe, soon as the ground warms up enough, and give me a hand with that?" Gabe asked. "Put some of those new skills to use, keep you from getting soft now that you're pounding a keyboard all day instead of swinging an axe. You aren't as good at it as I am, of course." He leaned back against the wall with a satisfied sigh. "But I can supervise."

Alec snorted. "I'm at least as good at it as you are. We'll have a fence-off. Bet you twenty bucks I'm faster."

"It also has to not fall down," Gabe pointed out helpfully. "But I'll take that bet. Mira can judge."

Another snort. "Oh, yeah. Because she's impartial."

She was laughing, her eyes dancing. "You realize what just happened, don't you?" she asked Alec.

"What? My brother just questioned my manhood?"

"Your brother just conned you into building half of my white picket fence. And you're supposed to be the smooth one."

He didn't answer that, because the door had opened again, and there was Desiree, in the same soft, snug shirt and jeans she'd worn yesterday, her hair falling in the ringlets he loved. And he was grinning like a fool.

"This is getting to be a bad habit," she said ruefully. "Second day I've slept in. Good morning, everybody."

"Two days isn't a habit," Alec said. "Sit. How's your grandma doing?"

"Good," she said as she sat. "Going home today like they thought, so that's good."

He got up and fixed her coffee, sat down again next to her. Saw Gabe taking it all in, exchanging a glance with Mira. Well, obvious to his twin wasn't the same as obvious to the world.

Mira finished her own coffee and stood. "I'd love to hang around with you guys, but I need to get ready for work. Don't want to be late."

"Yeah," Alec agreed. "You've got a pretty harsh boss, I hear. I imagine the consequences are dire."

"You don't want to know," she agreed solemnly.

"How's that working out?" Alec asked his brother when Mira had left the room. "Mira runs Gabe's office," he explained to Rae. "Since they moved up here."

"Since she figured out that we should move up here," Gabe corrected. "And the answer is, terrific. Marketing, administration, dealing with insurance companies, the works. We've got a couple other people in there, but she's the one making it all happen. Runs the whole practice for my partner and me. Marry an efficient woman, that's my advice, and my brilliant life plan too."

"Too bad we never thought of putting that in our personal ads," Alec agreed. "Could have got everything working out for us a whole lot sooner."

Rae laughed at that. "You guys never used a personal ad in your lives."

"I know what mine would have said, though," Alec told her.

"What?"

He smiled. "Tell you later."

Gabe pushed himself away from the table. "I've got to get ready too. Glad Alec brought you by, Desiree. Stay as long as you like, and come back anytime."

♡

"Let's go for breakfast, a walk by the river," Alec urged, turning away from the front door with Rae fifteen minutes later after saying a quick goodbye to Gabe and Mira. "Unless you want to cook, or to chance it with me. But I'm warning you, I'm not too good."

"Remember? Me neither. I'm sure I should be whipping you up Eggs Benedict or something, convincing you that I'm your Dream Woman, but I'm afraid it'd be more like your worst nightmare."

He laughed. "No mastery of the culinary arts required, as long as you aren't judging me on that score either. So," he made a motion towards the door, "eat? Walk?"

"It's like you're talking to your dog," she protested. "They both sound good, but we should really get back."

"It isn't even eight yet. Consider yourself still kidnapped, because I'm not nearly ready to let you go."

He had to grab her, then, didn't he? He had a point to make, after all.

"That shouldn't sound so..." she sighed when he came up for air.

"So what?" He gave her another long kiss, pulled her in just a bit closer with a hand under that gorgeous ass. Got a little distracted, sent his hand down the center seam of her jeans, and then kept it there, because that was where it belonged.

"So...sexy." It was another sigh, and she was moving under his hand, and he decided that what he *really* needed to do was take her back to check out those flannel sheets again.

So he did. Which made it quite a bit later by the time they actually got their breakfast.

♡

"It's really OK with Gabe for you just to take his truck like this?" she asked when he'd climbed in next to her after they'd restored themselves at the Chuck Wagon Café. Pancakes. He loved pancakes, and he wasn't about to figure out how to make them. Even if he'd geared himself up to do eggs, pancakes would have been out. So there he was. Restaurants.

"Of course it is." He turned the fan up, shivered at the blast, wished it didn't take so long for this monster to warm up. No new snow, but it was *cold*. Good thing there'd been plenty of warm clothes to borrow for this walk, because he really didn't want to take Rae back to the City yet.

"What if he needs it, though?"

"Then he'll call me, won't he? Or take my car."

"They didn't need it to get to work, obviously. Is it that close? Or do they have another car?"

He laughed at that, turned onto the main road toward the river. "The office is exactly two blocks from the house. They both went native on that show. They walk to work together, walk to the grocery store together, walk to the gym together and work out. They belong to the damn Rotary Club together, go to meetings and demonstrate Civic Responsibility. It's actually a little nauseating." At least it had always seemed that way before.

He made the left turn onto the river road. Perfectly clear, and the parking lot for the path probably would be too. He hadn't needed to take the truck at all.

The thought had barely crossed his mind before he was taking another corner, in amongst the pines now, and feeling the wheels sliding right out from under him.

Black ice, he registered as he steered into the skid, fought to keep the car under control, pressed down with a desperate foot and felt the antilock brakes engaging. A brief screech, one final fishtail, and they were clear.

"Huhh." He let out the breath he'd been holding in a relieved sigh. "That was a little too close. Thank God nobody was coming in the opposite direction."

"Stop the car."

The words came out strangled. He looked over in surprise, saw her face, white and rigid, her knuckles gleaming against the black handle of the armrest.

"Stop," she croaked again. "Please."

They had arrived at the entrance to the park, he realized with relief. He slowed even more, took a cautious left into the lot. Pulled into the first space he saw.

She was pulling at the door handle, frantic, before they'd even come to a complete stop. He popped the lock for her, saying, "Desiree, wait." But she didn't stop to listen.

By the time he made it out of the car, around to her side, she was leaning over the hood, her arms wrapped around herself. Not crying this time, but shaking violently. Silently, which scared him even more.

"Baby, no. It's all right. It's OK. We're fine." This was the second time, he thought desperately, and once again, he had no earthly clue what to do, so he did the only thing he could think of. Pulled her into his arms, turned her around, leaned against the car himself, and held her. Stroked his hand over her hair and murmured nonsense to her while she shook, and the tears came at last.

"Sorry," she finally got out, sagging against him. "I know..." She gave a little laugh. "Big overreaction. Is there a..." She swiped at her face. "A tissue box in the car, maybe?"

He let go of her with reluctance, did some searching. "More paper towels," he apologized, handing them to her.

"We have a pattern going." She still sounded much too shaky, but more like herself again.

"There's a bench down there by the river," he offered. "Want to go sit with me for a few minutes?" He reached into the car again, handed her a knit hat, pulled on his own. "As long as we don't freeze our...ears off."

"Yes," she said. "Sitting would be good."

♡

"I'm sorry," he said when they'd got there. The wood was cold beneath them, and he wished he'd thought to bring a blanket or something from the car, but he didn't want to go back and get it, leave her alone.

He turned a bit on the bench so he could look at her. "Maybe I was going too fast. I wasn't thinking about the possibility of black ice. With everything that's happened to you this weekend, I guess that was the last straw, huh?"

"It's not that," she said, her gaze fixed on the icy water flowing over tumbled boulders, the snow-covered banks. "Or maybe it was that, who knows. I'm sure it didn't help. You were driving fine. Not your fault. But I was in a car accident when I was little. The swerving and the screeching...they pulled me right back there. I'm the one who should apologize. You didn't bargain for all my childhood traumas this weekend."

He ignored that. "The back seat," he guessed.

"Yeah," she sighed. "The back seat. It was..." She swallowed. "When my mom died."

"Was she driving?"

She shook her head, her eyes still on the river. "No. My dad. They'd been having an argument, I think. At least, he was mad. But then," she said with a bitter little laugh, "he was usually mad."

♡

"I'm just saying, maybe you could ask him for another chance." Her mom's voice sounded small and scared, and Desiree twisted her hands together between her legs, pressed her elbows into her sides.

"I just *told* you." It was the Bad Voice, the really loud one, and she shrank a little further into the door. "He's been out to get me from Day *One*. He wrote me up for every little thing he could. And the second he found something he could use, some stupid rule that everybody breaks anyway, *bam.*"

Her father's fist hit the steering wheel with a *thunk*. The car went sideways, and her dad said a bad word, and there was a screechy sound.

"Chris. Slow down. Please." That was her mom. Desiree could see the side of her head, but she couldn't see what she looked like, because it was all dark. She wished her mom would look back at her. They'd been supposed to go see Santa Claus at the mall tonight. And then her mom was going to take her to get ice cream, even though it was cold outside, but that was OK, because it was a Special Occasion, and it was a Girl's Night Out.

They were supposed to go right from day care, but then they had to go a different way, because her dad had called to get picked up, and they had gone to his work instead, even though he usually didn't come home until she was in bed. And now he was driving, and he was mad. And Desiree wanted to ask about Santa Claus, but she didn't.

"Did he say you could file for unemployment?" That was her mom again, and her voice was quiet, and scared.

"Do you think I sat around and talked to him about unemployment? Should I have said, 'Oh, excuse me. Could you pretty please toss me a bone so my wife won't be on my fucking back when I get home tonight?'"

"Shh," her mother hissed. "Desiree."

"Do you think you could be just a little bit supportive?" Her dad's voice sounded mean. "Maybe take my side for once? One time? Is that too much to ask?"

"I just said..." Her mom's voice was wrong, wiggly, and Desiree knew that meant that she was going to cry, and she pressed her fingernails into her palms and bit her lip to keep from crying herself.

"I just wondered, are you going to be able to get unemployment," her mom said. "Because if you can't, we'll have to move again. We can't pay the rent on my tips. Not past January. Even if you watch Desiree until you get another job, so we don't have to pay for day care."

"Excuse me for not thinking it through, while I was sitting there getting fucking *fired*. But I'll tell you what. Since you have to have all the details, I'll show you the letter. And then you decide for yourself if there's likely to be unemployment."

Her dad's hand came out of the front, groping toward Desiree's leg. She shrank against the seat again, pulled her legs to the side. She could see his head now, because he was leaning over. His hand was grabbing all around, and then it took hold of a piece of paper that was lying on the floor.

And then the car was going the wrong way. They were going sideways, and there was the screechy sound again, and somebody was screaming. Her mom. Her mom was scream- ing. And then there was a really big bang, and Desiree felt the seatbelt yanking tight around her, and she hit her head hard against the window.

And it hurt, and she wanted her mom. But her mom didn't come.

And after a long time, some people were shining lights inside the car, and they talked and talked, and then they took her out and put her on a bed thing and put the bed in a place like a room, but it wasn't a room, because it was a truck. And her mom still didn't come.

♡

She didn't tell Alec all that, of course. Nobody wanted to hear all that. She just laid it out for him in a few bald sentences.

"Holy…Wow," he said blankly. "Sorry. I didn't know."

"Of course you didn't. How would you?" She was embar- rassed now. Oh, yeah. This was definitely the way to get a guy. Cry all over him, again and again. Yeah, she was sure men found that really attractive. No wonder she'd been single so long.

She stood up abruptly. "My butt's cold, and I'll bet yours is too. Let's walk, OK? Unless you want to get back."

"No, I want to walk." He looked a little disconcerted, and no wonder. But he set off with her down the packed snow of the path, took her gloved hand in his own.

"Not exactly what you had in mind," she suggested. "For your romance. Not quite walking barefoot on the beach."

"Exactly what I had in mind," he said firmly. "Being with you, that was the main part of the whole deal."

"Having me weep all over you," she persisted.

"Also fine by me."

She gave it up, walked beside him in silence for a few minutes.

"What was your mom like?" he asked at last.

It wasn't the question she'd expected, and she struggled a little with the answer. "I don't remember too much, mostly just images. Moments, feelings. She had curly red hair like me, and I remember that I thought it couldn't be so bad to have red hair, even though the other kids said so, because she did, and she was pretty."

"And she used to sing to me," she added after another minute. She couldn't seem to stop herself from telling him. The residue of terror and tears, she supposed. And she'd laid herself so bare to him this weekend, there didn't seem like much point in holding back now. "She had this rocking chair, and when I was sad, she'd put me on her lap, and wrap her arms around me, and rock, and sing me this silly song. After she died, I used to get in there by myself and rock, and sing the song, really softly, you know, so my dad wouldn't hear. But it didn't feel the same."

"No," he said, his voice coming out gruff. "I can see that it wouldn't."

"And I remember," she said with a laugh, "I used to think she was so fancy, because she had a black skirt and a white blouse, and a little black bow tie on a piece of black elastic. She called it "my tuxedo," and I don't know how old I was before I figured out that it was her uniform. She was a waitress, you see, like my grandma and me. My dad and I would go there sometimes to get her after her shift, and she'd bring me hot chocolate with whipped cream on top, and a maraschino cherry. Just like on my grandma's Jell-O salad." She laughed again. "That's probably why I still eat it, why I've never had the heart to tell her that I hate it."

"No," he said, "it's because you love your grandma."

"Yeah." She blinked a few stubborn tears back again. "That too."

"But," he said after a few more silent minutes, "you didn't go live with your grandmother after that? You stayed with your dad? Well, I guess that made sense."

"It didn't, not really," she admitted, "once I was old enough to think about it. It wasn't like he ever seemed all that crazy about me. He liked pretty girls, and I sure wasn't that. Not a very attractive child at all, really. But it would have been a hardship for my grandparents to have me. They didn't have any money either, though they had a place of their own."

"The mobile home."

"Yeah. So I wondered. I always thought," and the tears were there again no matter how hard she tried, choking her up, "that they just didn't want me quite enough. I went to Chico every summer for a couple weeks, though, during their vacation. I realize now that they saved it all up for when I'd come. Don't you think that shows that you really love somebody? If you save all your vacation for them?"

"I never thought about it," he admitted. "I guess it does, though."

"That's why I try to give my grandma nice vacations now," she explained, "because she never had them, just took care of me. Too bad she only wants to go on the bus to Reno." She laughed a little again, thinking about that. "But I do try."

"But you wondered," he prompted.

"Oh." She sighed. "Yeah. Turns out it was pretty simple. Money. My mom's Social Security. If my grandparents had been my guardians, if I'd even lived with them, been registered for school there, they'd have got the money. And my dad wasn't the best at holding down a job."

"But you did end up with them."

"With my grandma, yes. Because my dad had a girlfriend— well, another girlfriend, but one who made fairly good money, and she wanted to move to Arizona, had an offer of a good job down there."

"And you didn't want to go?"

"It wasn't just that." She swallowed against the remembered shame of it. "She didn't want me to come. But that was fine," she hurried on, "because you're right, I didn't want to go, and I finally ended up with my grandmother in Chico, where I wanted to be anyway, and where the school was better, and there were more AP classes, which made it so I could finish college in three years, which was pretty important, I'll tell you that. My grandpa had died by that time, and it was rough for my grandma, so the Social Security helped with that too, as long as it lasted, until I was eighteen. And once I finished business school, you know, I could help her out, and it's all been good from there," she finished in a rush. "The occasional Jell-O salad, you know, the occasional heart attack, but otherwise, happy endings."

She laughed a little, trembled with tension, or the release of it, she couldn't tell which. "There you go. My life story. Talk about over-sharing. Cue the violins, huh?"

♡

He didn't answer her right away. He couldn't. He'd thought she'd twisted his heart before. Now it was as if she'd ripped it right out of his chest.

"I don't even know what to say to all that," he said helplessly after a minute. "I'm at a total loss here."

"Hey," she said, giving his hand a little tug, "it's not *that* sad. I mean, look, here I am. Healthy, wealthy—well, reasonably, and getting better all the time—and hopefully wise. Lots of kids have a harder time than that."

"Oh, yeah? Not the way I see it."

"All you need is one person." She lifted her other hand, the one he wasn't gripping tight, and put up her index finger in its gray glove. *"One.* One person who thinks you're special, who you know you can count on to love you no matter what. I had two, my grandma and my grandpa. Lots of kids have *zero.* You know how many kids are in foster care in California? How many kids ought to be? You know how happy any one of them would be to turn eighteen and still have a place to live like I did? Somebody to believe in them at all?"

He was stunned at her passion. "That's the reason for the scholarship, then," he guessed.

"It's a little thing," she said, "but it's something I can do."

"So maybe that's where my foundation should be focused, you think?" he asked. "Something like that?"

She shrugged. "It should be wherever something's happening that you can't stand, I suppose. And that could be something entirely different. There are lots of sad stories in the world, lots of good causes. I'm not telling you which one matters most."

"And don't you think we'd better turn around?" she asked a bit plaintively. "Because I can't even feel my toes anymore."

discretion

♡

"Well, good morning, Merry Sunshine." Brandon looked pointedly at his Rolex when Alec walked into the break room in mid-afternoon. "We had a good weekend, did we?"

"You know where I was." Alec grabbed a Red Bull from the fridge and shifted his laptop case on his shoulder. "Rae's grandmother. We just got back."

"How's Dixie doing?" That was Joe, veering off on his way across the floor at sight of Alec and coming in to join them.

"Good as she could be." Alec popped the top on his drink and took a long swallow. It had been a fairly eventful day, one way and another, and he had a lot of catching up to do before he left tonight. "She went home from the hospital around noon today, and Rae's got somebody in to take care of her while she rehabs."

"Tough," Joe said. "On Rae, I mean."

"Yeah. It was."

"Uh-huh." Brandon took another swig of his own coffee. "Good of you to take her up there and hold her hand. You trying to tell us you're not hitting that?"

"Watch it," Alec warned, trying to keep his temper from flaring. *Deny, deny, deny.* "Rae's been with her sick grandmother, and I've been writing code in a waiting room. So watch it."

He wanted to drop it, so he dropped it. "You get what I sent yesterday?" he asked Joe.

Joe nodded. "Looks good. I got Michael going on it this morning."

And then Rae walked into the room, and Alec hoped she hadn't heard what Brandon had said.

He'd waited at her house for her to get changed, looked around her pretty living room in surprise, then driven down the hill with her, parked at his place. Had thought about changing himself, decided not to bother, and was still in his jeans and flannel shirt.

Not her, though. Her hair was up in that twist again, the sexy, snug top and jeans replaced by her brown and cream outfit. All covered up, and still looking so good to him. He did his best not to let his gaze linger, tried to remember what he'd been talking about.

"Hi, guys," she said, passing Alec without a blink and pulling the milk out of the fridge, pouring it into her mug and popping it into the microwave. "Any disasters during my unexpected vacation?"

"No," Joe said. "Alec says your grandma's doing better. Glad to hear it."

"Thanks."

"Nice to have Alec's company, too," Brandon said. "In that waiting room and all."

"Yes," she said, punching the button on the coffee machine. "It was."

Brandon stared at Alec accusingly as soon as she'd left the room again. "You lie like a dog."

"You stay with your folks?" Joe asked, ignoring Brandon's comment.

Alec forced himself to relax. "Yeah. Saw Alyssa for a little while too. She was up for the weekend, getting over a breakup."

"She OK?"

"Oh, yeah. Liss is a survivor, you know that. She was seeing a surgeon, someone she met on a sales call. He told her he'd just gotten through a rough divorce, hurting, scared to risk his heart. You know, the usual B.S."

"And he wasn't," Joe guessed.

"Nope. She ran into him on the Santa Monica Pier. With his wife." Alec sketched a half-circle out from his stomach. "About eight months' worth of not-divorced."

"Ouch," Brandon laughed. "That's gotta be awkward. What are the odds?"

Alec kept his focus on Joe. "He showed up at her place a couple hours later to 'explain,' can you believe it? Clearly didn't bother to get to know her very well during their brief romance, because you know Liss has a fairly good left hook."

That brought a satisfied smile to Joe's face. "He ran into a door, huh?"

"Yup." Alec tossed off the last of the Red Bull. "Gabe and I taught her well. Wonder how he explained that one at home. She was icing that hand all day Saturday." He tossed the can into the recycling. "Back to work. Come tell me what I've missed, Joe, when you get a chance."

"I'll come right now," Joe said, and they left the room together, leaving Brandon with his coffee. And all his speculation, Alec hoped, unanswered.

flowers and chocolate

♡

Desiree heard the voices outside, recognized Alec's. Here to pick her up, right on time, for their first big date. He'd taken her for a quick dinner after work on Wednesday, and then to his apartment for the night, which had all been, well, great. But, he'd told her, not good enough.

"I meant what I said," he'd told her very early Thursday morning when he was dropping her back at her house. "I want a romance. Tomorrow night, it's the real deal."

So here they were. Really, truly dating. And it was apparent that however well they might succeed in being discreet in the office, here at home, their cover had already been blown.

She unwound herself from her spot on the couch and stepped out through the French doors to find Alec, as she'd surmised, having a cozy chat with Javier across the hedge in the last dim glow of twilight.

"Hi," Alec said with a smile that cut right through the faint illumination provided by her porch light as he took in her clingy chestnut-brown knit dress, the shoulder bared by its asymmetrical neckline, her delicate heels. Her hot-date clothes, purchased just for tonight, because it had been so long since she'd had a hot date. "We were just talking about you."

"I'll bet." She eyed his stylishly cut black jacket and slacks, his usual trim white shirt. His own hot-date clothes, which she was sure he'd had more than a few occasions to use, but that was all right, because he looked so good in them. And just as a bonus, he had a satisfyingly large tissue-wrapped cone in his hand. "Did you bring me something?"

"I did." He held it out to her. "I almost gave them to Javier after all the nice things he said about the show, but I decided to save them for you."

"Mmm. Good of you." She wrapped her hands around the tissue paper, held the bouquet to her face and filled her nose with the sweet scent. "They smell wonderful. What are they? I can't see that well."

"Peonies," he said, and she could see the warmth in his eyes just fine. "Beautiful, just like you."

She looked across at Javier, saw his eyes go wide, the mouthed "Wow," and smiled happily back at him.

"Well, thank you," she told Alec. "For both. The flowers, and the compliment."

"That was good," Javier told him. "You're wasted on that show. Your brother got all the best lines."

"Yeah, but Alec took his shirt off more," Desiree pointed out loyally.

"Hmm. Good point," Javier conceded. "Tell you what, I'll watch till the end, then I'll let you know who was hotter."

Alec laughed. "I'll tell Gabe the challenge is on."

"So," Javier said. "What I *really* want to know is, did they get creative with the editing, or did you actually hate Scott as much as they're making it look?"

"No. I actually hated him more. At the point where you are now in the show, I was pretty much consumed by fantasies of getting some excuse to take him out."

"So did you?" Javier probed.

Alec smiled. "You'll have to watch and find out, won't you?"

Javier sighed. "Spoilsport."

"Hey," Alec pointed out, "I signed a contract. Even Desiree doesn't know."

"Oh, even Desiree, huh? All righty, then." She could see Javier storing that nugget up.

"And I've got to take this lady out to dinner," Alec said. "We have a reservation, and anyway, she gets cranky when she's hungry. Good to meet you." He reached across the hedge and shook Javier's hand. "Thanks for watching. Hope you keep tuning in. "

"Oh, I'll be watching," Javier said. "Don't you worry." He looked at Desiree. "Have a nice dinner, baby girl. And you were right, by the way. Absolutely habanero."

♡

"I'm not even going to ask," Alec said when she'd taken him inside. "Leaving that right there on the table."

She laughed. "Probably best. I'm going to have some interesting questions to answer pretty soon. Good thing for you that I don't kiss and tell."

She stretched to open the big cabinet above the fridge, was about to grab her stepstool from its recess, then realized she didn't have to. "Could you get down that big vase for me? Can you reach it?"

"Sure." He pulled it down with ease, handed it to her. "Benefits of a tall lover."

She had to smile at him, then. "Is that what you are? My lover?"

"I sure hope so."

She set bouquet and vase down on the counter, reached for him. "Then I think you'd better kiss me quick here, don't you?"

"No," he said, wrapping his arms around her lower back and pulling her close. "I think I'd better kiss you slow."

"Flowers," she said a few minutes later. "Water."

"Mmm." He pulled her curls aside, kissed the back of her neck, just under the hairline. "Got to get those flowers into the water."

She stepped back with reluctance, and a laugh, too. "Alec. I do. And I thought you said we had a reservation."

"Not for another half hour. I just wanted to get you alone."

She was unwrapping the flowers. "Oh. These are gorgeous. You shouldn't have." Eight huge, drooping heads in varied shades of pink, their lush clouds of petals wafting gentle fragrance, tendrils of green ivy twining between the blooms.

"I thought they'd match your house," he said. "Your secret feminine side, which, in case I haven't mentioned it, is one of my very favorite sides of you, though it has some fairly strong competition."

She let herself feel the pleasure of that as she ran the water, added the little packet of flower preservative, cut the stem ends carefully off, and arranged the blooms lovingly. Swept tissue, ribbon, and stem ends into the kitchen trash and wiped down the counter, then set the vase in the middle of her round oak dining table and stood back.

"Gorgeous," she said again. "Thank you." And she had to give him another quick kiss, just to show him how much she liked them.

"Well, I was kind of hoping that I'd get to see your bedroom tonight," he said. "So I decided I'd better pull out all the stops."

"Oh, are we going someplace romantic?" How much better could he make this?

"I hope you think so." He was smiling again. "And I chose someplace we could walk to, so I can hold your hand."

I want to bring you flowers. I want to hold your hand. I want to sweep you off your feet.

"But how about showing me that bedroom now?" he suggested. "Give me a little inspiration for the evening, make sure I work hard enough to charm you."

"Reservation," she reminded him.

"I said *see* it," he protested. "I didn't say *use* it. Yet."

♡

But when he saw it, he wasn't so sure. The crystal chandelier wall sconces were pretty, and so were the pale green walls, the glossy white trim, the soft, thick cream-colored rug with its pattern of roses around the border that stood beside the bed. It was all soft and warm and feminine, and made him want to stay. But the bed made him want even more.

"That's a fairly good bed," he told her.

"It's my dream bed. I bought it last year after I got my bonus. It reminds me of sleeping in the clouds." She laughed. "That's pretty fanciful, but it does."

"I can see that." The puffy white comforter and pillows, yes. "But you know, as a guy of the male persuasion, it kind of sends a different message."

"Oh, yeah? What message is that?"

He gestured at the drift of white net curtains at each corner of the four-poster. "Well, I can't speak for every guy out there, but to me...I look at those curtain things, one in every corner, conveniently right there at the bedposts, and I think..."

"Wait a minute," she said, and her mouth was hanging open a little. "You look at my pretty bed, and you immediately think *bondage?*"

"Well, yeah," he admitted. "I do. I'm a guy."

That forced another laugh from her. "It's like a whole different world. But check this out." She flipped off the light switch—sitting inside a curvy porcelain switchplate, of course, painted with more roses and edged in gilt, of course—leaving them in the dark. But only for a moment, because she was doing something at her bedside table now, and the white net was suddenly illuminated with dozens of tiny lights casting a glow through the fabric.

"You have a light-up bed," he said slowly.

"I do. Isn't it pretty?"

"It is. And I've got exactly what I wanted. Inspiration. Let's go out to dinner."

♡

He took her walking up the rest of the Filbert Steps, all the way to the top of Telegraph Hill, down the other side along the curving path. Another five minutes past stately buildings from the beginning of the last century, angular structures from more recent times, until they reached the lighted window, the hanging sign outlined in gilt that announced the tiny French restaurant tucked into a block of retail shops, more apartments rising above them in this densely populated old neighborhood.

Soft lights and candles, white tablecloths and red roses, the corner table he'd specified, Vivaldi playing softly in the background. And watching Desiree eat. The way her eyes closed when she tasted the first mouthful of perfectly fried sole, her sigh as she sipped from the glass of white wine the waiter had just refilled from the bottle set in its ice-filled gondola. It was all pure pleasure, and his own meal wasn't bad either.

"Now for the best part, at least the best part here," he told her when their plates had been whisked away, thick black decaffeinated coffee had been set in front of them in white porcelain cups. "Dessert."

"Oh," she sighed. "I don't think I can. Not if you don't want me to fall asleep on you. All that food, and the wine..."

"Just taste it," he coaxed. "Because here it comes."

"What? How..."

"I ordered it ahead of time," he explained. "Because it takes a while to prepare."

The waiter appeared bearing a dessert plate, in its center the white ribbed ramekin with its crusty brown dome, set it down

215

with a flourish. A dollop of vanilla bean crème fraiche in the center of the rich concoction, a sprig of mint garnishing the plate, just because it looked nice.

"Et voila," the waiter said, standing back. "Le soufflé au chocolat."

"Two spoons," Alec pointed out helpfully, holding up his own dessert spoon. "Help me out here, Desiree. You wouldn't want *me* to fall asleep."

"I don't think I can help myself," she admitted. "I've never had chocolate soufflé."

And, again, her eyes drifted shut as she held the first spoonful in her mouth, let the chocolate melt over her tongue, and he watched her loving it, and loved watching.

He walked her home, held her hand, kissed her in the light of a streetlamp at the very top of Telegraph Hill, the golden shaft of Coit Tower behind them, the lights of the City spread out beneath them, the suspension cables of the Bay Bridge rising and falling in a graceful arc, a silver necklace across the darkness of the Bay.

And then he took her home, put her on the white bed like a cloud, and made love to her, long and slow and sweet. Not using the curtains at all, because he didn't need to, although he did turn on those little lights, because he needed to see her.

There would be another time for the curtains. For tonight, he wanted to touch her, and taste her, and feel her touching and tasting him. He wanted her hands, her mouth against his skin. He wanted to hear her breathy sighs, and, later, her cries, to know how much she wanted him, and to know that he knew exactly how to touch her, how to kiss her, how to please her. He wanted to love her.

lift into your plank

♡

"That's it," he told her in the morning when they were drinking coffee and eating toast with jam in her comfortably upholstered dining chairs, the smell of peonies filling the air, the crystals in the chandelier overhead casting rainbows onto the wall next to them, the patio beyond the French doors all dappled sunlight and blooming lavender in terra-cotta pots. "I'm moving in."

"What?"

He laughed at her startled expression. "Nah, just kidding. But I like your house better than mine."

"Well, so do I," she admitted. "I'm sorry, I know it's the best address, and I'm sure it's all the latest thing, but…"

"It's cold," he agreed. "And not…comfortable. How did you get everything to look like this? Did it come this way, or did somebody do it?"

"Somebody did it. Me. With help from a contractor," she hastened to say. "It was all carpeted, and it had fussy wallpaper everywhere when I bought it five years ago. It took me three years to do all this, to get it exactly the way I wanted it. I moved a lot when I was a kid, and I wanted someplace that was…all mine."

"Security," he guessed.

"Yes," she said with surprise. "I guess, now that you say it… yes. Or maybe, you know…" She shrugged, a little embarrassed now. Why did she keep revealing herself to him like this? "Women, the nesting thing."

"Hey," he said. "I'm impressed, I'm not criticizing. All I did myself was write a check, and you saw how that turned out. I can't imagine how you had the time."

"I didn't do it all at once," she explained. "I went slowly, one room at a time when I knew what I wanted and I could afford it, and I found everything myself. My kitchen tiles, my light fixtures, my big bathtub, everything. I had magazine articles, and I looked at websites, and I went around and looked at open houses and stores and salvage places, and, well, everything, every chance I got. But the nice thing is, it's so small, it was doable. Javier and Philip designed the garden," she thought to add. "Because they're into that. That's why it blends so well with theirs."

"Turned out great," he said. "I guess if you get tired of making my life easier, you could go into business for yourself."

She laughed at that. "I could, if anybody else liked what I like. I think it's fairly obvious that my secret inner self is a 70-year-old grandma."

"No," he corrected her. "Your secret inner self is a pretty girl who likes pretty things. And I'm pretty crazy about your secret inner self."

"Well, thanks." Boy, did he know the right things to say. "But none of my selves can cook, so what do you want to do for breakfast?"

"Eat," he said promptly, making her laugh again. "What do you usually do?"

"I normally go over to the farmers' market in Ferry Plaza, Saturday mornings. Have a walk, get something to eat, pick up a few things for later."

"Let's do that, then, if you want company. I have to go into the office today, but what do you think about my coming back again tonight? Since, as we know, I don't like my apartment. Maybe we could even buy something and heat it up, and, I don't know, watch a movie? Or I could take you out again," he hastened to say.

"No, that sounds good. I have work to do too, but later—that sounds good."

♡

"So I'm wondering," he asked when they were walking back through the Saturday-morning quiet of the Financial District, comfortably stuffed with various delicious delicacies and laden with their purchases. Fruit, salad vegetables, artisanal bread and cheese, Greek and Vietnamese and Italian treats, each in its own little container, ready to be heated. "Why don't you cook, when you do everything else so well? I mean, I know why *I* don't. My mom did it for us growing up, and then I started working pretty hard as soon as I was out of school, and there were restaurants, so…" He shrugged. "Gabe learned how, but I never did. But I'd have thought you would've had to."

She hated this kind of question. It always made her feel like a freak. But then, he didn't cook either. And he hadn't judged her yet, so she put one more cautious toe into the water.

"I grew up eating frozen dinners," she tried to explain. "And school lunches. *Free* school lunches, and breakfasts too. Food never tasted all that…tasty. Sometimes I'd go to somebody's house, and they'd have this good food, you know? Mashed potatoes with little lumps in them that tasted like…potatoes. Gravy. In the morning, they'd have pancakes that fluffed up. I would wonder how they did that, how they got it all to taste that way, but I didn't have a clue. So I just figured, that was something some people knew how to do, but I didn't."

"Your grandma, though," he suggested.

"Umm…remember that Jell-O salad?"

"Oh. Yeah." He made a little face.

"Well, that's her best dish. That's her signature. So there you go. She's great, but cook? Not so much."

"And you never learned. Like me."

"Just like you, although I don't eat out all the time like you do. I eat a lot of salads, things like that. Energy bars," she said, and saw his smile. "And I can make eggs. But cooking needs special pans, and measuring cups, and ingredients. I don't have any ingredients. And I don't have time. I've hardly ever even used my oven. Maybe three times?"

"Really? You bought a blue oven, and you don't even use it?"

"Nope. There you go, my guilty secret. How often have you used yours?"

"I've heated things up," he admitted. "And that's about it."

"Well, you know," she said, "that's what they make the Ferry Plaza market for. So we can heat things up. You can be in charge of that."

♡

He was quiet for a few minutes as they reached the steps and began to climb. She'd been right, he hadn't seemed to judge, to her relief.

"So this is what you do?" he asked as they finished the first block's worth of stairs and started on the second. "For a workout, I mean? Walk the steps? Because I have to say..." he leaned back, shot a sly glance behind her. "It's working great for you, though I suspect you were naturally gifted to begin with."

How did he manage to make a too-tall, too-slender woman feel so sexy? That was *his* gift. Well, one of them.

"If you like it," she said, trying not to let her smile betray her foolish heart any more than necessary, "I guess you should tell my yoga teachers 'thanks,' because that's where it comes from. I mean, yes, I walk a lot too, but that's where the sculpting part comes from."

"Really? Yoga?"

"What, never heard of Yoga Butt?"

"Mmm, no. But I'm appreciating the hell out of it." Which made her feel even better.

"Three times a week or so. Drop-in, whenever I can make it. In fact, Saturday evening is one of the times I usually go, because it isn't as crowded. You know," she added with a little laugh, "just the lonely boys and girls going with Plan B."

"And you want to go tonight," he guessed.

"Well, yes, if you wouldn't mind. I'd be back by seven, so we could still do something after that, if that's not too late."

"No, I'm fairly sure I'll still want to do something."

"I mean, dinner."

"Yeah," he said. "Dinner too. But why don't I go with you? You can show me what it's all about. If they let men in, and if you don't have to wear special yoga clothes made of weird stretchy stuff. I don't look too good in tights."

"Men go. It's not ballet class." Really? He wanted to go to yoga with her? *That* was new. "And it's not fancy, it's Yoga to the People. You put your donation in a Kleenex box at the end. Shorts, and shirts are optional."

"Wow. I'm *definitely* going. Topless yoga girls? I am so there."

That time, she giggled. She *never* giggled, but she did it now. "No, sports bras. But I wear a tank top."

He sighed. "Well, that's sad, but I'm coming anyway."

"We should be discreet, though," she warned. "It's on Mission, lots of techies. And you don't exactly blend."

"Out of context," he pointed out.

"Still. You, the show…and, well, let's face it. You. Discreet. No kissing me."

"All right," he said reluctantly. "I'll just save it up."

"You do that." Boy, he made her smile. "And it's a ninety-minute class," she realized. "That might not be the best for your first time. We can do a different one if you'd rather, earlier in the afternoon. The others are only an hour."

"Hey, I'm in shape. I work out almost every day."

"I know you are. I've been watching you chop wood with your shirt off on TV, remember? It's a little different, though. Different muscles, and you're using them in different ways."

"Desiree. It's *yoga*. It's stretching. How hard can it be?"

♡

A half-hour into it, he would have laughed at those words, if he'd had enough energy left to do it with. An hour in, and he was holding on purely out of pride, hoping that he could finish the class, that he wasn't going to collapse in an ignominious heap on top of the puddle of sweat that had collected on his mat.

"Lower halfway," the instructor was saying now in a soothing voice that was rapidly getting on Alec's last nerve. "And hover in your plank. Move your right palm so it's centered under your body and turn onto the outer edge of your right foot, stacking your left foot on top of your right."

Alec figured it out, mainly because he could follow the girl next to him, shifted so he was supporting his weight on his right palm, the side of his right foot, slowly straightened his right arm. Put his left foot precariously on top of the right and wobbled more than a little, but he was doing it.

Except that it wasn't over. "Lift into your hip, and now, if you choose, raise your left hand to the sky," suggested the syrupy voice. "You might want to raise your left leg as well, find some variation in your pose."

Or you might just want to stay right here, Alec decided. All right, the twenty-two-year-old next to him, the one with the tattoos snaking over her shoulder, disappearing under the brief coverage of her sports bra, and emerging again to continue down her back, was doing it. Because she was clearly some kind of freak of nature.

But then they were on the other side, and Rae was doing it all, both arms in a graceful line, one long leg lifting into the air at a full forty-five-degree angle as if it were no problem at all. And he was sweating more than ever, and wondering who the hell thought this was a fun time.

♡

Desiree came slowly out of the depths of her shivasana, opened her eyes, wiggled her fingers and toes, then turned onto her side. A few class members were quietly rolling up their mats, preparing to leave, but she took her time, enjoying the moment. The 90-minute class was her favorite. She always emerged relaxed and rejuvenated.

The tinkling instrumental music stopped for a moment as a song ended, and she heard another sound amidst the rustles and shifting. A snore. She pushed up onto her knees and looked to her left.

Alec was on his back all right, and yes, he was relaxed. In fact, he was asleep.

Another snore, and she giggled. Put a gentle hand on his shoulder, gave him a little shake.

"Alec," she murmured, leaning close. "Sweetie. Wake up."

"Huh?" He raised his head with a start, looked at her above him. The startled look turned to a smile. "Uh…what?"

"You fell asleep," she told him.

"Oh. Guess it worked." He got up, moving pretty slowly, she couldn't help but notice, hung his rental mat on the ballet bar that ran along one wall. It dripped onto the hardwood floor, and she felt another giggle rising.

"OK," he sighed when they were outside again and walking to his car. "Consider my ass kicked."

She laughed out loud. "A little harder than you expected?"

"As always, Desiree," he told her, "you've outclassed me."

meeting in the conference room

♡

Desiree found her attention wandering, jerked it back to the speaker again. It was Alec who was doing it to her. Leaning back in his chair at the head of the table, one ankle crossed over the other knee, one hand lying casually across his thigh, the other hanging at his side. He seemed keyed up despite the relaxed posture, and when she looked more closely, she could see his fingers drumming a little on the dark fabric of his trousers.

She'd seen him in those pants before. In fact, she'd taken those pants off him before. Just a few nights ago, on the pale area rug that covered the floor of his equally pale living room.

She'd unbuckled the smooth black leather belt first, pushed its tongue slowly out of the nickel-plated loop, pulled it back to free the hole from its fastening prong, tugged with both hands to separate belt from buckle. And then had worked on his top button, pulled the zipper slowly down. She could almost feel the little metal tab she'd held delicately between her fingertips, the finely woven dark woolen fabric just barely abrasive where she'd grasped a handful to give her purchase.

But that was only part of the memory that had her staring at the strong, clever hand resting on his thigh. It was mostly the fact that she'd been naked at the time. And kneeling at his feet.

She realized with a start that his fingers had stopped drumming, and that his eyes were fixed on her face, his expression intent. And now he didn't look relaxed at all.

Probably wondering why she wasn't paying attention. She shoved away the awareness of the tingling in her breasts, between her legs, wriggled a little to settle herself into the plush leather chair, and turned her gaze resolutely to Mark, the sales manager for Advent PR, who was still droning away about his company's proposed campaign to an audience of Alec, Joe, and Brandon. And, this time around, Desiree too.

Alec thought she could contribute some insight to AI's marketing efforts, she reminded herself, and that was both a compliment and an opportunity to expand her work horizons in a way she'd never anticipated. He wasn't going to keep inviting her to these things if she couldn't even focus, let alone contribute.

"Everything you've talked about so far has been B to B," she said when Mark had finally made his latest point. "Going to the consumer is going to be the challenge, though, in terms of cost-effectiveness. Do you have a plan for that?"

"I'm glad you asked," he said, and she smiled a little inside. Mark had taken Question-Answering 101, it was clear. He shuffled papers a bit, clicked ahead a few slides, and began the next topic. On which she *focused.*

Until she felt the quick vibration of her phone under her hand and realized she'd been stroking it, rubbing her fingers along the raised plastic edges of its case. And how embarrassing was that?

She glanced down at the screen, and froze.

You're on this table tonight.

Her gaze flew to his face, and he stared impassively back at her for a second, then back at Mark again. He'd scooted his chair in a bit, and she couldn't see his hands anymore. Because they were under the table, texting her.

She could feel her heartbeat picking up, realized that her tongue had come out to moisten her lips.

Damn him. How was she supposed to pay attention now?

She couldn't help it. She sneaked another peek. Raised her eyebrows a little at him. Picked up her phone, scooted closer herself, and did her own stealthy thumb-typing.

You and what army?

She wasn't even pretending to listen anymore. She was just waiting for the buzz against her palm.

No army. Just me.

Ha, she texted back. *Think again.*

I am thinking. Haven't decided.

Startled, she shot another look at him. He was giving up that easily?

A smile barely touched one corner of his mouth, then he was looking at Mark again. It was an endless minute before she felt the buzz.

Which way you'll be facing.

And that was when she completely lost her focus.

♡

She told herself that she was hanging around because she had a lot to do. Went through her list, item by meticulous item, checking each one neatly off as she completed it. Heard the big space outside slowly emptying, and couldn't stop the drumming of her heart, or ignore the tingle that had long since become a steady thrum.

And still she didn't hear anything, or see Alec. For all she knew, he could have left already. He'd probably just been messing around today, passing the time. That *had* been a boring meeting.

She hadn't said that, not exactly. But when Mark had left and they'd all been sitting around the table afterwards, after Brandon had given his enthusiastic endorsement of his candidate and Alec had asked her what she'd thought, she'd been honest.

"It all looked professional enough," she said. "But if he's the best they've got, and he couldn't even hold my interest in this room, and I'm the client, what does that say about their ability to reach out and grab the prospect?"

"I agree," Alec said, his face betraying absolutely nothing. "Anything that's not grabbing you, Rae, isn't good enough. And he couldn't hold my interest either. I kept finding myself getting distracted."

Which was all true enough, and had probably meant no more than exactly what he'd said. Besides, they'd been nothing but careful in the office these past weeks, for the excellent reason that they needed to be. Their fantasies were just that, fantasies. And knowing he had the same ones she did…that was a nice thing to think about, on the nights he wasn't with her, and that was all it was. So she should just *stop*.

She was about to give it up and leave after all, the quiet convincing her that everyone had gone. She and Alec hadn't made any plans for tonight, she reminded herself sternly. She had no earthly reason to be disappointed just because he'd passed the time during a lackluster presentation by teasing her.

She jumped a little at the ringing of her desk phone, the sound harsh in the silence. Picked up the receiver before glancing at the illuminated display.

Conf Room

She cleared her throat. "Rae Harlin."

"Rae." His voice came out slightly tinny. She could picture him in there, leaning over to punch buttons on the speakerphone that stood in the center of the table. "Could you come in here a minute?"

"I'll be right there," she heard herself answer. Hung up the phone, logged off dutifully, shut the lid of her laptop. Stood up and went to her door, shut it behind her, and walked the thirty feet to the corner conference room.

She could see through the clear panel at the top of the frosted glass that made up the interior wall that the light was on in there, although the door was closed. Was aware of the rectangles of light showing in irregular patches from the facing buildings. Other late-stayers finishing projects, working hard.

She didn't knock. Just opened the door and stepped inside.

He was leaning against the credenza beneath the windows, arms folded across his chest, white dress shirt still trim and tucked in perfectly. His sleeves rolled a few careful times, his ankles crossed, the picture of casual ease.

But his face wasn't casual, and his eyes were burning into her.

"Shut the door," he said. "Lock it."

She turned, twisted the knob to its horizontal position, and faced him again.

"Just how wet," he asked her, "did you get?"

She swallowed. Decided that she was going to make him work for it.

"I don't know." She looked back at him, kept her gaze steady. "I haven't checked. Why don't you see if you're man enough to find out?"

He shoved off, uncrossed his arms. "What a good idea."

He came close, and she raised her chin a little despite her best intentions, prepared herself to be kissed. But he didn't do it. Instead, he grabbed her under her bottom and set her on the table. One hand dug into the twist of hair at the back of her head, and she could hear the *ping* as hairpins hit the polished surface of the table. With the other hand, he shoved her skirt up, then closed it around her thigh, just above the knee.

"I'm starting right here," he said. "Let's see if you tell me first, or I find out for myself."

Strong fingers gripped the back of her head, held it in place for him, and he was finally kissing her. Starting out gently enough, his mouth teasing out a response, urging her to yield.

She wasn't done, though. She kept her mouth closed, held her knees together as best she could. If he wanted to play seduce-the-employee, she was going to make the game good.

He wasn't having any of it. His tongue moved over her upper lip, then he was sucking her lower lip between both his own, pulling it inside, and her mouth was opening under his, and his tongue was in her mouth.

She got a little distracted by the slow, thorough kisses that left her mouth tingling and swollen as he went on and on, still holding her head exactly where he wanted it, but she did manage to notice that his hand was pushing her narrow skirt further up her bare thighs, moving behind her to pull her to the very edge of the table, then grasping her leg again. Above her knee at first, stroking slowly up as he continued to kiss her, his thumb on the sensitive skin of her inner thigh. She felt herself shifting her weight as he got closer, willing him to move faster, to hurry up and get there. If he noticed, he didn't show it, just took her mouth again and again until she could barely think, until all she could do was hang onto his shoulders and kiss him back.

He stepped back a pace at last. Pulled her to stand again, got both hands under her skirt, lifted it up to her waist, and put her back on the table.

"Spread your legs for me," he told her.

And this time, she didn't try to resist. She opened her thighs, welcomed him as he came to stand against her. Because she wanted to feel it, the press of him into her, only the fabric of her thong between the woolen fabric and her tender flesh.

And then he'd stopped kissing her, was pushing her onto her back, onto the hard surface, his hand still behind her head, keeping it from hitting the table. Her skirt was around her waist, and he had both hands around the waistband of the thong, was lifting her hips, pulling it down her legs, over the heels she still wore.

"Let's have a look," he said, and if there was dark satisfaction in his voice, well, he'd earned it. He had a hand on each thigh, was opening her wide, almost to the point of discomfort. And she'd never felt so open, so vulnerable.

"The answer is," he told her, "very, very wet. The answer is that you've been waiting for this all day. And I'm going to give it to you right now."

He was dropping down, out of her sight, leaving her staring up at the expanse of white acoustical tiles, the long, narrow light fixture. Until she felt the touch of his tongue, and nearly climbed right off the table. After that, she wasn't looking anymore, because she'd squeezed her eyes shut to concentrate on every delicious sensation. Slow, then faster. Stopping for a moment, then slow again. Harder, then softer. Never letting her rest. Never allowing her attention to wander even for a moment.

But there was more to come, because he had a finger inside her, then two, and was moving them in a rhythm that had her hips following along, and he was doing things to her with his mouth and tongue that had her past the point of moaning, where she could only express what she was feeling by crying out, louder and louder.

And if she'd been tender and tingling all afternoon, every bit of anticipation she'd experienced was paid off in one glorious rush of sensation, until she was bucking under his hand and mouth, her back arching against the hard wood. Keening, now, as wave after relentless wave slammed through her, hard and hot, and left her gasping.

She was still shaking when he rose into her line of sight again. His hands closed under her hips, pulling her up tight against him, and then the hot pressure was filling her, the climb starting again.

She reached out blindly with both hands, found the edge of the table behind her on either side, and held on as he moved inside her. Out so slowly, inch by careful inch, followed by a hard thrust that left her shaking. Over and over, and she was almost there, calling out again.

And then he pulled out altogether, and she was reaching for him, opening her eyes. And begging.

"Alec...No. Please. Come back."

His only answer was to reach under her lower back, pull her towards him. She stumbled in her heels when her feet hit the floor, but he still didn't speak. Not until he had turned her so she was facing the table, and was pushing her down again.

"Down on your stomach," he said. "Right now."

She turned her head to the side so her cheek came to rest on the wood, felt him pulling her back again, only her toes reaching the floor. He was lifting her, shoving her skirt up again, then pushing something underneath her so she lay on an incline, her bottom in the air, her feet dangling in the heels he still hadn't taken off. He guided himself inside with a hand on each of her hips, and it was slow again. But this time, his fingers came around between her legs, rubbing in time with his thrusts, sending her rocketing up higher with every stroke.

He took his hand away, and she cried out in dismay until he replaced it with the other one, keeping up the rhythm of his hips all the while.

She felt the tip of what must have been his thumb, hard and wet, inside...inside, his fingers closing over her bottom, holding on tight, and was shocked into stillness. But only for a moment, because his other hand was still moving over her from the front, and he was still thrusting into her, and it all felt too good, too strong.

"Alec..." she moaned. She had no purchase with her feet off the floor. She got her elbows under her, squirmed back against him, rested her head on her hands, and felt it all. "Oh...no... help."

He stopped. Everything, like a stop-motion video.

"Help?" His voice sounded hoarse behind her. "Stop?"

"Don't..." She got out. "Don't stop. Don't you dare."

She heard the soft sound of his laughter. And the movie started again. All of it. The hand, the thumb. And him. All of it, filling everything. Making her feel everything.

Her hands were slippery with sweat against the table, and she couldn't hold herself up anymore anyway. She reached out desperately for the edges again, gripped the smooth surface as best she could, put her cheek against the hard wood, and held on as he drove her higher.

"More," she gasped. "Alec. More."

So he gave her more, and then more still, and everything in her was tightening, winding up, higher and higher, until she was finally, blessedly, over the top. She heard herself crying out so loudly that she was very nearly screaming, the gasping groans as he joined her, and they were both there together, spinning down and down, out of control.

♡

Long seconds passed, the only sounds the moans she couldn't control, his harsh breathing. Then his hand was on her back, gentle, as he withdrew from her.

"How're you doing down there?"

"Uhh..." She couldn't answer. She realized that she was lying face-down on a conference table, her hands stretched limply at her sides, her legs dangling. That she was still wearing her blouse, that her skirt was around her waist, her underwear gone. What a sight she must be. She struggled back, impeded by something under her hips, felt his hands coming out to pull her upright, turn her around, pull her skirt down, set her in a chair.

He grabbed a handful of tissues from the box on the credenza, made a few adjustments. Picked his shirt up from the table where, she realized, it had been providing padding under her hips, and pulled it on. It wasn't looking nearly so neat anymore.

"Stay there," he commanded. "Give me a sec." He zipped himself up, reached down and handed her the underwear he'd tossed to the floor, then went to the door and unlocked it, pulled it shut behind him.

She sat in the chair, held the silky thong, and trembled. She should get up, she thought vaguely. Put her underwear on. Go to the ladies' room herself and clean up. But she honestly wasn't sure she could.

He was only gone a minute, then he was back with her, twisting the lock carefully shut again. He came over to her and pulled her up, then sat down again with her in his lap.

"Desiree." He smoothed a hand over her hair, which she could tell was falling down. "Baby. Talk to me."

She laughed a little, the sound husky and low. "I think...I'm still stunned. Did you really just do me on the conference table?"

She could hear the grateful relief in his answering laugh. She should probably look at him, she thought vaguely. But she'd shut her eyes, because lying against his chest felt so much like the only thing she could do right now.

"I think I just did exactly that," he said. He was kissing her cheek again, smoothing his hand down her back, along the silk of her blouse.

"Mmm. You did a really good job." She had her hand around his upper arm, over the swell of bicep, squeezing and stroking there. "I think I've been folded, spindled, and mutilated."

"Well, hopefully not mutilated. But folded and spindled... definitely." He kissed her again. "Come on. Let's get you cleaned up, go out to dinner. What do you say?"

Her legs were a little wobbly, still, when she stood up. But it had been worth it.

She saw the thick blue binder on the table, and stopped.

"What was that," she asked slowly, "underneath me?"

The flash of his white grin was her answer. He didn't even have to say it, but he did anyway.

"The employee manual."

past history

♡

"Just for the record, I don't think I want to have anal sex."
She got him just as he was sitting down, and he very nearly spilled the glasses of red wine he'd brought back from the bar. He caught himself, handed over her glass, and settled into the leather couch near the fireplace in Ziggurat's coziest corner, much quieter than usual at nearly nine o'clock on a Wednesday night. Quiet enough, discreet enough, he hoped, for a quick drink and dinner, because all he wanted to do was feed her fast, get her upstairs and into his bed, and hold her all night.

"OK," he said cautiously. "Want to elaborate?"

He could see even in the dim light that her color was rising, but she plowed ahead. "You're too big, and I think it would hurt."

"All right. Did you not like what I did after all, back there? Too much?"

Still embarrassed, still honest. "No. I mean, yes, I liked it. But I don't think I want to go any further with it."

"Well, for the record." He set his glass down so he could take her hand. The hell with discretion, because this mattered. "We aren't going to do anything you don't want. All you have to do is tell me."

He could feel the tension leaving the hand he held in his own, and sighed with relief that turned out to be short-lived.

"So you've done that before?" She studied her glass, took another sip.

"What? Which part?" He was starting to sweat now. Talk about your minefields.

"Anal sex," she said promptly. "Have you done it?"

"Uh...yeah. I could lie, I guess, but if you talked to somebody who knew better..." He gave her a rueful smile. "Unfortunately, some girls *do* kiss and tell. But I gather you haven't."

She laughed a little herself. "You pretty much exhausted the breadth of my experience by the second time. What else have you done?"

"What *else?*"

She dropped his hand, made an impatient gesture. "If I'm going to tell you what I don't want, I have to know what it is. What you're thinking you want to do."

"Uh...You should probably assume that I've done every-thing. Well," he hastened to qualify as her startled glance flew to his face, "I've never had sex with a man, and I've never hurt anybody. Or paid for it," he added as an afterthought. "But I'm a guy, Desiree. When it's been there to take, I've pretty much taken it. And if a woman's wanted something, I've pretty much given it to her. I've been around the block a time or two."

"Around the *block?*" she complained. "Sounds to me like you've cruised the entire neighborhood."

That forced a laugh from him. "Could be."

"And that's all right with you," she probed, searching his face. "To have me say that I don't want to do something."

"Absolutely all right with me." He could feel the ground getting a little firmer under his feet again. "Mandatory, in fact. Although if you tell me that you only want to do it in bed at night, under the covers, in the missionary position with the

237

lights out and your eyes closed, I might have to do some hard negotiating."

"And I take it," he added with a disappointed sigh when she was smiling again, "that this means I have to send the chickens back."

Which made her burst out laughing, and the relief filled him, and he grinned back at her and took another sip of his own wine, and thought, *Man, I love this.*

And that was when he heard the voice from behind him.

"Hi, Alec. How're you doing?"

He turned, already tensing. *Oh, no. Not quiet enough.*

"Hi, Debra. How are you?" He set his glass down, stood, and blessed his good memory. He could almost always remember their names. But the timing was…awkward.

The pretty Asian girl gave him a look at her perfectly straight little teeth, then smiled at Rae. "Hi, how are you? I'm Debra."

"Rae," she said. He didn't need to glance down to see that all her wariness was back, could feel her withdrawal as clearly as if he were still holding her hand.

"I haven't seen you in a while," Debra told Alec. "Have you been out of town?" *In other words,* he thought, *why didn't you call?*

"Just busy, I guess." *Please go away.*

"Well, I won't keep you," she said. "I'm meeting some people myself. But…" She reached into her purse, pulled out a business card, pressed it into his palm. "If you know of anybody who's looking for help with PR, give them my name, would you? I'm thinking about making a move."

"Nice to meet you, Rae," she said with another smile. And was off again with a toss of the shiny black hair, her hips moving in an easy glide under the short skirt.

Alec sank down again, reached for his glass. *When in doubt, drink.* Then changed his mind, set it down.

"So. Where were we?" he asked. "Just about to order some dinner, I think."

Rae ignored that for the pathetic attempt it was. "This would be the downside for me, then. Was that recent?"

"No." He sighed and looked at her again. "I told you. Months. Not since that first day I met with you." He flicked the card restlessly against the fingertips of the opposite hand. "And anyway, I just started wondering if what I've always thought of as my irresistible personality was actually some kind of networking."

A sharp laugh greeted that idea. "You mean that's never occurred to you?"

"Ouch. Some ego, huh?" He grinned, handed her the card. "But we *are* still light on the PR side, so if you're interested..."

She ripped it neatly down the middle and dropped the pieces onto the table in front of her. "No way, buddy. Not on your life."

two heads are better than one

♡

Somehow, after that, it worked out that he was spending every other night with her—and, all right, both nights on the weekend. Almost always at her place, just because his apartment *was* too big, and too cold, and too unfriendly, and her cottage was so much better on all counts. Not to mention that it had her in it, and if the choice was falling asleep alone, or falling asleep holding Desiree, well, that wasn't really a choice at all, was it?

But it was driving him a little crazy that he always had to invite her, or more accurately, invite himself. She never seemed to be counting on it, although she always said yes. When he brought a few things over so he wouldn't have to go home to change before work, she emptied a drawer for him in her tiny spare bedroom, and cleared space in its closet, and his toothbrush, his razor, his shampoo all found new homes in the feminine territory of her bathroom. But she didn't give him a key.

He could almost see her hovering, halfway out the door, ready to bolt. He'd had some kind of half-assed idea that he should try not being so available, maybe make her miss him a little, but then she took the weekend off to go see her grandmother, and even though he'd gone up to Truckee in desperation and helped Gabe build Mira a white picket fence, that had still been one hell of a boring weekend. And there he'd been on Monday night, right back with Rae again, and that had been the end of that one.

Meanwhile, he kept suggesting dinner, and he even went to a few more yoga classes. He figured she'd eventually realize that if it was Monday, Wednesday, or Friday, he was going to be around. So when he got that other call on a Wednesday afternoon a few weeks later, it didn't take him long at all to figure out how to respond.

At least he hadn't been thinking about her at the time. He wasn't that far gone. He was still able to work, and he swore when the distinctive chime of his phone broke his concentration. Damn. He'd been *this* close to getting that sequence.

He glanced at the screen, a moment of surprise followed by a faint but unmistakable sinking of the heart, a new emotion to associate with this particular name.

The phone chimed again, and he considered ignoring it. No, she deserved better than that from him. He picked up.

"Hey, Claudine. How's it going? Where are you?"

"In town. And I need to meet you for a drink tonight."

"Probably not the best idea," he said cautiously. "Things have changed a little in my life."

He heard the impatient sigh. "I got that last time, remember? No designs on your virtue, lover boy. But there's something you need to know."

"What? You got hot gossip?" His mind wandered back to that sequence again.

No answer for a couple of seconds. "Something you need to know," she repeated. "But not on the phone."

He sat up straight, the code forgotten. "Something about me, you mean. Personal, or business?" Rae? Were people talking despite their caution?

"Both, I think. Tell you tonight, in person."

"It's bad, then?"

"It could be."

"All right. Ziggurat at six-thirty?"

"No. Someplace quieter. More private."

"Look," he said cautiously. "You know I've enjoyed it, but…"

She sighed again. "I told you. Your beautiful body's ancient history to me. I'm trying to help."

"All right. But if it's something about the company, I'm bringing Des—Rae."

"Uh-huh. Because two heads are better than one. Right."

Claudine had always seen too much. And right now, she was seeing that he didn't want to meet her alone, without Rae, and have Rae learning about it and wondering why. And anyway, if it was something about the two of them, she needed to hear it too.

But probably not. Probably just another rumor started by a competitor, casting doubt on AI's progress. But even if that were it, Rae needed to be there to ask her own questions, because she'd think of something he wouldn't.

"Yes," he told Claudine now. "Because two heads are better than one, especially if one of them's hers. I'm bringing her."

♡

Alec saw Claudine coming in the front door of Dagustino's, touched Rae's hand to alert her. He'd chosen the North Beach restaurant where he'd taken Rae for that first late-night dinner. A back table again, same candlelight, same quiet intimacy, but a completely different mood. Rae tense beside him, not touching her wine. They hadn't been talking, just waiting. No point in speculation until they knew what they were dealing with.

He stood to meet Claudine, gave her a kiss on the cheek, watched her reach across the table to hug Rae. And she still looked good. She dressed much like Rae, in fact, though the clothes looked a little different on her curvier figure, and no question, the blonde hair that fell in carefully tousled waves half-way down her back was sexier. So why was there only one woman at this table that he wanted to take home tonight?

He forgot all about that, though, within seconds of the waiter delivering Claudine's martini and leaving the table again. As soon as he heard her news.

"What?" Alec stared at her, exchanged a startled glance with Rae. "Where does this come from?"

Claudine waved one manicured hand in a dismissive gesture. "Where do these things ever come from? It's not even a rumor. Just a whisper."

"That our code could be for sale." Alec felt the cold rage welling. "To whom?"

"Don't know that either. Sorry, all vague."

"But you believe it."

She hesitated. "It feels real. It feels bad. You know I have to go with my gut."

He nodded. Successful salespeople always did, and nobody was more successful than Claudine.

"The Chinese," Rae said. "Probably."

"That's usually who it is," he agreed. "But who'd have access, and how would they have got it? We've been careful, as careful as I've ever been."

Rae pulled out her phone, began taking notes. "I'll call Eric Lindquist over at DatAssure in the morning, get him to run some forensics. We'll think it through, start narrowing it down."

Claudine tossed off the rest of her martini and stood. "I'll leave you guys to it. Sorry to be the bearer of bad news. If I hear anything else, I'll let you know."

"Stay and have dinner," Rae urged. "Since you're here. We don't have to talk about this."

"But you want to. Anyway, I've got dinner plans of my own. Had to do a little reaching out, once I lost my San Francisco

Treat. And even if I didn't…getting a distinct fifth-wheel vibe here."

Alec looked at her sharply. "*That's* not out there, is it?"

She smiled. "Nope. Your secret is safe with me."

♡

"The Chinese," Rae said again when they were alone. "That's who's buying. They've got practically a whole industry built up around stealing code. And you know who they usually go for."

"Chinese nationals," Alec said. "Or Chinese Americans."

"And disgruntled employees, or former employees," Rae said. They looked at each other, said the name at the same time. "Simon."

♡

But when DatAssure came back with a name, it wasn't Simon's.

"I have to assume the guy's better at programming than he is at industrial espionage," Eric Lindquist said on Monday morning. "Or you'd have fired him the first week."

Rae studied the sheaf of papers Eric had handed across the desk, with Alec looking over her shoulder. "He used an *FTP site* to transfer the files? Isn't that…"

"Moronic?" Eric asked. "Yeah. On the other hand, it made for a pretty easy investigation. But then, you were watching for flash drives, right?"

"Could have put it in his underwear," Alec pointed out. "Stupid bastard."

Rae looked across at him, startled.

"Hey," he shrugged. "Obvious loophole. But what are we going to do, strip-search everybody?"

He was trying to play it cool, but inside, he was seething. Michael. Who'd been given this opportunity, this kind of access. And had paid them back with treachery.

"You'll want to talk to him, and, I assume, to fire him," Eric said. "Make sure there's nobody else in it with him. Be aware, though, it's going to be hard to prove, and hard to prosecute. But it doesn't look like you lost as much as you could have. I think we caught it early."

"I'll talk to him," Alec promised. "You don't have to worry about that."

"I have some recommendations as well," Eric said. "Ways to step up your security, on an ongoing basis. Just in case this isn't an isolated event. Because where there's a buyer, there's a problem."

He went on for ten minutes to outline scrutiny of the logs, extra layers of protection, and at the end of it, Alec nodded.

"Do it," he said. Signed the contract Eric pulled out, and left DatAssure's office with Rae.

"Time to bring everybody in," he said, reminding himself to slow to her pace for the walk back to the office. He wanted to walk fast, though. He wanted to hit something. He wanted to hit Michael, and to keep on hitting him.

"I agree," she said. "We need to tell Brandon and Joe, and the board too. It was one thing when all we had was a rumor, but with proof...we need to disclose."

He nodded unhappily. "Before we talk to Michael, even. Because Joe will want to be in on it, and the board will want to know what we're doing, and what we plan to do. Let's just hope," he said grimly, "that the son of a bitch talks."

♡

But when Michael was brought into the conference room, was sitting across the table from Alec, Joe, and Rae, he didn't admit anything. Just stared at them as if he were facing a firing squad, disbelief and horror written clearly on his young face.

"But I...I *didn't*," he stammered. "I wouldn't. You have to believe me. I want this job. I want to do this. Why would I risk my whole future?" He was babbling now. "It wouldn't be worth it. I wouldn't. I didn't."

"It's right here in the log." Alec pointed to the damning proof. "Your login, transferring the files. And you were here." He reached a hand out for the time record, and Rae handed it to him. "In the office. You did it, and we know it. Time to talk about it."

"There is one way out," Rae said when Michael continued his denials. She'd been designated as the Good Cop in this exercise. "If you tell us who you sold the code to, we can make this a lot easier on you. And if you tell us if anybody else was involved. Was this Simon's idea? Tell us," she coaxed, "and it'll be easier."

"But I can't." Michael was crying now, and Alec looked at him with disgust. Weak. A follower, not a leader. "I can't, because I don't know, because I didn't *do* anything! Why won't you believe me?"

"Tell us who you sold it to, you little punk," Joe growled. "Now." He looked meaner and bigger and madder than ever. The Bad Cop, and he did it well. Michael ought to be quaking in his boots, and from the looks of things, he was.

"Nobody." Michael was still crying, but he was defiant. "You can beat me up or whatever you want to do, but I can't tell you, because I don't *know.* Because I didn't *do* it. I swear I didn't. I swear on my...my mother's life.'

They kept at it for a while, but it was no use. The board hadn't wanted the police called any more than the three of them did. Having it hit the grapevine that their code had been compromised...People said that any publicity was good publicity, but they weren't talking about this kind. This kind spelled nothing but disaster.

In the end, Alec fired Michael to the tune of more tearful protests, watched Security walk him out, then went back to the conference room with the others for a postmortem.

"I don't know," Rae said, looking unusually unsettled. "He was pretty convincing. Do you think he's that good an actor?"

"No," Joe said. "I think Simon was in it with him, calling the shots, making it happen."

"He probably didn't realize everything Simon was doing," Alec agreed. "May not even have got a cut, who knows. A pawn, for sure, but he was part of it all the same. And of course he's upset. He's very, very upset that he got caught. That isn't hard to fake at all. We'll probably never know the whole story, but we have to assume the worst. This is too important to take chances."

That was the bottom line. They talked to the board about the additional measures they were taking, and Rae talked to the security desk about being even more thorough with their checks. That was all they could do, except to be grateful for Claudine's warning, and to hope that they'd seen the end of it. To hope, but not to know. And not knowing was no good at all.

just only me

♡

"How about going away with me this weekend?" Alec asked Rae a week later. The investigation and its aftermath had shaken even his optimism, and he didn't like how tense she'd been looking. It would be good for both of them to leave the City for a day or two, even if there were some work sessions involved.

They'd just come from his place, where they'd showered after another yoga session, during which he'd actually managed to balance on one leg, lean forward, stick both arms and his other leg into the air, and stay there, which he'd been fairly proud of. He didn't know what it was called, but he'd done it. And watching Rae in her stretchy little shorts, twisting her sweat-soaked body into those interesting positions, always gave him good ideas. But right now, he was taking her out to eat, which was another of his favorite things.

"I was thinking about Point Reyes," he said. "Remember that thing about walking barefoot on the beach? We haven't done that yet. I'm falling behind here."

"That sounds wonderful," she said with a little sigh, "but I told my grandma I'd come visit. It's the three-month anniversary of her heart attack, do you realize?"

"Yeah, I can certainly see why she'd want to celebrate that milestone."

She laughed, took another bite of roasted rock cod with Italian peppers, another sip of Chardonnay, and he watched her savoring both. "She does want to, though. A survival celebration, I guess, and I thought I could take her out to lunch on Saturday with the girls and Lupe, let them splash out a little. That's my big weekend plan."

"Well," he found himself saying, "I should probably visit my folks too. Why don't I take you, give us both some company on that drive? Much as I know you enjoy driving your clown car. We could go up Friday night, come back Sunday afternoon. Sound good?"

You are so screwed. Gabe's words after that Christmas lunch were right there in his head, loud and clear, and he knew why he was really offering. Because he didn't want to spend the weekend without her.

♡

And it was even worse than that, because he ended up taking them all to lunch. Rae and her grandmother, Lupe and Mrs. Sanderson and Mrs. Chang, and Mrs. Calhoun too, the fourth member of the pinochle group.

He wasn't even sure how it had happened. He'd started out by offering his services as a chauffeur so the ladies could have a drink, all except Rae, the other designated driver in the party. He'd ended up, somehow or other, at a big round table in Olive Garden with six women. And when he'd convinced Rae that she really ought to have a margarita or two and let him worry about the cars, with six *toasted* women who hadn't made more than a token effort at the "lunch" part of the outing.

"He was scampering down that corridor," Mrs. Sanderson was saying now, barely able to get the words out, her gray curls shaking, "naked as a jaybird, laughing his fool head off, with two nurses running after him, shouting, "Mr. Williams! Mr. Williams! Get back in here!"

The others were holding onto the table, tears running down their cheeks, and an older man sitting with his wife at the next table caught Alec's eye, shook his head with a resigned smile.

"This is...*empty*," Rae said when her laughter had subsided. She picked up the margarita pitcher and waved it in an extravagant motion. "That is so sad. Don't you think that's sad, Alec?"

"That's sad," he agreed. He raised a hand for the waitress. "Another iced tea for me, please," he told her. "And another pitcher for the ladies. Another virgin margarita for you?" he asked Dixie.

"Oh, I'd better." She wiped her eyes. "One's my limit now, and that's what's really sad."

"You know what, Alec?" Rae asked him, midway through the next round. She'd grabbed his arm, was looking up at him seriously.

"No, what?"

She snorted a little, worked her face into seriousness again. "You're very, very handsome. Everybody wants to go out with you, but you know what?"

"No, what?"

"They don't get to," she proclaimed. "Not any more. Just me. Just only me, did you know that?"

"I did know that." He grinned back down at her. "Just only you."

He turned to Dixie. "What do you think? Time to go?"

"Oh, honey," she laughed, "I think we'd better. Desiree's going to have a headache tonight, that's for sure. Never seen her so silly."

When the waitress came with the check, Rae lunged for it, missed completely, and Alec handed it back along with his credit card.

"I'm supposed to pay," she told him plaintively. "I always pay."

"Nope. Not any more," he told her. "Just only me."

♡

It was a bit of a hilarious effort sorting them into his car and the waiting taxi, but he managed it in the end. Sent Rae, Dixie, and a sleepy Lupe off with a word to the cab driver, installing Rae in the front seat, of course, and delivered the other ladies himself, with Mrs. Sanderson as his final stop.

"We had an unexpected change of plan," he told the old man who'd come to the door of the mobile home at his wife's rather noisy entrance. "I'm afraid your car's still at Olive Garden. If you want to give me the keys, I could get a cab back there to pick it up."

"Naw." Mr. Sanderson reached for the cane beside the door, grabbed a 49ers cap from the hanging rack and settled it over his scant white hair. "No need to spend good money on that. I'll go on with you, get it myself."

"They got a little loopy, did they?" he asked when he'd lowered his skinny behind in its tan slacks into the big car, pulled his cane in after him, and Alec had shut the door and got in on his side.

"Yes, sir," Alec said with a reminiscent smile, pulling out of the mobile home park and onto the main road. "They sure did."

"Well, you know, women need to have their fling now and then to be happy," the old man said with a chuckle. "You should see them on Pinochle Night. When it's at our place, I go on over to Stuart Grainger's and watch TV, 'cause those girls get *loud*."

Alec laughed. "Not too hard to imagine at all. They sure seemed to be having a good time today."

"Yup. They'll have enjoyed that, 'specially having Desiree take them out on the town. Desiree, now, she's got a special spot in everybody's heart. Always been a good girl, and she still is. She does our taxes every year, did you know that?"

"She does?" Alec asked, since Mr. Sanderson seemed to be expecting an answer.

"Yup. Ours, and Iris Chang's, and her grandma's too. Started out with Dixie's when she was, oh, 'bout sixteen. Dixie was all set to go to H&R Block like usual, but Desiree looked it up on that computer, figured it out. Smart as a whip, that girl. Dixie bragged on her, of course. We wasn't too sure, but Dixie got her check right enough, and Desiree said, now that she'd done it for her grandma, she might as well do ours too. Course, we tell her she doesn't have to bother, now that she's got that big job and all, but she does it just the same."

"I didn't know that," Alec said when the other man paused again.

"Yup. Always been smart like that. And hard-working? Phew," the old man said with a wave of one scrawny brown arm in its baggy white short-sleeved shirt. "Now, Dixie's a hard-working woman, don't get me wrong, but Desiree? You never saw her without some big book, full of math or what-not. That's when she wasn't working all the hours God sent to pay for that college. Hasn't forgot her roots, either. Visits, calls, and I know she sends up a check every month. Do anything for her grandma."

"Now, woman like that," he went on, as Alec had another light turn yellow on him, pulled to a stop, "woman who's had the kind of hard time she has, too, she deserves good things. I'm sure you got a big house to go along with this fancy car, and you ride around in limousines, drink champagne and what-not, but that's not what I'm talking about. I'm not talking about fur coats and diamond rings. I'm talking about a man to treat her the way she deserves, be good to her. Appreciate her the way a man should appreciate a good woman."

"Yes, sir," Alec said, putting his foot thankfully on the gas again. "You're right."

"I heard you was hanging around her," Mr. Sanderson said. "Now, I'm not saying your mama and daddy didn't raise you right. We're Lutheran ourselves, but everyone knows Reverend Kincaid's a good man. But who knows what kind of ideas you've gotten into, down there in San Francisco. Maybe you're thinking, just 'cause Desiree doesn't have a daddy who cares about her, you can go on and mess with her, break her heart. But she's got plenty of people who think the world of her, and I'm telling you here and now, you treat that little girl right."

Alec had a vision of a posse of senior citizens, chasing him down and beating him to death with their walkers if he screwed up.

"Yes, sir," he said again. "I will."

"And I'm sure you're thinking," the other man went on as if he hadn't spoken, "if you needed a lecture from some old man, you'd go on home and get it from your own grandpa. But young people today, they seem all mixed up to me. The girls think they got to run after the boys somehow, try to get them interested. They don't realize we was *born* interested. They'd do better to let us know they'd be doing us a favor by even noticing us, but they got it all backwards, maybe 'cause they don't have daddies at home, I don't know."

"Well, don't worry," Alec said, turning into the Olive Garden parking lot with a prayer of thanksgiving. "Desiree's got that down. In fact," he couldn't help saying, "maybe you want to have this conversation with her, about not messing with *my* heart."

"Huh." The sharp little eyes took him in from beneath the brim of the ball cap. "You fall in love with that girl?"

"Yes, sir," Alec admitted, pulling up beside the old Taurus. "I sure have."

The old man shook his head slowly, chuckled a little.

"Then, son," he said, reaching for the door handle and shoving it open, "Lord help you."

♡

"Your phone rang while you were gone," his mother said a few hours later from her spot at the stove when Alec had pulled off his running shoes, wiped his face on his T-shirt, and come in through the laundry room after a very long run that had shaken some of the cobwebs from his mind.

He went over and picked it up from the kitchen table, smiled, and pressed his thumb against the name.

"Hey," he said when she picked up. "Feeling better?"

He heard the rueful laugh. "Yeah. I took an *extremely* long nap, and I have a bad feeling it's going to be followed by an early bedtime." She did sound sleepy. "I can't believe I drank that much. And I'm pretty sure I remember that I left you to pay the bill. Let me know how much it was, and I'll pay you back, and for the taxi too."

"Oh, no, you won't. My pleasure. Getting six beautiful women the worse for wear? Are you kidding?"

"Wait a sec," he said, ignoring her protest. "My mom's hissing something at me." He held the phone against his chest, looked at his mother, and asked, "What?"

"Lunch," she said, gesturing furiously. "Tomorrow."

"I think my mom's inviting you to lunch tomorrow," he said, to the accompaniment of her emphatic nods. "You and your grandmother. And Lupe too," he went on, correctly interpreting his mother's circling hand.

"Oh. Let me check." She was gone a moment herself. "My grandma says yes, thank you, but Lupe goes to Spanish Mass, and she's having lunch with friends afterwards, so it's just us. And," she said, and he heard the resignation in her voice, "my grandma says she'll bring her Jell-O salad for dessert."

"Desiree," he said sternly, "you really need to learn how to cook."

She laughed. "Hey. You want to see us, or what?"

"I want to see you. And on that note, how's that couch working out for you? That can't be too comfortable. Want me to come get you tonight? You could sleep in Alyssa's room." He raised his eyebrows at his mother again, got her nod in return, and stepped back out into the laundry room, shut the door behind him. "And if I happen to wander in there during the night," he said more quietly, "well, as long as you can keep it down, nobody has to know about that."

"Alec," she said, and he could hear the giggle that he hoped was only partially the residue of the margaritas, "I wouldn't dare. Not with your dad there. We'd be struck by lightning or something."

"Gabe and Mira sleep together when they're here," he pointed out. "And they're not married."

"Yet," she reminded him. "Engaged is different."

"Well, we're engaged up here, remember? I told that nurse so and everything. That probably gives it the American Nursing Association seal of approval."

"No way," she said again. "You can fool some of the people all of the time, or so I hear, but I have a feeling you can't fool your dad *any* of the time. And you can't fool me either. And besides," she went on hastily as he was opening his mouth to say something, although he had no earthly clue what, "my grandma wants me here. But I'll see you tomorrow at church, OK? And then lunch."

And he had to be content with that.

♡

"She coming over tonight?" his mom asked, frying hamburger now, when he'd stepped back into the kitchen again.

"No," he said, setting his phone down on the counter and picking up the big knife from the cutting board, absently whacking the top off a green pepper. "She's staying there."

His mother went back to her frying for a minute.

"She thinks—" he said, then broke off.

She looked at him inquiringly. He rocked the knife back and forth, made a couple slices in the wood. "She doesn't think I'm serious about her."

"Hmm," she said. "You know, if you're going to stand there and wreck my knife, why don't you wash your hands and cut up those vegetables for me?"

"Uh...OK. How?"

"Onion first. Dice it. Little pieces," she explained. "And then the rest. For the carrots, think quarter-inch coins. Everything else, half-inch cubes."

He got through the onion and watched her add it to her hamburger meat, then set to work on the rest. His decapitated pepper was a bit of struggle, but he figured it out eventually.

"I don't know how she feels," he said when he'd started on the carrots. "I know how *I* feel, but I can't tell what she wants."

"Are you having a good time?"

"Of course we are." He frowned at Susie's back. "But it's not enough just to have a good time. Not anymore."

"You're afraid she doesn't want a commitment." She'd turned a little now, and he could see the smile.

"Are you *laughing* at me?" he demanded with a flash of anger the likes of which he hadn't experienced since she'd grounded him for sneaking out of his bedroom window, junior year. "It isn't funny."

"Well, it is, a little," his mother said calmly. "Don't you imagine this is the conversation a whole lot of women have had with their mothers about you over the years?"

"It can't have felt this bad."

"Oh, I don't know. I'll bet it felt exactly this bad, at least for some of them."

"Well, then, I'm sorry. I never meant to hurt anybody."

"Oh, sweetie." Susie turned from her work, wrapped her arms around him, and gave him a hug. She fit right under his chin, and he kissed the top of her head, noticed that she was going gray, and had a flash of how Desiree must feel, a sudden rush of tenderness combined with the certain knowledge that one day, he was going to lose his mother. And realized in that moment that things had shifted forever. That he was an adult, and that at some point in the not-too-distant future, he would be a parent himself. That it was all on him now, and that he wanted it that way.

"I know it's hard," his mother told him, stepping back again and turning to her soup, opening a carton and pouring in beef broth. "But if it's meant to be, it'll work out. You just keep on being patient, and keep on loving her. A good man who's going to be there for you through thick and thin isn't that easy to come by. You're a good man, and Desiree's a very intelligent young woman, and if you hang in there, she's going to see that. But she's got some pretty deep scars. Some old wounds. I don't think trust comes easily for her."

"I know that's why." He was chopping red potatoes now, still grappling with the wave of emotion that had swept over him. "But I can make it better for her. I can make it right."

"Well," she said, "if that's how you feel, you just go on and love her, and if it's meant to be, it'll happen."

"You sound like Gabe."

She laughed at that. "Well, I don't think that's such a bad thing. It worked out pretty well for him, didn't it?" She gave him a playful nudge, smiled at him with the happy optimism he'd inherited from her.

"And now that you've mangled my vegetables," she said, taking his cutting board and beginning to scrape the contents into her soup pot, "go take a shower. Because, phew. You stink."

He glanced back at her as he left the room, and saw the smile still on her face. He could swear that she was *singing*.

He pulled the sweat-soaked T-shirt over his head, tossed it onto the floor of his room as he passed it on his way to the bathroom, and wondered why everybody in the world thought that his suddenly, terrifyingly vulnerable heart was funny. Even his own mother.

♡

"So to recap, here's how I've spent my weekend," he said on the following evening. They were nearing the end of their long drive, the towers and cables of the Golden Gate Bridge glowing soft red against the black of the Bay beyond, flashing past the windows of the big Mercedes. "I've taken five old ladies to Olive Garden. I've listened to a lecture from a cranky old man about how I'm not good enough for you."

"Oh, yeah," he said at her look of surprise, "didn't I tell you about that one? Yeah, that was another fun time. But that wasn't all. I've gone to church. I've eaten more Jell-O salad. I've spent two nights in a single bed, aching to have a woman in there with me like I haven't done since my crush on Elke Christensen. The head cheerleader," he explained. "Elke was *hot.*"

"You couldn't get the head cheerleader?" she asked, and she was laughing. "I'm disappointed. My last illusion shattered."

"I was fifteen. Hadn't grown into my full potential yet."

"Well, that's a pretty good list," she admitted. "I'd say you've been amazingly restrained and virtuous."

"Yeah, I'd say so too. So," he asked as he took the turn onto Lombard, "don't you think, after all that, I deserve some kinky sex?"

He shot another look across at her, and she was still smiling. "Yes, I think you do," she said, "and I think I do too. I was at Olive Garden too, remember."

"You were. But at least you got drunk."

"Hey. Do you want kinky sex or not?"

"Oh, yeah," he assured her. "I want it."

And he got it. But not entirely the way he'd planned, though they got to the curtains, all right. He used them on her, and it was even better than he'd hoped. And then she used them on him, and that was pretty good too.

♡

"Guess I've had kinky sex now," she sighed, knowing that her foolish smile was right out there for him to see.

"Guess you have." And he was looking just about as happy and satisfied as she felt, so it didn't matter.

"Not quite the same as doing you on the conference table," she acknowledged, "but I gave it my best shot. And I think you enjoyed it, too."

She stayed where she was, kneeling astride him, just because it felt good up here. Bent down to give him a long kiss, felt his hands coming up to hold her waist, slide over her bare back, and loved it.

"Aw." He shrugged, grinned up at her. "I can take it or leave it."

"Oh, yeah?" She moved to swing her leg over him, but he grabbed her thigh, held on.

"Changed my mind," he said. "I can only take it. Come on down here and kiss me again."

"So who needs it, huh?" she asked against his mouth.

He sighed. "Yeah. That'd be me. Aw, hell, Desiree. Who am I kidding? Every single person I've talked to this weekend has figured it out, so I might as well say it. I'm crazy in love with you."

She sat back fast, and this time she *did* swing her leg over him, sat back on her knees beside him, busied herself smoothing out her hair. "Oh." She couldn't think of what else to say. "You are?"

"I am," and he was smiling at her now. "No doubt about it. I'm officially crazy."

"You..." She leaned down, grabbed her underwear from the floor by the bed where she'd dropped it. "Wow. You sure know how to make a woman feel good."

Just like that, the smile was gone. "You think I'm just talking? This is a big deal for me. I've never said that before."

Claudine's words were right there. *"I don't think the words 'I love you' have ever crossed those luscious lips, not unless he was talking to his mother."* But she remembered what they'd been talking about when Claudine had said it, too.

"And you've got me sweating now," he pointed out. "Waiting to hear you say it back."

"I'm..." She hesitated, busied herself pulling on her underwear, felt a little better when she had it on. "I'm pretty sure I feel...that way."

"*Pretty* sure?" He pushed himself up to sit against the pillows. "That *way?*"

She felt the panic closing in, shoved it back, did her best to be honest. "I love being with you. I miss you, the nights you're not here. And, OK, I'll say it. I'm crazy about you."

And even that was almost too much. She got up and found an undershirt in the dresser drawer, put it on. Didn't look at him, but could feel his eyes on her.

When she turned around again, he studied her face and sighed. "Well, this is awkward," he said. "Not sure what to do here."

"What do you usually do when a woman says that to you?" she asked. "What happens next?"

"Ouch." She could see the wince. "Yeah. Well. Sometimes they leave, sometimes they stick around, I suppose thinking that

I'll say it back eventually. Which I never have, which I guess is my answer right there." He was pulling on his own underwear now, his T-shirt too.

"Alec." He really looked hurt, and she couldn't stand that, so she sat beside him on the bed. "I'm just...I can't give my heart away like that. If I didn't know you..." She stopped, looked down at the curve of her thigh, ran her hand through her curls, messing them up again. "I mean, if I didn't know *about* you. If I hadn't heard so much about you, and from so many people. If I hadn't seen you in action on the show, the way you were with Chelsea. Talking to your brother, too, all the things you said."

"That was then," he said, "and this is now. I'm different. That's all I can tell you. I don't know if it *was* the show, or if it was seeing Gabe change. When you're a twin...you do what your twin does. You feel what he feels, you change at the same time. It's a hard thing to explain, but it's real. Or maybe that had nothing to do with it, and it was just you. The one right woman, coming into my life at exactly the right time, when I could recognize her, when I was ready for her. I don't know why it happened. All I know is, it's here, and it's real."

"I want to believe that," she said. "And I almost do. Because what I've seen, what you've been with me, it's...I don't know how *not* to believe that. Maybe I just need a little more time to be sure you mean it, before I can...let myself go."

She looked up at him, saw him looking back, his gaze steady on her, and admitted it. "I'm scared to say it. I'm scared to feel it. I'm scared you'll change your mind, and if I let myself love you...I don't know how I'd get over that. Because have you ever lived with anybody? Have you ever even had a serious relationship with a woman, one that lasted a...a year?"

"No. Have you, with a man?"

"No. No, I haven't."

"Then we're in the same place," he insisted. "New at this. Born-again virgins, trying it out together, seeing where we get."

She had to smile. "Born-again virgins? Is that what we are?"

"Yes." He was smiling back at her, and the relief, or some other emotion she didn't dare name…whatever it was, it was filling her now, rich, and strong, and…wonderful.

"Born-again virgins," he said again, "trying something brand-new. Think you could do that with me?"

She looked at him, all the strength and all the sweetness of him right there to read in his face, and made her decision.

"Yes. I think I could." She reached a hand out for him, felt his palm closing around hers, his fingers threading through her own. "Born-again virgins. I could do that. I could try."

all the time in the world

♡

"And that's it," Alec sighed nearly four weeks later, pushing away from his desk with both hands. "We're there." He looked at Joe, shoving back himself with his own satisfied smile, and laughed out loud. "And it's good."

"It is." Joe reached two massive arms over the shaved dome of his scalp, interlaced his fingers, and stretched. "We'll look at it again next week, start picking holes in it. But, yeah. It's damn good. What time is it?"

"Uh…" Alec looked at his monitor. "After eleven." The outer office long since emptied on this Friday night, even Rae having left hours ago.

"So, hey. We made it before midnight," Joe said. "I'm going home, working out, and crashing. And I'm not planning to drink another cup of coffee all weekend, or look at a single screen. Turn my phone off, stick the laptop in the desk, go climb a mountain or something. You?"

Alec had stood, was walking around the office now. He didn't feel tired, he felt energized, though he knew it wouldn't last. "Taking off too. Going someplace," he decided. "For sure."

Joe shut down, put his laptop away, swept the empty Red Bull cans and the pizza box into the wastebasket. "Going alone?"

"Haven't decided," Alec lied. He wished he could tell Joe, that he could trust him. But it wasn't only his secret to keep.

♡

And the next day, he was at Point Reyes. Taking Rae away for the weekend, walking barefoot on the beach holding her hand, just as he'd promised her. Everything in his life coming together, better than he could have hoped. And the open space, the salt in the air, the grainy firmness of the sand under his feet, the resonant thunder of waves hitting shoreline, the quiet, soul-deep pleasure of having her beside him for all of it—it was all carrying him up, so buoyant he could have floated away.

But in the afternoon, he got jumpy again. At first he'd thought it was just the unaccustomed idleness, being at loose ends after working flat-out for so long to finish the beta. Finally, though, obeying an instinct he couldn't explain, he went back to the inn with Rae, got the laptop he hadn't, after all, been able to leave behind, and drove to a place where he could change the folder's password. Thought about calling Joe and telling him he'd done it, but then, Joe had said he wouldn't even have his phone with him, let alone be online.

He'd tell him Monday. Monday was soon enough.

♡

The planner did the work at his kitchen table, as always. Transcribed the last careful character from the piece of paper lying next to him and waited, breath held, for the microsecond it took for the screen to appear. And then the smile bloomed. It stayed on his face as he located the folder containing the beta version of the code, clicked on it, and encountered the password screen.

He typed in the password. And watched the red-bordered box appear, with an additional note.

Password incorrect

Too fast. Too eager. He retyped, more carefully this time.

Password incorrect

He checked his caps lock. Off. Risked a third try.

Access denied due to multiple incorrect attempts. Please contact your system administrator.

He swore again. Sat and thought it through. And then went with Plan B.

♡

Alec took Rae out for a long, late dinner. They ate crab cake salad and blackened wild king salmon and tiny baby vegetables, and drank a whole bottle of chilled Chardonnay. Held hands across the white tablecloth and, afterwards, shared a delicate crème brûlée and drank snifters of Grand Marnier, just because it seemed like a good idea. Left the restaurant at last, its final customers, and walked the few blocks to the inn in no hurry at all, both a little drunk, and very happy. Tilted their heads back to see the stars overhead, clear and bright in the night sky here at the edge of the world, got a little dizzy, and laughed.

Back at the inn, they filled the huge soaking tub, lit all the candles, poured in the bath salts, and lay together in the warm, aromatic water. Slow kisses, languid touches, murmurs and sighs. Until the water cooled and they climbed out, toweled each other dry with huge, fluffy white bath sheets, pulled the quilt back on the big bed, and made long, slow, languorous love, quiet, and peaceful, and beautiful. And knew that they were each with the person they most wanted to be with, and that they had all the time in the world.

full disclosure

♡

That was Saturday. And on Monday morning, they were summoned to an emergency meeting of the venture capital board.

♡

The five faces around the table were grim, Alec saw, and he had a moment of disorientation, almost vertigo. The beta was finished, and it was the best work he and Joe had ever done. They were on the verge of something huge, a game-changer. He knew it. What could possibly be wrong?

It didn't take him long to find out.

"At 11:43 on Saturday night," Ron began without preamble, "Alec's credentials were used to log into the server, and the entire alpha version of the code was downloaded to a hard drive. You didn't know we were tracking that," he told Alec, "but ever since that first event, we've been doing our own separate, very detailed monitoring of your systems. And the primary thing we've been looking for is any downloading of the code. Maybe you'd like to explain, after our discussion of security, why you did that."

"I didn't," Alec said. The alpha was gone? He was always cool, but he wasn't cool now. He was sweating, his heart pounding with anger, and fear, and an overwhelming wave of relief that he'd changed the password on the beta.

Ron looked hard at him. "You trying to tell me that you gave somebody else access to your credentials, or that somebody guessed them?"

"Absolutely not. I've been changing my password every few days, and I've been randomly generating a nine-character series. Nobody could have guessed that."

"You can remember a random series that changes completely every few days?"

"I'm very bright."

"Then you must be bright enough to see that, if your credentials are secure, and nobody else could have downloaded the code, it had to have been you. Please explain why."

"I can't explain it," Alec insisted, "because I didn't do it. If somebody did, we have to find out who, and how, and right now. A keylogger, I assume, to capture my credentials. We need to trace that."

"Nobody could have shoulder-surfed you?"

"Again, absolutely not. Not even anybody in this room. I don't let anybody watch me log in." Except Rae, but it wasn't Rae. He needed to find out who. And then he needed to kill the bastard.

"It can't be a keylogger," Ron said, "because DatAssure has been all over the records, backwards and forwards, to check. So I'm sorry, Alec, but we're left with you. Denial isn't going to work. Tell us now."

"Why would I take my own code?" Alec asked in frustration. "Why are we wasting time on this?"

"Why would you take it? To sell it. I believe that's the usual reason."

"To *sell* it? Again, why? What would I get for it that I wouldn't get when we're bought out, or when we go public, whichever happens first? And why the alpha? Why wouldn't I take the beta?"

"Maybe you thought you'd get both. Maybe that's why you took the alpha. Tell the buyer it's the beta, and they go to market with it, get people excited about the idea, prime the pump. You come out in a few months with the much improved version, and you're paid twice, aren't you? You weren't counting on anyone finding out that both versions were your own handiwork, and that you'd been double-dipping."

For once, Alec couldn't think of an answer. His mind was always faster than anybody else's. He had the answer to the next problem while everyone else was still asking the last question. But right now, he had nothing. Because what Ron had said made a kind of weird, twisted sense, and he couldn't think how to refute it. Except to say that he hadn't done it, which was just about no good at all. And as long as the board was focused on him, they weren't solving the problem.

"It wasn't Alec." It was Rae's voice, and he looked up fast.

"I'm sure none of us wanted to think so," Ron said. "Unfortunately, there's no choice."

"It wasn't Alec," she said again. The tiger eyes were steady on Ron across the entire length of the table, two dots of color in her cheeks the only sign that she wasn't as cool as she looked. That, and the barely audible click of her ballpoint. "It isn't possible, and I can prove it."

"Rae," Alec said, urgent now. "No. Don't."

Ron waved at him to be quiet. "If she can prove it, I want to hear it."

"Desiree." Alec was standing now. She couldn't. He couldn't let her. "No. It's not worth it. We'll figure it out. Don't."

It was as if he hadn't spoken. "I know it wasn't Alec," she said, "because he was with me on Saturday night. The Pelican Point Inn at Tomales Bay, to be exact, which doesn't have internet access. He has the receipts to prove it, and he can show them to you."

The board members were looking at each other now, and nobody spoke for a minute.

"You're *kidding* me." That was Brandon, sitting on Rae's other side. The other man's face was flushed red, and his usual cocky smile was replaced by outrage as he stared at Alec. "Not only did you sell us out, but you slept with Rae just so she could alibi you? You'd do that to us, to Joe and me? Not that it's much of an alibi. How hard was that, to drive off once she fell asleep, log in from someplace else? She wakes up when you come back to bed and, what, you were in the bathroom?"

Rae didn't answer him, not directly. "What time did you say the code was downloaded?" she asked Ron.

"Eleven forty-three."

"He didn't drive anyplace else," she said. "At 11:43, Alec wasn't driving, and he wasn't logging in. He was making love to me."

And that's when Alec sat down. Because he had nothing to say. Because she'd put it all on the line. Everything she'd worked for. Her reputation. Her security. Her net. And she'd done it for him.

He sat and looked at her, her color still high, her eyes still blazing. And her pen still clicking.

♡

The quiet around the table was broken by Ron. "Well," he said, "now we have a real mess."

"No," Alec said. "Now we have some answers. You all know it wasn't me. And that it wasn't Rae either," he said as an after-thought. "Unless you think we were in it together."

"Which is a possibility," Ron agreed, "but a less likely one." He looked at Rae, the disappointment evident. "I can believe you've used some incredibly poor judgment, but it's hard for me to believe that two people whose integrity I would have sworn to are *both* bent."

"Thank you," she said quietly. "For that." Alec could see her shaking a little, and he wanted to hold her, to tell her it would be all right.

"Give us time to figure it out," he told Ron. "A few days. There's got to be an answer." He looked at Rae, and she nodded.

"More investigation," she said. "Interview everybody. Check financial records. We can do it, but we've got to move fast, contain the damage."

"We've got a mess here," Ron said again, shoving his chair back from the head of the table. "The board needs to discuss this. Could the four of you go into the outer office and wait, please."

Alec looked at the iron-hard set of the older man's features, and knew that argument would be fruitless. He didn't answer, just stood, and Rae, Joe, and Brandon followed his lead.

They sat for twenty endless minutes, unable to hear anything from the soundproofed room. Rae silent and poker-straight in her chair, her expression closed. Joe's face thunderous, which usually meant he was thinking furiously, and that he'd talk only when he was done thinking. And Brandon a pointed distance away, thighs spread, forearms on knees, staring at the floor.

And when Calvin Tang opened the door again and beckoned them back inside, his expression had nothing welcoming about it.

"Here's what we're doing," Ron said when they were seated again. "You're shut down." He held up a hand when Alec would have spoken. "For at least a few days, probably a week or more. Rae's right. Interviews, investigations, going through those logs with a fine-tooth comb. But none of you can be involved, because as far as we're concerned, you're all compromised until we can prove otherwise. We can't go forward with this kind of uncertainty, and we're too far in to think of cutting our losses without more investigation."

Well, Alec thought, that was one small mercy.

"So," Ron said, shoving back from the table, "go home. We've already shut the office down, and we've got the locksmith up there now. No access until the investigation is done. Your servers are being wiped as we speak. We can't take the chance that there's malware lurking on there, some kind of backdoor access. Everything's wiped and re-installed, and we're not starting up again until we've got the answer."

"The beta," Alec said.

"Oh, don't worry," Ron said. "We've got the beta. Let's just hope nobody else does."

♡

The four of them walked out of the conference room in silence, through the office, out the double doors and into the marble-lined corridor. They stopped in front of the elevator, and Alec pushed the "Down" button, still stunned. Still shaken to the core.

But when it came, Brandon stepped back.

"I can't do it," he said.

"What?" Alec stared at him.

"I can't ride with you. I can't stand next to you. I can't pretend this didn't happen. How could you do it?" Brandon demanded. "How could you sell us out?"

"You heard me. I didn't." Alec felt the helpless rage rising. How did you prove a negative? How did you prove that you hadn't done something? You couldn't, not if what Rae had done wasn't good enough.

"Yeah, I heard you," Brandon said, "and I heard what Rae said too. I heard that you got her to lie for you, or to work with you, or that you fooled her too. I don't know which one it was, and I don't care. I *trusted* you, man. I *believed* in you."

Alec stepped into the elevator, which was now protesting Joe's restraining hand with a loud, insistent pinging. Joe and Rae followed, but Brandon didn't.

"I'll wait," he said, and the doors closed on his confused, angry, wounded face.

Alec looked across at Joe. "Want to get out at the next floor? You want to avoid me too?"

Joe shook his head. "No. I'll ride."

He hesitated, though, when they got to the lobby. "We should talk," he told Alec.

Alec sighed. "Go home. We all need to clear our heads. Something will come to us. There's a way to figure out who did this. There's an answer. We just have to think of it."

He watched Joe leave the building. "My place?" he asked Rae. "Or yours?"

"Yours," she decided. "More central."

He nodded, walked out with her, turned right without thinking about it, his mind racing. "We know it wasn't me," he said slowly, "which means it has to have been someone who could get my credentials. Which means it has to have been someone with admin privileges."

"Or someone working with someone who has admin privileges," she suggested.

His feet were still carrying him, but he barely noticed. "Thomas. Chinese, admin privileges. What's the worst thing that can happen, security-wise? You compromise a developer, or..."

"You compromise someone in IT," she finished. "The very worst."

"We thought Michael was stupid, right, to use an FTP site to transfer the files?"

"Right. You're saying he wasn't. That somebody else was leaving breadcrumbs."

"And making us think that once we'd caught Michael, we'd solved it." He picked up the baton from her and ran with it. The question is, Thomas all along? Or Thomas and Simon?"

She'd stopped at the light, was waiting to cross Market. "No," she said, and she was grabbing his arm now. "No. I think that's still not it. Not quite. We need to go get your car. Because I think I know. I think I see. The only person. The person who makes sense, who fits. Using the person who could be used."

"Explain."

"What Brandon said, about how you slept with me so I'd alibi you. That you used me."

"What? You *do* think I did it? That this is all some kind of double bluff?" Confusion, and anger, and hurt, the sharpest pain he'd felt yet that day. He took a step back, and the light turned green.

"Alec. Wait. Listen." She grabbed him by the elbow and yanked him into the intersection and across the street with her. "No. I mean that's how he did it. A woman. Veronica. You look for the weakest link, right? She's the weakest link. We need to go see her. They sent everyone home already, right?"

"Right."

She had already pulled out her phone, was looking it up. "She lives in San Leandro. Come on. Let's get your car. I'll explain on the way."

a live goat to catch a tiger

♡

Two very long hours later, after Rae had coaxed, and explained, and been sympathetic and understanding to a point that had Alec's teeth gritting in frustration, they were still sitting around a small dining table with a swollen-eyed, tear-streaked Veronica.

"I'm so, so sorry," she said again. "I should have told you, Rae. After you gave me the job, and you've been so good to me. But he's a *partner*," she pleaded, "and he said it was a secret. He showed me a memo from the board about the security breach, and he said he needed my help to trap Alec. That he needed Alec's credentials so he could track what he was doing, could catch him downloading the code. That they didn't trust anybody else here, because Alec could have got to everyone, but that he knew he could trust me. I said I had to check with you, Rae. I told him so. But he said no, because..." She swallowed, looked down, "because you were compromised. Because you were..."

"Sleeping with Alec," Rae finished for her.

Veronica's blotchy face flushed an even deeper red. "Yes," she whispered. "Because Alec had seduced you, in order to get you to help him. But he said you didn't realize," she added hastily. "He never said you'd done anything wrong."

"So he had you install the rootkit and the keylogger, and then wipe it once you had Alec's login and password, and the password for the code folder," Desiree said.

"Yes. I did it as soon as Alec came in on Friday," she explained, still looking at Rae, avoiding Alec's eyes, as well she might. "It was only on there for five minutes. Then, when I had what I needed, I uninstalled them and ran the program to cover up that I did it."

"How did you know how to do all that?" Alec asked.

"He showed me how, a long time ago. When..."

"When you did it to Michael," Alec realized, his eyes meeting Rae's.

"Yes," Veronica said. "Because Michael was stealing too. But that's how I knew it was all right, don't you see? Because Michael was doing it, and we caught him."

"DatAssure caught him, you mean," Alec corrected her grimly. "After Rae and I got a tip and alerted them."

"No," Veronica said urgently. "He explained it to me. He's the one who figured it out, and that was why Michael was fired, because I helped catch him."

Alec ignored her. "We need to make that right with Michael," he told Rae. "All this time wasted. All this time..."

She nodded. "We will. Later."

"It was only five minutes," Veronica repeated, as if that would make it better. "And he said we needed to. He said it was for the *board*."

"And it didn't occur to you," Alec couldn't help saying, "that if the board had needed that information, they would have gone through their security consultants to get it, not the receptionist?"

She opened her mouth, closed it again, seemed to shrink into herself. Desiree glared at him, kicked his foot under the table, and he shut up.

"What else did he do to get you to help him?" Rae asked gently. "Veronica," she went on as the young woman began to cry again, "you've been victimized. You thought you were doing the right thing, but you were lied to. That isn't your fault. As long as you tell us the truth, you're going to be all right. You'll have a job. Not this job," she went on hastily, because now Alec was kicking *her* foot, "but I'll help you get something."

"He said..." The tears were flowing freely now. "That he loved me. That he was so glad he had me to help him. That after this was over, we'd be able to be together openly, not hide anymore. He's going to take me to meet his mother," she pleaded. "So you know he's serious."

"Have you heard from him today?" Rae asked.

"Not...not yet. When they told us the office was closed, to go home, I tried to call, but it went to voicemail. I thought they must have caught Alec. That it was over, and we'd be able to be together, like he said. But I haven't heard from him after all, and I don't know what to do."

The last part was a wail. Rae sat for a moment, thinking. Alec longed to tell Veronica that she might think about checking out the Society for the Aid of the Terminally Credulous, or start filling out her unemployment forms, but he sat still as well. And after a moment, Rae spoke again.

"Do you have somebody you could go stay with for a few days?" she asked.

"My sister." The sobs had died to sniffles now. "In LA."

"I think that would be a good idea," Rae said. "Call her right now, and tell her you're coming to stay. Today. The first flight we can get you on."

Another few minutes, and the call was made, to the accompaniment of some more tears, some confused non-explanations. And Rae entering the sister's name and number into her own phone, Alec noticed. Although he pulled her away for a few seconds during that phone call, because he had to.

"She's our best evidence," he argued from the entryway, keeping his voice low. "And you're planning to send her away? We should take her to Ron right now."

"I think she needs to be gone," Rae said, glancing into the room where Veronica was still talking. "Tell you later. But I've got it covered, I promise. Can you trust me?"

He hesitated a moment, but there was only one answer. "Yes. As long as you explain."

"Soon as we're done," she promised. "Wait. She's hanging up.'

"And now," she told the other woman when she was standing over her again, "you pack a suitcase, and Alec will drive you to the airport and pay for your ticket." Which Alec was not one bit thrilled to hear either, but Rae was clearly on a roll, so what the hell. "And you give us your phone. We'll call your sister on the way and tell her which plane you're on," she went on hastily when Veronica began to object again, "but we don't want to give . . . *him* any way to get in touch with you."

"But..."

"Do you believe me?" Rae demanded. "That he was using you? Come on. Talk and pack." She shepherded Veronica into the bedroom of the cheap apartment, and Alec followed, leaned against the wall.

"Yes," Veronica admitted, crying yet again. Alec didn't know where women stored all those tears, but they must have an extra reservoir somewhere, because the supply seemed to be inexhaustible. But she was getting down her suitcase from the top shelf of her closet, which was progress. The influence of a will greater than her own, he guessed. Although to be fair, just about any will seemed to be greater than Veronica's.

"And you want to help us now, don't you?" Rae coaxed, taking clothes from Veronica and packing them tidily into the case. "You want to clear your name, so you have a good future?"

Veronica nodded, pulling clothes haphazardly off hangers, out of drawers, handing them to Rae

"That's enough," Rae judged. "Toiletries. Bathroom. Come on."

"You just do what I say," she was telling Veronica when they returned, "and everything's going to be fine. But you can't call him. If you do," she said sternly, "I can't help you, and neither can Alec. Not anymore. You could even go to jail. Do you understand?"

"I can't…I can't go to jail." It was a whimper. "My parents…"

"You do what I say," Rae repeated, "and you won't. You give me your phone, you don't call him, you stay at your sister's until I call you and tell you it's all right to come home again. You listen to me, you do what I say, and you'll be fine."

♡

"You really think all that was necessary?" Alec asked when he'd parted with several hundred dollars for a last-minute ticket to LA, Rae had added Veronica's phone to the collection of items in her purse, and they were leaving Oakland Airport's short-term parking lot. "You think she would have talked to him again?"

"Who knows," Rae sighed. "And who knows what he would have done, now that she's not useful to him any more. He must know that she wouldn't stand up to any real questioning."

He glanced at her sharply. "You don't think she's in danger. You're thinking he'd actually hurt her, let alone, what, kill her? I don't believe he's capable of that. He may be a thief, but a killer? No. I don't believe it."

"Now that he's gone this far, who knows what else he'd do? I just feel like she should be out of his reach. We don't have enough yet. We haven't stopped him. And if his story was good enough, she'd buy it again, and she'd tell him we were here, and that we knew."

"I can't disagree with you there," he admitted. "What would make a woman suspend rational thought like that?"

"Looking for love."

There was no good answer to that one, so he left it.

"If we're going to stop him," he said, "we need a plan. Or should I assume that if I listen to you and do what you say, I'll be fine?"

"I do have an idea," she said. "We can't risk him muddying the waters any more. Doing something else to implicate you, or both of us now. And meanwhile, with the alpha out there...No. We need to do it now, and I think I know how. Head for your place."

"Huh." He moved into the right lane. Northbound, toward the Bay Bridge. "Then what?"

"Now we know, but we don't have the real proof, right? We don't actually have him with his hands on the code. I think I know how to get it, but I do need your programming skills."

"Oh, I get to contribute? Do I get to hear the plan too?" He knew he shouldn't be amused, because this was deadly serious. This was Desiree's reputation on the line, and his too, in the worst possible way. But his usual optimism was already back, because they had this, and they were going to be all right. He was sure, deep-down sure, all the way to his bones.

"You definitely get to contribute," she said, "because you're also going to be doing the talking. We have a few meetings to set up. I'll tell you what I'm thinking while we drive."

"All right," he said. "I'm driving. Tell me."

♡

Brandon met with them reluctantly, but he met with them.

"Joe?" Brandon sat back on his own white leather couch, his boyish face twisted with bewilderment. "First it's you, and now it's Joe? Are you sure?"

"A hundred percent," Alec said. "You know how much I hated to believe it. You know how tight we've been. He's been at my house every Christmas. He's like a brother, at least I thought he was. But I thought it through, and it was the only answer. And then I did some research of my own, I won't tell you what, and it's confirmed. But I need your help to prove it."

"Anything," Brandon said. "I'm sorry, man. I shouldn't have believed that it could have been you. But when I heard about you and Rae, that you'd hid that from us...it seemed like anything was possible."

"I shouldn't have," Alec said. "I should have trusted you. Well," he amended, "I should have trusted *you.*" He swallowed the anger at the betrayal and went on. "We were wrong, and we need your help, because we're both under a cloud now. We need a third party to verify this."

He pulled out his laptop, began pressing keys. "I've put a copy of the beta version onto my own drive. That's the bait. And this is the trap."

"What? How?"

"I give you access," Alec explained. "You're my independent witness. When he goes for it, I've got you to verify that I showed it to you, and that he accessed it. We can take that to the board. They'll believe us, if you're backing me. And once they've nailed him, the rest of us are off the hook. The code's safe, Joe's out of it, and we're all in the clear."

"But how?" Brandon objected again. "How will you know he's got it, or safeguard it once he does? And how did you get access to the beta? They shut us down."

Alec smiled, and the smile wasn't a nice one. "I always say Joe's the best, don't I?"

"You do. So, how?"

"He's not the best," Alec told him. "I am. I hacked Joe's accounts a long time ago. I guess I've never really trusted him as much as I wanted to think I did. And as for the beta..." He laughed. "You think I wouldn't keep separate access to my own code? That's what TrueCrypt is for. The file looks empty, and the partition is undetectable. But it's all there."

"They wiped the servers, though," Brandon protested. "I'm sure it's a done deal."

"Separate server entirely. It's there. Only Joe and I know, only Joe and I have access. Until now."

"All right. If you say so, though it still seems risky to me. The entire beta version, right out there?"

"It won't be out there," Alec insisted. "I'll intercept it. But you need a live goat to catch a tiger. Joe would spot it if the code were a fake, so it has to be real. But, all right, I didn't want to tell you, but I will. I've built in a booby trap. When Joe logs in, anything he downloads will be garbage."

"But that means the whole thing's garbage," Brandon said. "That you can't use it."

"No, *I* can use it. But Joe can't. He uses his creds, those land mines explode. But only if it's him."

"How are you going to tell him, though, so he buys it? Joe's no dummy either."

"He isn't," Alec agreed. "That's why I'm going to tell him it's you."

"*What?*"

"That's right." Alec shot a glance across at Rae, and she nodded. "I tell him this same story, except I tell him I'm trying to trap *you,* and that I'm about to give you access. And when he's got the beta, sitting right there for him to grab, with you all set up to take the fall for it? He's going to grab it. Whether the board thinks it's you or me or even Rae, that doesn't matter to him. He's imagining himself sitting back, pretending to be all wounded and depressed that he's having to start over. With who knows how many millions in some offshore account. Don't worry. He's going to take the code. I'll call you when the trap's set, so you can watch for it. We'll both be watching. Double proof."

He began typing. "I'm sending you my credentials now."

"Wait," Brandon said in alarm. "Stop."

Alec lifted his fingers from the keys.

"Email?" Brandon demanded. "Are you nuts? With everything else he's done, you think Joe couldn't get into your email? Write it down." He got up, grabbed a pad of paper from the kitchen table. "I'll use it, then I'll shred it. No electronic trace."

Alec had to laugh at that. It wasn't a cheerful laugh. "Man, you're right. What was I thinking? With everything that's been going on...I'm toast."

He copied the information down and shoved the pad across the stone coffee table to Brandon, then backspaced over the beginnings of his email, logged off and put his laptop away.

"And now," he said, getting up and watching Rae doing the same, "we go tell Joe. Wish us luck."

Brandon was still reeling, it was clear. "I just...I can't believe it's all happening. But, yeah. Good luck."

Talking to Joe was tougher. The same explanation, with one crucial difference. But that was the one that mattered.

When they finished, Alec was sweating. He got back into his car with Rae, leaned back against the seat, and sighed.

"Ron next," she prompted.

"Yeah." He started the car, put it in gear. "Ron."

♡

"How sure are you of all this?" Ron pressed, when they were sitting in front of the massive emerald-green marble fireplace, filled with a decorative floral arrangement for the summer months, in the drawing room of the venture capitalist's Pacific Heights mansion.

"A hundred percent," Alec assured him.

Ron's eyebrows went up. "No CEO B.S.," he warned. "You tell me a hundred percent, you better have something more than logic and deduction to back it up."

"Here it is," Rae said. She pulled her phone out of her purse, set it on the inlaid wood of the coffee table, and pressed buttons for her first voice memo. Veronica's words tumbling out through the tears, telling a story of seduction, lies, and the betrayal of a friendship.

"I assume," Ron said when Rae had pressed the "stop" button at last, "that you recorded those other conversations too."

"We did," Rae assured him, and played them for him.

"You know that wouldn't be admissible in court," Ron reminded them. "Recorded conversations without the recorded party's consent? No."

"It doesn't have to be, does it?" It was Rae who answered. "All it has to do is clear Alec with the board, and give you the background you need to monitor the trap. The trap is all the evidence you need to put him out of business, whether or not you prosecute."

"Which you realize we won't," Ron said.

"We realize it," Alec said. "Shareholder value in a company whose code has been compromised? Whose code has even been *rumored* to be compromised? That stock price just took a dive."

"That's right," Ron said. "Persona non grata in the industry, yes. Prosecuted...unfortunately, no."

"Clearing Alec's name," Rae said. "Preserving the value of all his hard work. That's what matters."

"All *our* hard work," Alec said. "*Our* names. Everyone's but his. That's it."

"When do you think he'll bite?" Ron asked.

"Fast," Alec said. "Depending where his buyer is, and how fast he can get in touch with him. He won't want to access the code until he's sure the trap is ready, and he won't send it until he's got the payoff. At least, that's how I'd do it."

"Hmm," Ron said. "Hope you never do embrace the dark side, because you'd get away with it, wouldn't you?"

"He can't," Rae said. She smiled at Alec, and he could see all the fatigue, all the nervousness and excitement there, because he was feeling exactly the same things. "He's constitutionally incapable of it, and you should have known it. Once a preacher's kid, always a preacher's kid."

"You'll forgive me if I've been less convinced of Alec's moral rectitude," Ron said. "And finding out about the two of you— that hasn't helped you one bit with any of us." He looked at her, seeming genuinely saddened. "Why, besides the obvious? I'd have said you knew better. You're the last person I'd have expected to risk your career for a…a thrill."

It was Alec who answered. "When you met Moira," he said, referring to Ron's wife of thirty-odd years. "If you'd been working with her at the time. How much would that have mattered?"

"Not much," the older man admitted. "Not much at all. You telling me that's what this is?"

"That's exactly what this is." Alec had Rae's hand in his now. "The real deal. And if you think Rae's judgment and integrity could be compromised by being involved with me, then all I can say is, you don't know her very well."

"No," Ron corrected, "looks like I don't know you. But I'm beginning to get the picture."

♡

The planner paced. Living room, dining room, kitchen, again and again. He should sit down, but he couldn't. When his phone finally rang, he lunged for it. An unfamiliar number. Of course.

"Yeah," he said.

"You got it?" No niceties, no greeting.

"No. But I will."

"You screwed up." There was contempt in the voice, and the planner was sweating even more. "They've shut you down, and I have to assume they're wiping the servers. I was hoping that meant you'd got it, but you're about to tell me that it means you got caught."

"Not me. Kincaid. They found the breadcrumbs, that's all."

"You left the breadcrumbs, but you didn't get the code?"

"I got all the alpha. A hundred percent. And—"

"I'm not paying you for the alpha." The tone was flat. "We're done."

"No, wait," the planner insisted. "I've got the beta version too, at least I will. I've got clear access to all of it, as soon as it's safe to take it. The board still thinks it could be Kincaid— well, him and Rae working together, which is even better—and Kincaid thinks it's—somebody else. It's a beautiful thing." He laughed, his confidence returning. "Whichever way it works out, the others are screwed, and I'm sitting pretty. And so are you."

The voice on the other end was silent a moment, then asked, "When?"

"Hours. That's all."

"Call this number when you have it."

"I'll call. You wire the money, and I'll mail the code, same as before. Twenty million."

"We said ten." The voice was sharp.

"And now it's twenty."

"Twelve."

"Twenty."

"Thirteen, and that's final. With twenty million, I could build from what I have of the alpha."

"You couldn't," the planner insisted. "You don't know what else we've added. It's massive."

"The basic idea's there," the voice said. "Thirteen. Take it or leave it."

The planner took it. Thirteen would do.

He was in the clear, he thought as he hung up. He was bulletproof, and once he implemented Part Two of his plan, he'd be bombproof. And with the company shut down and Alec and Rae at loose ends, Part Two was just about to fall into his lap. He could feel it. He could very nearly taste it. And it was going to taste so sweet.

14-millimeter wrench

♡

"One may smile, and smile, and be a villain."

"What?"

"*Hamlet,*" Alec explained. "It just popped into my head."

They were hiking, of all the bizarre things. Mid-morning, and they'd heard nothing. Which, they'd reminded each other, was what they had expected. But the prospect of waiting around all day for something to happen was too much, so they'd driven an hour down the Peninsula to Los Gatos, then up into the Santa Cruz Mountains to Castle Rock State Park.

"As close to remote as we can manage on short notice," Alec had said. "I need to be someplace where we can see the hills, and nothing else. There's nothing we can do now anyway. The trap's set, and we're out of the picture."

So here they were, taking a couple hours away from all of it, walking amidst the boulders and the redwoods, looking out over tree-covered ridges to the distant Pacific. Hardly anyone else around on this Tuesday morning, the weather mild down here, out of the San Francisco fog. Blue sky, warm sun, the song of wind in evergreens, a few birds adding their grace notes. Peace.

Except that they were talking about it, because they couldn't help it. The deception, the betrayal were too raw, too recent.

"I should have known," he said again. "I should have seen."

"You saw what he meant you to see," she said. "What he's been showing you for, what? More than ten years?"

"That's right. I thought we had loyalty. I thought he had my back, just like I had his. I *trusted* him. I have to wonder, has it always been like this? Or just lately? And why?"

"Envy," she said. "There's a reason it's one of the Seven Deadly Sins, isn't there? Because what's stronger than that, the feeling that somebody has what you don't, and you deserve more, and it's not fair?"

"Love," he said, and he didn't care how it sounded, because it was the truth, and he needed to tell her the truth. "Love's stronger. That's one thing I know for sure."

He tightened his hand around hers, feeling the emotions roiling inside in a confused, confusing mixture. Anger, and pain, and gratitude that he had her to share them with, to help him make sense of them.

"Not for him, I'll bet," she said. "I'll bet that envy burns so hot in him, it's burned all those other feelings away."

"If that's how he feels, I'm sorry for him."

She snorted. "You can be sorry for him, I guess. But don't let it influence what you do. Because I think he hates you. To do this…He has to hate you. And you need to remember that."

The planner pulled into the spot next to the Mercedes. Only a few other cars here on this weekday morning, he saw with satisfaction. And Alec had conveniently parked in the most remote spot, right at the end of the lot, not wanting to expose the perfect paintwork on his perfect Mercedes to a careless hand opening a door. Which was perfect for the planner too, because his own car would shield him from the other direction if anybody did come by.

No risk, no reward.

He reached into the back seat, pulled out the items he'd stashed there. Reminded himself that he'd practiced this, over and over, in the safety of his own garage. He'd been even smarter than he'd thought when he'd bought his own German car, and he felt the rightness of it again, as if every decision he'd made in his life had prepared him for this moment. He'd even done all his research at the public library. Nothing on his computer, and no way to prove that the unfortunate error that would cause the tragic accident hadn't happened…well, accidentally. How sad, two lives lost just because a mechanic had been a little careless. He'd thought of everything. It was practically risk-free. Part Two, locked and loaded.

He looked around again. Still nobody. It was all here, if he had the balls to take it. And he did.

"Showtime," he said aloud. He pulled on the work gloves and opened his door, covered the narrow gap between the cars, walked around the back of the Mercedes. Looked around one final time, and committed.

It was all about speed now. Get in, get out. He pulled on his headlamp and flipped the switch, laid out his blue plastic tarp, scooted himself under the big car, and got to work with his 14-millimeter wrench. Exactly the same as when he'd practiced, mere seconds to locate the right spot, only a few more to loosen the bolt to the left front caliper, and it was done, and he was scooting out again, folding up his tarp, switching off his light and pulling it off, walking quickly around the Mercedes with only a brief pause to reach under the rear bumper for the black box he'd hidden there weeks previously. He yanked it free, felt the magnet resisting as if it were unwilling to let go, as if it the device were asking to do a little more work for him.

God, he was good. He opened the door of his own car again and got in, tossed everything into the back seat, stripped the gloves off quickly, just in case somebody came by and noticed. Which nobody did, because this was all meant to be.

He drove for less than twenty minutes, pulled into the turn-out he'd scouted on the way up. Put the gloves on again and picked up his tarp, a hammer he'd left ready, and the magnetic GPS device, opened his door and laid the tarp down, the bulk of his car shielding him from the roadway. He destroyed the tracker with a few swift blows, bundled up the tarp with the pieces inside, put the hammer back into the car and removed the wrench.

He walked to the dumpster at the edge of the asphalt and opened it, tossed the tarp and wrench inside and pulled a couple bags of trash on top of them, wincing at the smell. Yanked his gloves off and threw them into the opposite corner, rolled his shirt sleeve down and used it to cover his hand, and closed the heavy cover again with a metallic *clang*.

Then he moved to his second turnout, less than ten minutes away, reached under the driver's seat for the police scanner, and turned it on. And waited.

♡

"Look out." Desiree grabbed for Alec's elbow, yanked him aside as they reached his car, sitting alone at the end of the lot. "That's nasty. People who walk dogs and don't pick up after them..."

He laughed a little. "Yeah. That would've been a good omen for today, huh?"

Once they were in the car, he pulled his phone out of his pocket. One bar at last, so he did a little clicking around.

"Anything?" she asked.

"Not yet. Hard to wait. Maybe we should have gone camping, what do you think?" He heard her laugh as he pulled out of the lot, looked across at her with a grin.

"Camping, huh?" She smiled back at him. "No need to go to extremes. Don't worry, it'll happen. He's not going to be waiting around. He's got to be itching for this. I'll bet we know something by the time we get home."

"Your place or mine?" He shook his head. "Can't believe I just said that. Proof of extreme stress."

"Mine, don't you think? Or we could go have lunch first, if we haven't heard."

He frowned, his attention caught.

"It'll be OK," she promised him again. "It's going to happen."

"Sorry." He'd turned onto Black Road by now, downshifted as he began the long descent to the freeway. "Brakes felt a little spongy there for a second. I just had the car in the shop, but I think I'm going to have to take it in again. But hey, the mechanic probably has a boat payment to make, so it's all good, right?"

"Besides, you know you want to drive my car," she teased again.

"Oh, yeah. I always wanted to join the circus. Think I'll go for the loaner." He took another corner, and the tires screeched a little.

"Alec." He could sense her grabbing for her armrest. "Please slow down."

He shifted all the way into first, felt the transmission jerk in protest, heard the protesting rev of the engine, loud even in the normally whisper-quiet interior. And felt the car slowing, but not enough. Not nearly enough.

"Something's wrong," he said as they went around another corner too wide, too fast, with another screech of tires. "Brakes." Because he'd just put his foot all the way to the floor, with no resistance at all.

His heart was pounding, the adrenaline pouring through his body, every sense screaming at him. He pulled the emergency brake. Another jerk, another brief slowdown, just in time for another sharp curve, and they made it around that one too.

"Alec," she was saying, her voice high with tension, but he barely heard her, all his attention focused on the road ahead. Still miles to go, and too much weight, too much momentum. No safe way to stop.

Another corner, more precarious this time. He almost lost control, the big car fishtailing, and it was now, or it was over.

Not her side of the road, not slamming her into the bank. His side, the downhill side. His mind ran through the physics in microseconds. Nothing but trees down there, second-growth cedars and redwoods. He needed a glancing blow that would swing the car around, take some of the impact. Not on the driver's side, because that would turn the car in the opposite direction, and she'd be the one who hit. That glancing blow had to come on the right corner of the hood. And it had to be now.

The next curve was coming up, and he knew they wouldn't make it. He drove deliberately over the curb, down the bank, felt the tires bouncing, the front end jolting over the uneven ground, and heard her start to scream.

He held onto the wheel with all his strength through the jarring bumps, aimed for one specific tree, for the car to strike it in one specific spot. Felt his body jerk at the impact as they hit, the seatbelt yanking tight, but it was nothing to the force of the airbags slamming into his face, his chest, his knees, harder than he could ever have imagined. And then the car began to swing around, exactly as he had envisioned it.

He saw the trunk of the tree, larger and larger, approaching the side window, the only place he could still see, as if it were all happening in slow motion. And heard Desiree's continuing scream only dimly, from a long way away.

His last thought before the thick trunk met him was a prayer of gratitude. That she was screaming. That she was alive.

♡

Desiree heard the voice, and thought for a confused minute that she'd died. That this, finally, was heaven, and that there really were angels.

"Mr. Kincaid." There it was again. "Your airbags have deployed. Are you and your passenger injured? Do you need assistance?"

She tried to answer, but only a croak came out.

"Mr. Kincaid. Do you need assistance? Are you injured?"

"Help," she managed to say. "Please. Help."

"Help is on its way."

She tried to look, but the airbag was in her face, and she could only see that he was pressed into his own bag, and that he was still. She listened with all her might, and heard nothing. Not a word. Not a moan. She tried to hear him breathing, but she couldn't, not over the pounding of her heart.

"Alec," she got out. "Alec. Are you all right?" But there was no answer.

She felt the tears on her cheeks, hot and salty, and she was trembling with cold. She was cold, and her chest hurt, and her head hurt as if something were pounding into it. And she couldn't hear a thing.

But after a while, she did hear something. She heard the sirens, closer and closer. And the voices. People were there, then, pulling her out of the car, putting her gently onto a board and strapping her down, passing her up the steep bank and into the waiting ambulance, and she could see the flashes of its whirling red lights even with her forehead fastened to the board. They were loading her carefully inside, and the big vehicle was starting on its way to help, to safety.

And the tears were still there, and the cold. Because during all that time, she'd been calling for Alec. But Alec hadn't answered.

the smartest person in the room

♡

"Desiree."

He was saying her name in his dream, and he was whirling, carried to the surface of consciousness, then back underneath, now rising again.

"Desiree."

A long time, or a short one, and a hand was touching his, a woman's voice in his ears. "Alec. Sweetie. I'm here."

He opened his eyes, tried to turn his head, but it hurt, so he didn't.

"Alec."

Her face was above his now, and it was his mom.

"Desiree," he said again.

"Sweetie, she's all right, and so are you." Her hand was clutching his, and there were tears on her cheeks.

"Where...What..."

"You were in an accident," she said. "A car accident. You've just come out of surgery, but you're going to be fine. You're going to be just fine."

She was crying, and he wanted to do something about it, but it seemed too hard. So he shut his eyes again and drifted some more, and after a while, she was walking beside his bed, which was rolling now, pushed by somebody he couldn't see, through brightly lit corridors, into a big elevator, down another corridor and into a room, and he was being shoved onto another bed, which got through the fog in his head, because it hurt.

He could see now that his right arm had tubes leading to it, and his other arm was encased in plaster from bicep to fingertips. His entire body ached, but the pain was gentle, held at a distance, and everything around him kept approaching and receding, coming in and out of focus. The white walls, the TV mounted in the opposite corner, a nurse doing something to the plastic bag hanging on the metal stand at his right side. And his mom.

"Desiree," he said again. "Where...is she?"

"Here," she promised. "In the hospital."

"OK?"

"She's going to be fine."

He shut his eyes, because keeping them open was too much work, and the nurse was talking to his mother, leaving the room, and he opened his eyes again and his father was there, and Gabe too, filling the space between his bed and the empty one beyond.

But he was still so tired, still floating. And Desiree was all right. So he just closed his eyes and let them talk.

Desiree's wheelchair came to a stop as Dixie paused outside Alec's door and called out, "Knock, knock. Visitor for the patient."

The two solid figures blocking Desiree's view turned, shifted, and she saw him. His black hair was still the same, but that was all. His face was almost unrecognizable, his left eye puffed shut, the fierce red bruising extending up his forehead, down his cheek. Adhesive tape across his nose, his lips swollen and marked by black lines of stitching. But none of that mattered, because he was alive.

Gabe and Dave moved to the end of the bed where Susie sat, and Dixie wheeled Desiree close, close enough so she could reach a hand out for Alec's where it lay on the bed, the fingers taped to a device that was probably measuring his pulse, tubes running to the crook of his elbow and fastened with more tape. She touched his hand, and he looked at her out of his one good eye and tried to smile.

"Hey," he said, his voice weak, "you should see the other guy."

She laughed, and it hurt, so she stopped. "We both made it," she said. "Because of you."

"We'll leave the two of you alone for a while," Dave decided. "Come back in a few minutes."

"Grandma," Desiree realized, "you should go rest."

"Gabe's found us a hotel," Susie promised. "I'll take her there right now."

"I'll see you later tonight, honey," Dixie said, bending to touch her papery cheek gently to Desiree's, squeezing her hand. "You take care."

"Where are we?" Alec asked when the others had left.

"Los Gatos. It was a short ride. I guess you don't remember it."

"No. What day?"

"Tuesday afternoon. It's been about six hours since the accident." She didn't tell him how long those hours had been for her. She'd share that later, when he was in shape to hear it.

He looked at her from the corner of his one good eye. "You look...bad. In a wheelchair."

She would have laughed, if she could have. "Just to get down here to see you, because walking hurts. Some bruises, a couple cracked ribs, a mild concussion that's more like a bad headache, that's all. They'll discharge me any time now. You're a whole lot more beat up than I am."

He tried to shift, winced. "What's wrong with me?"

"Let's see. One concussion, *not* mild. Two broken bones in your left arm, which now has a pin in it—that was your surgery. Three broken ribs, which are probably going to hurt the most. And a whole lot of bruising. You don't look pretty, but you're going to be all right."

He was barely listening. "We still don't know," he said. "What happened. The code."

"Yes, we do. I called Ron a half hour ago, told him what happened, and he told me that the code had been accessed. It's all over."

"Good." He closed his eye and sighed. "That you're on it. Because I'm falling asleep again."

"You rest," she said, holding his hand a little more tightly. "I've got this."

"The car, though." The blue eye opened again. "Can't have been an accident."

"No. Too coincidental, and too extreme. He did it."

She caught the shift in his expression as he looked beyond her. She tried to turn to the door, was stopped again by the sharp pain in her side. But she didn't need to turn after all, because here was Brandon, advancing into the room, hesitating at the sight of her.

"Rae," he said with surprise. "You're mobile, then?"

"Oh, yeah." Her throbbing skull and aching ribs were telling her that it was past time for another pain pill, but that didn't matter. "And Alec's better off than he looks too. It'd take more than a little car accident to do the two of us in. We're hard to kill."

"Man." Brandon sprawled into the chair Susie had vacated near the foot of the bed with a sigh. "You look like shit."

"Feel like it too," Alec said.

"I'm so relieved. I thought I was going to be out of a job." Brandon laughed a little, ran both hands over the thighs of his

297

dark indigo jeans. "No, seriously," he went on after a moment, "I was just…" He shook his head. "What a relief. I came as soon as I heard. It's so good to see you guys."

"Who told you?" Rae asked. "About the accident?"

"Huh?" He blinked at her. "Who? Joe. He called me. Didn't realize you'd sprung the trap, I guess. Still pretending. But then," he caught himself, "that doesn't matter now. What matters is that you two are all right."

"Interesting," she said thoughtfully. "I didn't realize he knew yet." She looked at Alec.

He moved his head a fraction as if to shake it, stopped. "No. My dad said he'd call. A few minutes ago."

"You mean…" Brandon hesitated a moment. "No. It can't be. Even he wouldn't have done that."

"Done what?" she asked.

"You're suggesting that he caused your accident? No way," Brandon insisted. "I don't believe it."

"No," she said. "Neither do I. Joe wouldn't do that, and he didn't. Give it up, Brandon. We all know how you knew."

"What?"

"You knew," she said, "because you did it."

"*What?*" He stared at her in disbelief.

She paid no attention to that, because Brandon was good at lying. So good at pretending. But she wasn't buying it, not anymore. "I don't know how," she said, "but they'll find out. You knew where we were, how? You didn't follow us, or we'd have noticed. It was too rural up there, too empty. So it had to be some kind of tracking device on Alec's car, which they'll find too, because I've already told them to look for it. They'll take that car apart, I'll make sure of that. You knew that we were on top of a mountain, and you tampered with Alec's brakes, which you'd probably been thinking about for a while. I don't know if it was always part of your plan, or if it just seemed like the finishing touch, but it'll come out in the investigation, because as soon as the police get you in that room and start to question you, you're going to cave."

"You're crazy." He made as if to rise, seemed to change his mind, sat back down again, stuck his legs out in front of him, leaned back in his chair. "Why the hell would I do that?"

"Oh, I don't know." She kept her own posture relaxed with an effort even as her mind raced. She'd had six long hours to think this out, though. She might not know exactly how he had done it—yet—but she knew why. Her hands curled and moved inside the pockets of her robe, wanting to hit him. To beat him for what he'd done. Everything he'd done. Everything he was. "Because you wanted to cover up the theft of some computer code, maybe, get rid of the people who'd foolishly given you the password, so they couldn't tell anyone that they'd done it? Pretty pathetic attempt, though, as usual. A Mercedes is a well-built car. Not like, you know, that second-best thing you've got, that little BMW."

She saw him flush, was glad her taunt had hit home. "I think you'd better have them check you for brain damage," he said. "Because you're nuts. And dude," he told Alec, "I'm sure she's a firecracker in the sack and all, but seriously, you can do better."

"No," Alec said. "I can't. Shut up."

Brandon laughed. "What, you tell her you're in love? That how you got in? I don't think that's going to last long. Not once she finds out what a dog you are, catches you sniffing after that next piece of tail."

Desiree barely heard them. "But then," she went on after staring down at her lap, thinking some more, "maybe you figured that even if you didn't kill us, it would be enough just to muddy the waters, give yourself an excuse to quit. All that delay and confusion, you know, with Alec injured, that cloud still hanging over his head, and Joe's too now? Maybe you'd have got lucky and we both *would* have had brain damage. So unfortunate for us, and for the company, and for you, of course, having to move on after all your hard work. You could've just slipped away, wouldn't even have had to hide. You're here now to make sure we don't know, to see if you need to get out right away, do that hiding after all. Or to make sure we haven't found out yet that the code's been taken. If we had, what? You'd be joining us in mourning the fact that Joe was too smart, that he figured it out, that he somehow got the undamaged code after all. Too bad it's too late. Too bad we've already figured it out, because as usual, you haven't been smart enough."

"You think it's too late?" He laughed again. "You already gave me access, remember? Maybe you two are the ones who aren't smart enough, did you think of that? If it *was* me, and I'm not saying it was, that code would be long gone, nothing you could do about it, and no way to pin it on me."

"Why?" Alec asked, and as much as she knew talking hurt, asking this question had to hurt more. "Why, when you've been my partner for so long? When you've gotten so much from working with me?"

"So much? Brandon stared at him. "So *much?*" The mocking laughter was gone. "What do you mean, so much? What have you ever given me besides your leftovers? Joe's your partner. Joe's the best, and I'm some guy tagging along, getting the crumbs. You got any chick you wanted, and I got her fat friend. Rae was too good to have lunch with me, but as soon as you snapped your fingers, she was lying down and begging you for it, wasn't she? Because you've always made sure you got all the money, and all the credit too. You're the one doing the interviews, giving the presentations, taking your shirt off on the reality show. You live in the Millennium Tower, and where am I? Some second-class place, always. *Always.* Because for every million you got, you gave me maybe, what, a fifth? A tenth? *Maybe,* if I was a very good boy and kissed your ass enough. No matter how much I did for you, I was never going to hit the big time, never going to be the one raking in fifteen mill at one shot, because you were there taking it all."

"Because you didn't earn it," Alec said. "You want fifteen million, you go have the idea. You go build the company. You didn't earn it, and you don't deserve it."

"Like hell I don't. You *owe* me, and you know it. And now you're trying to pin this on me, but you won't, because I'm too smart for that. Because I'm one step ahead of you, and I always have been."

He smiled, and it was ugly, the mask fully fallen away now, the envy that had twisted his soul for so long right there to see, the boyish features distorted into something nasty and vicious. He made Desiree sick. Her nostrils were full of the stink of him, and her stomach curled in disgust.

Her mind all but screeched to a stop as the thought registered. She took another sniff. Looked at the soles of his shoes, visible as he sprawled in the chair near the foot of the bed, and felt the memory click into place. Of her pulling Alec by the elbow as they approached the passenger side of the car, helping him avoid the pile of dog poop with its clear mark right smack in the middle, where some unfortunate soul had put his toe into exactly the wrong spot. A mark that was a perfect match for Brandon's left Ralph Lauren.

"You've got dog poop on your shoe," she told him.

"*What?*" He stared at her, then turned his foot sideways to check it out.

"I don't think that's going to help you," he said with a smirk, relaxing with an obvious effort into his casual posture again. "Someday in the not too distant future, I figure I'll be able to buy about, oh, a hundred thirty thousand pairs just like it."

"Good job with the division," she said admiringly. "That's what they promised you? Thirteen million? I don't think you're going to be seeing that. In fact, I don't think you're going to see anything but the inside of a prison cell. Two counts of attempted murder, I think that's what they're going to call that."

"What are you talking about?" He was still trying to brush it off, but she could see the sweat starting to form on his upper lip. Brandon had never been nearly as cool, nearly as smart as he thought he was.

"I got my MBA at UC Davis," she said.

He looked at her like she'd lost her mind, and Alec was staring at her too, out of his one good eye, but he kept quiet.

Brandon didn't, though. "So? Is that supposed to impress me? Not exactly a Tier One school, is it? I got mine at Stanford, or didn't you know that? You know what UC MBAs call Stanford MBAs?" He laughed as if he'd never told the joke before. "Boss."

She ignored that. "You know what else UC Davis has? A vet school."

"Oh, you're a vet too? Is there no *end* to your talents? What are you going to do, get your horse and kick me to death?"

"And you know what they have at that vet school?" she asked. "The only animal forensics lab in the United States. Did you know that canines secrete their DNA in their feces? I read an article on it. And do you know what that means?"

"That you're desperately trying to stall me?" The sneer was still in place, though it looked a little less certain now. "So you can think of something, something that isn't there, to keep me from getting away with it?"

"You aren't going to get away with anything," she had the satisfaction of telling him. "Because you don't have the right code. You've got a fake, with your fingerprints all over it, and Joe, and Ron, and I imagine the whole rest of the board already know about it."

"You're lying." The color had crept up, and his posture wasn't relaxed anymore, but he was still in there swinging. "Nice try, but it's already gone. You're too late."

"No. You're the one who's too late, because Alec lied to you. Joe would've seen it, because Alec was right, you need a live goat to catch a tiger. But you're not a tiger, are you? To catch a weasel, a dead goat works just fine. And your fingerprints are all over that dead goat. But it's even worse than that, because you've put your footprint into something so much nastier."

She saw him struggling to make sense of what she was saying, felt a rush of contempt so strong it nearly overpowered her. "You were always going to fail anyway, though," she told him, "because you can't do anything else. You're so jealous of Alec you can't stand it, because you know that he's so much more than you could ever be. He's better-looking than you, sure. He's more charming too, and women like him better. But that's not all. He's smarter than you, and stronger than you, and braver than you, and kinder than you. And he's a better man than you. He always has been, and he always will be."

"You..." He could hardly get the words out. "You set me up."

"Yes," she said. "We did. But that isn't what's going to do you in. If you'd stopped with the code, you'd have been all right. You didn't even take much of a risk with that, did you? You knew that even if you didn't manage to steal it, even if you failed—which you must have realized, in some sad, pathetic corner of your sad, pathetic little mind, that you would—even if the worst happened and you were found out, you wouldn't be prosecuted, because nobody would want it to leak out that the code was ever compromised. You knew it'd be swept under the rug, and you could just slink away like the weasel you are. But in the end, you didn't even leave yourself that way out. You managed to screw it up beyond redemption."

"Because," she said, and had the satisfaction of seeing his face turn ashen as she went on, "when you stepped in that pile of dog poop in the parking lot, doing whatever you did to Alec's car, you placed yourself at the scene of the crime. Checkmate, Brandon. We win."

He stood up, hardly seeming to know what he was doing. Took a couple steps toward the door, then stopped. Straightened. And turned. "Nice try. But *you're* the one who's screwed up. This hospital has an incinerator. All I have to do is dump the shoes, and my ass is free. Thanks for the warning, though." He sketched a salute. "Guess you aren't quite as smart as you think you are. But then, we already knew that, didn't we? Your MBA's from Davis, after all."

He smiled at the pair of them, turned back to the door again. Took one step, came up short at the sight of Dave and Gabe Kincaid coming into the room. It wasn't just the size of them. It was the expression on their faces.

"You forgot one other thing, too," Desiree said. She pulled her hand out of her pocket at last, held up the item that had been inside it all along, and, finally, pressed the "end" button on the call she'd pocket-dialed. "That no matter what I'm doing, no matter where I am, I always carry my phone."

♡

The interviews took hours, especially since the detectives kept having to wait for Alec to wake up. But at last, Brandon had been taken into custody, his shoes duly confiscated. Only time would tell whether he'd stay there, because he hadn't talked, had called an attorney and clammed up. But then, the pressure hadn't really begun to be applied, because there was still that little matter of code theft, and he'd have to be considered a flight risk. Release on bail, she had a feeling, was going to be a tough prospect. One way or another, Brandon was history.

And for now, he was gone, and she was alone with Alec in his room again. She was dressed this time, discharged, aching, and exhausted, but wanting to say goodbye before she joined Gabe in the waiting room to be taken to the hotel. Where she could lie down again, and where, she had a feeling, she was going to be very well taken care of. By her grandmother, and by Susie, who were both waiting there for her.

"I'll come back in the morning," she promised, still holding Alec's hand, because she couldn't bear to let it go.

"I'll be counting on it," he said, the words still a little slurred from his split lip, his voice slow from the Demerol. "And on my mother making you sleep past seven, and making you eat a good breakfast. She'll probably feed you in bed. Just warning you. She's going to fuss."

"Yeah." She smiled. "I might have missed out for a few years there, but I think I'm going to get a fair amount of mothering tonight."

"Not just tonight. You're going to get it from now on."

Her heart swelled a little more at that, and she squeezed his hand. "You're so tired too. I'll go, and let your dad and Alyssa come back and sit with you."

"Wait," he said. "Something I have to say."

"Alec. It can wait."

"No," he said. "It can't. Because there's one thing I've always known, and I need to tell you what it is."

"All right. What is it?" She smoothed his dark hair back with a gentle hand.

"I've always known I was the smartest person in the room."

"Oh." That wasn't what she had expected. Not at all. But he was still so beat up, and so doped up, too. There'd be plenty of time to talk later.

He wasn't done, though. "And now I know I'm not, but it doesn't matter. Know why?"

"No, why?" she asked, and her heart had begun to pound.

"Because," he said, "I'm smart enough to love the smartest person in the room."

305

She started to lean over him, was brought up short by a sharp protest from her ribs, and contented herself with stroking her fingers over the single unmarked patch of skin near his ear.

"Well, that's good," she said with a smile, letting all the tenderness show. No doubts, no fears. Not anymore, and never again. "Know why?"

"No, why?" He smiled back at her, even though she could tell that hurt too.

She looked into his one undamaged dark blue eye, the only familiar feature in his wreck of a face, and surrendered the last remnants of a heart that had long since been his.

"Because," she told him, "she's smart enough to love you right back."

epilogue

♡

It was six weeks later, and his cast was off, his ribs were mostly healed, and they were in Idaho. After a stop in Chico for Gabe and Mira's wedding, of course, because Alec was the best man.

Standing up with his brother, seeing the look in his eyes as Mira walked down the aisle on her father's arm, had moved Alec in a way he would have been astonished by just a year earlier, when he'd seen the two of them meet for the first time. He watched Gabe take Mira's hand and, as always, felt what his twin was feeling. But it was so much more this time, because he recognized the emotion, and he welcomed it.

It was a bit of Old Home Week all the way around, because so many of the *America Alive* cast members were there to celebrate with them. When the bride and groom stepped out for their first waltz to Hank and Zara singing one of their earliest hits, Alec didn't think there was a dry eye in the house.

"Good Night, Irene" might have been a bit of an incongruity, the song that had typically meant the end of an evening, not the beginning of a life together. But it was right, Gabe reminded Alec and a few of the others afterwards, because it had been their very first dance together.

"And," he said, Mira's hand in his, "the night I knew for sure that I was going to marry her."

"Then?" she protested, her eyes shining with laughter and love. "You'd barely kissed me."

"You don't have to touch the stove," Gabe said with a sly glance at his brother, "to know that it's hot."

Alec looked for Rae, because he needed to dance with her, as best he could with all his tender parts. She was with his mother and sister, and Joe too, and he smiled to see it. Joe took a while to get there, but when he was in, he was all in. No more distance. There were still going to be three partners, but one of them was going to be Rae.

"This is a fine day."

He turned to look into the wise eyes of Stanley Douglas. Standing, of course, with Alec's father. They'd taken to each other immediately, because they were two of a kind. Same size, same build. Same way of seeing right through the barriers to what lay beneath.

"It is," Alec agreed. "They're good together."

"Yes, they are," Stanley said. "And they aren't the only ones." He nodded in Rae's direction, exchanged a speaking look with Dave. "Looks to me like the player's met his match."

"I'd try to deny it," Alec said, "but I'm afraid it's a lost cause. My playing days are over. Get your trading cards now, I guess, because they're about to become collectibles."

The rumble of Stanley's laugh filled their corner of the big hall. "This time, son, I think you've got it right."

♡

That had been a good time all the way around, especially after getting the news that Brandon had given up his buyer. Which wasn't the Chinese at all, but a competitor who, Ron had assured Alec, was going to find his life made infinitely less comfortable.

"Let's just say," Ron said, "that he's not going to be able to afford any more transactions like that, once the SEC gets through with him." And Alec reminded himself once again never to cross Ron. Power moved in mysterious ways, and so did Ron.

He'd have been a lot more worried about Brandon, even though Desiree had been right about the animal forensics lab, if it hadn't been for that other mistake.

"The lesson we take from this," he had told his family around the dinner table, its leaves expanded to fit its rapidly growing numbers, "is that stealing's one thing, and you might even get away with murder. But never, ever try to cheat the IRS."

"What he got for the code," Joe guessed.

"Not just that. Turns out he's been sheltering income for years, as soon as he started making any. They were already checking into him, and that criminal investigation, and a little work in the background by Ron Jacobs too, took it all up a notch. Seems Brandon started out at the screaming edge of that line, and eventually crossed right over it to the tune of quite a few millions that, I'm told, are likely to translate into some fairly good jail time."

"Well, the IRS got Al Capone in the end, when nobody else could," Desiree said. "So I guess Brandon was small potatoes."

Alec's return to work had gone slowly, for all that. The pain was one thing, but the lingering effects of the concussion had made him forgetful, slowed his thought processes. He'd been forced to take a big, if temporary, step back, let Desiree and Joe handle things. Which they'd done, of course, including hiring Michael again. The apology had helped with that, and the raise had helped more.

So that was all good, and Alec was eager to get back into it, especially now that the new software was in the midst of its testing phase, and the beta users were every bit as excited as he'd thought they would be. The buzz had begun in earnest, and it was only going to get bigger and better, because he already had ideas about the second generation. But he was going to be implementing those ideas with some differences, he'd already decided. It was fine to have life be all about work when there wasn't anything in the world you'd rather do, but he wasn't there anymore, and neither was Rae.

And now they were in Idaho, taking another week after the wedding for themselves. Two days to drive from Chico to Boise, staying in motels and eating in diners with antlers on the wall, then they'd started up the twists and turns of Highway 95 through the mountains and the forests, beside wide rivers and tumbling creeks, into the rolling hills and farms of the Palouse. They'd taken turns driving, because he was still sore, and she was still scared. The accident had stirred up too many old memories.

"You don't have to do this," he'd told her at the very beginning, when her own ribs had healed enough for her to get behind the wheel. "At least not right now. We can hire somebody to drive me until I can manage it again. And to drive you too. Or just stay out of a car altogether until you're ready."

"I'm not going to be crippled by that fear. I need to be able to ride in a car, and I need to be able to drive a car, too. And I'm going to." Her knuckles showed white against the wheel of her little clown car, which he'd squeezed into with a few grimaces, but she'd felt more comfortable in it for her first time than in his new Mercedes.

"You're allowed to have some fears," he said. "You don't have to overcome everything."

"Yes," she said. "I do. I need to learn to sit in the back seat, too. But if you'll sit with me while I do it all, that'll help. Just... be there."

"Always," he promised. And he was, and it helped. She was shaking and white that entire first time, but she did it, and she was doing this too. Driving, and sitting beside him while he drove. It got easier every day, and on the way home, she'd already told him, she was going to try the back seat.

But right now, it was the highway and the back roads out of Moscow, past the site of the show, and on to the campground in the cedars.

"Are you sure?" she'd asked doubtfully in the University Inn that morning. "Camping? I know you brought all the stuff, but are you sure you're strong enough? Do you even know how?"

He had to laugh at that. "If there's one thing I know how to do by now, it's camp. You saw the show. And besides, you know, I was a Boy Scout. In fact," he said with a little embarrassment, "I'm an Eagle Scout. I have merit badges."

That made her laugh. She looked at him grinning back at her, and laughed some more. "I'm going to have to get your mom to show me a picture," she decided. "How come I never read that in an interview?"

"Secrets," he said, "deep and dark. And, alas, secret no longer. I can build a fire. I can pitch a tent. I can tie knots. And I want to do it. I needed to come back here where this whole thing started, because I feel like it's been a..." He made a circular motion with his hand.

"A journey," she guessed.

"Yeah. A journey. And it feels like the journey should end with camping."

So they camped. He pitched the tent, and he built the fire, and he cooked her a Boy Scout special. A hamburger patty, sliced potatoes and carrots and mushrooms and onions, seasoned with salt and pepper and wrapped in layers of foil, laid on the grill over the fire to cook, eaten off paper plates.

But they did have wine, because he wasn't *that* much of a Boy Scout. And later, they climbed into the sleeping bags they'd zipped together, and made the kind of love they'd nicknamed "porcupine sex," because, like porcupines, they did it very, very carefully.

"I need you to hurry up and heal." She was curled against him, her hand on his chest, kissing his shoulder. "Because I need to be on the bottom again."

He smiled at that, turned his head and kissed her cheek. "Well, I've got my ribs on the special Advanced Mending Plan, because believe me, I need you to be on the bottom too. Don't worry. I'll be doing you on the conference table again before you know it."

"Mmm. Will it be as much fun, though, now that everyone knows about us? Now that we don't have to be so discreet about it?"

"Well," he considered, "I guess we *could* let people watch, if you need the thrill." Which made her laugh and hit him, gently, of course, and he laughed too, and held her, and they fell asleep in their sleeping bag, only the netting between them and the clear, star-dotted North Idaho sky.

She slept all the way past seven, and by the time she was dressed and had joined him at the picnic table for the mug of coffee he handed her, he'd already done a morning's work.

"Sit." He waved his spatula at one of the folding chairs by the fire, which he already had going against the morning chill, though he was using the stove this time around. "And prepare for Meal Two out of Two that I know how to cook."

"What is it? Eggs?"

"Nope. Rainbow trout." He flipped the crispy fillets onto a plate, added one of the cinnamon rolls they'd bought the day before, and handed the plate to her. "Breakfast, courtesy of yours truly, bona fide outdoorsman. Took the bones out for you and everything."

She seemed to notice the fly rod leaning against the picnic table for the first time. "Did you *catch* these?"

"I'm not sure your amazement is very flattering. I may not have many skills, but I do know how to write code, and chop wood, and build a fence, and fish for trout. I even know how to cook them."

"And run a company," she pointed out.

"And run a company," he agreed with a smile. "And love you. There you go. My skill set."

"Well, if it's going to be as limited as that," she said, and there was color in her cheeks now, "it's a good thing you do all those things so well."

She looked down, took a sip of coffee, set her mug down on the ground and took a stab at the trout with her fork. Her eyes widened as she took a bite. "Wow. It's really good."

"Fresh does make a difference. And that fish was swimming an hour ago."

"I'm impressed. You must be trying to soften me up or something."

"Could be." He sat on the bench, leaned back against the wooden table, and looked at her. Sitting in her folding canvas chair and eating the fish he'd caught for her, her auburn curls in wild disarray, not a speck of makeup on her honey-colored skin, one of his flannel shirts pulled over her T-shirt against the morning chill. And he'd never seen anyone who looked better to him.

"I wanted to do this differently," he said.

"No," she protested. "It's good."

"I mean, *this.* I wanted to wait until we were home again. I wanted to take you on a helicopter ride over the Napa Valley, and have music and champagne, and have the ring bought. I wanted to give you the romance, and the memory. I had a whole plan. But then, you've been messing with my plans since the day I lost my place in line to pick up your Tic-Tacs."

She didn't seem to have heard that. She was staring at him, her fork in the air, the fish forgotten.

"But I need to do it now," he said. "So I'm going to. Desiree, I love you. And I know I'm not a hero, although I wish I could be that for you, because you deserve a hero. I'm sure you could look around and find a better man, someone who's always done right, someone with steel in his soul to match yours. But I promise you this. Nobody is ever going to admire you more than I do. Nobody is ever going to be there for you the way I will. And nobody is ever going to love you more. At those things, I'm the best, and I always will be."

"Oh. Alec." She'd set her fork down, and her nose was getting red, and her curls were a mess, and he loved her so much his heart hurt with it.

"There's nobody better," she told him. "There's no better man. You risked your life for me, and if that's not a hero, I don't know what is. You're the man I want. It's you. It was always you."

"Then I need to ask you." He was choking up too, but it didn't matter, not anymore. "I need to ask you to marry me, and work with me, and have my babies, and help me make someplace beautiful to come home to, someplace with you in it. Because I need to give you a good life. And I need you with me, because if I don't have you, my own life won't be any good at all."

She was smiling back at him, and her heart and soul were in that smile, offered to him along with all her strength and all her courage, and he knew that he'd be spending the rest of his life trying to make hers better. Trying to make it beautiful.

"Well, then," she said, and he could see her trying for her usual brisk tone, but it wasn't working too well, because her voice was trembling.

"If you need to ask me," she managed to say, "I guess you'd better go ahead and do it. Because I love you too. And I need—I need so much. I need so much to say yes."

The End

Sign up for my New Release mailing list at
www.rosalindjames.com/mail-list to be notified
of special pricing on new books, sales, and more.

Find out what's new at the **ROSALIND JAMES WEBSITE.**
http://www.rosalindjames.com/

"Like" my **Facebook** page at facebook.com/rosalindjamesbooks
or follow me on **Twitter** at twitter.com/RosalindJames5
to learn about giveaways, events, and more.
Want to tell me what you liked, or what I got wrong? I'd love
to hear! You can email me at **Rosalind@rosalindjames.com**

by rosalind james

Cover design by Robin Ludwig Design Inc.,
http://www.gobookcoverdesign.com/

Turn the page for a preview of the next book in the series!
Read on for an excerpt from
Asking for Trouble
(The Kincaids, Book Three)

killer tuesday

♡

Alyssa Kincaid's Tuesday started out badly. And then it got worse.

She'd begun to hate Tuesdays anyway, the last year or so. When the past weekend was a memory, the next one four long days away. When her Sunday-evening pep talk, about how this week was going to be different, had proven fruitless yet again in the face of another meeting with her sales manager.

"I'm seeing the calls," Tim was saying now. "But I'm not seeing the orders for Mylexa."

"I'll meet my quota," Alyssa insisted, trying not to get rattled at the sight of the graph behind his desk showing all his reps' numbers. Hers weren't bad, she reminded herself. Not the best, but still right there in the middle. A solid performer. So she didn't have the killer instinct. So what?

"Your quota includes Mylexa. You're supposed to be pushing it." Tim bent his head over the contact report, giving her a great view of his new hair plugs. One hateful, pudgy, micromanaging forefinger stopped at an offending line. "Olsen's office. Where's his order?"

"His order's right there."

"For Mylexa. Where's that?"

The recklessness came over her like a rising tide. "Not there. Because I told him to stick with Zylase."

"*What?*"

"It's a better drug. You know it is, I know it is. And Dr. Olsen knows it too."

"And manufactured by the competition," Tim said, his heavy face mottling red. For a pharmaceutical company employee, he didn't exactly walk the walk. "Did somebody neglect to tell you that you're supposed to be pushing *our* drugs?"

"My way's working pretty well so far, isn't it? I have credibility. Ask any of my doctors. They know I'll tell them the truth, and if I say it's good, it's because it's *good.*"

"I don't care about *credibility,*" Tim snapped. "I care about numbers. Yours are down this month."

"Most people's are down. It's December."

"Electra's aren't." His lips were drawn thin with displeasure, his face seeming to swell above the tight collar that squeezed his fat neck.

Because Electra makes every doctor she calls on think he's about to get lucky, Alyssa didn't say. *And half of them probably do.* She'd been so excited when she'd been hired by Moreau Industries, into what was by far her best-paying, most prestigious job ever. But it hadn't taken her long to realize that most pharma reps were young, female, and good-looking. Just like her. And now she knew exactly why that was.

"I'm not going to prostitute myself for sales," she said. "I'm not going to mislead anybody, I mean," she added hastily. Too much honesty was not necessarily good policy, even for her.

She didn't fool Tim, though. "This job isn't about saving humanity. It's about getting sales any way you can. I don't care if you have to give the guy a blow job in his office. Do what you have to do, just get the sale. That's what it's about. That's what you're paid for."

And that was it. That was what turned another bad Tuesday into the last Tuesday.

She shoved her visitor's chair back and stood abruptly, reaching for her wheeled sample case. She could feel her cheeks flaming, the wave of anger heart-high now and rising fast, about to push her past the point of no return. "Find somebody else for that," she got out. "I quit."

Tim looked startled. He didn't want her to leave, she realized with a mixture of astonishment and satisfaction. These were just his normal bully tactics, what he thought of as motivation. Well, they sure didn't motivate her. Except to motivate her right out the door.

"You'd better rethink that right now," he said. "You're not going to get another job that pays like this. You don't get an attitude adjustment, you're not going to make it anywhere, doing anything. You're sure as hell not going to make it in sales."

"I'll take that chance." She turned, started to wheel her case out, then stopped in realization. Hitched her shoulder bag up and left the case where it was, laptop, samples, and all. "Have a nice life."

Her indignation carried her through the long drive in the usual creep of traffic on the 10 to Santa Monica, but then the doubts started closing in. They were raging in full force by the time she pulled into the smoothly paved parking lot of the white-stuccoed garden apartments set in the midst of towering palms and landscaped grounds, grabbed her purse, and stepped out into another gorgeous Southern California day. Up the curving white sidewalk and through the glossy green front door of an apartment she wasn't going to be able to afford much longer. Not unless she got a new job right away, one that paid as well as the one she'd just walked out of. Which, right now, didn't look too likely.

She picked up the phone to call Dennis, because she needed to tell somebody, needed somebody to tell her she hadn't been an idiot, and that was your boyfriend's job, right?

Which was when her Tuesday went from bad to worse.

"So you just quit?" he asked her incredulously. "What the hell, Alyssa! You don't quit a job until you have another job, didn't anybody ever tell you that? That was just unprofessional. You never, *ever* do that, walk off like that."

"What else could I do, though, after he said that?"

"I don't know, let it roll off you, like every other rep does with their sales manager? And started scouting other jobs?" Dennis repped for a software company, had been in the industry for years, moving smoothly from one position to another when he got restless or something wasn't working out, always seeming to land in a better spot. He'd been more than a boyfriend, he'd been a mentor, too. She'd met him on a Sierra Club outing, and over the past few months, the relationship had changed from casual to something more.

He was still talking. "Why didn't you think it through before you did that?"

"I was supposed to overlook what he said? Are you serious?"

"I've heard worse. Sales managers are all assholes. It's part of the job description. Quitting was bad enough, but it's December. Who hires in December? You aren't even going to be able to start looking for a month."

She was getting mad now. He wasn't even going to be out-raged for her? "I don't want to do the job anymore anyway," she said, and recognized the truth of it. "I can't sell things I don't believe in. It feels like...pimping."

"No." She heard the frustrated exhalation of breath, the *Alyssa screwing up again* sound that she'd heard so many times in her life, and felt her temper ratcheting up higher. "It feels like sales."

"Helping the customer make the best decision is sales," she insisted. She was walking up and down the black-and-white tiled floor of her little kitchen now, pacing in her agitation. "This is pimping."

She had to calm down, she told herself. She got too hasty when she lost her temper, the events of today being a sterling example. "Anyway. I can't do the Utah trip, that's for sure. I'll have to eat the plane ticket, but you should be able to get the hotel room refunded, right, almost three weeks out?" They'd planned a ski vacation for before Christmas, a trip that had loomed large and promising on her horizon. Their first real vacation together, doing one of her favorite things.

"Oh, come on," he said. "Don't bail on me now. It's not that pricey, just your half of the room and some meals, lift tickets for a few days. And all right, maybe I overstated. You'll have a job within a few weeks, I'm sure."

She waited for him to suggest that he could help out. He could afford it, and then some. But he didn't.

"I need to save my money," she said when no offer was forth-coming. "I'm sorry to spoil your vacation too, but maybe we can do something local instead." He was bound to be disappointed, she reminded herself. And he wasn't obligated, after all.

He hesitated so long she thought she'd lost the connection. "Dennis?"

"Well, I'm sorry too. I'll miss you, of course, but I think I'll still go," he said. "I've been looking forward to it, and the snow's great this year. Who knows when I'll get the chance again?"

She actually held the phone away from her ear and stared at it for a minute. "You're going to go without me," she was finally able to say.

"I said I was sorry. But I'm not the one who quit my job in a huff because my boss was mean to me. It isn't really fair of you to expect me to cancel my plans because of your—somewhat naïve, I have to say, idealism."

"I thought we were building a relationship here. I guess I was wrong. I guess we're not."

"What, I'm supposed to say, 'Alyssa, right or wrong? I'll take care of my woman?' I respect you too much for that. We're two independent people."

"I see. Not a couple. Well, all right, fine." And the temper was right back again. "That pretty much tells me everything I need to know."

"What, you're going to break up with me because I won't cancel my hard-earned vacation for you, because you had a snit fit? That's just childish."

"No. I'm going to break up with you because you're selfish. Because you don't care that my boss insulted me so badly I had to walk out. Because you don't support me. And that's not my idea of how a relationship works."

"You're just setting yourself up to be disappointed, then," he said, and she could hear the anger in his voice now too. "Over and over. The world doesn't revolve around you and what you want and how you think things ought to be."

"No. But my world has rules. And when you break the rules, you're gone." And with that, she hung up.

Minus one boyfriend. Minus one job.

acknowledgments

Many people assisted in the research for this book. However, any errors or omissions are my own. My sincere thanks to (in alphabetical order):

Computer security and software applications: Carol Chappell; Dave Gilbert; Drone 74E83EED; Steve Pryor, Verity Systems

Fashion: Erika Iiams, Department of Family and Consumer Sciences, University of Idaho

Legal issues: The Hon. Barbara Buchanan

Mercedes-Benz mechanical issues and safety: Kris Klein, Mercedes-Benz of Oakland; John Wansick, Fairmount Auto Service

San Francisco real estate: Jeffrey Marples, Managing Broker, Spinnaker Real Estate Group.

As always, my heartfelt thanks to my awesome critique group: Barbara Buchanan, Carol Chappell, Anne Forell, and Bob Pryor.

And, of course, to my husband, Rick Nolting, for reading what I write, and for not being embarrassed about being married to a romance novelist.

Cover design by Robin Ludwig Design Inc.,
http://www.gobookcoverdesign.com/